TEXAS RANGERS STONE & MCKINNON

ALSO BY PATRICK LINDSAY

Opening the Frontier: Spencer and Son

Chance Reilly Series

Chance Reilly

Gibson's Gold

Agua Caliente Canyon

Latigo Series

Latigo's Choice: Taming the West

Latigo's Chance: Boomtown Gold

Latigo's Trouble: Meltdown in Leadville

TEXAS RANGERS STONE & MCKINNON

PATRICK LINDSAY

WOLFPACK
PUBLISHING
· EST 2013 ·

Texas Rangers Stone & McKinnon
Paperback Edition
Copyright © 2025 (As Revised) by Patrick Lindsay

Wolfpack Publishing
1707 E. Diana Street
Tampa, FL 33610

www.wolfpackpublishing.com

This book is a work of fiction. References to historical events, real people, or real places are used fictitiously. Any similarity to real persons, living or dead, is purely coincidental and not intended by the author.

All brand names and product names used in this book are trademarks, registered trademarks, or trade names of their respective holders. Wolfpack Publishing is not associated with any product or vendor in this book.

Paperback ISBN 979-8-89567-076-7
Ebook ISBN 979-8-89567-075-0

TEXAS RANGERS STONE & MCKINNON

MIKE STONE

PROLOGUE

NEAR AUSTIN, TEXAS—OCTOBER 1877

Miles Young lay under the shade of several post oak trees, watching the activity in front of him through a pair of binoculars. Miles considered himself a survivor, and considering the things he'd seen and experienced during his seventy-five years, survivor was an appropriate description. Take now, for instance. Miles owned this land together with his old partner, Zeb Statton. It was a bit small, as far as ranch country in Texas was concerned, but they'd owned this land for nearly twenty years. Miles wasn't sure where Zeb was these days, but Miles had decided to come back to this property and settle down in the years he had remaining. He had come back to this land, only a few miles from Austin, and had planned to build a little house right here on Walnut Creek.

The problem had started just as soon as he returned. He had a building place in mind, here, right on the creek, with a small natural pasture behind the house, as he imagined it. The pasture was surrounded on three sides by steep, hilly terrain, and he'd figured he could run a few cows on that pasture without too much work being involved. When he'd come back to the land and started scouting the building site though, he'd noticed right away there were other people on the property.

Being a cautious man, he hadn't ridden up to identify himself and demand that they leave the area. For one thing, that little pasture made a natural hideout which made him think right away he might be dealing with outlaws. And now, watching through his binoculars, he was pretty sure he was looking at none other than Sam Bass, of train robbing fame, making a camp right here on the property he shared with Zeb Statton.

Feeling confident he wouldn't be spotted from his current position, Miles laid down the binoculars, crawled farther back into the trees, and lay on his back while he considered the current situation. Sam Bass had some reputation as a gunfighter and had a considerable reputation as an outlaw and train robber. Earlier in the year, his gang was said to have stopped a Union Pacific train carrying a gold shipment from San Francisco. The robbery took place in Nebraska, or so they said. The Bass gang was said to have made off with over $60,000, by far the largest train robbery anyone had ever heard of. The rest of the story he'd heard said that the gang had split up and that Bass had come back to Texas.

Miles had seen the posters of Sam Bass. He rolled over, picked up the binoculars, and looked at the group of men in his pasture down there. Yep, he thought, that sure looked like Sam Bass. He sighed and rose to a crouch, moving silently back through the trees to his horse, where he untied the reins from a low-hanging tree limb and mounted. There was a saloon back along the road to Austin that needed his attention right now.

———

Hunched down on a stool at the bar, Miles reflected that things could be worse. He hadn't been seen, and he couldn't imagine that Sam Bass and his gang had any interest in his little piece of property. He would just keep his head down and let them pass on through. He started to feel better, and after one beer, he switched over to whiskey. As he ordered the second one, a conversation from a couple seats over caught his attention.

"...Sam Bass, somebody seen him in town yesterday... don't know what he was doin'..."

Miles finished the second whiskey and unconsciously leaned a little closer to the conversation.

"You know he'd have a lot of gold...won't put it in no bank, though. Might rob a bank." A wave of laughter followed.

"What would you do if'n you had all that gold? I'd bury it, that's what I'd do."

That thought hadn't occurred to Miles, and it didn't make him all that happy. If Bass buried some gold on his property and Miles found it, that would mostly be good. He wouldn't want to get caught digging it up, though. Besides, Bass would be likely to stick around his property for who knows how long? Miles just wanted to build a little shack on the property and live out his years peacefully. A worse thought occurred. What if word got out that Bass had been on his land and people just started to think that gold was buried there? There wouldn't be a minute's peace, and trespassers would constantly dig up the place.

The bartender came along and offered a refill on the whiskey. Miles reluctantly passed on that and ordered one more beer for the road. His big mouth had been probably his worst enemy in life, and the problem doubled when he'd had too much to drink. A couple more whiskeys and he was likely to be talking about seeing Sam Bass on his land. After nursing the last beer for about fifteen minutes and hearing nothing more that concerned him from the other customers, he climbed off the barstool, mostly steady on his feet, and made his way outside to his horse. He would camp out under the stars tonight and see what things looked like tomorrow.

———

Sunshine filtered slowly through the trees the next morning. Miles opened one eye, then the other, feeling only a slight headache. He was thinking about getting up and getting himself some food when he registered the sound of hoofbeats...quite a few of them. He rolled over and took stock of his surroundings. He lay in a small clearing in the middle of a circle of trees, and he couldn't see any movement. He could hear some water splashing, though, in addition to the hoofbeats.

He glanced to his right. Walnut Creek lay in that direction. It seemed that several people were passing by, maybe wading through the creek. He took a chance and rose slowly to his knees, looking down toward the creek. Now he could see several men, just their shoulders and up from his viewpoint, facing mostly away from him and walking their horses down the creek, no doubt to be sure they left no tracks.

Miles lay back down, pulled his hat over his eyes, and waited. Quite some time passed until he was sure he'd heard no more activity for at least the last fifteen or twenty minutes. Only then did he get to his feet and pull his boots on. Walking down to the creek, he watched from behind the trees and could see no one in either direction. He stood indecisively for a moment, then walked over to his horse, mounted, and rode out to the secluded pasture where he'd seen Sam Bass and his men. Mindful of the conversation from the saloon, he rode back and forth on the land for quite some time, looking for any signs of digging. He found none.

Satisfied, Miles rode back down to the creek bank, looking at the level spot he'd picked out as a place to build his shack and live out the rest of his days peacefully. He stared down the creek as far as he could see, then back out at the pasture behind him. He sat down on the creek bank and thought for a while. Finally, his decision was made. He would build his shack and hope the Bass gang never came back. Even if they did, he couldn't imagine what they would want with him. He certainly wouldn't raise any objections if they wanted to hide out for a while. He'd lived this long in some very untamed country by not causing trouble.

Miles decided today would be a good day to ride to Austin and get himself a wagon and some building supplies. This should work out fine. As long as, he reminded himself, he watched himself at the bar and didn't start talking more than he should.

CHAPTER ONE
CABIN STANDOFF

NEAR AUSTIN, TEXAS—JULY, 1882

I squatted down beneath the window of the old man's cabin, straining to see into the scattered oak trees outside. The fading light didn't give me much help as the sun continued to set into the hills to the west. There were flashes of light here and there, followed by the sound of rifle shots and the thud of bullets digging into the walls. Lucky thing Miles had built himself a solid cabin with good thick walls. I rose slightly from my crouch now and then and squeezed off a shot just to keep 'em on their toes. I could hear Miles in the back, getting off a few shots himself. It was enough to keep them from storming the cabin from the back, but I was afraid Miles had little left in him. He wasn't a youngster, and he'd taken a bullet when they had first opened fire.

I wasn't even sure how I'd wound up in this spot. This was exactly the kind of thing I'd been trying to avoid since I'd come to Texas just a few months ago. My name is Mike Stone, and I moved to Texas after a shooting in Cimarron, New Mexico. I had been doing my job as a deputy sheriff

—nobody seemed to question that fact. Unfortunately, the man I had shot had carried a certain reputation as a gunfighter, and I had taken him down before he'd even gotten a shot off.

The people I trusted the most, my uncle and the sheriff of Cimarron, a man named Chance Reilly, had told me I was already gaining a reputation as a gunfighter myself after just the one shooting. With that comes the need to defend yourself against fools trying to gain that same reputation for themselves. So, I'd come to this area around Austin, hoping to use the little experience I had as a ranch hand to find some work. I had it in mind to keep my head down and stay out of confrontations just like this one. If I couldn't make a place for myself in Texas, maybe I could get by for a couple years until memories faded back there in New Mexico.

I chanced a quick peek through the window and received a quick volley from outside for my efforts. I wasn't really sure you could call it a window, actually. It was a square peephole cut into the wall, but it served a good purpose today. I dove face down to the floor, hearing multiple shots hit the edges of the window, and one or two even reached the wall behind me. I wasn't even sure how many of them were out there.

I crawled on my hands and knees to the other window/peephole at the far side of the cabin. While they were still shooting at the place I'd just left, I raised up quickly and spotted a man crouched over, running for the cover of a large tree just at the edge of the clearing. I sighted down the barrel of my Winchester and dropped him where he was. Then I threw myself down on the floor again as they targeted my new position.

I checked the ammunition in my rifle, wondering how either one of us was going to get out of here alive. I heard the old man firing in the back and shook my head again at how I'd gotten into this spot. These last few years hadn't actually been anything I would have expected. My family came from farming stock, and we were known as pretty peaceful people where I'd come from, back in Missouri. I had left home a few years ago to tend the bar for my uncle at his saloon in Cimarron. After a while, I had gone to work for a rancher in the area, going along on a cattle drive to Abilene.

When I'd been working on the ranch for a few months, I asked my boss to show me how to handle a gun. He'd taught me well and told me I had unusually fast reflexes. I had thought little about it at the time. Then he'd been pressed into duty as the sheriff. I had convinced him to let me help out as his deputy. That had led me to the gun trouble, but my boss was also a good friend and they were threatening his family. Not to mention, they had wounded my uncle trying to hold up his saloon. After the gunfight in the streets of Cimarron, I had come here. Twenty-four seemed a little young to be getting a fresh start, but that's what I was doing.

Miles was a kind old guy I'd met in a saloon not far from here. We'd had a couple beers together, and he had told me about the frontier as it had been when he was young. I had run into him at the general store a few times and we'd stopped to talk. I found him to be funny and thoughtful at the same time. He seemed alone out here in this cabin, and I'd helped him haul some timber and groceries out here a few weeks ago. Then today, just a few hours ago, a little boy had come to me outside the general store in town and handed me a note. The note was from Miles, asking me to come out to see him at his cabin when I could make the time. Whoever these guys were out there in the woods had opened up with their guns just a few minutes after I'd arrived.

I could hear Miles calling me from the back. I fired a

couple shots out the front, just hoping to hold them off long enough to see what he wanted. Then I crawled to the back room, where Miles was lying on his cot. I could see he didn't have much time left. I was pretty sure he had taken that shot through the lung, judging by the ragged, labored breathing I was hearing. He looked pale and weak, though his eyes were still alert. It occurred to me I didn't even know his last name. Everybody just called him Miles, and it seemed to fit. He grabbed my hand with his own, and the strength he still had in his grip surprised me. His lips worked open and shut, and he talked in a hoarse whisper.

"Mike," he said. "Not many youngsters like yourself have the time and respect to pay attention to an old man. Now I got somethin' I need to tell you before I die."

I looked at the floor uncomfortably and began to shake my head.

He stopped me with a wave of his hand. "They got me through the lung and I've lost a lot of blood. There's too many of 'em, and I don't have the strength to get out. You still can, but just listen for a minute."

I nodded and waited, listening uneasily to the gunshots outside. They could choose to rush the cabin at any minute. I rose and fired a quick shot blindly through the gun notch in the wall above Miles's cot, then settled back down.

Miles's whisper sounded pretty feeble. I was hoping his story was a short one as my mind worked on the problem of how to get the two of us out of here. It had gotten a little quieter out front, and that worried me. Miles motioned toward his canteen, so I tilted his head back and poured a little water down his throat. He gathered his strength and started to tell me his story.

"I moved around most of my life, never settled down

anywhere until I built this cabin a few years back. Spent the winter of '45 holed up in a cabin near Ft. Bridger."

I glanced at him in some surprise. I'd had no idea he had been a mountain man in his time, but there was no telling what lay behind a man. I nodded impatiently, wondering how dark it was getting out there.

Miles grabbed my hand again. "Anyway, the reason my partner and I got trapped in that cabin was we'd piled up a pretty good number of pelts. Neither one of us had ever had much money, and we was just too stubborn to leave those pelts behind." He coughed for a moment, then went on. "My partner's name was Statton. We hung on through bitter cold and through snowfall deeper than you can imagine. Four months we were holed up in that cabin. Managed to shoot a deer now and then and steered clear of the Utes. Finally, we slogged out of there, carrying those furs on our backs. Five hunnert dollars apiece, we had."

I gave him a little more water and took a short, crouching run to the front of the cabin. A quick glance showed me one man crouched at the edge of the trees, gathering himself for a dash to the cabin. I snapped off a quick shot through the peephole and saw him grab his leg and fall back behind the trees. I crawled to the back again, eager for Miles to finish his story.

When I reached the cot, Miles was waving some paper around. "Statton and I never had money—not before or after. We couldn't waste this money like we'd wasted everything else, so we bought this land. One hunnert acres. He pressed the paper into my hand. I'm givin' it to you."

I started to protest, but he shook his head and coughed in short, explosive barks. "Yours," he said again. "Unless Statton's still alive or willed it to somebody. I ain't seen him or heard from him in fifteen years. You'll have to share if'n he's done something with his half."

I could see it was useless to argue with him, and besides, he probably didn't have anybody else to give it to. I would have to try to find out something about Statton, though. "This Statton," I said, "what was his first name?"

"Zeb," he told me. Then he grabbed the front of my shirt. "One more thing," he whispered. "This is important. There's rumors about money buried out there by Sam Bass."

I'd been glancing back toward the front, thinking about firing a couple more shots out there. I turned back and stared at him. "Sam Bass?"

Miles nodded and grinned faintly. "Yeah. You heard of him, huh?" I nodded. Miles waved a hand in the air again. "Nothin' to those rumors," he told me. "Bass was here, all right, not long after that big train robbery in Nebraska. His gang was out there." He waved vaguely toward the pasture near the cabin. "I watched 'em out there. They stayed a few days. Didn't bury no gold, though. Didn't bury nothin'. No treasure."

I nodded, saying nothing as a fresh burst of gunshots peppered the walls of the cabin. Miles collapsed back on the cot. "Problem is, I got a big mouth when I've been drinking," he said finally. "I said somethin' at the saloon the other day about Sam Bass being on this land a few years ago. Stupid, I know." He waved toward the sound of the gunshots. "That's prob'ly why they're out there. They think there's treasure."

I got to one knee and grabbed Miles by the arm, looking toward the front door. "We've got to get out of here now," I told him. "It's getting dark, and we can't be trapped in here."

Miles pushed my hand away and shook his head. He pointed at the papers in my hand. "Put those in your pocket," he told me. I did so. Then he pointed at a crate in the corner of the room. "Now," he said, "push that over to me and pull the lid off."

I glanced at the crate, then looked back at Miles. "We've got to get out of here now," I told him again.

Miles shook his head one more time. "There's a way for you out of here," he told me. "Just push that crate over here and I'll tell you about it."

I hesitated, then I shrugged and pushed the crate over. I pulled the lid off, then ran back to the front in a crouching run. They didn't seem to be charging us on this side. Probably the bullet I'd put into one of them slowed them down a little. Plus, I'd shot that first one, and he hadn't moved since. I was pretty sure he was dead. I had a feeling they would come from the back side and move around the sides of the cabin to the front.

I ran to the back again, noticing that Miles was lying back against the wall of the cabin. His pillow lay beside him, his hand under the pillow. The crate lay open beside the bed. Miles pointed to the wall where the crate had been. In my hurry to push the crate to him, I hadn't noticed a hole in the wall. The crate had concealed it.

Miles pointed to the hole in the wall and the open space behind it. "Mike," he said, "there's a tunnel out of here. I lived in the woods most of my live, and I was a little spooked about Sam Bass coming back here to start with. I could never abide the idea I might be trapped in here. So, I made a tunnel. You take that tunnel out of here. It goes down a few feet and curves around to empty out by the creek, around the bend. They won't see you. You take what I gave you and get out of here."

"I can't just leave you here," I told him. Even as I spoke, I could see flecks of blood around his mouth. The lung shot was taking him out, I realized. Still, I hesitated, looking at Miles in frustration. "What are you going to do?" I asked him. "There are still way too many of them for you to take out."

Miles gave me a small, slow grin. "No," he told me, "I can take them out, all right." He lifted the pillow. He was holding several sticks of dynamite in his right hand. I stared as he reached into his shirt pocket with his left hand and pulled out several matches.

CHAPTER TWO
ASH MCKINNON

I stared at the matches, then the dynamite, then slowly lifted my eyes to Miles's face. He wore a faint, wry grin as he nodded toward the tunnel. "I can hold them off for you, but you don't have much time, and neither do I." He gave another short, explosive bark. There was blood on his lips now, and he was much paler than he'd been just a few minutes ago. He pointed at the tunnel with the hand that held the matches. "It's time. You need to go right now. Just pull that crate in front of the wall after you get in there."

I hesitated, looking again at the dynamite and noticing the long fuses for the first time. I wondered if he planned to light them and put them under the bed after the men outside broke into the cabin. It seemed like an awful way for Miles to die, and I didn't want to leave him there. I was big and strong enough to carry him out of there, but they would kill us both instantly if we came through the door.

I had no illusions I could pull him down a tight tunnel with me. He didn't look like he would survive the trip anyway, and he seemed to read my thoughts. "I'm not strong enough to go down that tunnel." He reached back into his pocket and brought out several more matches. "These are to light the lantern you'll find just a few feet inside the tunnel. Now go."

I grabbed the matches and dragged the crate behind me to the mouth of the tunnel. I crawled in feet first and pulled the box to the wall.

The darkness was almost complete once I was inside. I needed to turn around in order to see where I was going, which proved to be a challenge. I managed to sit down in the narrow confines of the tunnel, pushing my feet overhead in the air, then twisted to get on my knees, facing down the tunnel. I lit a match and saw that the path sloped downward and slightly to the right. I held the match out and searched for the lantern he'd mentioned. I saw it at the bottom of the slope and crawled down there, using a second match to light the lantern.

The dim glow from the lantern showed me a tunnel not much wider than my shoulders. At six foot one, I was several inches taller than Miles and could only move forward if I bent over almost completely. My head brushed the ceiling even so, and my shoulders often scraped against the sides of the tunnel. A feeling of near-panic settled over me at being so closely pressed on all sides, but the thought of Miles back up there with that dynamite got me moving.

There was a musty smell in the corridor and some eerie shadows were cast on the wall by the lantern. A few small, furry shapes scurrying out of the way in front of me told me that rats had found the passage. My back was feeling cramped and stiff after I'd gone only a few yards, so I got down on my knees and made a little progress by crawling and lifting the lantern and setting it back down every yard or so. The sounds of pounding and splintering of wood came to my ears then, and I realized they were probably breaking down the door out there.

I picked up the lantern again and rose to my feet, shuffling along as fast as I possibly could. If Miles touched off that dynamite while I was still in this tunnel, I knew I could be trapped in here. I pushed myself down the tunnel, my shoulders sore and a little raw from scraping against the sides. I ignored the fresh pain in my back as I worried that my fastest pace might still be too slow. Every step I took, I feared I would hear the sound of an explosion.

When I smelled the fresh air and felt the breeze on my face, I knew I'd made it. Then the light from the lantern shone off some tree branches. The mouth of the tunnel narrowed down significantly, so I pushed the lantern out through the opening and crawled the last few yards on hands and knees again. When I emerged, I collapsed on my face in the grass and sucked in the fresh air gratefully. I could hear and see the water gurgling in the creek in front of me. I crawled to it and scooped several handfuls into my mouth.

I could see no one around me, and my first instinct was to run for my horse and ride back to town as fast as I could. I was beginning to worry a little about Miles, though. If they had broken through the door and taken him prisoner before he could light the dynamite, there was no telling what they were doing to him back there. They might even torture him, trying to get information about buried gold that didn't exist. I kneeled indecisively at the creek, listening for sounds from the cabin.

When the explosion came, it was deafening. I hadn't been smart enough to stay flat on the ground, so I was knocked sideways to the dirt by the blast. I risked a glance upward and saw a spout of yellow fire climbing into the sky back there where the cabin had been. As the debris began to rain down, I rolled over onto my stomach and covered my head with my hands. Dirt and small chunks of wood fell on me for probably a minute or two.

I stayed on my stomach until the pieces of wood and other debris stopped falling, and the only sound I could hear was the crackle of the fire. I pushed myself to my feet and looked in the direction of Miles's cabin. There was only the glow of a few small fires here and there. I took a few steps in that direction and saw no sign of life. I stood there quietly until I felt sure that all the attackers had gone into the cabin and gone up with the blast. Miles had made his last stand.

I felt a little empty and discouraged as I stood there, wondering what to do next. It dawned on me that my horse would have never stayed hitched to the tree branch I'd tied him to after that explosion. I had a feeling that none of the outlaw's horses would still be there, either. It was five miles back to the hotel in town. I took one last look at all that remained of Miles and his cabin, then turned and started the long walk to town.

———

When morning came, it took me a minute to sort through what had happened last night. It all seemed like a bad dream for a minute, but that crawl through the tunnel and that huge explosion from the dynamite were real enough. I wondered idly how many sticks Miles had set off to make that big an explosion, then got out of bed to figure out what I would do now. I poured a little water in the basin to shave, remembering that the horse I'd had last night had been borrowed from a ranch just down the road. He had probably found his way home by now, but if not, I would have to go find him or make good with the owner.

I finished cleaning up and walked outside the hotel, pulling the papers from my pocket that Miles had given me last night. I shuffled through them, not knowing much about owning land—didn't really even know if this land was mine now, legally. I only had Miles's word for that. I also had to find out what I could about this guy Statton, who owned the other half of the land. How was that going to work?

I sorted through the papers I had. The first said *Abstract of Title* and said something about one hundred acres located on Walnut Creek, apparently bought from the state of Texas. The next set of papers looked like a survey of the land...those looked good enough. The third paper was just a handwritten note that said, *I give this here land to Mike Stone*. It had Miles's name scrawled at the bottom. I shook my head at that last one.

I was pretty sure I had seen a lawyer's office somewhere on this street. I walked along for about five minutes, then stopped at a sign that said *Jacob Peters, Esq*. I pulled the money I had left out of my pocket and counted it. Four hundred seventeen dollars left from what I had brought from New Mexico. Well, I thought, first I'll find out about the land, and then I'll look for a job. One hundred acres probably wasn't enough for a cattle ranch. My half would only be fifty acres, and that definitely wasn't enough. I couldn't afford to buy the cows, anyway. I pushed the door open and went in.

Jacob Peters was seated at a desk in the middle of a small office. His desk was littered with paper. He squinted at me through a cloud of cigar smoke as I came in, then waved at an empty chair across from the desk. I shook his hand and introduced myself, then took the seat he offered. I pushed the papers across the desk and told him I needed to know if I legally owned the land and, if not, what I needed to do. He took the papers, offering no comment, and shuffled through them, mumbling a few things to himself as he did so. As I thought, the last paper brought him to a halt. He took the cigar out of his mouth and stared at it for a minute.

After a while, he looked back up at me, then shoved a blank piece of paper across the desk at me. "This will be a lot easier if we can get Miles in here to fill out a legal document," he told me. "Can you get Miles to come in here with you?"

I told him that wouldn't be possible.

He eyed me sharply. "Why not?"

I explained what had happened at the cabin last night. His eye grew large, and he puffed on the cigar a few times.

"Does the sheriff know about this?" he asked.

I admitted that I hadn't told him yet.

Peters nodded and pushed the blank piece of paper a little closer. "I want you to write that you certify that you are Mike Stone and that Miles gave you these papers," he said. "Then report what happened to the sheriff and give me about a week. I'll get the sheriff's word that he has been out to Miles's place and that Miles is assumed to be dead. Then I'll record this at the county office. You know you'll still share this land with Zeb Statton, or whoever he might have willed it to?"

I agreed that I was aware of it. Peters charged me five dollars for his work. That seemed little enough for fifty acres of land, so I paid him and left the office in search of the sheriff.

Luckily, I had met the sheriff before and had actually been introduced to him by Miles one night in the saloon. Even so, I wasn't feeling good about reporting what had happened last night. I found him at the jail, sitting at his desk. He questioned me pretty sharply about what had happened. I told him what Miles had said about him talking at the saloon about Sam Bass and the speculation about buried gold at the property.

Since he was going to find out pretty soon anyway, I told him that Miles had willed me the property. That didn't seem to surprise him. It turned out that Miles had told him he intended to give me the land—he just didn't think it would happen so soon. The sheriff said he would go out to look at the property and asked where I was staying, in case he needed to find me. It was a relief when I finally walked out of the office.

Standing on the street outside the jail, my thoughts turned to what I'd been thinking about before my visit to Miles last night—I needed to find some work. My best bet was to work on a ranch in the area, or maybe to work as a hand on a cattle drive up the Chisholm Trail. Both were going to mean I had to have a horse. I thought about the money I had left in my pocket and retraced my steps toward a livery stable I'd passed on my way here. There had been a *horses for sale* sign in front.

When I reached the stable, there was a paint horse that looked like he might have a little mustang blood in him. I stood with my hands in my pockets and looked him over, trying not to look too interested when the owner walked up.

"Can I do something for you?" he asked. He followed my gaze to the paint horse. "Good horse, that one. Two hunnert dollars."

"How much?" I asked, trying to sound as shocked as possible.

"Two hunnert," he repeated, but I thought I heard a little pleading tone.

I shook my head. "Too much for me." I started walking away.

"One hunnert ninety, and I'll throw in a blanket and bridle."

I turned around and ducked under the fence into the corral. I checked the paint's mouth and led him around the corral a couple times. "One seventy."

The livery stable owner shifted from one foot to the other for a moment. "One eighty, and I got an old saddle I'll throw in."

I patted the paint on the shoulder and looked around at the man. "Let me see the saddle and I'll try him out for a while."

Ten minutes later, I'd handed over the money and left the horse with him for a few more days. On the way out of the stable, I stopped and looked over my shoulder. "What's his name?" I asked.

He looked up from where he was working, shoeing a chestnut mare. "Guy that sold him to me called him Blaze."

I repeated the name softly. "Blaze it is," I said to myself.

————

I nursed a beer in the local saloon that night, reflecting that I'd seen Miles in here as often as not, but obviously, I wouldn't be seeing him anymore. My idea was to look around for work, so I watched the doors, feeling pretty sure I would remember a few of the ranch hands who had dropped in here before. I hadn't really struck up a friendship with any of them, but maybe they could at least tell me if any hands were needed on the ranch where they worked. After a while, I spotted a group of three coming in and remembered that they worked on a ranch a few miles west of here.

When they sat at a table near me, I approached and asked if I could join them. They looked neither friendly nor unfriendly, but one of them waved at an empty seat next to him. I gave them a minute to order their drinks and then introduced myself. They went around the table in a hurry, firing off names. There were a couple names I never got, but the one who waved at the chair was named Ned. There was a Jim in there somewhere, and I had no idea about the other two. They seemed more interested in drinking than talking, which wasn't surprising.

I asked where they worked and was told the outfit was called the Lazy R and was located a couple miles to the west. After a couple minutes had passed, I explained that I was hoping to find work at a ranch in the area and asked if they needed any hands at their ranch.

Ned glanced around at the others. None of them offered a comment. Ned shrugged, took a pull from his beer, then grabbed a pencil and a slip of paper from his pocket. "I'm the boss—it's my ranch," he told me. "I just hired a couple of these guys last week." He pointed at the two whose names I still didn't know. He stopped to jot down his full name on the paper, then wrote *Lazy R* beneath it. "I don't need anybody right now, but I never know when I might. You can check with me in a couple weeks if you want to."

I put the paper in my pocket, thanked him, and moved over to a stool at the bar. A maybe was better than nothing.

I ordered another beer at the bar and started in on it, glancing over my shoulder from time to time to keep an eye on the door. Suddenly, a large shadow appeared in front of me, and I turned to see a man about my age. He was, I guessed, a couple inches taller than my six foot one, and probably twenty to thirty pounds heavier than my one hundred ninety. He wore a friendly grin, and when he spoke, he sounded like he came from somewhere deep in the hills. He held out his paw and gave me a handshake that was somewhat painful.

"Ash McKinnon," he told me. "Can I set?" I nodded, and he settled onto the stool next to me and then ordered two beers. "Saves time," he explained. "I'm thirsty."

When the beers came, he drained half of one of them with a single gulp, then wiped his mouth with the sleeve of his buckskin jacket. He looked over at me. "I heard you askin' about work," he said. "I think I can help. If'n you know anything about cows, maybe we can help each other."

He had my attention. "I've worked on a ranch," I told him, "and I helped with a cattle drive from Dodge City to New Mexico. Tell me about yourself."

Ash's face lit up with a smile. "I'm from a place you never heard of, back in Tennessee. Town called Ford's Creek, up on the hills near to North Carolina."

Well, I thought, I was exactly right about where he was from.

"I come...came out here lookin' for work, too," he said. "I got hired on for a cattle drive, even though I don't know all that much about 'em—we had one old milk cow. But the trail boss figgered I could lift things, and push wagons out of the mud, and maybe learn about drivin' cattle."

I began to see a glimmer of hope. "What cattle drive?" I asked.

McKinnon grinned and killed the other half of the first beer. "Ever hear of King Ranch?" he asked.

"Sure," I said. "Down near the Mexico border. Over a half million acres, they say."

McKinnon nodded enthusiastically. "That's the one. They got a herd they're drivin' up the Chisholm Trail starting in a few days. Boss said I could meet 'em here in Austin. I figger if I could get a job on that drive, you can for sure. Pays thirty-five a month, prob'ly take two months." The second beer disappeared, and he wiped his mouth on the other sleeve. "Trail boss is named Jud Campbell, and

I'm gonna meet him at Sholz Garten saloon in Austin next Tuesday night. He'll have the herd bedded down near the trail, outside town."

I was wondering about the part where we could help each other when he explained that one, too.

"There's more," he said. "Campbell says we can buy some cows here and add 'em to the drive if we want to. Says we can buy longhorns for around four to five dollars here and sell 'em for more than twenty in Kansas. Profit is ours."

I did a quick calculation of how much money I had left and how many head I could buy.

Ash looked at me sideways. "I figger to buy about sixty or seventy cows and take 'em up there. But I need a partner to help me take care of 'em and show me how to do my job. I'll give you ten of my sixty cows if you'll be my partner and do that for me." He waved at the bartender for another beer.

I turned at looked at him. "You don't know me," I said.

He shrugged. "I think I usually have a pretty good hunch about people when I meet 'em. I have a good feeling about you. Do we have a deal?"

I stared at him for a moment, then chuckled. "Why not?" I extended my hand, and he crushed it with one squeeze. I decided I wouldn't shake hands with him again except for emergencies, but I left feeling pretty good about my new partnership.

CHAPTER THREE
SARAH STATTON

S t. Louis was a fresh experience for Sarah Statton, but then, she'd had a lot of new experiences lately. Take that train ride from Philadelphia, for instance. Now there was an experience. Foul-smelling soot filling the air, sparks flying, and the continual jolting and clacking of the wheels over the rails. She had found St. Louis to be very unlike her hometown of Philadelphia, though the differences were not entirely the ones she had expected. St. Louis had all the trappings of a city—hotels, restaurants, and businesses. The people, though, she found to have more of a pioneer nature. They were cattle-men, farmers, and riverboat gamblers, among other things. It was a wide-open town.

The porter on the train had recommended that she stay at the Planters House, and that was where she had come. Now she was standing at the window of her hotel room, watching people hurrying down the street under-neath flickering streetlamps. She wondered where they were all going. Not for the first time since her journey had begun, she was also wondering whether she should have come here. Maybe it would have been better to stay with her father in Philadelphia.

It was her uncle's will that had brought Sarah here. News had come to her by wire three weeks earlier of the death of her uncle, Zeb Statton. It was the first news any of her family had received concerning his death. For that matter, it was the first news of any kind they'd had about Uncle Zeb for a good many years. The attorney probating the will informed her that she, Sarah Statton, had been named as Zeb's sole heir and suggested that she come to St. Louis. The contents of the will, according to the attorney, were rather confidential, and he did not wish to entrust anything to the mail.

Sarah's father, Major Tom Statton, was against her coming here, though not because of the potential dangers of the journey, as she had at first suspected. Tom Statton remembered his brother as an eccentric man. No telling, he said, what might be in that will, but he was almost certain it wouldn't be worthwhile. What his brother considered worthwhile, the major said, would only be worthwhile to Zeb Statton. At Sarah's insistence, however, he had reluctantly put her on the train to St. Louis.

Her uncle Zeb was almost a stranger to the family. It had been eighteen years now since any of them had actually seen him. He'd spent much of his life in the mountains of the West, so far as they knew, trapping, drinking, fighting Indians, and exploring. They'd even heard he had married an Arapahoe squaw, but didn't know whether or not to believe it. Whenever Uncle Zeb's name came up, her father only smiled and shook his head. Uncle Zeb, he said, was the wild man of the Statton family. The only time he had ever spent close to home had been a brief stint in the coal mines of West Virginia.

Sarah herself still had some vivid memories from that

visit made eighteen years ago. Only six years old at the time, she could remember sitting on his lap by the hour, listening to stories about fighting bears and savages. She'd thought he was the most fascinating man she'd ever seen. A small smile crossed her face as she looked down from the hotel window. She had little to compare him to at age six, but she still had a lot of curiosity about her uncle Zeb. She remembered that he couldn't seem to stay in the house for very long before he would get up and prowl around outside, taking long walks in the streets of Philadelphia. The only time he seemed to stay inside for any length of time was when he was telling Sarah his stories.

It had seemed at first to be highly unusual that he would choose an heir based on a little girl he remembered from eighteen years ago. Then again, maybe there had been no one else to name in the will. His had been a solitary life. And, she reminded herself, Uncle Zeb was a highly unusual man.

The mystery wouldn't last for long, anyway. Sarah crossed over to the bed in her room and pulled the wire message from her luggage. It came from the attorney who had contacted her, Bill Pearsall, with offices on Locust near Third Street. She tossed the wire back onto the bed. She would see about the will tomorrow.

———

The early morning fog from the river was just beginning to clear away when Sarah left Planters House the next morning. She noticed, as she had yesterday, the wide-open, frontier atmosphere of the town. She was getting used to it already. It was a vibrant, alive kind of environment. Being the daughter of an army officer, she was used to some rough-and-ready living, but it had also been an orderly life in a certain way. This was entirely different.

Sarah walked down Fourth Street. The clerk at the hotel had told her it was just a few blocks to Locust. He'd also warned her against straying over to the French section of town, Carondelet. *Vide Poches* he'd called it. Empty Pockets. She would take that advice. She'd had enough adventure on this trip already without adding robbery to the list of new experiences.

Sarah came to Locust and turned east toward the river. A block later, she stood in front of an unimpressive office building. The sign on the door advertised the law office of Bill Pearsall. With a quick glance around her, she pushed open the door and went in.

The office was cramped, with paper strewn haphazardly about. There was just one desk in the outer office. Sarah faced a rather small and harried-looking man of about forty, who seemed to have a habit of swallowing nervously every few seconds. Seeing Sarah, he set down a sheaf of papers and hurried out from behind the desk.

"Jeremiah Keene, ma'am. Can I be of some service to you?"

Sarah held out the wire from the law office. "I received this wire from Mr. Pearsall concerning the will of my uncle, Zebulon Statton. I sent an answering wire, so Mr. Pearsall should be expecting me."

A faint shadow of recognition seemed to come into the clerk's eyes at the mention of Sarah's name. "Oh, yes," said Keene. He shot her a sideways glance, and his Adam's apple seemed to bob nervously in his throat several times. Did she make him nervous, Sarah wondered, or was he just one of those nervous little men who never seemed to calm down?

"Follow me, please."

Keene led the way to an inner office, knocked, and waited for an answer. When it came, he ushered Sarah inside. She found herself in an office almost as small as the one outside. A window was propped open on the east side to allow some breeze in from the Mississippi River, but it was stiflingly hot and stale in the office, anyway. Muggy, thought Sarah, that was the word for it. A large man rose from behind the desk, shirt sleeves rolled up and collar open.

"Miss Statton. I'm Bill Pearsall. Been expecting you. Sit down, please."

Sarah took the chair he offered and gratefully accepted a glass of water. She noticed that Keene was still standing in the doorway and felt some irritation. She wanted a private audience with Pearsall about her uncle's will.

Pearsall, following her gaze, waved impatiently. "That will be all, Keene." Keene left, but Sarah noticed his disappointment.

Pearsall watched as the door closed behind Keene, a frown of concentration on his forehead. After a moment, he turned to his desk and began shuffling through papers in some side drawers. Various scraps of paper floated to the floor to be scooped up and jammed back in the drawers indiscriminately. Sarah watched in some amusement and fought down the urge to ask about his filing system.

"Ah," he announced at length. "Here it is." Pearsall triumphantly pulled a brown paper package from the drawer and slid it across the desk.

Sarah examined the package with care. The package had the name of the law firm on it and was sealed with wax. She looked up at Pearsall. "Have you seen this?"

Pearsall nodded affirmatively. "Your uncle came in here with all the contents of that package in a box. He dumped it on my desk and asked me to make a will, which I did. I'm serving as the executor as well. Naturally, I saw the contents of the will and the package. I considered that his letter to you was personal, and I didn't open it. I can assure you that no one else has had access to the will."

Sarah nodded, wondering about that last piece of information he'd volunteered. She hadn't asked about anyone else seeing it besides Pearsall. She broke open the seal and pulled out the contents of the package. Ten gold pieces fell from the envelope and rolled around on the desk. She examined these briefly and saw they were ordinary twenty-dollar gold pieces. The next item in the package was a map, drawn on a tanned hide. Sarah turned it over and studied it carefully. They had drawn it with painstaking care, and it appeared to be an area in Texas, close to the town of Austin. It was a rather small area, judging by the detail. Setting the map aside, she turned her attention to the other document she found, which was a note from her uncle, sealed in an envelope. She read.

Dear Sarah,

  I give this land and the map to you becuz my other kin ain't no account excep yore Pa, some. You was my favrit only you probly cain't remember me.

  This here land is in Texas, near Austin, as you can see from the map. It is good land. I buried some stuff in a spot along the creek. I marked the spot on this here map with a X.

  Foller the map and watch out fer injuns.

Love to yore Pa.
Zeb

Sarah looked up to find the attorney's eyes on her. She glanced at the envelope that had contained the letter. It had been sealed, but anyone could have read it and put it in another envelope. She got up and walked over to the window. She could see the riverboats loading at the docks, the huge paddlewheels motionless. She turned back to the lawyer. "What do you think of all this, Mr. Pearsall?"

Pearsall smiled, not unkindly, and cleared his throat. "Well," he began uncertainly, "your uncle Zeb was a very, uh, colorful man, Miss Statton. It was hard to know what to make of him, most of the time. He didn't seem to have much use for people or to be very comfortable with them. He struck me as an honest man, though, and from the way he talked, I believe he cared for you. Does that help?"

She shrugged, though she was somewhat encouraged by what seemed to be an open and honest assessment of her uncle. She debated within herself for a moment, then asked the real question on her mind. "Do you think it would be worth my while to go to Texas to see this property?"

The lawyer stalled behind a cough and seemed more evasive this time. "Well, fifty acres—possibly one hundred acres if the other owner isn't accounted for—isn't a great deal of land, but you may find that you like it and want to stay."

Sarah nodded absently, then put her cards on the table. She glanced behind her to make sure the door was closed. "In his letter to me, he said he buried some things near a creek bed down there. Does that change your answer?"

Pearsall reached his hand out toward the map and glanced up at Sarah. "May I look at it?" Sarah nodded. Pearsall examined it, replaced it on the table, and drummed his fingers thoughtfully on the desk. "What's valuable to one man might not mean much to another, or there could be actual value there." He glanced at the map again. "Creek beds can change course over time, of course, but not that much time has gone by."

"Right," Sarah responded. She gathered together the materials on the desk and replaced them in the package.

Pearsall was looking out the window, still thinking. "Maybe looking at the land itself would be your best reason to go or not go."

Sarah collected her thoughts, then nodded in agreement. No telling what her eccentric uncle had buried. It could be something of value, or it could just be some old keepsakes. There didn't seem to be anything further to be gained here, so she thanked the attorney and turned to leave. Pearsall came out from behind the desk to escort her to the door. She left, feeling Keene's eyes on her back as she passed through the outer office.

Once outside the law offices, she paused, feeling very much let down. Hundreds of miles she had come for this, and it wasn't what she had hoped for. Somehow, she had believed there was a lot of money hoarded all these years by this strange uncle of hers. Returning home empty-handed was an unbearable thought. Still, there was the land. One hundred acres—or fifty acres—was worth a lot more in Philadelphia than it would be in Texas, but it could be some good property. And at the very least, she had the ten gold coins.

Sarah trudged back toward the hotel, turning over in her mind what she knew about her uncle Zeb. She had been such a little girl when she had seen him, and yet she had been the apple of his eye. She found that she couldn't shake the feeling that he wouldn't play such a cruel trick on her as to leave her a will for some worthless property.

By the time she had reached Planters House, Sarah had come to two conclusions. One, she wouldn't decide on what to do about her uncle's will until she'd had taken a day or two to think about it. And two, there was a man with blonde hair and strange gray eyes who had followed her back from the law office. She had no idea who he might be.

———

Jeremiah Keene had waited until his work at the law office was over, around five-thirty, before he hurried down to the street to meet his cousin. Louis Sharpe was his first cousin on his mother's side of the family. Keene didn't trust him. Truth be told, he was more than a little scared of Louis and desperately wanted to be rid of him. The last four years with Sharpe in prison had been a welcome break, but now he was back. Those gray eyes gave him the chills sometimes. He was hoping the information he had might change his life.

When the old mountain man had come to the office, carrying a box full of stuff, Keene had immediately been interested. He had seen Pearsall take the old man's box home with him that evening, so he'd had to wait a couple days for his chance. A few days later, Keene had gone into Pearsall's office while the lawyer was out to lunch. He had found the old man's box in a drawer in Pearsall's desk, along with the will prepared by Pearsall. Keene had gone through all of it, including the letter, which he replaced in another envelope and sealed when he was done reading. He only had a chance to take a quick look at the map before Pearsall returned.

Sharpe hadn't been in town at the time, but Keene knew he came through St. Louis from time to time. It had been an incredible stroke of luck that Sharpe showed up just two days before this girl Statton came in for her appointment about the will. Sharpe had agreed to meet in the café across the street from the law office after Keene was done working today. Keene had been vague about the purpose of the meeting. He crossed the street and entered the café, looking around as he did so. Sharpe wasn't there yet, so Keene took a seat at one table and waited. He had little information to add to their earlier meeting, two days ago, when he had explained about the old man's will, but he hoped to be rid of the blackmail payments he'd been making for the last two years.

Sharpe appeared a few minutes later and slid into a chair across from his cousin. Keene said nothing but watched Sharpe's face as he placed an order. He suspected that Sharpe had followed the girl after she left the office, deciding whether he wanted to pursue this. When the waiter was gone, Sharpe glanced around at Keene and nodded briefly. "I'll check it out," he said. He stood up to leave.

Keene threw up a hand to stop him. "And our... arrangement. Is that over?"

Sharpe cast a glance back at him with those cold gray eyes. "We'll see," he said, then left.

———

The next evening, lingering over dinner in the Planters House dining room, Sarah came to her decision. She hoped the land itself looked promising enough to give her a new direction in life. Failing that, maybe what her uncle had buried in the creek bed would be worth the trip.

Sarah puzzled over the man who had followed her from the law offices yesterday. He was a complete stranger to her, and he had been waiting outside the hotel when she left this morning on some errands. She had taken a couple of detours and ducked in and out of a couple shops but didn't feel entirely sure she had shaken him off the pursuit. His appearance was very neat, even dapper. She supposed he could be considered attractive, with the exception of those eyes. There was something in those eyes that bothered her. She wondered whether he was a dangerous man. Her instincts said yes.

Sarah's father, being a military man, had taught her

how to take care of herself, and she was glad for that now. Her decision was made, she was going to Texas to check out that land and to look things over. And she had decided to trust absolutely no one. She looked around for the waiter and asked what she owed.

Sarah paid the bill and mounted the stairs to her room slowly. She gasped in surprise when the door swung open. Someone had ransacked her room. Hurriedly, she checked her luggage to reassure herself that the map and note were still there. They were. She drew her revolver from her purse and checked the room carefully. There was no one there.

CHAPTER FOUR
HIRED

I sat across a table from Jud Campbell, trail boss for Richard King of the King Ranch. We were seated at the Sholz Garten saloon in Austin. Ash McKinnon sat next to me, though he had already been hired for the drive. Campbell stared at me over his beer mug, then looked over at Ash. "You vouch for this guy?" he asked.

Ash nodded his head enthusiastically. "I do, Cap'n," he said.

Campbell transferred his stare from me to Ash. "You can call me Jud, or Campbell, or Boss," he said. "Not Cap'n." Ash nodded. "How long have you known him?"

Ash squirmed on this barstool, which was a tough thing to do for a man his size. "Since yesterday," he finally admitted.

Campbell snorted into his beer but let that one pass. He transferred his stare back to me. "You done this before?" was his next question.

"I have," I told him, and explained about a drive I'd made with three others to buy cows in Dodge City and bring them back to Cimarron, New Mexico. He asked me a couple questions about Dodge City, probably just to verify that I'd been there. I answered them pretty easily, and he nodded.

He sipped his beer. "How many of the herd did you get back to Cimarron?"

I had to tell him we'd lost three-quarters of the herd in a flash flood at the Colorado River.

He only nodded sympathetically. "Can't control nature," he said shortly. He studied my face as I finished by explaining my duties at the ranch in Cimarron. "Ever use a gun?" he asked bluntly.

I looked down at the table for a moment, then looked back up at him while I explained about the man I'd killed in a gunfight as a deputy sheriff. He registered a surprised look, then glanced over at Ash and back at me.

"I think you'll do," he said, extending his hand. "You've done this before, and I like a man who can look me in the eye and give me a straight answer." I shook his hand. "How many horses do you have?" he asked.

I winced a little. "One," I told him. I didn't mention that I'd only bought Blaze the day before.

He nodded. "Okay. You'll need at least three or four more, but we can provide those from the ranch. Lots of young cowboys can only afford one horse." He finished his beer and stood up. "We leave day after tomorrow. Ash here can tell you where to meet us. You can run some of your own cows with the herd if you want." He set his beer mug on the table with a thump, picked up his hat, and disappeared.

———

The next morning found me riding to a local ranch west of town, where Ash told me we could buy some cows to put in with the herd. It had been a dry year, which meant the rancher might be inclined to let go of a few head at a cheap price. I had counted up what I had left from the money I'd brought from New Mexico, and I figured I could buy twenty-five head if I could get them for five dollars apiece. Ash had promised to give me ten cows in return for helping him learn how to take care of his cows and how to do his job on the drive.

We turned in when we saw a sign for the Rocking R ranch, just a little east of where Campbell was staging the herd for the drive. We found the ranch owner saddling up in the stable area and introduced ourselves. He looked up only briefly. "How many head do you boys want?"

We had already talked that one over. "Eighty-five," I answered quickly.

He nodded. "I can do that. It's been a dry year, but I still need five dollars a head for them."

We exchanged a quick glance and agreed. He led us out to a large pasture and showed us some cows he had already separated out. We rode around and looked them over. There were a few that I thought looked a little old for the drive, and I pointed them out. The owner who gave his name as Bill, drove those off. The remaining cows looked a little thin from the drought, but they were all longhorns and I knew they would hold up well on the drive.

Bill called in a young cowboy who turned out to be Bill's son, and he and Ash drove the remaining cows into a corral while Bill and I both took count. We agreed on a count of eighty-five head. Ash and I pooled our money and paid. Bill volunteered the help of his son to drive the cows to the area where Campbell was staging the herd to begin the drive tomorrow.

We arrived after about two hours. I'd had some concern about being able to identify our cows at the end of the drive, but it turned out that ours were the only ones with the Rocking R brand. We thanked the young cowboy for the help and reported to Campbell after merging our cows with the rest of the herd. Campbell introduced us to most of the other men on the drive. It staggered me to find out the size of this drive. We had a crew of fifteen cowboys, plus the cook and Campbell. We had 3,000 head of cattle to drive a distance of 1,000 miles. Campbell expected we would be on the Chisholm Trail for two to three months, depending on weather and any difficulties we might have. I decide not to ask about the difficulties until later.

———

Louis Sharpe sat in a saloon across from the Rocky Mountain House and toyed with his empty whiskey glass, thinking about the twists and turns his life had taken during the last five years. He'd ridden with Sam Bass, including that time several years ago when they had robbed the Union Pacific train in Big Springs, Nebraska. His lips curled into a smile as he waved for another whiskey. What a haul that had been. He'd ridden with Bass for only a short while after that, leaving the gang after he had buried most of his take from the robbery in a creek bed at that place in Texas.

His smile turned to a scowl. He had intended to get back there and dig up his money a long time ago, but he'd tried one more train robbery with a couple guys he didn't know out in Arizona. The result had been a four-year stay in the Arizona Territorial Prison. What a nightmare that had been. He would never forget the incredible heat, just laying out there on the rocks. He'd passed out a couple times when they had to break up rocks, exposed to that blazing sun. His mind returned to the present as the waiter brought his whiskey and he downed it in one gulp. He was never going back to that place, or any other prison, ever again. He would go down shooting this time. And, he reflected, he was superb with his guns.

Sharpe crossed the street to his room at the Rocky Mountain House and considered his next move. He'd trailed the girl to watch her buy a ticket for the stagecoach and knew she would leave for Austin tomorrow. He considered riding on the same coach just to unnerve her, but he decided against it. He had copied the map when he had broken into her room, so he knew where she was going. He had been there before, anyway, but the map would still help. Besides, he didn't like stagecoaches. He would take a Union Pacific train to Kansas City, then switch to the Union Pacific Southern Branch to get down to Austin. He could bring his horse more easily on a train car.

He considered the coincidence that he was returning to the same property he'd been at with Sam Bass just a few years before. He'd left that money there from the train robbery... He stared out the window. His interest in the land in Texas didn't really have all that much to do with what that old coot might have buried there. He was, however, pretty disturbed at how close the old man's hiding place might be to his spot. That was a lot of money he had down there, and he didn't want anybody else digging it up.

The land would make a great hideout, too. Sam Bass had planned to return there and use the place as a spot where he could come after pulling a job. The opening into the back of that valley through a narrow notch in the hills made it ideal as a base of operations. Bass had also planned to dig a hideout into the side of one of those hills. He could do the same for himself. Well, he could hire a couple guys to do the digging. Until then, there were plenty of trains and banks to rob in Texas.

He considered for a moment whether the information

from Keene was any good. Keene was a weasel of a man, but he was probably too scared to cross Louis. At least, that's how he'd always figured it. Plus, Sharpe knew about the child his cousin had fathered with a woman not his wife. He could always threaten Keene with that information.

He thought back to his original meeting with his cousin about this property. How long ago had that been?

———

They'd met just a couple weeks ago at the saloon by the Rocky Mountain House. It was a regular procedure for Sharpe when he was in town and when he'd decided to squeeze Keene for some more money in return for keeping quiet about the boy. He'd been blackmailing his cousin for several years. This time, though, seeing him for the first time in four years, something seemed to be different. Keene was even more nervous than usual. He sat opposite Sharpe and shifted this way and that on his chair until Sharpe had grabbed his shoulder and pinned him where he sat.

"What is it, Keene? We've been through this a dozen times. I don't like the sight of your face any better than you like mine. All you have to do is pay me your money and get out. That way, you don't get hurt. You don't want to get hurt, do you, Keene?"

Sweat glistened on Keene's forehead, and his face was pinched with anxiety. "Well, uh, that's the problem. The money, I mean." Sharpe remained deceptively quiet. He'd found that to be more effective than shouting. Only a slight tic at the corner of his gray eyes gave away the anger he felt building inside him. "I think," he hissed, "you'd better explain yourself. I'm the only one who decides when you stop paying. And, of course, there are many ways to pay. Money is the least painful."

Keene was sweating profusely now. How long, Sharpe wondered, had it taken him to gather the courage to do this?

"I mean," Keene quavered, "that I have a proposal for you. A business proposition. You can accept it and turn me loose, or you can turn it down and do your worst to me. Either way, I'm not paying you another penny. You've bled me dry. And I've risked my job getting information for you for the last time. If Mr. Pearsall catches me going through some of that confidential information, I'll be discharged. And at my age, I'd never find another position as good." Keene opened his mouth as if to say more, then changed his mind. He settled back in his chair and seemed to brace himself for the worst.

Sharpe sat back and studied Keene through narrowed eyes, letting the tension build and, with it, Keene's anxiety. Maybe he'd underestimated Keene after all. This was more resistance than he'd ever expected. Of course, every deal dried up eventually. He made a quick evaluation of the situation, and his instincts told him Keene meant what he said about not paying anymore. Not that Sharpe cared about having Keene beaten, of course. That could be arranged very easily. He knew a couple good people right here in St. Louis. But if there was no more money forthcoming afterward, it was a waste. Sharpe hated waste.

The sounds of drunken trappers and riverboat hands carousing at the Rocky Mountain House filtered through into the saloon. Long minutes passed. At length, Sharpe decided. "Okay, Keene, if your information is good enough, I might just let you off the hook. Go ahead. I'm listening."

Keene let go an involuntary sigh of relief and licked his lips nervously. "And you won't say anything to my wife about Juanita? Or the boy? I need some sort of reassurance from you about that."

Sharpe smiled mirthlessly. "There are no assurances, Keene. If it's good enough, I said. I'm still waiting."

Keene inhaled deeply and took the plunge. "You know I work for a lawyer—Mr. Pearsall." Sharpe nodded impatiently. "Well," continued Keene, "a few months ago, an old trapper came into the office to make out a will. Mountain man, name of Statton. I, uh, happened to hear Statton talking to Mr. Pearsall about his will.

"Listening at the keyhole, Mr. Keene?"

Keene smiled uncertainly and waited for some reaction to his story. When he saw there was none forthcoming, he plowed on ahead. "I've been on the lookout for something like this—information to sell to you—for some time. Well, anyway, I could hear enough to know that man Statton was leaving everything to his niece. Something about some land, a map, and maybe some money he buried on the land. In Texas, near Austin."

Sharpe gave Keene a long, hard stare. "You don't have any idea what he buried there, do you?" Keene squirmed uncomfortably in his chair. Sharpe shrugged. "Go on."

The softening of the other man's tone encouraged Keene, and some of his nervousness evaporated. "Of course, after that, I was watching for my first chance to slip into Mr. Pearsall's office and find out what was in that will. He had taken the box home that night, and I saw nothing of it for a few days. Then Statton came back to town to sign the will. Mr. Pearsall went to lunch after Statton left, and I found the package with Statton's things, including the will."

Sharpe settled back in his chair, his face was impassive. Keene took a sip of his beer and continued, "The will and Statton's materials were easy to find. Right there in the top desk drawer. It was sealed already, but I know where he keeps his seal, so I went ahead and broke it open. There was a sealed letter inside, which turned out to be a note from Statton to his niece. I read the letter and put it in a different envelope. There was the will, of course. Also, ten gold coins."

The part about the ten gold coins revived Sharpe's attention. He leaned forward. "Only ten?"

Keene nodded. "Only ten, but the letter said something about burying his valuables in a creek bed." Sharpe nodded, his lips pressed into a thin line. Keene hesitated, not sure which direction to take with the story. "There was a map, also, drawn on a tanned piece of hide. I started to draw a copy, but Pearsall came back before I could do that. This is as much as I could copy." He passed over a piece of paper.

Sharpe's face was totally impassive. "What good is any of this to me?" he asked.

Keene took a moment to regroup. Sharpe leaned forward impatiently. "How much property?" he asked.

Keene pointed at the will in Sharpe's hand. "One hundred acres. There is a partner somewhere who owns half, if he's still alive."

Sharpe looked at the partial map for the first time. His face registered surprise, and he looked up sharply at Keene. "Is this some kind of joke?" he asked bluntly.

Keene, confused, sat back in his chair. "Absolutely not. That's what the map looked like. What's wrong?"

Sharpe stared at him for a moment, then looked back at the map. He'd been on this property recently, he was pretty sure. He looked back at Keene, then realized that Keene would have no way to know that.

Sharpe looked at the map again, piecing things together in his head. He was almost certain this was a map of the property where he'd hidden out with Sam Bass and his gang after the robbery of the Union Pacific railroad. He couldn't be sure, but what Keene had copied sure looked like it. Sharpe hadn't trusted the crew he was riding with. He hadn't really known any of them before the robbery, and they were all carrying all that money from the robbery. He'd sneaked off down to the creek bank one night and had buried most of his take from the robbery. He'd be going back there anyway for the money, and maybe to use it as a base of operations if he could put a crew together in Texas.

Sharpe looked back up at Keene, nodded, and toyed with his bottle of beer. "Is there any more to this story?"

Keene kept a wary eye on the beer bottle in Sharpe's hand. He half expected it to land against his skull any moment, and he wanted to protect his eyes. He needed his eyes for his job.

"Statton died just a couple weeks ago, and now the niece is coming to see Pearsall about the will. You let me know where I can reach you, and I'll tell you when she comes. You can follow her or do whatever you like. I'm sure you'll know how to make some money out of this."

Sharpe said nothing for a long moment, and Keene kept his eyes on the table. "Agreed," said Sharpe.

Keene looked up, unable to believe his good fortune. "You mean I'm free? No more payments for your silence?"

Sharpe shrugged and nodded. "If this information turns out to be worth something."

Keene sighed with relief and rose from his chair. He had taken only a few steps toward the door when he heard Sharpe call his name. He froze, then turned slowly around to look into those ice-cold gray eyes.

"Mr. Keene, cousin or not, you'd better hope the girl shows up. And you'd better hope this is worth my while. I'm a man who hates to waste his time."

Keene gulped nervously. "She'll come." Keene left the saloon and disappeared into a crowd out in the street. He could only hope the land and whatever the old man had buried would be worth it. He had walked out with a feeling he might be betting his life on it.

———

Sharpe turned from the window in the room, his mind coming back to the present. He had told Keene this afternoon that he might let his cousin off the hook. He smiled mirthlessly. Picking up his hat, he headed downstairs to the bar.

CHAPTER FIVE

CATTLE DRIVE

S arah braced her feet against the floor of the coach and prepared herself for yet another rough stretch of road. They had been bouncing around in this coach ever since they had left St. Louis, or so it seemed. She'd been making a mental comparison between this trip and the train ride from Philadelphia to St. Louis and had concluded it wasn't much of a tradeoff. She gave a slight edge to the train ride. She had gotten rid of soot and flying sparks, but dust had replaced those by the bushel. No more clacking over the rails, but there seemed to be a lot of rough roads. On the train, though, she'd been able to stand and stretch, maybe walk around a little. On the stage, she just had to wait for the next stop to eat or change horses.

She had sent a wire to her father before leaving St. Louis and could only hope he wouldn't be too upset about the trip to Texas. Maybe he was getting used to this sort of thing by now. Being an army kid whose mother had died when she was only twelve, Sarah had grown up in a hurry out of necessity. Major Statton had realized years ago that he had a very independent daughter. Despite that, Sarah knew that this trip was a little adventuresome, even by her standards. She made a mental note to write a letter to her father the first chance she got.

She leaned back and looked out the window. They were still in Missouri, and it was a rolling, wooded countryside they were passing through. Ash, oak, and poplar trees were pushing buds into the spring sunshine, and here and there, she saw a dogwood blossom. She watched absently as a few blue jays and orioles chased each other from limb to limb, disputing territory and scolding. It was a serene setting, but her mind was busy with the property in Texas. Was the other owner still alive? If not, had he willed the property to someone else? If so, how could she find that person?

The matter of the ransacking of her hotel room remained unresolved. She suspected it had something to do with the man who had followed her a couple times— the man with the cold gray eyes. She could only hope she'd seen the last of him when she got on this coach to Texas. She hadn't seen him since he had followed her around in St. Louis.

There were just too many questions to resolve right away. They came to a gentler stretch of road and bouncing mercifully ended for a while. She leaned up against the side of the coach and drifted off to sleep.

———

I awoke at daybreak, just out of habit. I laid in my bedroll for just a minute, thinking about the new adventure I was about to have, just a little surprised at the new turn my life had taken. My family was in central Missouri. I guess the new description of my family would be *hard-scrabble farmers*. My dad, mom, and sister were still eking a living from the land. My brother and I had gone to New

Mexico to help our uncle with his saloon out there. A shooting in Cimarron, New Mexico, had eventually brought me here.

I stood up and stretched. I was big enough to take care of myself, which was a good thing because I'd had to do that for almost all my life. I had my father's build, with dark eyes and hair like my mother. My grandma claims I'm handsome, but I don't know how much stock you can place in that idea.

There only seemed to be a couple of people stirring, no doubt because the drive didn't start until tomorrow. I glanced over at Ash's bedroll. I didn't really need to look to know that he was still asleep. The snoring had probably kept the cows awake last night. I pulled on my boots and walked over to where the cook was putting breakfast together. I offered to help, mainly because I had learned it was a good thing to stay on the cook's good side during a cattle drive. He looked like he might be making biscuits, which was a good sign.

The cook's skills on my last drive had been limited strictly to beef and beans, as far as I could tell. This cook's name was Morty. I pulled some bacon out of the wagon for him and, of course, some beans. Some things never change.

I heard my name being called and turned around to see the trail boss, Jud Campbell, approaching. I dropped the crate of canned beans at Morty's feet and walked over. Campbell squinted toward the herd, then glanced over at me. "You were on a drive from Dodge City to New Mexico, right?"

I nodded. I heard footsteps and glanced back to see two hands approaching us.

Campbell stopped and introduced everybody. "Mike, this is Bevins." He pointed at a tall, rather stooped man a few years older than me.

I extended my hand, which Bevins ignored after fixing me with a sour expression.

"This is Porter," Campbell continued, indicating a short, compact, dark-haired man about my age.

Porter nodded at me and said nothing.

Campbell turned back to me. "We'll have you and McKinnon and another man named Red..." He stopped and looked around, apparently looking for Red. Not seeing him, he turned back around. "...riding point when we start out tomorrow," he continued. Looking over and Bevins and Porter, he pointed in their direction. "You can ride drag." With that, he walked away.

Riding drag was generally considered to be the worst job on a drive. You got nothing but the dust raised by all those hoofs in front of you. If any of the herd lagged or tried to break away, you had to round them up and bring them back. You were the last one to get to camp and maybe had to hope there was some dinner left when you got there.

Bevins had opened his mouth to protest, but Campbell was already gone. They both shot an angry glance at me and left.

I shrugged and headed back toward where I'd left McKinnon, raising the rafters with his snoring, when I heard my name called again. I turned to see a rangy redhead walking my way. It didn't take a genius to figure out this was probably Red. He erased all doubt when he introduced himself as Red Corbin.

"McKinnon described you to me," he explained. "I told Campbell to assign the three of us together on the jobs. Hope you don't mind. It's a long way to Kansas, and I'd just as soon get along with the guys I'm working with." He extended his hand as he spoke. He seemed to take me in with a frank, shrewd glance as we spoke, and I had the feeling those eyes missed little.

"You're the one that killed Juarez Chico, over in New Mexico, right?" The question came as a total surprise, and my mouth dropped open.

"How do you know that?" I demanded.

He made a dismissive gesture with his hand. "Until recently, I did some work for the state of Texas," he said a bit evasively.

I searched my mind for an explanation. Suddenly it dawned on me. Some kind of law enforcement. "Rangers," I guessed.

"Texas Rangers." Red nodded and gave me a disarming grin. "Nobody else around here knows. You'd probably like to leave that in the past."

I nodded.

"Your secret's safe with me," he said. "Let's get some chow."

————

The drive started at sunup the next day. We got 'em moving with a small pack we separated out and began pushing north. The others fell in line, with a little help from the cowboys in the rear. We saw a big bow-legged longhorn steer push to the front right away and figured we had our lead steer. He must have had a six foot spread on those horns. We named him Butch, and he took to the trail like he'd done this before.

Campbell had explained that we would go north to Ft. Worth on this first leg, keeping the Trinity River to the east of us by several miles. We didn't want them to be close enough to stampede for the water, but it would be there whenever we needed to take them over and water them. We were covering flat grassland for as far away as I could see, which was a big change from where I came from in Cimarron, New Mexico. I was used to mountains and a lot of greenery. Still, it was friendly country for driving cattle to market. The miles passed pretty uneventfully for a couple of days.

On the third day, we heard hoofbeats coming up and turned around to see Jud Campbell approaching. We rode over to meet him and kept the horses drifting north with the herd as we talked.

"I've heard," he said abruptly, "that we may have herd cutters trying to take some cows. Either just before we get to Ft. Worth or just after. We're only a couple days away now." He looked around at us. "Red, I know you've worked for the Rangers." He looked at Ash and me. "You boys are too young to have fought in the war. Stone, I know you've got some experience at sheriffin'." He looked over at Ash. "McKinnon, you're always bragging about how good you are with that Winchester. Can you really hit anything with it?"

Ash drew himself up to his full height in the saddle. "I can," he announced, "hit a mosquito at fifty yards. We've got a lot of mosquitos in Tennessee," he added unnecessarily.

Campbell was in no mood for joking. "What if the mosquito turns out to be a man? And he's got a gun out and he's trying to take the cows. Can you hit that?"

McKinnon dropped his joking expression and leaned forward. "I've got sixty cows back there myself, and it's how I plan to make a start for myself out here. You can count on me."

Campbell looked at him and smiled briefly. "I believe I can, at that. You boys keep your eyes open up here. I'm leaving you in the lead until after we get a couple days out of Ft. Worth." Then he left as quickly as he'd come.

We stayed alert and scanned the horizon constantly for the next two days, but we had no trouble. By the end of the third day, we bedded the cows down a couple miles to the west of Ft. Worth and were looking forward to a couple days in town before we headed north again.

———

The coach rattled to a stop in the station yard, raising a thick cloud of dust that filtered in and settled over the passengers. Sarah was sure that every piece of clothing in her wardrobe was now carrying about a one-inch layer of dust. The stagecoach driver's head appeared in the coach window, and he spoke cheerfully, as always. "We'll be here for about a half hour to change horses an' have a bite to eat. Food's waitin' for you in the station house."

Sarah accepted the driver's arm as she dismounted from the coach. She picked her way across the yard and into the station house. Finding a seat on a long bench drawn up to a rough-hewn table, she looked at the food they placed in front of her. Cautioning herself not to complain, she was nevertheless dismayed at what she saw in front of her—tough steaks on dirty plates. Even by army food standards, she thought, this just wasn't good. These plates looked even dirtier than the ones at the last stop. Sarah wondered what kept the attendant so busy he couldn't even get around to washing plates. Did he spend all his time fighting wild Indians, or what? She fought down about half her steak before pushing it away.

The stagecoach driver came in and sat down at her right elbow. He must have gotten used to the food and plates long ago, Sarah decided. He actually seemed to like it. Small amounts of juice from the steak splashed onto his checkered shirt as he ate, contributing to the stains already there from meals past. They were cheerfully disregarded. After a while, the driver pushed back from the table, and noticed for the first time Sarah's half-eaten steak. He turned a sympathetic grin on her. "Food's not much what you're used to, is it ma'am?"

Sarah smiled and shook her head. "No, I guess it isn't," she answered.

"Yeah," responded the driver. "It taken me a few months to get used to it, myself. Had to, though. It was either that or starve. I guess my stomach's ruint now. I actually kinda like it."

Sarah laughed, and the driver pressed on with the conversation. He probably didn't get too many women on this route. Sarah had been the only woman on the coach since leaving St. Louis, and they were now approaching northwestern Arkansas.

"Will you be going all the way to Ft. Worth, ma'am?"

Sarah glanced around her, noticing that none of the other three passengers seemed at all interested in her answer. That reassured her. She'd been pretty jumpy about being followed in St. Louis. She turned back to the driver. "Yes, then I'll take another stage to Austin."

The driver asked a few more questions that were a little too personal for Sarah's taste. She answered evasively, then excused herself after a while to walk around in the yard a bit before they had to re-board the coach. When the driver called for the passengers to take their seats, Sarah sighed philosophically and took her place inside again. Time to be bounced around some more. If only these seats were padded just a little more. This was going to be a long ride.

———

Louis Sharpe took his horse to the most convenient livery stable near the Rocky Mountain House Hotel, then walked a few blocks to the Union Pacific Railway depot. He would have preferred to ride the stage with the girl because he didn't want to let her get out of his sight. He didn't entirely trust the information given to him by Keene. Unfortunately, he'd probably been a little too careless in following the girl around for the last couple days. Who would have thought that an eastern girl from the city might catch on to somebody trailing her through the streets of St. Louis?

He approached the window for a train ticket. He planned to take the Union Pacific Southern Branch west to Kansas City, then board a train going south through Kansas and Oklahoma to Ft. Worth. From there, he could board a train for Austin. Tickets in hand, he walked to a bench and settled down to wait for his train.

He stretched out and made himself comfortable, as best he could, reviewing the events of the last few days in his head. She must have spotted him when he followed her to the Planter's House that first morning after her visit with the lawyer. Right away, she'd started dodging him, looking over her shoulder, making pursuit difficult. Of course, he had to know if she really planned to make the trip to Texas. It would suit his purposes much better if she just went home and left the land empty. He wasn't sure, so he had broken into her room and copied the map. He knew where the land was situated, but he might as well check to see what the old man had buried by the creek. Breaking into the room had been risky, he had to admit. Still, he had been able to stay with her at a pretty safe distance until he had seen her board the stagecoach this morning.

He had actually hoped to find out something about the other owner of that land. There had been a shack on the river down there, and maybe somebody living in that shack. He needed to know more about that. He'd found nothing in the girl's room about the other owner. If she had any more information, she had taken it with her. On her guard all the time. Maybe he should have done it differently. Maybe he should have tried a little romance. Something told him this one wouldn't have fallen for it.

———

Morning dawned hot and humid, and the stage rolled out early. The trees and rolling hills of the earlier part of this trip had given way to occasional rocky bluffs and lakes and rivers. They were somewhere in Arkansas, the driver had said. The wheels of the stage bounced along the well-worn ruts of the trail, raising clouds of dust. Sarah held her handkerchief over her nose to filter out the worst of it. She was relieved when the stage made the first stop of the day to water the horses.

The stage stop was nothing more than a shack for the stage employee, a well, and a water trough. The passengers climbed down from the stage one by one, grateful for the chance to stretch their legs and for a drink of water to cut the trail dust from their throats. Sarah stopped just outside the stage and accepted a cup of water carried over to her by one of the other passengers. As the only woman on this trip, she was getting the royal treatment from the others.

The stagecoach driver moved off to help the stageman water the horses while the man riding shotgun on the stage had disappeared into the shack. The shotgun rider was a recent addition who'd come on board just this morning, and there had been much speculation among the passengers about what they carried that required the shotgun rider. The strongbox had rattled a little when they'd lifted it this morning, so they were guessing it was gold that the man was guarding.

Sarah tipped the last of the water into her mouth and had just started to carry the tin cup back to the well when she saw the four mounted men. They hadn't been there a moment ago, and she looked around to see where they'd come from. A jagged, rocky ridge a hundred yards to the east of the station offered the only concealment, so they must have come from there.

Her gaze returned to the mounted men, and it came to her with a slight sense of shock that this was a holdup. She'd read about this sort of thing, but it didn't seem real, even now. All the men had pulled bandannas over their mouths, and they had their rifles pointed at the passengers.

The man doing the speaking was a short, stocky man seated on a powerful bay. He was brief and to the point. "Ain't nobody gonna get hurt here, unless we got us some heroes. Generally, we bury the heroes. If'n there's time for the burial. Now, here's the way it works. Two of us stay right here and keep you covered so nobody gets antsy with their weapons. One watches the horses. The other two"—here he jerked a thumb at the two men on his left —"will take your valuables. Don't hold nothin' out on us. Ma'am."

He'd tipped his hat with the last word, and Sarah realized he was speaking to her. She couldn't help but smile a little at the situation. Politeness in a crook who was preparing to rob her. That was a new one. The two outlaws he had pointed to dismounted and began to check the male passengers for weapons.

Sarah found she was still thinking clearly, and three points came to mind forcibly. First, they hadn't bothered to check her for weapons, and she knew how to use her revolver if she could get to it. Apparently, they had decided she was harmless. Second, they had forgotten or overlooked the man who had been riding shotgun, he was now in the shack. At least, that was the last place she had seen him. No doubt he was looking for a chance to use that shotgun of his if he could do it without harming the passengers. And third, the drifter who had claimed to be a cowboy, standing to her right, was preparing to do something rash. She could sense it from his posture and his unrelenting glare at the robbers.

The stare from the drifter gave way to a wild light in his eyes. He submitted to having his gun taken, but his face was deadly pale afterward. Standing next to him, Sarah was acutely aware of his fist clenching and unclenching down there at his side. There was a nervous tic in one of his eyes, and he was breathing in quick, shallow spurts. Things were about to boil over into serious trouble, she felt sure.

CHAPTER SIX

MEETING SARAH

S arah watched as the two dismounted outlaws split up, and while one of them carried the confiscated guns back to his partners, the second approached the drifter to take his wallet. The drifter let out a strangled cry of rage, hauled back his clenched fist, and swung.

It was a futile act to begin with, and it was over almost before it started. The outlaw ducked instinctively when he saw the movement, and the drifter's punch swung wildly over his head. The outlaw then drew and reversed his gun, stepped forward, and struck the drifter across the temple with the butt of the gun. There was a dull thud as the drifter slipped to the ground.

Sarah moved in quickly. "What have you done to him?"

The outlaw, on edge, swung around to cover Sarah, and her eyes widened in genuine fear.

"Put that thing away," she commanded. "Or do you intend to go around here shooting unarmed women?"

Embarrassed by her words, he mumbled under his breath and dropped the gun back in its holster.

Sarah dropped to her knees beside the drifter. "You

don't mind if I try to patch up your handiwork, do you?" She hoped the forced outrage in her voice would cover the tremble. Now came the tricky part. She had to get the gun out of her purse. She looked up to find the man on the bay horse watching her intently. His rifle, though, was still aimed at the stage driver. Sarah opened her purse and caught his eye. "I have bandages in my purse," she told him. "May I do what I can to bandage this man's head?"

The outlaw on the bay horse hesitated, then nodded.

Sarah reached into the purse and withdrew the gun. She pointed it at the man on the bay horse. After that, things seemed to happen too quickly, and not at all the way she had planned. She had thought that when she covered the man with her revolver, he would sit still or maybe drop his Winchester. Then the shotgun rider in the shack could cover the outlaws who had dismounted. Instead, the man on the bay horse swung his rifle toward her. When she saw the gun begin to move, Sarah pulled the trigger and shot him cleanly through the chest.

Pandemonium broke loose. Sarah watched in horror as the stocky man on the bay horse lurched over backward and landed in the dust. His horse reared and raced away. At the same instant, the shotgun boomed from the shack, and the shot blew the second mounted man loose from the saddle. Sarah swung her revolver to cover the man who'd hit the drifter, and he backed away with hands held high. "Don't shoot, lady," he croaked, "I'll ride."

Sarah nodded, feeling immense relief at not being forced to shoot again. The shotgun boomed one more time from the shack, and the last outlaw, out near the horses, pitched over onto his face, rifle clattering to the ground. There was a receding drum of hoofbeats as the man Sarah had let go made his escape.

One of the other passengers, a Dallas banker, Sarah

remembered, helped her to her feet. "Are you all right, Miss?" he asked. "You're looking awful pale."

Sarah nodded, then dashed out behind the well where she was suddenly sick. She came out and leaned against the side of the well, waiting for the trembling to pass. That gun of hers had never been used for anything but target practice before. It all happened so suddenly it didn't seem quite real.

The corpses over there looked real, though, and one of them was there on her account. The man riding shotgun came from the shack, shotgun cradled under his arm. "That was a brave thing you done, Miss," he told her. "You gave me the chance I needed to open up with old Betsy here." He patted the shotgun. "Didn't a one of the passengers get hurt, neither."

Sarah managed a small smile, but the bodies were being carried out behind the shack now, and she stared with dulled eyes. The stagecoach driver grabbed a shovel and dug. Were there any others buried out there, she wondered? She transferred her gaze to the shotgun rider. "Did we really have to shoot, do you think?"

The man looked at her closely, then braced his shotgun against the wall and kneeled down beside her. "You listen to me, ma'am," he admonished, "you only done what you had to do. Don't forget that, and don't go worryin' yourself about the man you shot. He was bringing that gun around on you when you pulled the trigger. I saw it. If you hadn't shot him, you'd be dead right now in his place. You defended yourself, that's all. Okay?"

Sarah nodded and pulled herself together with an effort. "Of course," she said, "You're right. I'll be fine." They both stood on their feet and the stage tender came forward.

"Stagecoach driver's about ready to go," he told them.

"I know the guy that got away, and he might have some friends who'd like to try this again. You folks better get out of here as fast as you can."

"What about the injured man?" Sarah noticed he still lay where he had fallen.

"He'll be all right. I'll take care of him. I've had plenty of practice doctorin' out here at this stop." He shook his head. "One of the dumbest plays I ever seen. Could have got the lot of us kilt, swingin' with his fist like that." He walked over to help carry the drifter toward the shack, muttering to himself the entire way.

Sarah smiled despite herself and walked back over to the stage. When she had boarded, they rolled out.

———

After they had been back on the trail for about an hour, Sarah found that some of the shock from the robbery had faded. She knew she would never forget seeing the man on the bay horse topple to the ground. She also knew he would have very likely killed her had she not fired. The other thought that lingered in her mind was the man she'd let go. The fear in those eyes as he backed away from her gun. She had never seen anyone scared of her like that. And the lie bothered her, too. She had told him she was unarmed.

It wasn't a useful way of thinking. Sarah shook her head, impatient with herself, and turned to find the Dallas banker watching her sympathetically. "It's not still bothering you, is it, Miss? Self-defense is a way of life out here. I'm a banker myself, but I carry a gun sometimes, and I'll use it, if need be."

Sarah shook her head again. "It's bothering me a little less, I guess. Maybe I just need to think about something else. Tell me about something else. What do you know about Austin?"

The banker smiled quizzically. "You're going to Austin?" Sarah nodded. "I'll be there for a while, at least."

"Well," he began, "it's the state capital, you know. It's going to grow, I think, because of that. I've been down there a couple times. You'll like it there." He went on for a few more minutes about Austin, then they talked about the West, about Philadelphia, and about the army. Eventually he nodded off to sleep. After the stagecoach driver finally announced that they were about two hours away from Ft. Worth, Sarah also drifted off to sleep.

———

I'm a small-town boy, so Ft. Worth was just about the biggest thing I had ever seen. Ash McKinnon and I had come into town after we'd bedded down the herd outside of town. Several of the others headed for a saloon first thing, but Ash and I mostly walked around, staring at all the people. We found out they actually had street cars running, so we caught a streetcar from the courthouse to the railroad station, then walked back to where we had started. We went into the courthouse and found out the population of Ft. Worth was over nine thousand people. Ash said he wasn't sure he'd actually seen nine thousand people in his entire life.

Jud Campbell had cautioned us against going down to Hell's Half Acre—an area maybe five blocks long and three blocks wide that started down around Tenth Street. He said the area had been cleaned up some over the last six or seven years, but a guy could still get in a lot of trouble down there. He said Ft. Worth had a marshal several years back named Long Hair Jim Courtright who had arrested or shot several of the troublemakers. Word was he cut the number of murders in town by half, but had extracted money from the businesses for doing it. Anyway, he lost the election somewhere along the way and didn't live here anymore. Campbell said Courtright wore two guns facing forward and was quite a gunfighter. I couldn't really picture how he would draw with the guns facing forward. I guess he must have reached across with the opposite hand to pull it out.

We found a saloon near the courthouse and walked in for a beer just as the sun was setting. Ash asked me what I wanted to do with my money after the drive ended. I shrugged. "I don't have enough money to start a ranch. I don't have enough property either. Fifty acres won't be enough."

Ash glanced up in some surprise. "You own fifty acres?"

I explained how I came to have the fifty acres after Miles had died.

He nodded and looked down into his beer. "You said you were a deputy sheriff for a while. Want to do that again?"

I stared out the window and thought about the day I'd killed Juarez Chico in the street in Cimarron. I didn't want to do that again.

Finally, I turned and looked over at Ash, who was still waiting for an answer. "I wouldn't mind being a part of something bigger. If you're sheriff or deputy sheriff and an outlaw comes into town, maybe several of them, you might be the only one around to stop them. That wasn't much fun."

Ash nodded, then fell silent for a while. "We could do some more of these drives and make some money. Only they say the railroads will take the place of these drives after a few years. We could still do it for a while, though."

That was a thought. Maybe we could. I grabbed my

hat and rose from the table. "I'm going to find a place where I can get a bath and a shave," I told him.

Ash looked surprised again. "You're kidding."

"No," I said. "Bath and a shave."

Ash stared at me. "When was your last bath?"

I searched my brain. "I guess the day before we left on the drive."

Ash shook his head and waved for another beer. "You go ahead. I'll keep just fine till we get to Kansas."

I chuckled and left the saloon. I had to ask directions a couple times, but I finally found a place for the bath and shave. We would head back out to the camp to take our turn on guard duty after a couple hours, then the drive would start again in the late morning tomorrow. I knew that I would be back in Ft. Worth for a while in the early morning. Campbell had asked McKinnon and me to come in and pick up the payroll at the bank before we broke camp. He said he didn't want the men to get their hands on the pay while they were anywhere near Hell's Half Acre. I had to grin at that one.

————

Louis Sharpe stretched out as best he could on the rail car and watched the slightly undulating southern Oklahoma landscape flash past through his window. He planned to beat the girl to Austin and keep an eye on the stagecoaches coming in. He'd had to admit to himself that he couldn't be absolutely sure the property was the same one he remembered. It was a crudely drawn map, and he hadn't been there in five years. When he was sure, he could dispose of the girl if he wanted the place as a hideout.

Actually, he corrected himself, there could be one other owner he needed to take care of. He'd done this sort of thing before. It made no difference to him whether the victim was a man or a woman. He would just have to be more careful if it involved a woman. It would have to be an accident. No problem there. People always had accidents out here in the West. Especially these Easterners. An accident while riding her horse. Maybe even a staged Indian attack would do just fine.

His thoughts turned to whether or not he wanted to bring in any help on this. He knew of two others who had been with the Sam Bass gang who, the last he knew, were in Ft. Worth. Maybe he could look them up when he arrived. If there turned out to be trouble with the unknown partner on the land, or if it looked like he was going to get his hands dirty in dealing with the girl, he could use them. They didn't need to know what any of this was about. If things worked out, maybe he could use them for some robberies.

After he had set up on this property in Austin, he could go on back to St. Louis and see Keene again. If Keene could keep his ear up to the keyhole at the lawyer's office and find out more things like this, it could be very profitable. Better than the blackmail, even. Keene could be a sort of junior partner. Sharpe's lip curled up in a smirk. He would be a partner that didn't get paid—if this brief trip turned out to be worthwhile. If it was a hoax, Keene would be a dead man. Sharpe didn't allow himself to be double-crossed more than once. It was bad for business.

The train pulled to a stop, and they passed the announcement along that this would be a fuel stop, and there would be no other stops before arriving in Ft. Worth. Passengers were invited to stretch their legs for one hour, after which they needed to be back on board for the final run. Sharpe got up and moved to the exit. He would look up those two gun-hands while he was in town. You never knew when it might come in handy.

———

Sarah stood in front of the only hotel she had found since getting off the stagecoach and carrying her suitcase around for the last several blocks. The words *Ft. Worth Hotel* were displayed on the sign in front of her. Nothing about the building looked very promising. Several boards appeared to be loose on the front steps, and the entire building could use some paint, as far as she could see. Still, she hoped to get a good night of sleep or two before leaving on the last leg of the trip to Austin. Not for the first time, she wondered if she had made a good decision in coming down here.

After checking in, she found the room to be a little better than what the building had seemed to promise her from the outside. The bed seemed to be pretty comfortable, and her room faced away from the street below, so it might be fairly quiet. After washing up for a few minutes, she walked down to the front desk and asked about the locations of the telegraph office in Ft. Worth. She had told her father in her previous wire that she would stop here, and she was eager to see if she had received an answer. The clerk directed her to an address on Eighth Street, only a few blocks from where she was.

She found the telegraph office without too much trouble, noting the hum and clatter around her as she walked in. The arrival of the railroad just recently had probably turned Ft. Worth from a sleepy little town to a hub of activity. She stepped up to the desk, gave the clerk her name, and waited anxiously while he searched for a message for her. Her hopes were flagging when the clerk gave a triumphant snort and snatched a message from a disorganized pile under the counter. He pushed it across the countertop to her. Her words of thanks were drowned out by the man in line behind her announcing his name to the clerk.

Sarah took the message and left the office, seating herself on a bench in the morning sunshine as she eagerly opened the message from her father. Major Statton was, as usual, brief and to the point in his message to her. She leaned slightly to lessen the glare on the sheet of paper and read: "Sarah, received your wire on the morning of the fourth instant. Stop. Glad you are well. Stop. Have received orders for transfer. New post in Ft. Lowell, Arizona. Stop. Passing through Ft. Worth train station on the morning of the twenty-fourth instant. Stop. Meet me if you can. Stop."

Feeling encouraged at the news from her father and excited about seeing him again soon, Sarah decided on the spot to pack up her bags and take the train to Austin for the last leg of the trip. She packed within a few minutes and checked out of the hotel, picking her way around the steps in need of repair in front of the hotel and reaching the street. She looked at the directions she'd gotten from the clerk to get to the train station and turned south. Instantly, she froze. The man with the gray eyes was directly across the street, staring at her.

Feeling panic, she turned to see two cowboys coming down the street toward her. They were both big men. She grabbed the arm of the one closer to her, slightly smaller than the other, with dark, curly hair and a friendly, attractive face. "There you are," she blurted out. "You're just in time to walk me to the train station."

CHAPTER SEVEN

HERD CUTTERS

W e were within about a block of the bank—I could see the First National Bank of Galveston sign above the front doors. Ash and I were carrying a case apiece to carry the money back to our horses. I figured we would have no trouble getting it back without being held up, but I was wearing my gun belt this time, and I would feel better when we were back at camp.

I caught a quick impression of a beautiful, auburn-haired girl who was elegantly dressed, at least to my eyes, coming up on my right, and I stepped aside a little to give her room to pass. To my astonishment, she grabbed my arm and said something about walking with her to the train station. I spun around, swept off my hat and said something that sounded like *whaaattt?* Ash spun too, no doubt as surprised as I was. I could only hope I wasn't staring at her like he was.

She stepped in and wrapped her arm around mine, smiling up at me, but I could see a little fear in her eyes. "Please," she said in an undertone, "there's someone over there who I think has been following me all the way from

St. Louis. Will you please walk me to the train station and stay with me until I get on?"

I reached down and lifted the bag she had been carrying. "It would be my pleasure," I assured her. I looked around for whoever might be following her, but she pulled me back around to face her.

"Don't look, please. Just get me to the station." We turned and walked in that direction.

I noticed that she seemed to chatter nervously for the first block. We passed by a man who was across the street, leaning against the wall of a building, appearing to study some papers he was holding in his hand. Her nervousness seemed to decrease after we passed him. She clung to my arm as we walked, and I must say I was really enjoying it. I glanced back at Ash and saw that he was trailing behind us. Knowing Ash, he was probably looking around to see if she had any friends who needed help. We reached the station, and I watched her bags while she bought a ticket, then walked her over to where the train was boarding.

She handed her bag to an attendant, then turned back to me, smiling and patting my cheek with her gloved hand. "Thank you," she said simply. "You've helped more than you know. I'm Sarah Statton, by the way."

I took off my hat again, not sure if that was the thing to do or not. "Mike Stone," I told her. I pointed at Ash and introduced him as well.

Sarah nodded at Ash, then smiled at me again. "If you get down to Austin sometime, maybe I'll see you."

My eyes widened slightly with surprise, and maybe a little excitement. "I'm from Austin," I told her. "I'll be headed back down there after we finish this cattle drive."

It was her turn to look surprised. Then the train whistle sounded and there was no more time. "Look me up, Mike Stone," she said, and then she was aboard and the train was moving.

I stood and watched as the train pulled away. And to think the most exciting thing I'd expected to do today was to carry the money back to the cow camp. I turned and looked at Ash, who was also watching the train pull away. He took off his hat and scratched his head, then replaced the hat.

"I think," he announced, "I'm going to go and get me a bath and a shave, too."

"You do that," I told him. "The cows will appreciate that all the way to Kansas."

———

Sharpe kept his distance, staying about a block and a half away from the train station. He hadn't really planned on catching today's train, anyway. He had been just as surprised as the Statton girl looked when they had seen each other on the street. He hadn't expected to cross her trail again until they both arrived in Austin.

He was a little puzzled about the two men who had accompanied her to the train station. Both wore a gun belt, and they seemed to know her, or at least the dark-haired man seemed to know her. If she had a protector or two down here, that would change everything. He continued to watch as she boarded and left. The two men turned and began walking back in his direction. He turned and looked the other way. He made it a point to be recognized as little as possible.

After both men had passed by on the street, Sharpe crossed and entered a run-down saloon on a side street. Two men sat inside, mostly in the shadows, each working on a whiskey. They looked up and nodded in recognition when Sharpe walked across and joined them at the table. He knew them only as Pete and Kendall. Whether those were their actual names, Sharpe didn't know and didn't care. They had been with Sam Bass at the same time he had, and he knew he could count on them to do whatever he needed, so long as he paid them sufficiently.

Without preamble, Sharpe looked across the table at them. "How many of you are left, and what are you doing?"

The two looked at each other and exchanged a shrug. "There are four of us left from the Bass gang around here," Pete told him. "Perkins is making noise like he's in charge, and we think the other two plus a couple new guys are gonna rob a train somewhere. We might join 'em. They'll be watching for train robberies after what we did before. We'll see."

Sharpe absorbed the information silently. The other two watched his face. Finally, Kendall asked the question on their minds.

"You got somethin' for us?"

Sharpe hesitated, then shrugged. "Maybe. I'm not sure just yet. If I do, it would be a few days' work down near Austin." He stopped and tried to decide how much he was willing to pay them. "Pay you maybe a hundred dollars for a few days' work. You interested?"

The two exchanged glances. "What would we have to do? Rob something?"

Sharpe shook his head. "Nothing like that. You might need to make a couple people go away. Pretty simple stuff."

Both outlaws nodded their heads. "Okay. Let us know."

Sharpe nodded, tossed off his whiskey, and watched while the other two left.

Sharpe sat moodily at the table, angry for the hundredth time, he was sure, about the split he had gotten after the Union Pacific train robbery. There were six of them, and Bass said he split the money evenly. Sharpe had gotten $6,000—300 twenty-dollar gold pieces, but the newspaper reports later said that $60,000 had been taken. His cut should have been $10,000. He swore under his breath and looked around, waving his empty glass in the air. Sam Bass was dead now, killed here in Texas. No chance to get even. Sharpe wondered, though, if Bass might have buried something on that creek bank in Texas. It might be worth his while to look around after the property was his.

————

Sarah leaned back into her seat on the train. The clack of the rails was familiar to her because she had come to St. Louis from Philadelphia by train. She was glad she had switched from the stagecoach for this last leg. She glanced into her purse. Sarah had eight of the twenty-dollar gold pieces from her uncle left, plus about as much that she had brought with her. She would need to decide pretty quickly whether she would stay in Austin. She could teach school to make some money if she needed to.

She turned and looked out the window, feeling worried once again that she had seen the same man who had trailed her in St. Louis. It seemed like a pretty big coincidence that she would see him on the street in Ft. Worth. She believed she had gotten rid of him. She had watched from the train window and knew for sure that he hadn't boarded this train. She had checked behind her several times during the walk over to the station and hadn't seen him again. Maybe that was the last she would see of him. Somehow, though, she still felt a pretty big concern about whether she would run across him when she got to Austin.

She leaned back again and closed her eyes. That young cowboy had been helpful. Very gentlemanly and pretty handsome to boot. A small smile crossed her lips. So, he was from Austin. Something about him...she had a feeling he might be looking for her around the town down there. Another small smile played across her face. Eventually, the rhythm of the wheels on the rails caused her to doze off to sleep.

————

We moved out of Ft. Worth around midday. Campbell told us not to get used to it—he assured us we would pull out at daybreak the rest of the way. I guess he wanted the boys who had spent a lot of time at the saloons to recover. By mid-afternoon on the first day, it was getting hot. I shed my coat, tying it onto the saddle, and I was already pretty happy we were doing this drive in the late spring, not the middle of summer. I pulled out my canteen for the first of many swigs of water, thinking back to the girl I had walked to the train station.

Sarah Statton was the name she had given, and she would be in Austin. A small smile crossed my face, and Ash McKinnon, riding next to me, snorted loudly. "Still thinkin' about that girl, I see," he chortled. "You'll be lucky if she recognizes you when you get back to Austin. Think she's got a sister?" he added as an afterthought.

"If she does, I'll introduce you," I said, "but only if you've had another bath and shave."

I was saved from hearing Ash's reply when we heard an approaching horse. We all three reined around to meet Jud Campbell, who had ridden forward to talk to us. He spent no time on chit-chat, as we had learned on the first day or two of the drive.

"Next water is the Red River, due north," he told us. "I

hope to make it there in four days, so keep 'em moving. They'll stampede for it when they get a whiff of the water, so be careful about being out in front after a couple more days go by." He opened his mouth as if to say something, then seemed to hold off on saying it. Finally, he waved for us to lean in and listen up, as if there was anybody else we'd be listening to out there in the middle of nowhere. "I'm still expecting herd cutters," he snapped. "So, keep your eyes peeled. They could come up out of a dry wash here or there. And one of you best be out front scouting as you go." He reined his horse around, then turned back. "If cutters show up, keep an eye out behind you too. They might have friends working this drive." Without further explanation, he galloped off.

We exchanged puzzled glances after Campbell returned to the herd. The first part was clear enough. McKinnon volunteered to ride scout for us, and Red and I agreed to that immediately. The second part was the confusing part. Campbell had hinted that herd cutters might work in partnership with one or more cowboys working on the drive. I thought back to the first morning, when I'd met Campbell. There were two men I'd met that morning, Bevins and Porter by name, who'd been very obviously unhappy about riding drag and pretty hostile toward me ever since. Could it be they were unhappy about riding drag for more than one reason? Did they want to be upfront when or if the herd cutters showed up?

After Ash had ridden out with his Winchester to scout up ahead, I told Red my thoughts about Bevins and Porter. I wasn't sure if we should keep an eye out for those two or if I was just suspicious of them because none of us liked each other. I explained that thought to Red as well.

He grinned at the last comment and seemed to roll the idea around in his head for a while. "You could be right about them," he said after a while. "Some people are just sour, but those two don't even try to get along with anybody else. I know that most of us have a few cows of our own on this drive. Those two don't have any. We'll keep an eye on them."

We rode along for a while, then Red asked, "How long were you a deputy sheriff?"

"Less than a year," I told him. "Why?"

Red shrugged. "Your instincts about Bevins and Porter might be right on."

———

It was the morning of the third day out when the herd cutters came. Ash was out scouting to the northwest when they came out of a dry wash to the east. There were three of them, bandannas pulled up over their mouths, and they held rifles in our direction as they came up on us.

The one in the lead pulled up abruptly and spoke for the three of them. "We're taking some cows," he said, gesturing with his rifle toward the herd coming up behind us.

None of them had their rifles trained directly on us, and when he moved the barrel away from me, I drew and fired in one quick movement. He toppled off his horse backward, triggering his Winchester in the air as he did so. The one next to him tried a snapshot from the hip as I swung to cover him, and my second shot took him off his horse as well. He fell into the dust as his horse reared and trotted away. The third man dropped his rifle and raised his hands as Red covered him with his pistol.

I heard hoofbeats behind me and swung, pistol still out, to cover Bevins and Porter as they rode up. They hadn't expected to find two dead herd cutters. I could see the confusion on their faces. Porter moved to pull his pistol, but Bevins reached out just in time to stop him. It was a good thing, because I was in no mood to take any more prisoners. I kept my Colt .45 out of the holster, though not aimed directly at them, as I heard McKinnon galloping in. When he came alongside, Winchester at the ready, I risked a glance backward and saw Red taking the third man prisoner. There was an awkward silence as we heard another horse approaching. I could see it was Jud Campbell.

Campbell took in the situation with a quick glance. He dismounted and looked at the two men I had shot. "Two shots fired, both men shot through the heart. Dead as Caesar, I'd say." He looked at me and noted that my pistol was still out.

With another glance at Bevins and Porter, I slowly re-holstered the gun.

Campbell swung his glance to look at them also. "What were you doing here?" he demanded. "It's a long way back to the drag positions."

They exchanged a glance, then Bevins spoke for them: "We were coming up to talk to Stone and Red, and got here just in time to help stop the cutters."

Campbell stared at them, then wheeled around to look at Red and me. "That right?"

I shook my head. "They got here after the situation was...handled. If they were coming to talk to us, I don't know why."

Campbell jerked his head toward my partners. "Red, McKinnon?"

Red shook his head. "It's like Mike told you. Didn't look like they were coming to help. Looked more like they might want to draw on us."

Campbell stared at them for a long time, then rode over to them, reaching into his saddlebag as he went. He pulled out some gold coins and gave a few to each man. "You're done," he said. "Ride out now. I have paid you what you have coming."

Bevins looked at me, his eyes shining with hate. His hand hovered above his pistol. I stared back at him, my right hand resting on my thigh. "You think you're a big man, Stone? I'd take you down, but you have too many friends here."

Red chipped in: "I'll make sure it's a fair fight. Just the two of you, if that's what you want, Bevins."

Bevins stared at Red, then at me. "Think you're a big man, Stone?" he repeated.

I thought about that one for a second. "I think I'm big enough to handle you, Bevins," I said mildly. "Your choice."

He remained frozen where he was for several seconds, his hand still hovering above the holster, staring at me unblinkingly. Finally, he relaxed and moved his hand away from the gun. "This isn't done," he told me. Then the two of them wheeled their horses around and rode away.

I turned to find the eyes of the three others on me. Campbell shook his head, then motioned toward Ash. "McKinnon, you big galoot. Help me load those two dead men on the horses. I'll get somebody to bury them." He glanced at me and shook his head again. "Two shots, two dead men. Who was that outlaw you killed in New Mexico?" Then he waved his hand. "No, I don't want to know." He led the horses away with the dead herd cutters. The third one, tied to the saddle, rode behind.

Red never mentioned the herd-cutting incident again, but I knew those eyes missed little. He seemed to sense that I didn't want to talk about it. The next day, around mid-afternoon, the herd picked up the pace. They bellowed, then broke into a trot. We made sure we were well out of their path when they stampeded toward the

Red River. We followed behind, then waded the horses in well upstream of the herd. I splashed several hatfuls of water on my head, enjoying the coolness of the water and the fact that the first major leg of the drive was over. Indian Territory and Kansas were still ahead of us.

CHAPTER EIGHT
THUNDER AND LIGHTNING

Sarah stood in the train station in Austin, her bags at her feet. She was relieved to have finally reached her destination, but also a little uncertain about how she wanted to proceed now that she was finally here. She moved out to the street, looking around her, then slowly became aware of a young boy standing beside her, cap twisted in his hands.

"Ma'am?" he said.

Sarah looked at him in some surprise, uncertain of what to expect.

"Ma'am," he continued, "if you're looking for a place to stay, my Ma runs a little boarding house down the street"—here he pointed down the road—"and I can take you there on my buggy if'n you'd like me to." He finished by pointing at a small buggy drawn by an elderly-looking horse at the side of the street in front of them.

Sarah looked at him in surprise. He said nothing further, just stood there twisting his cap in his hands. It occurred to her that this might be a pretty good way for the woman to get business for her boarding house. The boy could look for arriving passengers who didn't seem to have anybody meeting them or any place to go. It also occurred to her that if she could find room and board at a nice place for a reasonable rate, it would solve a big problem for her. She looked again at the boy standing next to her. "What's your name?" she asked.

"Daniel, ma'am." He continued to twist the cap in his hands.

"Daniel, I'm Sarah. Why don't you take me to see your boardinghouse?"

With a nod and a small smile, he helped her load her bags onto the cart and set off down the street.

A mile or so later, the boy pulled up at a long, rambling house at the side of the street. The house appeared to have a fairly fresh coat of white paint, with a small, waist-high fence surrounding the property. Flowers peeked out of a few window boxes at either side of the front door. Daniel stepped down from the buggy and stood uncertainly beside it, waiting for some reaction from Sarah, who also alighted, taking in the house and yard.

"Daniel," she said eventually. "Could you just watch my bags for a few minutes while I take a look and talk to your mother?"

Daniel nodded his agreement and took a seat in the buggy.

A middle-aged, graying woman wearing an apron promptly answered Sarah's knock at the front door. There was flour on her arms up to the elbow. She wiped her hands on the apron before reaching out to shake Sarah's hand. She glanced past Sarah to the buggy in the street and smiled. "I see that Daniel must have spotted you at the train station. Do come in."

Sarah stepped into the hallway. The woman closed the door and said, "My name is Judith Kirk, but you can call me Ma. Everybody else does around here. Can I assume you have some interest in finding a place to stay, Miss...?"

"Sarah," she responded, "and yes, I would like to find a place to stay at a reasonable cost."

The woman nodded and led the way down a narrow hallway, stopping at an open door and leading the way in, then crossing the room to open the curtains. The sunshine revealed a small but clean and neat room with a single bed and dresser. A pitcher of water stood on a sideboard under a mirror. There was a small closet in one corner of the room. Sarah made a circle around the room, testing the bed for a moment, then standing to look at the woman.

"The washroom is down the hall," she answered without being asked. "You would share it with the one other woman who lives in this hallway. I have four other boarders right now," she added.

Sarah nodded, her hopes rising. "And meals?" she asked. "And price?"

Ma, looking encouraged, answered promptly. "Two good meals served every day," she answered. "Breakfast, from six-thirty a.m. to eight a.m. Dinner, from five-thirty to seven p.m. I cook everything myself." She pulled at the apron, trying to read Sarah's expression. "Three dollars a week," she added.

Sarah hesitated only briefly. "Deal," she said. "Can I move in now?"

In answer, Ma turned, walked down the hallway, and threw open the front door. "Daniel," she called. "Bring those bags down here to the empty room." She turned to face Sarah. "You probably didn't have breakfast this morning. I can't let a new boarder go hungry on the first day. Would you like something?"

———

Over some fresh fruit, biscuits, and tea in a sunny dining room, Sarah told the woman a bit about her past and how she had made the trip to Austin. She mentioned the property left to her by her uncle, but mentioned nothing about anything buried on the land or the man who had followed her in St. Louis.

Ma listened to all of it, sipping at her tea thoughtfully. When Sarah finished talking, she appeared to be choosing from a few questions in her mind, then simply asked: "What do you need to do now?"

Sarah sat back and stared at the wall. She needed a horse, but didn't really want the expense of buying one. She probably also needed to take her uncle's will to a lawyer and see if some sort of filing needed to be made on the land.

Sarah began uncertainly: "Do you think there's a livery stable or someplace where I could rent a horse for a day now and then to go out to see the property—"

She stopped as Ma waved her hand in the air and pointed toward the back of the house. "We have a horse besides that old thing Daniel hooks up to the buggy. You can borrow her and the saddle and bridle if we're not using her."

Sarah stared at her, trying to find the words to thank the woman, feeling more than a little surprised by the generosity from a stranger. Ma waved her hand in the air again. "That's how we do things down here in Texas. We help our neighbors. What else do you need?"

Sarah wondered how she had been lucky enough to come to this house. "Well," she said, "I probably need to see a lawyer about my uncle's will and the property."

"Lawyer." Ma was up from the table and standing in front of a tall cupboard next to the wall. She opened a drawer and was rewarded with a small shower of paper. She fished among the scraps of paper, muttering "lawyer,

lawyer" under her breath. "Aha!" She turned, triumphantly holding out a scrap of paper. "Here's a lawyer. I used him for something a few years ago when my Jeremy passed. He did all right for me."

Sarah glanced at the paper. "Jacob Peters," she repeated to herself. She glanced up. "Is he far from here?"

Ma pointed down the road. "About half a mile," she said.

Sarah thanked her for the breakfast and stood up. "I can use the walk," she said and headed down the hall to find her uncle's will in her bags.

———

Sarah had gone only a few hundred yards down the street when she heard the clip-clop of hoofs pulling up behind her. She looked back to see Daniel approaching her with the buggy.

"Do you want a ride, ma'am?" He was staring at the street, glancing up to meet her eyes once in a while. Sarah suppressed a small smile. Did she have an admirer?

"Daniel," she said, "I can walk. It isn't far."

"I don't mind giving you a ride," came the answer.

"Doesn't your mom have something she needs you to be doing?" she asked.

"No, ma'am, I've done my work."

Sarah chuckled and stepped up to take a seat in the buggy. "Okay, Daniel, thanks for the ride," she told him. "Just drop me off and then go home to see if your mom needs you for anything."

———

Inside the office of Jacob Peters, Sarah fought her way through a cloud of cigar smoke and pushed a few documents across the desk. She laid down a document called *Abstract of Title* from the state of Texas, a map of the property, her uncle's will from the attorney in St. Louis, and last, the letter from her uncle Zeb. Peters read through all of them with few comments, stopping only to chuckle briefly at her uncle Zeb's letter. Peters finished reading them, looked up, and began to speak, then stopped and looked again at the map. He opened a desk drawer, rummaged through some papers, and pulled out a folder. He opened the folder and examined a few documents in it.

Sarah was feeling uneasy about the situation when Peters looked up at her. "Everything seems in order," he assured her. "I can file this claim for you."

Sarah breathed a small sigh of relief.

"You do know, don't you," continued Peters, "that two of you own equal parts of the original one hundred acres?"

Sarah stared at him. "I knew there could be another owner, a former partner of my uncle."

Peters extended a document from the folder he had pulled out. "Your uncle's old partner willed his half to a young man who was in here a few weeks ago. Let's see..." He sorted through the folder. "The other owner's name is Mike Stone. Young guy, tall, dark hair. Do you know him?"

Sarah's head came up, and she stared at Peters again. A dozen thoughts seemed to go through her mind at once. Finally, a small smile touched the corners of her mouth. It looked like she would cross paths again with that cowboy she had met in Ft. Worth.

———

We were well into the Territory now, after about six weeks on the trail. We had found good water at the North Canadian and Cimarron rivers, with a few streams to help us out in between. The cattle were now broken to the trail, and we were moving forward at a good pace every day. There had been no incidents since the attempted herd-cutting north of Ft. Worth. I was feeling we would make it to our destination of Newton, Kansas, without more trouble. Both Red and Jud Campbell told me not to relax. And, in fact, I knew from the drive I had made from Dodge City back to Cimarron, New Mexico, that trouble could come when you didn't expect it.

Taking my turn on night duty, I thought about the end of this drive and my plans for afterward. The Arkansas River and Kansas lay ahead of us, and even Jud Campbell had admitted we might finish the drive in a couple more weeks, making it a pretty quick drive. Red had told me he would recommend both Ash and me for joining the Texas Rangers, and I had to admit it sounded pretty good. It might be a good job for me, and maybe I could save up and decide what else I would want to do.

Glancing up at the moon and seeing a little gray light dawning in the east, I knew my shift was about over. I moved Blaze, the one horse I owned and had brought on this drive, around the back of the herd and thought about whether Morty the cook had any coffee going over at the chuck wagon. The closer I came to the chuck wagon, though, the more I realized the stillness in the air and the smell of rain closing in. I glanced uneasily at the sky. I could see several riders moving out toward the herd, so I rode on in and dismounted.

Accepting a cup of coffee from Morty, I could see Jud Campbell and Red approaching me. There were a few low rumbles rolling in, and Campbell looked worried. "Thunderstorms will spook cattle," he began, breaking off his thought and staring out toward the west. A jagged streak of lightning suddenly illuminated the sky. "Let's mount up," Campbell said, turning toward his horse.

Suddenly, a deafening clap of thunder broke the

morning silence, and the cattle bellowed. The rumble of movement reached our ears. "Stampede!" Campbell screamed, and I sprinted for my horse.

I had never unsaddled Blaze after reaching camp, so I grabbed the reins, swung aboard, and touched him with the spurs in one long, rolling motion. He leaped ahead as I jammed my boots into the stirrups and we raced out into the night. I could hear Jud and Red just behind me. I knew what we needed to do—we needed to turn the leaders if we could. If we could turn them back toward the herd, we could cause them to mill and stop the stampede. Otherwise, there was no telling how far they might run and how many cows we would lose.

Blaze had speed, and a quick glance back told me I had gained a little ground on Jud and Red. Small bits of hail stung my face as the sky was streaked by lightning again, and I heard another crack of thunder. The ground flashed by underneath in the pale morning light, and I could only hope that Blaze didn't come down on a gopher hole or other hidden danger underneath us. Getting thrown at this speed could be the end of me. I could see the leaders up ahead of me now, we would be abreast of them soon. I could see the lead steer, the one we'd named Butch, running out front with several more bunched behind him. Now came the most dangerous part of all.

Another glance back told me that Jud and Red, and behind them, a couple other riders, were moving over toward the herd in an effort to turn them. I had to do the same. Blaze seemed to know what I wanted as I nudged him over. We moved toward the lead steer and the others just behind them. I waved my hat and shouted as we moved closer, and it seemed almost miraculous as they pulled away toward my right. We stayed with them, moving a little slower now that we had caught the front of the herd but moving ever so slightly toward them as the herd turned.

I knew that the herd was spread out over the length of probably half a mile, so we made a wide, sweeping turn. I didn't feel the sharp sting of hail in my face and on my arms anymore, though the rain had opened up and made it difficult to see, even as the dawn brought a little more daylight. I thought maybe the pace was slowing a little. There was still an occasional streak of lightning in the gray sky, but the thunder seemed to have stopped. Riders appeared behind the stragglers at the end of the herd, off to my right. They swung wide and began helping us push the herd around. Finally, there was a confused mill of animals in no particular direction, with an occasional sickening thumping noise where two or more steers collided.

I pulled up to give Blaze a rest and to let my pounding heart slow down. Ash materialized out of the gloom, he had been one of those who had come behind the tail end of the herd to help push the leaders back into the stragglers at the rear. We watched as the herd slowly settled down. We would have to separate out Butch and the herd leaders later and get them back on the trail. For now, we were quite content to sit in the pouring rain and let them come to a complete stop.

——————

The last major stopping point and watering hole was the Arkansas River. We stopped there to let the cattle get plenty of water and to rest and water the horses. It was just a couple more days from there. We were all getting pretty eager to finish the drive. Ash and I took a count of the cattle we had brought up the trail with us. Of the original twenty-five cows I had brought on the drive, I still had twenty-two. Ash had lost eight of his original sixty-five. He had agreed at the start of the drive to give me ten cows in return for teaching him the ropes on the drive. We agreed he would give me eight after his losses.

We drove them into the holding pens in Newton exactly two months after we began the drive. Even Campbell seemed less grumpy than usual at the early date we'd brought them in. Newton didn't turn out to be much of a town, but the Atchison, Topeka, and Santa Fe railroad ran through there and would carry out cows back east. Campbell sold the herd for twenty-seven dollars apiece, so I had myself a stake of six hundred dollars profit in my pocket after the drive. Ash, Red, and I headed for the first saloon we could find to spend some of our profits.

After ordering a round of whiskey for us, Red tossed his down and looked at the two of us. "I'm going back to the Texas Rangers when I get back," he told us. "I had a chance to make a little money on this drive, so I did, but now I'll be going back." He paused while I ordered beer for the table. "Now," he said, "what do you boys plan to do?"

Now, there was a question that needed some thought. I knew I was going back down to Austin first, to check on my property again, and I had it in my head to look for that auburn-haired girl I had met in Ft. Worth. Beyond that, though, I didn't know what to do. I looked up at Red and shrugged. "First, I'll go back to Austin to check on some property I inherited," I told him. "The attorney was preparing some title papers for me. After that, I'm not sure."

Ash turned out to have fewer ideas about what to do than I did. He leaned back and took several huge gulps from his beer, wiped his mouth with his sleeve, and looked at both of us. Finally, he leaned back and stared at Red. "Beats me," he said. "Maybe I'll trail along with him for a while." He nodded his head in my direction.

I chuckled and waved a hand in the air. "Sure," I said. "Why not?"

Red grinned, then went over to the bar to get a piece of paper and a pencil. He came back to the table and wrote down his name and an address on the piece of paper. I looked at it. The address was in Austin. "If you have any interest in joining the Rangers, either of you, come and see me."

We both nodded, and I tucked the paper into my shirt pocket. It was something to think about.

CHAPTER NINE

INHERITANCE FOR TWO

S arah had expected to go out and view her inheritance within the first few days, but found that it was a full week before she made her way out to the property. After settling in for the first day or two, Ma Kirk, her landlady, had told her that Daniel's school needed a new teacher for the rest of the class year. Sarah remembered mentioning the possibility of school teaching during that first breakfast with the landlady, and Ma had come to her during the evening meal last night to let her know about the vacancy. Sarah had already decided to stay in Austin long enough to find out what she wanted to do with the land she had inherited.

The school building itself was unremarkable when Sarah went in the next morning. It was a one-room wooden building with a couple long rows of wooden desks. Thirteen students were attending, ages six through twelve. The outgoing teacher was there, along with a committee of three who hired and paid the teacher and made sure the school kept going. It turned out that Ma Kirk was one of the three on the committee, so Sarah had no trouble in getting the job. She was pretty sure she was the only one the committee had to choose from, so they seemed happy to welcome her as the new teacher. Sarah agreed to finish the school year over the next two months. They agreed to talk later about next year.

It was the weekend before she made a trip out to the land she had inherited. On Saturday morning, she borrowed her landlady's horse and followed her uncle's map out to the property. The first thing she noticed was what appeared to be the remnants of a house or shack, built along the curving banks of Walnut Creek. She dismounted and led her horse alongside the creek, seeing bits of wood strewn about over a wide area, along with a good-sized crater in the ground.

She wandered around the area, eventually hitching her horse to a tree and returning to explore the crater a bit more. She noticed what appeared to be a partially collapsed tunnel leading away from the crater and toward the river. Picking up a piece of wood, she dug a bit at the opening and saw steps leading down into the ground. She dropped the wood and jumped down to the edge of the creek, then walked along the bank, searching the side of the small bluff running alongside. Eventually, she saw what she was looking for—a tunnel that emptied out onto the bank of the creek.

Whoever had lived there had apparently wanted an escape route out of the cabin. Her uncle Zeb hadn't lived on this property, as far as she knew, so it must have been his old partner. She wondered if he had met his end in this explosion, or whatever had caused that hole in the ground. Returning to her horse, she pulled out her uncle's map again and began looking for the place where he said he had buried something in the creek bank. She pulled in the reins and balanced the map on the saddle horn, studying the land around her and turning the map until she felt she knew where to find the area marked by the X on the map.

She first rode away from the cabin through a small meadow, admiring the pockets of wildflowers she saw as she rode through. She followed the curve of a hillside deeper into the property, then finally turned and retraced the path she had taken back to the site of the old cabin. She consulted the map one more time, then rode her horse down into the creek bed, splashing through the water as she tried to match the landmarks on the map with what she saw in front of her. She studied the trees on her left, trying to match them up with a large oak tree her uncle had marked near the X on the map. She evaluated the surrounding ground. She felt pretty sure she was close to the area that her uncle had marked.

Sarah dismounted and walked along the creek bank, seeing nothing that really showed a spot where her uncle had dug, but she wasn't really expecting that. Several years had probably gone by, and no doubt the creek had overflowed its banks a time or two, erasing any natural depression left by the digging.

After retrieving her horse and touring the land a little more, she decided not to do any digging today. She didn't have any high hopes about what her uncle had buried. She would find it another day. The land, though, was a very pleasant surprise. The creek, the hills, the meadow... she could see herself living here. The other owner of the property, though, Mike Stone, had a say in this whole thing. They owned the property equally, as far as she could tell. The lawyer, Jacob Peters, expected Stone to come by to pick up a document when he returned to town. She would leave Peters a note with her address, asking Stone to come by and discuss the division of the land.

Reaching the site of the original house, she swung the

horse along the banks of Walnut Creek, then took the trail back to town. She was completely unaware that she had been watched the entire time.

————

Louis Sharpe emerged from the thick stand of trees where he had concealed himself, watching the girl through his binoculars. He knew why she had walked the creek bank and looked around—she was obviously looking for the place where her uncle had buried whatever that was he had buried. He didn't care about that too much. Eventually she would probably find it, but he was more concerned about her finding what he had buried. He wanted to follow her back to town, but first, he was curious about what she had been looking at down where the old shack site was located.

After the girl had disappeared from sight, he went to his horse and started down toward the remains of the old shack. He took his time getting there, letting the girl get a good head start. He had actually arrived in town several days ago but had had no luck in picking up her trail before today. Knowing she would eventually come to the property, he had waited until today, had ridden out here just before morning light, then concealed himself and waited. Now he had confirmed that she was in Austin, and it looked like she was planning to keep the land. He would deal with that later.

Riding up to the crater in the ground, he dismounted and kicked around among the dirt and pieces of wood. This place, he thought, was looking better and better. It didn't look like it would be that hard to reconstruct a shack and maybe dig a hideout in those hillsides up there, in case he needed that.

After reaching the trail to town, he could see her up

ahead but held back and followed at a distance. This girl had seemed to be pretty good at picking up anybody trailing her. When he felt sure he would be too far back to raise any suspicion, he trailed her into town. When she stopped outside a small building and went inside, he remained several blocks back. Eventually, she came out and continued on her original course. He followed, pausing outside the place where she had stopped. It was a lawyer's office, he noted. He would pay it a visit after dark and see what he could find there. He then followed her until she stopped at a boarding house. Sharpe made a note of the address, then rode away. He would give it a couple hours before he broke into the attorney's office.

———

I was chugging back to what I now considered home—Austin—on a train rather than horseback. Blaze was on the train in a livestock car. I'd done enough riding in the last couple months to give myself a break from it for a few days. I couldn't quite believe how quickly and easily I was covering the same ground I'd spent two months covering with the cattle. Ash McKinnon rode in a seat across the aisle from me, leaning back and snoring. That man could sleep anywhere.

I pulled the sheet of paper from my pocket that Red had given me, idly twisting it between my fingers as I looked out the window. Fifty acres wasn't enough to start a ranch, and the $570 I had left in my pocket wasn't enough to buy more land and stock a ranch. I was leaning more and more toward going to see Red, but first, I wanted to see my lawyer and go to see the land again. I was hoping the lawyer had some ideas on how to divide the land with the other owner. I had it in my head that I could build a pleasant house for myself on the site of Miles's old place, but that would have to be worked out. I turned a few ideas over in my head and eventually felt myself drifting off to sleep. Hopefully, I would snore less than McKinnon over there.

———

A couple days later, at mid-afternoon, the train rattled into the station at Austin. I stood and stretched, eager to get away from the confines of the railcar. I retrieved my bags and went down to claim Blaze when he was led out from one of the livestock cars. Ash and I mounted up and rode off down the street. We were looking for a place to stay, and I also intended to stop in at the lawyer's office. We passed a decent-looking hotel just a couple blocks from the lawyer's office, so Ash stopped in to get us a couple rooms while I continued for two more blocks and went in to see my lawyer.

I could see right away that Jacob Peters hadn't cut back on the cigars. I fought my way through the cloud of smoke and found a chair opposite his at the desk. He shook my hand briefly, then rummaged through a pile of papers on his desk. He extracted a couple of them and pushed them across for my inspection. I'm not any kind of expert at this, but the papers appeared to say I'm the legal owner of fifty acres of land. I nodded and pushed the documents into my pocket. I had already paid him when I first came to see him, so I stood. Peters held up a hand to stop me.

"The other owner of that property was here several weeks ago. She wants to talk to you about the land and how to divide it up."

I stared at him. "She?"

Peters nodded. "Yep." He rummaged through some

more papers before extracting one, inspecting it, and pushing it across the desk. "Name is Sarah Statton."

I went back to staring at him. "Sarah Statton." It was more of a statement than a question.

"Yep. You know her?"

I thought back to the auburn-haired eastern lady at the train station in Ft. Worth. I was sure that was her name. I looked at the paper he had just given me. It had the name Sarah Statton and an address on it. I looked up. "I think I do know her. Kinda auburn-haired, pretty, dresses like she's from somewhere back east?"

He nodded. "Yep. That sounds like her." He looked at me, cigar jammed into his mouth, a small smile curling up at the corners of his lips. "Maybe you should go see her."

I nodded absently. "I guess I will."

I walked out to the street and unhitched Blaze, looking again at the address on the sheet of paper. It was on this same street. I was guessing it was a little farther along. I wasn't sure how far. I could hear a horse approaching and looked up to see Ash reigning in his horse next to me.

"Everything good?" he asked.

I nodded. "The other owner of the property is that girl who asked me to walk her to the train station in Ft. Worth."

Now Ash was staring. "The girl from Ft. Worth."

I nodded.

"The pretty one."

I nodded again.

Ash pushed his hat back on his head and stared at me like I was crazy. "I think you got the Texas cattle fever on that drive," he said eventually.

I shook my head. "Nope."

He pushed his hat back a little farther. "You fell off your horse and landed on your head."

I shook my head again. "Nope."

He took off his hat and fanned himself a couple times. "Well," he said, "you were out in the hot sun a lot. Did you wear your hat every day?"

In way of an answer, I took up the reins and swung up onto Blaze. "I'm going to see her now at the address she left for me. You can tag along if you want to."

He mumbled something else about the hot sun but fell in beside me as we set off down the street.

About a mile down the road, as we approached a long, rambling house, I looked up to see a woman coming down the street from the opposite direction. A young boy walked beside her, carrying several books in his arms. I knew it was Sarah Statton. She looked familiar to me. I dismounted and swept my hat off my head. She looked at me uncertainly for a moment, then broke into a smile.

"You're Mike. Mike Stone. I remember you."

I nodded. "Yes, ma'am," I said awkwardly.

"Sarah. Just call me Sarah." She looked over at Ash. "I'm sorry, I know you walked with us to the station, but I can't remember—"

"Ash," he said, also sweeping off his hat.

She took in both of us with a beautiful smile, then turned toward the house. "Come in," she said. "We have so much to talk about. Did you see Jacob Peters?"

"I did," I told her.

She glanced back to see Ash still standing beside his horse. "Ash can come too," she told me.

"Well," I said, glancing back.

She gave me a quick glance. "We don't want to leave him out here," she said.

"Okay," I said, shaking my head. "I've only been around him on the cattle drive and in a couple of bars. I guess he has some company manners I haven't seen yet."

Her laugh rang out, and I laughed with her. "He'll be

fine," she assured me, patting my arm. "Come on, Ash," she said. "Join us."

Inside the house, Sarah introduced us to someone who called herself Ma. Ma made quite a fuss over us, seating us at a table in a sunny dining room, then serving us tea and cookies. Neither Ash nor I was quite sure how to handle the teacup. I decided to hold it by the handle, even though the handle seemed really tiny. I noticed that Ash opted to grab it with both hands. The slurping noise he made was barely noticeable, so I began to relax. He attacked the cookies with enthusiasm. Ma smiled and went for more cookies. Sarah watched me as I kept one nervous eye on Ash, and she laughed again. I decided I could get used to that laugh in a hurry. It made me smile. She leaned toward me a little. "We have a lot to talk about, Mike. Do you have any plans for that land?"

I set down my teacup and managed to get two cookies from the next batch that Ma brought before Ash could swoop in on them. "I had thought," I began, then stopped. What if she wanted to build something on that old home site?

"Go on," she urged me.

"I had thought maybe I could build myself a house where Miles's old house stood. The one that blew up."

"Okay," she said. "I think you should. I don't plan to build anything right away, and I could always build something down the creek a little way. We could be neighbors."

I nodded. "I don't know how to divide up the land," I said finally. "We both own it equally, but nothing says which part is yours and which part is mine."

She smiled, and I noticed she had a way of watching my eyes as I talked. "That's true," she said. "I don't think we need to figure that out right now. We both own half of it. Build your house on that site if you would like. If you want to run a few cows on it or something, that's fine with me too."

I smiled a little, wondering if this was a little too good to be true. I was really warming up to the idea of a pleasant house on the creek, a few fat cows out in the pasture, and a neighbor like her. Ash looked a little jealous, and I can't say I blamed him. I looked into the bottom of my empty teacup, searching for the right words. "This all sounds wonderful," I finally said. I looked up to find her watching my eyes again.

"Stay right there," she said. "There's something I want to show you." She disappeared down the hallway.

I exchanged glances with Ash and waited until I could hear her footsteps returning down the hallway. She seated herself again, then placed an old, tanned piece of hide on the table. I picked it up and examined it, noting that it was a crudely drawn map. There was an *X* marked along the side of what appeared to be a creek bank. I set the map back down on the table and looked up at her.

"Is that a map of the property we own?" I finally asked.

She nodded. "There was a letter from my uncle along with this map. He says he buried something there, but didn't say what. The thing is, I probably need some help to find the spot, digging, and maybe lifting whatever is in there."

I began to wonder why she was telling me.

When I said nothing, Sarah turned to me and placed a hand over mine. "Would you help me with this?" she asked.

"You barely know me," I said. "Are you sure?"

She sat back, thought for a second, then nodded. "I don't really know anybody around here," she said. "I probably can't do this by myself, depending on what he buried and how deep it is. We own the land together. I think I can trust you. So yes, this is what I want to do."

I agreed that I would help.

Sarah looked over at Ash. "Ash, what do you think about this?" she asked.

Ash looked at me. "Are you part Irish?" he asked me.

"Not that I know of," I told him. "Why?"

"Because," he said, "you might just be the luckiest devil I know."

CHAPTER TEN
UNCLE ZEB'S TREASURE

L ouis Sharpe leaned on his shovel and wiped a sleeve across his forehead to soak up some sweat running down his face. He cast a glance at the overhead sun. How could it be this hot already? It was only late spring. After a short breather, he resumed his digging. He had marked this place pretty clearly. He had buried about five thousand dollars worth of gold coins here when the Bass gang had come here more than five years ago, after the train robbery in Nebraska. He had always known he would come back to get it, but those years in prison had delayed his return. Besides, he believed that part of Bass's undoing had been the way he'd spread those gold pieces around after the robbery. Sharpe believed in keeping his head down and staying out of sight.

His midnight visit to the attorney's office last night had rewarded him with the information he was seeking. He was just a little uncertain about what he wanted to do next. He had gone through multiple boxes and folders of information, finally rifling through the loose papers on the desk. It was there he found the information about Sarah Statton and the property where he was now standing.

He didn't find out much about her that he didn't already know, including where she was currently living. He had already known that. He did find, though, that the other owner of the property was someone named Mike Stone. That was a little additional complication, but he wasn't really worried about it. He could make two people go away just about as easily as one. It had also occurred to him he could pretend to be Mike Stone for purposes of laying claim to the property later on. It was, after all, a pretty isolated area out here.

The moist ground on the creek bank sucked at Sharpe's boots as he continued to dig. His shovel struck something solid on his next effort. He pitched the shovel out onto the ground, then kneeled down to sweep the remaining dirt away from the box he had buried. After straining to pull the old wooden box out of the ground, he climbed out of the hole to retrieve his shovel, using that to lever the box out of its position. He then jumped back down into the hole, pulled the box free, and tossed it out. He pulled the lid open to reveal the two hundred fifty gold pieces he had left in there. After putting a few in his pocket and about one hundred more in his saddlebags, he returned the wooden box to the hole in the ground and covered it back up.

Sharp stood back and viewed the area where he'd had the gold. He scattered a few leaves in the area and satisfied himself that no one would know he had been there. His gold was buried at least a hundred yards down the bank from where he had seen the girl looking around, so he wasn't as worried that she might find it. He remounted and turned toward Austin, with the goal of taking an afternoon train up to Ft. Worth.

He had satisfied himself that he wanted to use this site as a hideout for future operations. It wasn't the Hole in the Wall in Wyoming, which he had used a time or two, but the narrow, almost invisible entrance through the hills, with the property ending at the creek on the other side, would serve ideally. He was a long way in distance and several years removed from the big train robbery in Nebraska. He had decided to work Central Texas.

Taking the trail back to town, Sharp decided he would try to establish contact again with Pete and Kendall, the two he had met with last week in the Ft. Worth saloon. They might be interested in coming down and working for him here. They might also be tied into other ex-members of the Bass gang. If there was anything in the works that sounded like it might be worth his while, he might throw in with them one time to get a better stake to establish operations down here around Austin. Sharp kicked his horse in the ribs and moved out at a spanking trot. He didn't like to waste time.

––––––––

Several hours later, Sharpe signed in at the hotel he had used before in Ft. Worth. It was just a few blocks down the street from the saloon where he had met up with Pete and Kendall before. He had a feeling he could find them there again. He threw his bag into the room and headed down to the saloon. Pushing through the batwing doors, he stood for a moment and let his eyes adjust to the dim light. Peering through the smoke, he saw what he was looking for: they were seated at a table in the corner. Pete beckoned to him to join. He walked over and took a seat.

––––––––

The sun was out on a beautiful Sunday morning in May as Sarah and I rode out toward the property. I was driving the buggy and ancient horse we had borrowed from Ma Kirk. Sarah rode next to me on the buggy seat, and there were two freshly purchased shovels in the buggy, along with a few burlap sacks, a pick we had borrowed from Ma, and a bulging picnic basket. Ash was on his horse, trotting alongside. I had persuaded him to come with the promise of the picnic lunch. He cast frequent mistrusting glances at the shovels and burlap sacks as we proceeded. The boy Daniel had begged to come along, but his mother had told him he had chores to do at home.

We stopped first in front of the old shack, and I recounted briefly for them my story about the night old Miles had blown his place up. Ash whistled softly and walked over to examine the old tunnel running out to the creek. He examined what he could see of what was left, then walked down to the opposite end where it emptied out to the creek bank.

"You might want to shore that up with some boards across the top of it," he told me.

I considered that briefly, then shook my head. "I don't know why I would need it," I told them. "Old Miles had lived out in the wilderness and was worried about Indian attacks. He wanted a way out other than through the front door. Strange, the way this turned out." I looked back at the remains of the tunnel, which seemed to have held up remarkably well. "I don't have any desire to be back down in there."

Sarah turned and walked back over to the buggy. "Is it time to do some digging?" she asked.

Ash's head came up. "Dig?"

I looked at Sarah and pointed in Ash's direction. "Look at him," I said. "Did you ever see somebody more qualified to dig for some buried money?"

Ash let out a loud moan. "I came for the lunch," he explained.

Sarah chuckled. "Ash," she said. "Are you telling me that a big, healthy man like you can't help out a little, digging here and there?" He rolled his eyes and heaved a resigned sigh. "You can have two helpings of the chicken," she said. "And I brought a chocolate cake that Ma baked this morning."

Ash brightened visibly. He smiled at Sarah, gave me a withering stare, and walked over to his horse. "I can dig twice as much as he can," he promised, pointing back in my direction.

We stopped at the first promising area that looked like what we saw on the map. There was a large oak tree leaning out as the creek took a quick turn toward the south. Ash and I each grabbed a shovel and began digging into the wet ground near the water. After fifteen minutes, we both had a healthy sweat going but had little to show for our effort other than a lot of mud and a few rocks. I stopped and leaned on my shovel, gazing down the creek bed. After a couple more minutes, Ash stopped and joined me. We both looked over at Sarah. "There are some other possibilities, right?" I asked. She nodded and pointed farther down the creek bank. "There are a couple more spots I noticed down there."

We clambered out of the hole we had dug, threw the shovels in the buggy, and rode down to the next site. The area curving inward was sharper and more pronounced. I was optimistic as we climbed up the bank and began digging. After a few minutes, the sound and feel of the shovels striking something hard underneath the surface rewarded us. We widened the hole and, after a while, could see the outline of a wooden box, maybe two feet square. After a few more minutes of digging, I jumped down into the hole, reached down, and heaved the box out under the trees.

There was an old rusty lock on the hasp of the box. I smashed it with my shovel several times and it opened. Sarah came over and I stood aside for her to reach down and open the box. Inside were a few letters wrapped inside a piece of tarp. They were yellow with age and badly weathered. Sarah opened one, pulled it out, and read a few lines. A small smile creased her lips.

"What do you know?" she said. "Uncle Zeb had a sweetheart. I would never have guessed."

She set the letters aside and reached back into the box, pulling out a chain with a locket on it. She opened the locket, and we saw the faded image of a woman's picture inside. "I guess this was her," Sarah said. She gazed at it for a few more seconds, then set it aside. She reached back in once more and gathered fifteen gold coins. She put them down on the ground, sorted through them, then gave one each to Ash and me. "For your trouble," she said.

I protested and tried to return the coin, telling her we had dug for only a few minutes, but she wouldn't hear of it. "It's not just for today," she said with a smile. "I'll probably need help on some other things. Who knows how much help I'll need?"

I chuckled and put the coin in my pocket. Ash looked at the coin in his palm, then looked at Sarah. "Will this help involve diggin'?"

"Maybe," said Sarah. "But if I meet a nice single girl, I'll introduce you to her."

Ash still looked undecided.

"Okay," said Sarah, "a nice, pretty, single girl." Ash grinned and stuffed the coin into his pocket.

We spread a blanket on the ground among the wild-flowers in the meadow, and Sarah pulled out the contents of the picnic basket: fried chicken, potato salad, freshly baked bread, and the chocolate cake she had promised. The digging and working with the pick had worked up quite an appetite, and we fell to it with a will. At last, I moaned with satisfaction and collapsed on my back on the blanket. Ash seemed to have run up the white flag over there as well.

"Everybody had enough?" Sarah asked.

I moaned. "I know I'm done." I raised my head to look at Ash. "I sure hope he's done. He ate an entire chicken and three-quarters of the cake."

Ash's face wore an injured expression. "Only three-quarters of a chicken," he said. "And half the cake."

Sarah's laugh brought another smile to my face. "My mistake," I said. "It was hard to keep track, what with all the chicken bones and icing flying around."

Ash snorted, mumbled something about accepting my apology, then rolled over and fell asleep on the blanket.

I helped Sarah pack up the picnic basket, then she took my hand and pulled me to my feet. "Let's take a walk," she said.

I kept a firm hold on her hand as we walked over to the edge of the meadow and took a seat on the hillside, looking down toward the old shack and Walnut Creek. Sarah took my hand in both of hers. "I will finish school for this year in another two weeks," she told me. "I'm going back up to Fort Worth in a few days, to see my dad." She saw the surprise on my face. "They have transferred him to a post in Arizona," she explained.

I nodded.

"Do you think," she said, "that you could come with me? You know the trouble I had traveling down here from St. Louis, and there was that man with the pale gray eyes in Ft. Worth. I'd feel better if you came."

A long, slow smile spread across my face. "What a good idea," I said.

Sarah laughed and rested her head against my shoulder. We sat there for a long time, looking out across our land.

————

I mostly occupied myself with plans for a cabin on my property during the next two weeks. I borrowed Ma's buggy and took some boards out to the site. I cleared away the wood and debris on the site of the old cabin, and I built a little cross and marked a grave site for old Miles down the bank of the creek a little way. I drove some stakes into the ground to mark out where the walls would go in for the cabin. I had planned on two rooms plus a loft to sleep in, but Sarah talked me into making it three rooms plus the loft. I went down to the creek bank and rolled some heavy stones into the tunnel exit down there. I also went back up to the building site and made a few efforts to disguise the entrance to the tunnel. I didn't have any use for it, and I didn't want people or varmints crawling up the tunnel and into my house.

In between trips to work on the house, I scouted out Austin a little and got to know my way around. One day, I was riding home after a little time spent exploring the ranches in the area when it crossed my mind to check in with Red and let him know where to find me. I stopped, dismounted, and rooted around in my saddlebag for a while, finally finding that piece of paper with his address. I asked directions a couple times and finally found my way to a rooming house. I asked the lady who came to the door if I could speak to Red. She told me he hadn't been in for a couple days, but I could leave a message and she would give it to him.

She gave me some paper and a pencil, and I sat down on the porch to write a message for Red. I told him I would be in town for another week or so, then gone for a few days to Ft. Worth, then back. I gave him the address of the hotel where Ash and I were staying. I couldn't think of anything else I needed to tell him, so I gave the note to the lady and rode home.

CHAPTER ELEVEN

EAGLE PASS ROBBERY

L ouis Sharpe followed the other five men along Weatherford Street, riding slowly east out of Ft. Worth. They rode single file in order not to attract any undue attention. Pete rode directly in front of him, and Kendall was one man ahead of Pete. Perkins, from the old Sam Bass gang, rode in the lead and in fact pictured himself as the leader. This plan was his, and Sharpe was willing to ride along. The plan was to rob the Texas and Pacific train when it pulled into the Eagle Pass stop, a little north and east of Ft. Worth. In general, Sharpe preferred to rob banks. Banks couldn't roll away while you were in them. He had pointed out to Pete and Kendall that the Bass gang had in fact been lucky during the Nebraska train robbery. The vault had yielded little, but they had accidentally discovered boxes full of gold coins on their way out of the train.

Perkins, though, claimed to have information that the luggage in the express car would be worth their while. Vaults these days tended to have time locks on them that made the robberies more difficult, and there might not be enough money in there to make it worth a robbery. Sharpe was willing to ride along and share in the loot from the luggage, if there was any. First sign of difficulty and he would be out of there. Then maybe he could put together a crew, starting with Pete and Kendall, to pay a visit to some banks around Austin and San Antonio.

When the buildings of Ft. Worth had receded behind them, the gang rode in a tighter formation. Sharpe kicked his horse up alongside Pete and Kendall and spoke in low tones. "If anything goes wrong, I'm out," he told them. "I won't even hang around to divide up the loot. I'd advise that you do the same."

Kendall glanced over quizzically. "Just what do you mean by *wrong*?"

Sharpe slowed his horse a bit to avoid being overheard by the men in front of them. "I mean if anybody gets trigger-happy and starts shooting. The law doesn't like robberies, but what really puts them on your trail is if somebody gets hurt or killed. You don't want any part of that."

Pete and Kendall glanced at each other and nodded.

Sharpe passed a piece of paper to Kendall. "If we get separated and you want to work with me down south, you can probably find me here." The paper contained the name of the hotel where Sharpe had last stayed in Austin. Kendall glanced at it and put it in his pocket.

The few miles to the Eagle Pass station passed quickly. Sharpe could make out a small building next to the rails they had first seen about a half mile back. Perkins gathered the group in a small grove of oak trees, largely shielding them from the station. Sharpe, through binoculars, could make out only one man moving around inside. Perkins glanced around the group, then pointed at Sharpe. "You go around the other side of the station—take care of the attendant in there. Then stand outside like you're ready to board. The train will stop for sure if the engineer sees a passenger."

Sharpe nodded. That suited his purposes perfectly. He mounted and swung a wide circle around the station.

The attendant looked up curiously when Sharpe entered. "Train boards on the other side," he said briefly. "You'll need to bring your horse around over there."

Sharpe nodded, keeping his head down and avoiding eye contact. When the attendant turned, he drew his gun, reversed the grip, and hit him sharply on the back of the head. Sharpe tied his wrists and ankles, stuffed a rag in his mouth, and dragged him out of sight behind the station. Leaving his horse out of sight, he walked through the station and stood in front as if waiting for the next train.

A whistle announced the incoming train before Sharpe noticed it, shielding his eyes against the glare of the late afternoon sun. He noticed that someone else had ridden out from the grove of trees. He assumed it was Perkins. He had to admit it was smart to come one or two at a time, helping to avoid suspicion. As the train approached, he saw a third man move out from the trees. Sharpe knew that his job was to take out the conductor. Perkins would deal with the engineer. The others would find the express car and roll both doors open.

The train pulled to a stop, and the conductor appeared in a doorway in front of Sharpe. "Where you going?" he asked as Sharpe approached the car.

"Marshall," Sharpe responded, naming one of the closer destinations.

"Seventy-five cents," the man responded, holding out his hand.

Sharpe dropped a twenty-dollar gold piece in the outstretched hand. The conductor mumbled his irritation at making change for such a sizable amount, dropping his head and searching in his coat pocket for change. Sharpe struck him with his revolver butt, lowering him to the ground outside the train car. After a few moments, the door to the express car rolled open and Sharpe entered. Pete and Kendall stood outside the car, holding the horses. Perkins's other two men were dragging luggage to the center of the car. Sharpe then sent them to the passenger cars, telling them to keep everyone in their seats. The men still in the express car began opening the bags and dropping what they could find into a large burlap sack. Sharpe did the same.

Perkins appeared and took charge, emptying what he could find and motioning at the other two to drag more of the luggage out. After just a few minutes, Perkins wasn't finding what he had expected. As his frustration mounted, he muttered something about robbing the passengers and moved forward into the passenger cars. Sharpe looked up uneasily. This had the potential to be a lot of trouble. After a few more minutes, a gunshot sounded from one car. Sharpe lost no time. He dropped the burlap sack, ran from the train car, across the station, and mounted his horse. He dug in his spurs and galloped away.

———

We rode side-by-side on the train from Austin to Ft. Worth, watching the countryside roll past us. We had each packed a bag and planned to stay for two days before returning home. On the way up, Sarah explained to me that she had stayed in touch with her father by telegrams since she had left. I wanted to meet Major Statton, but as much as anything else, I had to admit to myself, I was really looking forward to spending time with Sarah.

Eventually I dozed off to sleep. When Sarah nudged me awake, I could sense that the train was slowing. I looked out the window to see we were pulling into the station. I had spent a couple days in Ft. Worth at the start of the cattle drive, but as we walked away from the station toward Main Street, I could see right away that Sarah was much more familiar with big towns like this than I was. She laughed when I insisted on riding the streetcar—the walk was just a few blocks—but she came along with me.

There were people pulling carts with barrels of what they called *artesian water* for twelve and a half cents per barrel. I persuaded one seller to sell me a cup of water for a penny and Sarah burst out laughing at the look on my face.

"It just tastes like water," I protested.

"It's well water," she told me.

By the time we found our hotel on Main Street, registered for rooms, and left our luggage, it was early evening. We found a café just a few blocks from the hotel and enjoyed a leisurely, quiet dinner. Sarah told me for the first time about the attempted holdup of her stage on the way down from St. Louis. She could no doubt see the look of surprise on my face when she told me she had shot one robber. She looked away, and I could see she was still struggling with it. I reached out to cover her hand with mine.

"You did what you had to," I said.

She looked back at me, a small smile returning. "How about you?" she asked. "Have you ever had to do anything like that?"

I shifted uncomfortably and hesitated.

She gave my hand a squeeze. "What is it, Mike?"

I began by telling her of the short time I had spent as a deputy sheriff in New Mexico, then finally told her I had killed a man in a gunfight who was wanted for robbery and murder.

"So," she said softly, "You did what you had to, too."

We left the café and moved out to find a bench on

Main Street. We sat on the bench and held hands, watching the cowboys, buggies, and horses on the paved street—that was something else I hadn't seen. We could hear the occasional loud shouts and even a few gunshots coming from the area south of us. Sarah turned her head in that direction and pointed down the street. "What do you think is going on down there?" she asked.

"Hell's Half Acre," I answered. "No telling exactly what is going on. Some cowboys on the drive went down there when we came through town. They didn't look too good the next morning."

Sarah laughed and leaned her head on my shoulder. "We'll stay here," she decided.

———

We had breakfast near the hotel the next morning, then agreed to meet back in the lobby while I looked around town for a little while. When I returned to the lobby, Sarah was studying a small piece of paper that she held in her hands. A blanket was tucked under one arm. I looked over her shoulder at the paper, which appeared to be a map.

"What's that?" I asked.

She folded up the paper and handed me the blanket. "It's where we need to go this afternoon," she told me. "I asked around before we left about things we could see and do while we're here." She took my hand and led us out of the lobby in a northeasterly direction. After a walk of about fifteen or twenty minutes, we came to a grassy meadow. I could hear water burbling from a spring nearby, and there were several people picnicking on the grass.

"It's called the Cold Springs," Sarah explained. "I was told it is a popular place for people to picnic and just enjoy a nice day." She took the blanket from me and spread it out on the ground. She laid down on the blanket and patted the spot next to her.

I stretched out next to her, propped myself up on one elbow, and we talked about where we would go and what we would do from here. Sarah, a bit to my surprise, told me she had already decided to stay in Texas and hoped to live one day on the land she had inherited. She already knew I wanted to build a house on the property. I told her I might have an offer to join the Texas Rangers. A small smile crossed her face, and I paused.

"What?" I asked.

She shook her head. "Nothing, really," she said. "My dad is in the army, and you remind me of him a little. I think you would do well if you joined the Rangers." She looked at me speculatively for a moment. "I think my dad would like you," she said.

After a while, we walked over the springs. Sarah kneeled down and scooped up some water. Then I did the same. As I pulled back from the water, my hand came down on a loose rock and I lurched forward a little, steadying myself and trying to pull back to the bank. Sarah grabbed my arm to steady me and I half-turned as I came back onto my knees. We were suddenly face-to-face by the rushing springs, both kneeling. Impulsively, I leaned forward and kissed her. I pulled back, searching her face.

"Wow," she said, her eyes smiling into mine.

"Wow, indeed," I said, then leaned forward and kissed her again.

We stayed at the Cold Springs until the sun had begun to set and shadows were stealing across the meadow, then walked back and had dinner at the same café we'd eaten at the night before. Morning found us hopping on the streetcar to meet Major Statton at the train station.

"He's on the twelve o'clock train from Texarkana," she told me. "We have about an hour before his train leaves."

We were on a two o'clock train back to Austin, so we had our bags with us. As we saw the train pulling in, I shifted from one foot to the other and back.

Sarah glanced over at me. "Are you nervous?" she asked.

"I guess I am," I admitted.

"I think I like that," she told me, then took my arm. "Nothing to worry about," she told me. "He's going to like you."

He wasn't hard to pick out when he stepped off the train. He was in full dress uniform and carried himself like the lifelong army officer he was. Sarah stepped forward to give him a hug, the resemblance between them was obvious. When they had hugged, Sarah motioned to me and I stepped forward. "Dad, this is Mike Stone."

He gave me a firm but friendly handshake, then glanced at Sarah with a quizzical expression. "Mike is my new neighbor," she explained. "I asked him to come with me so I wouldn't have to travel alone."

His expression changed to a smile, and it struck me again how much they were alike.

Sarah led the way to a picnic table in the station yard. Major Statton took a seat on one side of the table while Sarah and I sat on the other. He asked his daughter to fill him in on what had happened. Sarah began by telling him about the meeting with the attorney in St. Louis. I noticed she left out the part about being followed. She'd told me she didn't want him to worry about her—I said nothing. She came to the part about shooting the would-be robber at the stagecoach stop, and her father's mouth dropped open in surprise. *So much for not worrying him*, I thought.

He looked at me. "Mike, were you with her?"

I shook my head.

Sarah put her hand on my arm, a move not unnoticed by the major. "I didn't meet Mike until I got here to Ft. Worth," she explained. "It was a chance meeting here near the train station. He was on a cattle drive to Kansas. I found out later that he is the other owner of the property down there."

The major looked surprised again, looking back and forth at us.

"Two old mountain man trappers were partners and bought the property," I explained. "One was an old man who lived in a cabin there on the land. He left his half to me. His partner was your brother."

Comprehension dawned in his eyes, then he laughed a bit at the coincidence of it all. He turned his gaze to me. "So, Mike, you've been on a cattle drive to Kansas. Tell me a bit more about what you've done."

I talked briefly about my childhood, then about going to join my uncle Sam in Cimarron, New Mexico, then finished by explaining that I had worked at a ranch and also served for a while as a deputy marshal.

He listened without interrupting, then asked: "What brought you to Texas?"

I hesitated briefly, but I had a feeling he would want a straight, direct answer. I explained about the gunfight in the street in Cimarron and how I didn't want to be known as a gunman. I'd come here to get a new start.

He nodded approvingly. "So, you've not had anything like that happen since coming here, I guess?"

My eyes dropped to the table, and I hesitated, but I had already decided to tell the straight truth, so I told them both about the herd cutters I had shot on the cattle drive. It was Sarah's turn to look surprised. I hadn't gotten around to telling her that story yet.

The major listened to the story without so much as a

blink. "They had their guns on you when they came out of the draw, right?" he asked.

I nodded.

"Then it was you or them. That's all there is to it."

Sarah patted my arm. "There was a Texas Ranger on that drive. He wants Mike to join the Rangers."

Major Statton studied me, a faint smile on his lips. "Are you going to do that?" he asked.

I shrugged a bit. "I might," I said. "I'm going to talk to them about it when we get back."

Statton nodded. "Well, he said, standing as a train whistle sounded, "we can always use another good man in the army."

"Oh, no," said Sarah, standing and linking her arm through mine. "Don't go stealing my neighbor. I need him down there on the land."

The major chuckled, extended his hand to shake mine, gave Sarah a hug, and turned toward his train. He stopped just before boarding, looked back at me, and pointed at Sarah. "You take care of her," he told me, then climbed up into the train. He waved from the window as the train moved away, and Sarah squeezed my shoulder.

"You see," she said. "I told you he was going to like you."

Afterward, we strolled toward the train station, bags in hand. I was tremendously excited about the possibilities in front of us. I was, I had to admit, more than a little sad that the trip to Ft. Worth was over. I knew that I would remember these last three days for a very long time.

CHAPTER TWELVE
RECRUITING STONE

T hey stopped only long enough to split up the small amount of money they had stolen from the train. Each of them had stuffed a watch or piece of jewelry in their pockets. Perkins only cared about dividing the money. He dropped the bag on the ground and stared at the two he had sent into the train car to take money from the passengers. They answered to the names Roy and Leo. Perkins didn't know which was which and he didn't care. He fixed one with a furious gaze.

"Who shot the man in the train?"

Neither man answered. Perkins pulled his gun and placed it under the chin of one of them. He repeated the question.

Leo, the one with Perkins's gun under his chin, swallowed nervously. "Hide-out gun. One of them had a hide-out gun. He came up with it and I shot."

Perkins continued to stare for a long moment, then dropped his gun back into his holster. "Dead passenger," he mumbled. "Just what we needed."

Perkins turned to the job of dividing the money, then

stared around the circle. There were only five of them. He looked over at Pete and Kendall. "Where's Sharpe?"

Both men shrugged. "Don't know. He took off."

Perkins snorted, then picked up the burlap bag. "His loss." He counted out the money five ways.

Pete and Kendall didn't follow as the others mounted up. Perkins wheeled his horse around and motioned at them impatiently. "You coming?" he shouted.

Both men shook their heads. Pete cleared his throat, then spoke slowly. "Maybe it's better if we split up." Perkins thought that one over for a moment then wheeled and put the spurs to his horse. Pete and Kendall watched as the three men rode away. The two of them would head south. Sharpe couldn't be all that far ahead of them.

———

Red left the bank in Austin, his cattle drive money tucked away safely in his account. What he really wanted to do still wasn't within reach. He wanted to buy a saloon. It didn't have to be right here in Austin, but he wanted to stay in Texas. He probably had less than half of what he needed, but he had it in mind to look for a partnership in a saloon somewhere. He would keep his eyes open for a chance. Meanwhile, he needed to get back to work, which meant reporting to his captain, Leander H. McNelly. McNelly had been a captain of the Rangers for the last twelve years, leading a group called the Special Force of Rangers. Red considered him to be tough but fair.

Tucking a few gold coins into his pocket that he'd taken out of his cattle drive money, Red unhitched his horse and rode away. He had a good idea of where to find McNelly, seeing as how Red had already found out that McNelly was in town. There was a small boarding house where McNelly kept a room, and he worked out of that room when he had to fill out reports or do any of the other paperwork he hated. Red knew that paperwork always put McNelly in a foul mood, but Red knew how to handle that. He broke into a small grin, happy because he didn't have McNelly's job and never wanted it.

Red mounted the steps to the boarding house, let himself in, and walked down the hallway to knock on McNelly's door. He heard a faint, gruff "Yeah?" and pushed through the door. McNelly sat at a familiar long, scarred wooden table. He was turned, facing ninety degrees away from Red, with the morning sun spilling over his shoulder and revealing paper scattered in various piles on the table. He was writing and glanced up only briefly.

"Have a nice vacation?" he asked sarcastically.

He and Red both knew that McNelly couldn't afford to lose Red. Letting him go for the cattle drive was McNelly's gruff way of acknowledging that. Red walked around the table to face McNelly and waited.

McNelly grabbed a wire and what appeared to be two Wanted posters and shoved them across the table at Red. "Train robbery at Eagle Pass station, near Dallas," he said without preamble. "Passenger killed. You take some boys and take care of it."

Red knew full well what McNelly meant by taking care of it. If the robbers didn't come back peacefully, they would come back dead. He looked at the two sketches. The man named Perkins he was somewhat familiar with. Perkins had been a part of the Sam Bass gang, which would not sit well with McNelly. The dead passenger really wouldn't sit well.

Red looked at the other sketch. The man's name was Louis Sharpe. He didn't look familiar to Red, so he studied the sketch for a while, trying to memorize the face. He glanced up at McNelly, who hadn't stopped writing. He liked to get the paperwork over with as soon as possible. Red cleared his throat, thinking about his question before asking. "This Sharpe, was he a part of the Bass gang as well?"

"Yeah, we think so. For a short while," came the reply. "Look at the eyes," continued McNelly. "They say you'll never forget the eyes when you see him. Kind of deadly pale gray, they say. Said to be extremely good with a pistol."

Red replaced the posters on the desk. McNelly waved in his direction. "Keep 'em. Take care of it."

Red nodded, folded the posters, and put them in his pocket. "How many men can I have?"

McNelly glanced up only briefly, looking a bit apologetic. "Two."

Red stared. "Only two?"

McNelly nodded. "You know they're cutting back the Force a little now. Plus, I just lost a couple guys. Two is all I can spare right now."

Red thought a moment, hesitated, then said: "I know a couple guys we could probably hire and use to help out on this."

McNelly paused and looked up. "Who've you got?"

Red leaned his knuckles on the edge of the table. "Couple guys who were on the cattle drive with me. Both young, but good guys. Guys you want beside you in a fight."

McNelly said nothing, lowering his head and writing again.

"First one," Red continued, "named Ash McKinnon. Fantastic with the Winchester. Big guy. Could really handle himself if things get rough."

McNelly grunted. "The other one?"

"Name is Mike Stone. Came down from New Mexico

just a few months ago. Worked as a deputy sheriff for a little while."

McNelly nodded, then turned over a piece of paper and continued to write.

"This guy Mike Stone," Red continued, "killed Juarez Chico in a stand-up gunfight in Cimarron, New Mexico."

McNelly stopped writing and looked up. "Juarez Chico?"

Red nodded. "Stand-up gunfight. Word is that Stone put three bullets in him and Chico only got off one shot into the dirt."

McNelly looked down and started writing again. He paused and looked out the window. "Get those boys in here," he said.

———

I walked into the lobby of our Austin hotel with Sarah in the early evening. We were pretty much fresh off the train from Ft. Worth and planned on a little dinner right after we had each dropped off our bags. Sarah assured me I would be welcome at Ma's table, though I might owe Ma a couple chores sometime. As we came through the door, it surprised me to see Red and Ash seated in chairs, looking at a couple of posters. Sarah and I crossed the lobby. They stood to greet us.

"How was your trip?" asked Ash, then got a look at the grin on my face. He waved a hand in the air. "Never mind, I don't want to know," he said glumly.

Sarah laughed and linked her arm through mine. "We need to find a girl for Ash," she told me.

"There's not enough money in the world," I mumbled.

Ash assumed his usual injured expression and Sarah gave me a nudge in the ribs.

Red interrupted the proceedings to get right to the

point. "Mike, I'll tell you what I just told Ash. I'm here to offer you a job with the Texas Rangers. Special Force unit, Captain Leander H. McNelly commanding. Ash, here, has already accepted."

It took me a moment to process it. I looked at Ash, who nodded. I looked over at Sarah, who smiled and gave my hand a squeeze. "Okay," I announced. "I'm in."

Red reached out to shake my hand and gave me a badge. "We leave in the morning," he told me. "Train robbery at Eagle Pass station, between Ft. Worth and Dallas. Six men in on the robbery. We're mainly looking for these two." He passed a couple posters to me.

The first was a man named Perkins. I'd never seen him, but didn't really expect that I would have. I pulled up the second poster for a man named Sharpe. He looked a bit familiar, but I couldn't place him.

I was about to return the posters when Sarah gasped, reached over, and grabbed the second poster. "That's him," she exclaimed.

I looked at her blankly.

"The man who followed me in St. Louis! The one I had seen in Ft. Worth when I asked you to walk me to the train station!"

Red moved us over to the entrance of the hotel, letting the sunshine spill on the image of Louis Sharpe. He held the poster out at arm's length. "Sarah, are you sure?"

Sarah studied the image for several seconds, then nodded her head.

Red pulled the poster back and began folding it up, lost in thought.

"You can't really see his eyes in the drawing," Sarah began.

Red's head snapped up. "Pale gray, deadly eyes?" he asked.

"Yes!" Sarah exclaimed. "That's exactly what they're like...pretty scary."

Red fished some paper and a pencil out of his shirt pocket. "When did you see him last?"

Sarah thought back, then looked at me. "It was that day in Ft. Worth, when we met."

"Day before the cattle drive left from Ft. Worth," I filled in.

Red nodded and scribbled that down. "And before that?"

"Just a few days before, in St. Louis." Sarah went on to describe how she had seen him outside the attorney's office, then had been followed around St. Louis, concluding with how her hotel room had been broken into.

Red put the poster, paper, and pencil away, clearly puzzled. "And you haven't seen him since..." He looked up at Sarah. "You're sure you haven't seen him around here?"

Sarah nodded emphatically. "Definitely not. And I was looking, believe me."

Red cracked a small smile. "Yeah, I guess you would have been," he conceded. "Do you think it could have been coincidence, seeing him in Ft. Worth?"

Sarah nodded again. "I think it's likely. I don't think he even saw me." She thought for a moment. "I don't know what I have that he would have really wanted. Maybe he didn't find whatever he was hoping for when he broke into my room, then moved on."

Red nodded, looking only partly convinced. He looked over at me. "You got any thoughts about this?" he asked me.

I reached out and took the poster again. "Wanted for train robbery." I looked up. "Is that the big Bass gang train robbery in Nebraska?"

Red nodded.

"Nothing about him since then?"

Red shook his head. "Nothing since."

I gave the poster back, slipping my arm around Sarah after I did. I stared out the door thoughtfully. "I'm not happy this guy that followed Sarah turns out to be so dangerous...maybe he's been operating in Missouri since that big train robbery?"

"Likely," Red agreed. "Has done nothing big enough to add to this old poster. We can talk a little more later about why he's in Texas and how to go after both of them." He looked over at Sarah, then at me. "You probably want to take her home."

I picked up Sarah's luggage and turned for the door. Red stopped us, handing a piece of paper to Sarah. "This," he said, "is the address where you can reach our captain, name is McNelly. Leander McNelly. I'll tell him what you've told me before we leave town. If you see this man Sharpe, or have any trouble at all, go straight to Captain McNelly. There's nobody better than him."

Sarah took the paper and gave Red one of those dazzling smiles. "I'll be fine, and thank you. If I see Sharpe or have any trouble, I'll go see the captain."

———

The boy, Daniel, was waiting for us outside the hotel with the buggy. He had met us at the train station and waited while we met with Ash and Red. I put Sarah's luggage in the buggy and mounted Blaze to follow them out to the boarding house. It was a ride of only a few minutes. I reflected that I was becoming pretty familiar with the road out to Sarah's place. I wondered what she would think if she knew I already had ideas about a future with her.

Dinner turned out to be a group of eight of us around

Ma Kirk's table, and I barely stopped shoveling food long enough to suck down some air now and then. Ma watched me and seemed to delight in watching me chow down on her cooking.

"A little hungry, are we, Mike?" she asked.

I downed the last of the chicken I was eating and wiped my mouth with the napkin she'd laid out. "You have no idea," I told her. "I was eating beef and beans three times a day for a couple months there."

A general chuckle went around the table.

"Nothing else?" Sarah asked.

"Well, once in a while, there was something that Morty, the cook, called biscuits. I got hungry enough to eat 'em after about a week on the trail."

Ma passed some food in my direction, but I waved both hands in the air.

"If I eat any more," I told her, "my horse Blaze will get a sore back just carrying me home."

Sarah took my hand, and we stood up from the table. I could see she wanted to talk, so we moved toward the front porch. We stopped when Ma called my name. She was coming from the kitchen with two napkins tied up at the top. I was pretty sure what was in them, based on the wonderful smell, but I asked anyway.

"Cookies," she told me. I looked at the two little bundles she gave me. "One is for your friend Ash," she said.

I shook my head. "You'll never get rid of him now," I advised her. She only laughed as she waved us out the door.

We went out to the porch, and the conversation turned more serious. Sarah took a seat on the bench, and I sat next to her. She turned a little to watch my face as we talked. "You looked a little upset, back there at the hotel," she said. "Are you worried about this man, Louis Sharpe, and whether I'll be safe?"

Well, I thought, she seemed to have gotten right down to what I'd been thinking about. I nodded immediately. "He's a dangerous man, and I'll be riding out of here in the morning. Maybe I should stay here with you."

She took my face in both her hands. "I'll be fine," she said. "I haven't seen him in over two months. I don't think he ever came down here—he's been robbing trains up north. I'll go to Captain McNelly if anything happens." She let go of my face and searched my eyes. "Okay?"

I nodded my head reluctantly. "Okay," I said.

We walked over to the edge of the porch and I stepped down, then turned around to face her. She draped her arms over my shoulders and I put my arms around her waist. "Just go do your job. Then come back here to see me," she told me.

A brief smile spread across my face. "You've got that," I said.

We kissed a few times, then I crossed the yard and climbed onto Blaze. Sarah stood on the porch and watched as I rode away.

———————

I met Red and Ash by the front desk at the hotel, as planned. I was a few minutes late and took the expected ribbing from them about Sarah. I told them they were just jealous, and we eventually moved to the saloon down the street to plan how we would go after what we were now calling *The Perkins Gang*. We ordered a round of beers and settled down to the subject we'd come to talk about.

Red put the posters on the table and pointed at them. "Where do we start looking for these guys?" was his first question.

We both stared thoughtfully at the posters. "How long ago did they rob the train at Eagle Pass station?" asked Ash.

Red took a pull from his mug. "About a week and a half ago," came the answer.

"So," I said, following up on Ash's question, "they've had time to leave the area up there, we just don't know if they would do that or stick around."

Red nodded absently, pushing the posters back and forth on the table. "We don't know where either of them is from, where they might have family or anything like that."

"So, if we don't start looking for them up there, around Ft. Worth or Dallas, we don't have any idea where to start," Ash mused.

Red nodded. "That's what I think," he said.

I nodded my agreement.

"We can show these posters around in a few places, ask if anybody has seen them," Red continued, "but if they just go into hiding for a while, we're not likely to turn them up."

"How much money did they get from that last train robbery?" I asked.

"Not much," Red admitted. "They might need to strike again pretty soon, but we don't know where or what they will do. The Bass gang mostly robbed trains, but these guys might decide they need to do something else now. They know we'll be watching the trains."

I pushed my beer mug around in a circle, staring absently at the table. After a moment, an idea took shape in my brain. "What if we gave them a good reason to rob a train?" I asked the other two.

Ash regarded me sorrowfully. "I'm back to thinkin' you were out in the hot sun too much without a hat," he told me.

Red just stared at me. "Explain that," he said finally.

I nodded, still putting things together in my head. "What," I asked, "would be one of the biggest, most used train routes in that area?"

Red shrugged and thought for a minute. "The Texas Pacific railroad line from Texarkana to Ft. Worth gets a lot of use," he said finally. "Why?"

I waved for another beer and leaned forward, elbows on the table. "These gangs that rob trains, they try to get information about which trains might have the most money on them, right?"

Red nodded his agreement, comprehension dawning in his eyes. "I think I see where you're going," he told me. "We find a way to give them a false tip that this train running from Texarkana to Ft. Worth will have a lot of money on it. We'll have to say exactly which day, I guess. We can figure there's a good chance they'll try to rob it that day, assuming they're still around that area up there."

"Yes!" I sat back, pleased with myself, and took a long pull from my beer.

Red leaned back in his chair and shook his head. "There's still a big problem," he told me. "That's a pretty long route, and there are several stops along the way. Even when we meet up with my other two guys, Sims and Walters, up there in Ft. Worth, we won't have near enough guys to cover everything. Actually," he said, thinking it over a little more, "at least one of those Bass gang robberies was after they had just blocked the tracks —pushed rocks and logs and stuff onto the tracks and forced the train to stop. Then they rode up and robbed it. They could do something like that at several points along the route."

I leaned back, feeling disappointed, and went back to staring at the table. The others fell quiet as well. Suddenly

I sat up and slapped my hand on the table. The others looked at me hopefully. "That," I said, "is why we'll be riding the train!"

Red absorbed that idea for a moment, then he grinned at me, leaned over, and slapped me on the back. "Stone," he said, "I think maybe you should have my job." He rose from the table. "You boys stay here and finish your beer," he told us. "I'm going over to the telegraph office."

CHAPTER THIRTEEN

T & P TRAIN

I t was about three days later, in the early evening, when the three of us rode into Ft. Worth. We rode down Main Street and I looked around me, thinking how different everything seemed this time. We pulled up outside the same café where Sarah and I had eaten a couple times. I wondered, as I dismounted, how she was doing.

We entered the café and were waved over to a table where two men were waiting for us. They made introductions all around. As I had expected, the two already at the table were Sims and Walters. We sat down and everyone ordered food.

"Now," said Red, looking at Sims and Walters, "tell me if you've done what I instructed in the telegram."

Both men nodded. "We have," said Sims. "We had a guy at Texas and Pacific Railroad pass the word around that there would be a large gold shipment on the Texarkana to Ft. Worth train next Tuesday, the twentieth."

Red slapped his hands together in delight. "How much money did you say would be on there?" he asked.

"Eight thousand dollars," said Walters. "Enough to make them really want to rob that train, but not so much they'll think it's too good to be true."

"Excellent," said Red. The food came, and we all dug in.

———

Perkins sat at a table in the White Elephant Saloon in Hell's Half Acre. Actually, the White Elephant was a block outside the Hell's Half Acre area, but the gambling houses were just a short walk and the entertainment here suited him. The occasional gunfight inside the saloon didn't really bother him. He had shaved his mustache since the train robbery, and he kept his hat pulled down low over his forehead. He didn't know if they had recognized him in last week's train robbery, but he didn't like to take chances.

He looked up enough to glance across the room. The two men who had stayed with him after the robbery, Roy and Leo, were both over there. Roy was deep in conversation with somebody, head down, both of them glancing around from time to time as they talked. Leo was coming back to the table, a bottle of whiskey in one hand and three glasses in the other. He halted as a fistfight broke out in front of him. He circled the fighters and set the whiskey down on the table. Perkins watched the fight with interest, but it was over quickly. A solid, short punch to the jaw sent one man to the floor. Waiters picked up the fallen man and tossed him out the doors into the street. The other fighter walked back to the bar and resumed drinking.

Leo poured drinks for both of them, and both had finished the first glass when Roy walked over and joined them. Roy sat down, poured himself a drink, and glanced over as the man he'd been talking to left the saloon.

Roy tossed off his drink, slammed down the glass, and looked at the other two with excitement. "I've got great news!" he announced. Perkins sat silently and waited. Roy poured himself another drink. "The T&P train from Texarkana to here is gonna have eight thousand in gold coins on it! On the twentieth," he added.

Perkins's face didn't change expression. "You want to rob another train, right here in the same place?" he asked incredulously.

Roy pressed his idea. "Old train," he said. "No time lock on the safe. Eight thousand dollars, right there in the express car." He stopped and waited for a response from Perkins.

Leo took up his case. "Eight thousand is a lot of money," he pleaded. "We could split it up and still have..." He grabbed a piece of paper and a pencil. He pushed the point of the pencil onto his tongue a few times. The pencil hovered above the paper. "We could split it up and still have..." His brow furrowed in thought. Perkins snatched the pencil and paper away in disgust.

"How do you know this?" he demanded of Roy.

Roy inclined his head to indicate the door. "That guy I was just talking to, the one that left a minute ago. He works for the T&P railroad. I told him I'd pay him twenty dollars if he ever had a great tip for me. This is what he just told me."

Perkins remained unconvinced. "You believe him? He tells the truth?"

Roy nodded his head vigorously. "I swear it, boss. He wouldn't lie to me." He broke off in mid-thought, waiting for Perkins, who tossed off his drink and stared at Roy. They had made little money on the last robbery, and what money they had didn't stay with a man for very long in Hell's Half Acre.

Perkins poured himself another drink. "I'll think about it," he said gruffly. The other two exchanged a glance, shrugged, and went back to drinking.

———

Sharpe led the other two, following the path of Walnut Creek around the curve of the hills, keeping an eye out for a fold in the hills, where one hill butted up against another as it sloped down to meet the creek. An old dry creek ran between the two hills, hidden by a small stand of oak trees and some underbrush.

The casual observer wouldn't suspect that the bed of the dry creek led into the property Sharpe had decided he would take for himself. When he saw what he was looking for—a large oak with a limb recently severed by a lightning strike—he led the way out of the creek bed and through the trees. They rode single file through a narrow, winding notch between the hills, following the dry creek bed until it ended at another larger stand of oak trees.

Sharpe continued to weave his way among the trees until the trees gave way to a green, open meadow flanked by hills on both sides. He pulled up and allowed Pete and Kendall to catch up with him. They came alongside, reined in, and glanced around them. Sharpe pointed to the south, across the meadow.

"The creek bends around and flows across the front of the property, down there." He shifted his arm, pointing to the southwest. "There is a road over there leading into Austin. Less than five miles from here."

Kendall nodded, looking over his shoulder at the path they had taken. "So," he said, "we come from whatever job we've been on, circling to the north if we need to, then ride through the creek to cover our tracks until we ride in through the notch in these hills. If anybody had followed us that far, they'll probably think we've gone into Austin."

Sharpe nodded, studying their faces for a reaction.

Kendall removed his hat and mopped his forehead with his sleeve. "Sounds good to me," he said, "when do we start?"

"Soon," Sharpe answered. "We'll do a couple banks." He turned, leading the way back down to the meadow, past the site of an old ruined shack, and onto a road leading to the south.

The other two followed wordlessly. They'd learned to recognize the times when Sharpe didn't want to be bothered with conversation or questions.

The road led into a town, and Pete and Kendall had little trouble figuring out that this would be Austin. Sharpe rode until he spotted a saloon on his right. He hitched his horse to the rail and went inside. Pete and Kendall followed, joining Sharpe at a table.

Sharpe downed two whiskeys before he began talking. "That property is owned by an eastern woman named Statton," he began. He filled up his glass again. "Actually, it's owned by the woman and a cowboy named Stone. I don't know if they both plan to keep half or what they plan to do with the land. If we're lucky, they'll just let it sit there for a while and not try to build or live on it."

Pete shifted in his chair and cleared his throat, preparing to say something. Sharpe fixed him with an icy stare from those gray eyes, and Pete fell silent.

"Say it," Sharpe barked.

Pete hesitated. "Well," he began, "it looks like a good hideout and all, but we can't use it if people are there all the time, building a house or something..." He fell silent again when he saw the anger in Sharpe's eyes.

"Doesn't matter," Sharpe interrupted. "They probably won't do anything with it until we're ready to move on."

Pete and Kendall exchanged glances, and Kendall stuck his neck out. "What do we do if one of them moves out there and we're trying to use it to hide?" he finally asked.

Sharpe downed his fourth glass. "We do what we have to do," he answered without hesitation. "I'll bet that place gets real quiet if the owners disappear. We keep it quiet. We'll keep an eye out for 'em. I know where the woman lives. Or we could grab her on the road between here and there. Not that hard. The cowboy, too. I know what he looks like."

Kendall nodded and reached for the whiskey bottle. Pete said nothing as he reached for a refill also, but his mind was churning. He'd never hurt a woman before, and he didn't want to start now. Maybe it wouldn't come to that.

————

Perkins didn't like to bring in somebody new before a major job, but he didn't feel he had a choice in this case. With only two men remaining from the Eagle Pass robbery, and just a few days before the train ran from Marshall to Ft. Worth with the large payload aboard, he needed two more men. He needed them not only for the robbery but to help pull the logs and rocks across the tracks. He had decided to ambush the train en route. After this one, he knew he needed to lie low for a while, and he planned to be rid of all these guys.

He was in a saloon in Paris, Texas. The town was larger than he had expected, the population being around four thousand people. Building the railroad through here a few years ago must have brought in a lot of people. He sat at a table with Leo, one of his guys from the last job. They were waiting for Roy, who had stayed behind in Ft. Worth to find a couple new guys.

Perkins wasn't comfortable staying there in Ft. Worth any longer, so close to the last robbery site. He knew that his poster was still around in a few sheriff's offices. He could only hope it wasn't being circulated.

The batwing doors opened, and Roy came in, followed by a couple cowboys, judging by the clothes. Perkins waited, expressionless, as Roy brought the newcomers over. Leo pulled over a couple extra chairs, and they crowded around the table.

Roy made the introductions. "Perkins, Leo, this is Bevins, and this is Porter."

Perkins ignored the proffered hands and poured himself a drink instead. He tossed it down and stared at the two men. "Either of you ever rob a train before?" he asked.

The two men looked at each other and shook their heads. "We've done a bank," Bevins offered. "Not a train, though."

Perkins let that one soak in for a moment, then passed the whiskey bottle across the table. "What've you done lately?" was the next question.

They each shrugged, toyed with the whiskey glasses briefly, then Porter answered. "We were on a cattle drive to Kansas. Part of the drive, anyway." He lowered his eyes and occupied himself with the whiskey.

Perkins's irritation was clear on his face. "Part of a cattle drive?" he prodded.

Porter tossed off the drink and nodded. "We planned to cut the herd and sell some cows. Had three partners who were supposed to take out the cowboys on point while we joined up from the rear." He shook his head, both men clearly angry with the outcome.

Perkins's temper was growing by the minute. The last statement hung in the air. Bevins looked over at Perkins's face and volunteered to finish the story.

"The other three came out of a wash to take 'em by surprise, like we planned, but...they got shot. Two of 'em did," he finished. "The other one got taken prisoner. We took our pay and left."

Perkins stared at them. "You got fired from a cattle drive?"

"Not fired," Bevins lied. "We just left."

"It was all over by the time we got there," Porter chimed in. "Nothing we could do. He'd already shot 'em."

Perkins continued to stare. "One guy shot two of yours after they took him by surprise?" he asked incredulously. There was a long silence.

"He got lucky, that's all," Bevins finally said.

Perkins shot an exasperated look at Roy, clearly unhappy with these new recruits. The problem was that he had only a couple days left. He'd been counting on Roy to bring somebody in, and these two were the only ones he had. He heaved a resigned sigh and decided to proceed with his plans.

After a round of beer had been brought to the table, Perkins explained his plan. "A few miles to the east of here," he began, "the track takes a really sharp, blind turn to the left. We're going to block the tracks there and pull the robbery when the train stops." He glanced around to be sure no one else seemed interested in their conversation, then continued. "There are a lot of big trees there, we're going to have to chop a few of them down tomorrow. We'll leave them out of sight, so the people in the noon train tomorrow won't see anything. Come day after tomorrow, we'll get out there early and drag the trees across the tracks. We should be able to harness a couple horses to help. Then we'll roll a couple of those rocks on the tracks."

Perkins stopped and drained half his beer with one gulp. He looked over at Leo. "Leo, you're going to get up around the turn and wave a red flag at the train so it can slow down before it hits the curve. We don't need the whole thing jumping the track and turning over on us. I'm going to take out the engineer first, then I'm coming back to the express car." He looked at Bevins and Porter. "You're going in the express car first, get it secured." Finally, he swung around to Roy. "You'll go through the passenger cars. Leo can join you when he gets there. No robbing." He fixed a glare on Roy. "If you shoot anybody, I'll shoot you."

Roy opened his mouth to speak, then thought better of it.

Perkins swung back around to look at Bevins and Porter. They were less than excited about it, judging by the looks on their faces. Perkins couldn't really blame them but would never admit it. He planned to make them do most of the hard work, chopping down trees and dragging them. He had also put them in the most dangerous position, boarding the express car first. If there was an armed guard on the train, he would be in the express car. Perkins planned to let the two new guys draw any gunfire that might come before he got on the train himself.

Perkins also planned to shortchange the new guys on the take, but they didn't need to know that. He had given Roy strict instructions not to tell anybody how much money was on the train. He mentally subtracted the amount he wanted to keep for himself. "There's going to be five thousand dollars in that express car," he told them. "That's one thousand for each of us when we're done." He saw their eyes light up at the thought of that much money.

Roy and Leo exchanged a glance over the heads of the

others. Both were wondering how that extra three thousand was going to get divided.

Seeing a little hesitancy still in the eyes of Bevins and Porter, Perkins gave them a little reassurance. "We've got a guy that works for the railroad," he told them. "It's an old train and an old vault. No time locks. We'll make the guy on duty in the express car open it for us. I'll have a couple sticks of dynamite in case we need it. We're going to get on and get off. No stopping to take Grandma's necklace from a couple passengers. We'll leave before anybody knows we were there. A thousand dollars for a couple mornings' work." He stopped and looked at the new recruits. "What do you say?"

Greed won out, as Perkins had known it would. Bevins and Porter didn't even stop to consult with each other. Both nodded.

"Okay." Perkins drained the rest of his beer and stood. "I'm outta here. Stay if you want to, just don't get drunk and do something stupid that's gonna get you remembered around this place." He turned to leave, then turned back. "One more thing. We split the dough right after the robbery, then we split up. Only two together. Makes it harder to track us. I'm going by myself. This should be enough to live on for a while. If you're smart, you'll get a long way away from here before you do any big spending." He turned on his heel and left, the batwing doors swinging back and forth behind him.

CHAPTER FOURTEEN
AMBUSH

Perkins drove them hard the next morning. They all took a turn with an axe on some tall oak trees, but Perkins saw to it that he himself took the shortest turn, and Bevins and Porter had the longest turns. When they had felled four trees, all at least thirty feet tall and with thick trunks, he called a halt. All of them picked a tree still standing in the woods and slumped down the side of it to rest against the base. Perkins felt the sweat rolling down his cheeks and waited for his pulse to slow down. This had been harder work than he'd imagined. He pulled a watch from his pocket and checked the time: ten o'clock. He wanted to be away from here before the daily train came through at twelve.

He pushed himself to his feet and threaded his way through the trees to a place where some large rocks lay near the rail bed. He assumed someone had blasted them out when the tracks were originally laid. They had been left conveniently close to the tracks, though it would involve rolling them uphill for a short way. He wanted to add the weight of the rocks behind the tree trunks before the train came tomorrow. He assumed the weight of the tree trunks was enough to stop the train, but he wasn't taking any chances. He bent and pushed at one rock, feeling rewarded when it rolled. Two of them could handle it tomorrow.

Perkins wheeled around when he heard a sound behind him. He turned back to test the weight of a couple more rocks while Leo walked up. Perkins was ninety percent sure it was about the money split tomorrow. He proved to be correct in his guess.

Leo kicked idly at one rock. "We're still expecting eight thousand dollars tomorrow, right, boss?" Leo began.

Perkins stared down at where the rails disappeared into the distance. He couldn't wait to be rid of all four guys. "Sure," he said after a lengthy pause. "Eight thousand dollars. The three of us will each wind up getting two thousand apiece. The new guys get only one thousand. That's if you don't mess up and tell them how much money is in there."

Leo continued to kick at a rock, clearly only partly reassured. "What if there's more than eight?" he persisted.

Perkins, rapidly losing patience, turned and leaned in uncomfortably close. "We split anything above eight thousand three ways, okay? You, me, and Roy."

Leo nodded and backed away. "Sure, boss, sounds good." He turned and walked back into the trees. Roy was waiting to talk to him back there. Perkins turned his back and walked the distance from the bend in the tracks to where he planned to board the train. He planned to make sure he was the only one counting the money tomorrow, whatever it took. Sometimes robbers got shot during train robberies, didn't they?

———

Perkins was worrying that they hadn't started early enough. Sunup would have been better than the eight thirty start they'd gotten. He pulled the watch out of his pocket and checked it. Ten o'clock sharp and they didn't have the first tree dragged across the tracks yet. The tree trunks had to be dragged out of the woods, and the branches were catching in the trees and underbrush when they tried to drag them. They had brought a couple extra horses, and they were going to need them. Why hadn't he thought to chop off the branches yesterday? They had two axes between them and took turns chopping away the branches on the fallen trees.

Finally, they had chopped away enough from the tree closest to the tracks to give it another try. Perkins climbed onto his horse. He wrapped a thick rope around the saddle horn. The other end of the rope was wrapped around the tree and secured. One of his other men was mounted and likewise had a rope from the saddle horn back to the tree. Perkins kicked the horse in the ribs and shouted, as did Leo, mounted on the other horse. The three men on foot did what they could to push the tree along. Perkins heaved a sigh of relief as the tree slid out of the woods. They dragged and pushed it up the slight incline to the rail bed, then dragged it across so the trunk of the tree lay squarely across the tracks. Perkins called a halt and led the horse back down into the woods while the others removed the rope.

Leo and Porter took the axes and began chopping away branches from the second tree. Perkins motioned at Bevins and led the way to a sizable rock that sat near the tracks. Perkins motioned at the rock.

Bevins stared at him. "You've got to be kidding," he snarled.

"We're moving the rock," Perkins snapped. "Now get down here and put your back into it."

Bevins remained where he was, staring levelly across the fifteen feet that separated them.

Perkins's hand drifted down near his gun belt. He hooked a thumb over the belt and returned the stare.

"You'll have one less man to do this work if you shoot me," Bevins said. His hand inched closer to his gun.

"I'll just throw your body onto the tracks with the trees. Maybe they'll stop if they think you're still alive."

Bevins stood motionless.

Perkins was aware of the other three drifting out of the trees to watch. Finally, Bevins shrugged, turned and walked toward the rock. "Bevins!" Perkins snapped. "Unbuckle your gun belt and drop it. I'll give it back when it's time."

Bevins paused, his back to Perkins, then he slowly unbuckled the belt, dropped it, and stepped away.

Perkins picked up the gun belt, tossed it into the woods, and joined Bevins. Together they pushed the rock, straining with the effort, until they had positioned it behind the tree trunk.

They continued in teams of three and two, chopping tree limbs and pushing the rocks. When enough tree limbs had been removed to haul the tree to the tracks, they all joined in. They continued to hitch two horses at a time to the trees. When there were four tree trunks and five sizable rocks positioned on the tracks, Perkins called a halt. It was just twenty minutes until twelve noon. They gathered briefly to cover instructions one more time, then Leo pulled a large red piece of an old blanket from his pocket, mounted his horse, and rode up around the bend to take his position.

———

We had ridden the afternoon train today, the 19th, from Ft. Worth to Texarkana. Tomorrow, we would be taking the return trip to Ft. Worth, expecting the attempted robbery during that ride. As the time drew closer, I questioned my plan, wondering what might go wrong. I was worried about the safety of the passengers.

The railroad had cooperated with having us ride the train. Fear of having remnants of the Bass gang robbing their trains had probably caused them to agree to that. They weren't willing to empty the train and send it through without passengers—they didn't seem to be all that convinced that a robbery would actually happen. They had agreed to stop selling tickets at the time we approached them with the plan.

We would group the passengers on board in one car. We would have a man at both ends of that car. We had alerted the engineer to be on the lookout for any obstruction on the tracks. We'd had to explain why, so he was in on the plan, but no one else on the train knew.

We were grouped now in a café in Texarkana, going over the plans we had for tomorrow. Sims and Walters would be posted in the passenger car, front and back. Nobody was going to get past them to threaten the passengers. Ash, with his trusty Winchester, was assigned to the engine. If nobody came to the engine, he would cover the express car from outside the train. Red and I were going to be in the express car. We would have to explain our presence to the attendant assigned to the car before leaving tomorrow. When and if an attack came, he would be under strict instructions to keep his head down and stay on the floor.

Red looked around the table, wanting to be sure everyone was clear on his job tomorrow. "Ash," he said, "if they try to board someplace where the train must slow down, your job is to stay in the engine. If they try to board while we're stopped, especially if the track is blocked, you probably have little to do, so get down to the express car as fast as you can." He looked around at Sims and Walters. "The passengers have to be protected at all costs. If there's an attack, they keep their heads down and stay in their seats. And nobody gets past you guys into that car. Clear?"

Sims and Walters nodded simultaneously.

He turned to me. "We don't have any windows in the express car. We let them get in the car, then we arrest them. If they draw on us, we shoot to kill. Us or them. Right?"

I nodded.

Red's gaze dropped to a paper on the table in front of him, where he seemed to have some notes. "We have a few stops between here and Ft. Worth. Obviously, we're on our toes when we stop. There are a few places where we slow down for turns, but no hills to climb, so I doubt they'll try to board us while we're moving. If there is a really sudden stop, assume we're about to be robbed." He stopped and scanned the sheet, then folded it up and put it in his pocket. "Train leaves at ten thirty. If you're late, you need to be thinking about your next job after the Rangers. Any questions?"

There were none. Red stood and looked around. "Everybody get plenty of sleep."

———

I was awake before dawn, pacing around the room in the hotel. After a while, I took it outside. I walked up and down the streets in Texarkana until I was tired and the sun was up, then went back to last night's café for some breakfast. Red and Sims were already in there, so I joined them. Nobody seemed to have a lot to say this morning. Even Red seemed a little keyed up. The hours crawled by until it was finally after ten o'clock and we boarded the train.

There was nothing in the safe at all. There were probably a few valuables in the passenger luggage we had, but other than that, there was absolutely nothing to rob back here. The train pulled out on time, and it wasn't long before I wished we had windows in this car. With nothing to look at and no idea what was going on outside, I was wishing that Red had assigned me anywhere else but in the express car.

The first hour was uneventful, but we'd expected that. The biggest stop we would make before Dallas was in Paris. I knew that stop was coming next. Also, I knew there was a very sharp turn in the tracks just outside of Paris. I rehearsed in my mind what to do if we stopped at the turn.

We pulled into the Paris station and stopped. I squatted on my heels in the car's corner, straining to hear anything that might be going on out there. I could hear nothing. I glanced over at Red, who was doing the same thing in the opposite corner, near the door. The attendant, I noticed, had a couple large beads of sweat on his forehead. He'd been told he should open the door if someone pounded on it, then back away with his hands in the air. I looked again, and the sweat was rolling down his cheeks. I supposed it wouldn't hurt if he looked nervous.

The train whistle sounded, and we pulled forward slowly, then gathered speed until we had the familiar click-clack sound and rolling sensation under our feet. I sighed, feeling a bit disappointed. I wondered if they were coming today. I looked over at Red, who simply shrugged and crouched back down on his heels. I did the same in my corner. The attendant wiped his forehead with his sleeve and left off sweating for a while.

Another half hour passed. I was seated now, my back

against the side of the car. The rhythmic motion of the train would have made me sleepy, but I was far too keyed up for that. I thought I felt the car slowing down, and I half rose from my seated position. Suddenly, the brakes were slammed on so hard that I went tumbling to the floor, sliding toward the vault. I threw up my arms to protect my head and was rewarded with a sharp blow to my left arm. The train continued to shudder as it sharply braked. Finally, we stopped completely and there was the sound of a crash coming from up front. Red, who had been protected against the slide by his position up against the front of the car, came up and started over to check on me. I stood and waved him off. My left arm was a little numb, but my gun hand would be fine.

―――――

Outside the train, Perkins, Roy, Bevins, and Porter waited under cover of the trees. When they could hear the train coming, they all drew their guns and watched for the locomotive to appear around the bend. They heard the squeal of the brakes as the train came around the corner, and the sound intensified as the engineer caught sight of the barricade. The train was decelerating quickly, but there was still a crash as it hit the barricade and came to a full stop. Perkins waved his gun in the air and the four outlaws broke from under the trees.

Perkins charged toward the engine, noticing from the corner of his eye that Leo had barreled around the bend on his horse, having accomplished his first task in slowing the train with the red flag. He would proceed now to the front of the passenger cars. Perkins re-focused on the engine. As he drew closer, he could see the engineer slumped across the controls and motionless. Realizing that the man had probably been pitched forward and knocked cold by the collision, Perkins pulled up and reconsidered. He moved on to the express car. He reined around as Leo passed behind him.

———

Roy galloped toward the passenger cars. He could see a full car as he passed the first one, then he pulled up, puzzled. The passenger cars behind the first one seemed to be empty. He wheeled his horse around and rode up to the back of the first passenger car. He leaped onto the step and yanked open the rear door, gun at the ready. As soon as he entered, he felt a gun in his ribs.

"Drop the gun," he was advised. The gun was pushed meaningfully into his ribs.

Turning his head slightly, he could see the badge on the man's chest. Roy dropped the gun and lifted his hands in the air.

———

A few seconds later, Leo swung his horse to the front of the first passenger car, ran up the steps, and charged through the door. The first sight that caught his eye was the image of Roy at the back of the car, hands in the air. His eyes dropped. Roy's gun was on the ground. A second later, Leo felt a gun at his back. He received the same advice that Roy had received about what to do with his gun. Leo shrugged, dropped his gun, and raised his hands. Moments later, they were both on the floor of the car, hands tied behind their backs.

———

Back in the engine, Ash sprung forward to check on the engineer, who had been thrown forward abruptly, colliding heavily with the windshield. Ash lifted him back into his seat, patting his cheek and calling his name. The engineer moaned but made no move to open his eyes. Ash grabbed his canteen and splashed water on the engineer's face. His eyes fluttered open, and he began returning to consciousness.

Ash left the water in the man's hand, then leaped down from the engine and began running toward the express car. He could see one of the outlaws in front of him, riding toward the car. Beyond the man on the horse, he could see two dismounted men. One appeared to be hammering on the door of the express car with the butt of his gun. Ash put his fingers to his lips as he ran, cutting loose with a shrill whistle. His other hand lifted his Winchester.

———

Perkins, startled by a loud whistle from behind him, wheeled his horse around and saw a man running toward him, carrying a rifle. The sun reflected the glare from a badge on the man's chest. Perkins didn't hesitate. He drew and fired even as his horse was wheeling around. He knew in an instant it had gone high. The horse, startled by the sudden turn and the shot, reared slightly. Perkins fought to get his mount back under control while he lifted his gun for another shot. He saw the rifle coming up...it was the last thing he saw. McKinnon's shot lifted him from the saddle, and he landed on the ground, dead.

CHAPTER FIFTEEN
EXPRESS CAR STANDOFF

We collected ourselves in the express car and looked around. The attendant had a lump on his forehead. He had also apparently been thrown sideways after the sudden stop. Blood oozed down from the lump, mingled with sweat. I asked in low tones if he could open the door. He nodded. After a few more seconds, there was a hammering sound from the sliding door in front of us. A voice demanded that we open the door. Red nodded at the attendant and he stepped forward. I could see his hands shaking from where I stood.

The door slid open slowly, and the attendant stepped back, hands in the air. He backed away from the door, and two men stepped up and followed him inside. Both men had guns drawn and bandannas pulled up over their faces. As they stepped in a little farther, Red stepped forward from the corner of the car behind them. "Hands in the air," he ordered.

The man closest to Red complied, lifting his hands. Red stepped forward and took his gun. The man closer to me, though, swung toward Red, gun out.

"Hold it!" I yelled. "I have you covered. Drop the gun."

The man swung his head toward me. The gun hand didn't move. "Your choice," I told him. "You can drop that gun in the next three seconds, or I'll blow you right back out that door."

Outside the door, there were two gunshots. We all flinched a little in surprise, but I kept my gun covering the man in front of me.

He stared at me for just a moment longer, then slowly lowered the gun and dropped it on the floor. I thought he somehow looked familiar to me. "Pull the bandanna down," I told him.

He did so, and I took a half step back in surprise. It was Bevins from the cattle drive. Red yanked the bandanna down on the other man, and I could see that it was Porter. Red produced a short length of rope and began tying Porter's hands. The sound of a crash in the car's corner suddenly distracted met. I looked over to see the attendant sliding down the side of the car. He had passed out.

Movement back to my right brought my focus back to the prisoners. I could see Bevins's hand disappearing into a vest pocket. Then he pulled it back out. *Hideout gun,* my brain screamed at me as the short revolver came out of Bevins's pocket. He lifted it in my direction. I swung my gun back up and fired two quick shots. The first drove Bevins backward. He teetered at the edge of the door, revolver still in hand. My second shot knocked him back out through the door. I could hear him landing heavily at the edge of the tracks.

Red shoved Porter to the floor, planted his knee on Porter's back, then half-swung to cover the open door. He looked at me and motioned toward the door with his head. I remembered the two gunshots from outside and began to slog my way toward the open door. I put my back against the metal of the door, then half crouched and swung around, gun out in front of me.

A familiar voice greeted me: "Easy, pard. We done got this one wrapped up." I looked over to see Ash, his Winchester slowly moving away from the dead body of Bevins. "Ain't nuthin' left to do but bury these boys," he advised me.

I looked past him to see another dead body on the ground. I wondered, not for the first time, if Ash could turn that southern boy accent off and on whenever he pleased. I suspected that he could. I grinned at him in relief. "Who's that over there?" I asked, pointing my Colt at the body behind him.

"Looks like the poster for Perkins," Ash told me. "He took a shot at me and I didn't take it none too friendly."

Ash looked at the man I'd had just shot in the express car. He tilted his head, trying to decide if he knew the man. "Bevins," I told him. "Porter is inside with Red."

Recognition dawned on his face as he looked again. "Well, if that don't beat all," he observed. "He wanted to take you on, back on the cattle drive. I guess he got his chance." He lowered the Winchester to his side as Red pushed Porter out of the express car.

Behind Ash, I could see Sims and Walters emerging from the passenger car, pushing two men in front of them, hands tied behind their backs.

Red stood beside me at the door of the express car, looking around. He stepped down and prodded Porter with the barrel of his gun. "Five of you, all together?" he asked.

Porter nodded sullenly. I holstered my gun and went back to check on the express car attendant.

We left the three prisoners tied up and stowed them in the express car. Red moved among the passengers, telling them we were Texas Rangers and that we had captured all the train robbers. They had no doubt heard the gunshots, but nobody seemed in a mood to ask questions. Ash and I moved up front to the engine where we found the engineer re-starting the engine. He climbed down and examined the front of the locomotive, telling us after a while that he thought the train could probably make it to Dallas if we could clear the debris from the tracks.

We used the robber's horses to drag the trees away and, with the help of a few passengers, soon had the rails cleared. The engine moved forward with a groan, and there was a loud grinding noise of metal on metal the rest of the way. But we limped into the Dallas station at about three o'clock that afternoon, a couple of hours behind schedule. All the passengers were safe and well, except for a few bumps and bruises.

The Dallas sheriff came down to the station with one of his men and relieved us of our prisoners. Our job was done on this robbery, but there was a worry growing inside me. We hadn't seen or heard of Sharpe being involved with this one. Where was he? Red promised me he would check with Captain McNelly when he sent a telegram about this afternoon's attempted robbery.

———

We were gathered, standing in the lobby of our Ft. Worth hotel. Red passed around a telegram from Caption McNelly, telling us how pleased he was with the capture of the train robbers and the safety of the passengers. He said he would inform the governor of our success. I squinted at the telegram to make out the governor's name. It looked like it said Oran Roberts. I hadn't heard of him, but I was pretty new around these parts. It wouldn't hurt to learn his name.

Red gave us a few minutes to read the telegram and soak up the congratulations, then waved his hands. "Some of you remember," he said, glancing at me, "that there was another Wanted poster for a man named Louis Sharpe. As far as we know, he was in on the Eagle Pass robbery, but obviously wasn't there today. McNelly says we haven't heard any more about him. The last he knew, Sharpe was still up in this area. So McNelly wants us to keep looking around here for a few days. We'll pass the poster around in Hell's Half Acre and see if anything turns up. If not, I'll get further instructions from McNelly."

I was disappointed, but we had no more news about Sharpe. The boys seemed to move toward the saloon down the street to celebrate our success. I watched them go, twisting my hat in my hands, then moved to join them.

Red pulled me aside. "Mike," he told me. "I know you're worried about Sarah, and I understand why. I'm just going to ask you for two days up here. We'll try to get his scent up here, and if we don't, I promise you can go back down to Austin after two days to check on things. If you're worried enough, I'll even send McKinnon down there with you. Deal?"

I nodded in relief and shook Red's proffered hand. Ash glanced back at us, then fell in alongside as we moved down to the saloon.

———

Louis Sharpe had dismounted from his horse on the main street of Round Rock, Texas. There didn't seem to be a lot going on, but he had counted on that. He glanced down the street as Pete wandered into the general store. Kendall had already gone into the bank to check things out. Sharpe had planned to make this a practice run today, but after riding over fifteen miles, they all felt like going home with some money.

"You're a stranger around here, aren't ya?" The voice seemed to come out of nowhere and into Sharpe's ears. He jumped slightly and turned to look. A wizened old lady stood behind him, her face not coming up to a height much above Sharpe's navel. He looked down in annoyance. She had a red, sunburned face, and she wobbled a little on her feet as she chewed on something, then turned and spat. Sharpe waved his arm to send her away, but she stood her ground stubbornly, her bright blue eyes boring into his.

"Stranger, right?" she asked again.

Sharpe muttered under his breath and turned around, waiting for Kendall to step out of the bank.

"Are ya here to see Sam Bass's grave?" she bellowed. This time, she had his attention.

Sharpe swung back around. "What?"

"Grave of Sam Bass, I said." She gestured at the street behind him. "He got kilt right out there. Shot it out with the Texas Rangers, he did." She nodded emphatically.

"You're crazy," Sharpe said in disgust, moving to push her away.

"I was here," she insisted, "under that boardwalk over there." She pointed across the street. "They buried him in a graveyard outside o' town." She pointed again.

"Molly, maybe you can come with me and stop bothering the man." A woman had emerged from a storefront behind them and began shepherding the old woman away, who was still mumbling things under her breath.

"She's crazy," Sharpe repeated, watching the two of them move away.

The woman turned before they entered her shop. "Molly's not quite right in her head," she said apologetically. "I'm sorry she bothered you." She hesitated. "She's right about Sam Bass, though," she said. "The Rangers killed him in a gunfight in the street out there about four years ago." She turned and went into the shop. Sharpe stared after them.

"We could take it right now if we wanted to." Kendall's voice was in his ear, causing him to jump again. He wheeled back to see Kendall staring at him quizzically. "Did you hear me? There's no guard, it's an old safe. Somebody told me the sheriff went out to somebody's ranch and won't be back for a couple hours. We could take it now, easy."

Sharpe pulled himself together and mulled things over, finally deciding. "Get Pete out of the café," he said. Kendall turned to walk away. "Hey," Sharpe interrupted him. "Did Bass get killed in this town?"

Kendall looked puzzled. "I dunno," he said, looking around him. "He got killed in a little town somewhere around here. Why?"

Sharpe shook his head and waved Kendall away. He didn't like coincidences, but this job sounded too easy to pass up.

Pete was moving toward him now, leading his horse. Kendall lounged against the wall of the barbershop across from the town bank. Sharpe walked toward Pete, who paused and appeared to be adjusting his saddle as Sharpe walked past.

"We take it today," Sharpe said as he passed. "You go in first and go over to one cage. I'll be right behind you. Kendall watches the door and the horses."

Pete nodded, then turned his horse and led it to the hitching rail outside the bank. He stalled for a couple minutes, pretending to search for something in his saddlebags. Sharpe continued down the street and repeated his message to Kendall.

Sharpe turned casually, returned to where he'd

started, untied his horse, and led it across the street. When he reached the hitching rail, Pete walked up the steps and into the bank. Kendall, whose horse was already outside the bank, began crossing the street. Sharpe looked in both directions, then entered the bank.

"Hands in the air," Sharpe shouted, pulling his revolver.

Pete pulled his gun also and covered the two cages.

Sharpe advanced toward the safe in the back. "Everybody on the ground," he yelled. "Except you." He grabbed a young woman who had the misfortune of being closest to him. He placed his gun under her chin. "Who here can open the safe?" he demanded.

She cut her eyes toward a tall, thin young man who was getting up from his desk and falling to the ground. Sharpe let go of the young woman and pointed his gun at the young bank officer she had indicated. He crossed the ground between them in three strides and lifted him from the ground by his hair.

Sharpe leaned in, whispering but making sure they understood his tone through the bandanna covering his mouth. "You'll open this safe in the next thirty seconds, or I'll kill you," he hissed. "Understand?"

The man hesitated only a second, then nodded, finding Sharpe's intent completely believable.

It was a matter of just a few seconds before the safe was open. Sharpe pulled a burlap sack from under his vest, then reversed his gun and knocked the young man unconscious. He took one quick look inside, then yelled at Pete, who was stuffing money from the cages into his pockets.

"Leave that," he yelled, "get over here." Unless Sharpe was mistaken, there were several thousand dollars in this safe. Pete held the bag while Sharpe stuffed it with money.

In less than two minutes, the safe was empty. Sharpe couldn't believe his luck.

They ran from the bank and out to the porch. Kendall held their two horses, rifle cradled in the other arm. They mounted and waited while Kendall untied his horse. A bell sounded from inside the bank, and Sharpe cursed under his breath. Finally, Kendall was mounted, and they galloped down the street, heading south and out of town.

Crack! The rifle shot took Sharpe completely by surprise. *Thunk!* The bullet had whistled by, very close to him, he was sure. He pulled his gun and swung around, looking for the rifleman. Kendall, just a few steps behind him, fell out of his saddle and landed heavily in the street. Sharpe spotted a man on a rooftop across the street and fired off two quick shots. He heard a muffled shout and felt sure he had at least wounded the man. Then he and Pete put the spurs to their horses and galloped away. They didn't slow down until they were a few miles out of town and Sharpe felt sure there was no pursuit.

————

Sheriff Thompson returned to Round Rock about three o'clock that afternoon. He had left behind a very peaceful town, but found total chaos when he returned. The bank, he learned, had been robbed of about three thousand dollars. Several citizens were trying to form a posse, but apparently, the robbery had taken place at least an hour and a half ago. He told them the trail was cold. He would get in touch with the Rangers. Old man Dickens had climbed to the roof of his feed store and succeeded in killing one robber. They had at least gotten the corpse out of the street and over to the undertaker. Dickens had taken a bullet through the shoulder and was being cared for by the doctor.

The sheriff dispersed the crowds of people, who were gathered in the street and talking among themselves. He worked his way along the street, stopping off into shops from time to time, asking if anyone had seen the men and if they could provide a description. He paused outside the barbershop, frustrated. No one in the bank had gotten a good look because of bandannas, and apparently, no one else had, either. He felt a persistent tapping on his shoulder and looked around, then down. It was old Molly. Crazy Molly, they called her around town.

"What is it, Molly?" he asked impatiently.

"I seen him."

Thompson stared at her. "Saw who?"

"The main bank robber guy. I seen him. Talked to him." She shifted excitedly from one foot to the other, overjoyed at her newfound importance. "I done tole him about the Sam Bass killing and everythin'."

Thompson looked at her, unconvinced. The door to the dress shop opened, and the proprietor came out.

Thompson waited. "Yes?"

"Molly was talking to a man out here in front of the shop. I think maybe he was one robber."

Thompson moaned slightly. One witness in town, and it had to be Crazy Molly. "All right, Molly," he said resignedly, "let's go look at some posters."

————

Inside the sheriff's office, Molly hinted strongly that she would like some whiskey, but settled for coffee while Thompson placed one poster after another in front of her. Molly considered each one carefully, apparently intent on making this last as long as possible. She felt she was important for a change. At last, Thompson placed the final poster in front of her, relieved that the process was at last over.

Molly's hand slapped down on the last poster so suddenly that Thompson jumped. "It's him," came Molly's shrill shout. "That's him. I tole you I seen him!"

Thompson's eyes went from the poster to Molly, then back to the poster. "You're sure?" he asked skeptically.

"Sure as I'm sittin' here. Won't never forget those eyes, I won't."

Thompson saw her to the door and thanked her, then slipped her a dollar and told her to get a good meal. He returned to the desk and sat down, staring at the poster. The name at the bottom said Louis Sharpe. Thompson drummed his fingers and stared out the window for a few seconds, then came to his decision. He picked up the poster and walked to the telegraph office.

CHAPTER SIXTEEN

CHASING SHARPE

L eander McNelly rode slowly up to the hitching rail outside the boarding house where he kept a room as an office. He dismounted, feeling generally pleased with the meeting he'd had with the governor this morning. His news that one of the two known remaining members of the Bass gang had been killed in an attempted train robbery had been excellent news for the governor.

McNelly was sure that the governor would be letting the newspapers know. The news that no civilians and no Rangers had been hurt was further good news. McNelly remained for a moment beside his horse, breathing in the crisp morning air and enjoying the moment. After a couple of minutes, he reached into his saddlebag and removed a single Wanted poster. He turned and climbed the few steps to the boardinghouse porch.

One benefit of keeping an office in a boarding house, he reflected as he walked down the hallway, was that he could have a meal there if he came in early or stayed late to work. This morning, he'd planned on only coffee, having eaten breakfast at home, but the smell of eggs and bacon wafting down the hallway was proving a little too much for him. He patted his stomach reflectively. His wife wouldn't be too happy with him if she knew he'd eaten two full breakfasts, but he didn't really need to tell her, did he?

He rounded the corner into the kitchen and the boarding house owner lit up in an ear-to-ear smile. Captain McNelly was her favorite renter. If anybody caused her any trouble, she would casually point out the captain to them the next time he came into work. It worked better than anything she'd found in the last fifteen years to keep renters honest and paid up to date. She jumped from her chair and began filling a plate with food. McNelly protested, but only feebly. She put a plate heaping with eggs, bacon, biscuits, and gravy under his nose and hurried over to the coffeepot. McNelly smiled a little resignedly and tucked into the food.

Thirty minutes later, feeling absolutely stuffed but satisfied, McNelly took the one poster he had placed face down on the table for breakfast and strolled down the hallway to his office. Opening the door, he saw a stack of telegrams on the floor. Frowning slightly, he bent to pick them up and dropped them on his worktable. That was more paperwork than he'd counted on, but he would not let that spoil what had started out to be a splendid day.

McNelly walked over to the window and basked for a moment in the warm sunshine streaming through. He opened the window to get some fresh air circulating, delaying having to start on those telegrams on his desk for as long as possible. McNelly realized there was one thing that was spoiling this morning. He glanced down at the poster he still held in his hand. If there was one thing that displeased the governor, it was the fact that the man in this poster was still at large. It was the one remaining member of the Bass gang who was still out there somewhere. McNelly turned the poster over and stared at the face, then at the name at the bottom of the poster. "Louis Sharpe," he muttered softly to himself.

He turned and tossed the poster onto the table, then walked around and seated himself. He reached for the pile of telegrams and worked his way through them. Luckily, nothing seemed to demand his personal and immediate attention. His spirits rose again. He frowned briefly at the telegram from Red, they could not turn up anything about Sharpe up in the Ft. Worth area. Apparently, he had moved on from there. Now they would have to cast a wider net.

McNelly reached for the last telegram, glancing at the name at the bottom. It came from a sheriff in Round Rock named Thompson. He wasn't familiar with the name. He read the telegram and half rose from his seat. He stopped to re-read the message, then grabbed his hat and broke into a run on his way down the hallway. Sharpe was right here, right under his nose. He slapped his hat on his head as he trotted across the porch, then jumped onto his horse and headed for the telegraph office.

———

Louis Sharpe, unaware of the activity just down the road in McNelly's office, lay against the side of a hill on the property he thought of as his own. Yesterday's robbery had been quite a success—they had taken over three thousand one hundred dollars from the bank in Round Rock. He'd had no idea that a small-town bank could have so much money in it. He wondered idly how it had all come to be there. If it was a common occurrence for banks in Central Texas to hold so much cash, he had a brilliant future here indeed.

Kendall's shooting had been quite a shock, mainly

because it had come so close to him. In fact, the shooter might have been aiming at him. After all, he had been the one carrying the money bag. Losing Kendall meant he was a little short-handed for future jobs, but he was planning to lie low for a while, anyway. Kendall and Pete had been saddle partners for a while, and Pete seemed upset about the loss, but he would just have to get over it. If he didn't, he could take his money and go.

He had sent Pete into town to get some provisions, enough to last them for at least a week or ten days. That's how long Sharpe figured he needed to stay out of sight. The truth was, he was a little worried about being seen in town yesterday. Not during the robbery or even afterward. He had worn his hat low and had kept his bandanna over his mouth at all times once they went in the bank. He was worried about having been seen before the robbery. He hadn't even planned on robbing the bank that day when they went into town, so naturally, he wasn't using the bandanna then. Now, the crazy old lady in the street and maybe the lady who had come out of the dress shop had seen his face.

Sharpe shifted uncomfortably and pushed himself up to his feet. He had chosen a spot around a fold in the hills, not visible from the creek down below, as a place to dig himself a little hideout. So far, he had done little digging. He planned to get Pete to do most of it. He paced around a bit, remembering the old lady in Round Rock. He would have gotten rid of her a lot sooner, but she'd surprised him by talking about Sam Bass getting killed there. He was pretty sure there was a poster out there with his face on it from his days of riding with Bass. He didn't need the Rangers coming after him, too.

Bad luck he had pulled the robbery in a town associated with Bass's name. That one train robbery in Nebraska had put a lot of lawmen on his trail back then. He wondered if the old lady could identify him, or whether anybody would believe her, even if she did. Probably not, he decided. Even so, it was one more good reason to lie low for a while.

Sharpe grabbed a shovel and began stabbing it into the hillside. His idea was to dig in far enough to have a place to sleep and cook some food, if the fire were built out near the opening. Also, they might bury some of their take from the Round Rock bank in the back. Sharpe still had some money buried along the creek bank as well. Pete would never know about that, of course. Sharpe had gone down there yesterday and dug down just enough to satisfy himself that the money was still there. He continued to dig for about thirty minutes, finally calling it a day and laying back down against the hillside. He looked at the growing pile of dirt outside the hideout, he would have to get Pete to haul that away.

Sharpe stood and walked around the fold in the hill, intent on washing his hands down at the creek. A splash of color and some movement caught his eye. He dropped to the ground and looked toward the creek again. Someone was walking around by the remains of the old shack. Sharpe rose and half crouched, half walked back to his saddlebags. Digging around in his gear, he came up with his binoculars and walked back to a vantage point where he could lie down and watch through them.

It was the girl—that Statton woman, walking around and doing a little digging down near that shack. She appeared to be planting some flowers. Sharpe lay motionless and watched for about a half hour. At the end of that time, the girl walked over to her horse, mounted, and rode away. Sharpe walked down for a closer look at what she had done down there.

———

Sarah had secured the horse and buggy for the day, and with them came the assistance of her little helper, Daniel. She couldn't help smiling about that one. She'd felt uncomfortable about it at first, but now she understood—he just liked to help her. He had loaded a few boards onto the buggy, along with a shovel and a couple other tools. It was understood he would come out to the property and help for a while, then come back to do chores for his mother at the boarding house. Sarah would ride her horse out there and have her own ride back.

As they were getting ready to leave, Ma Kirk came out of the boarding house with two small rose bushes wrapped up in burlap sacks. "If you're going to fix up the site a little for him, I think these roses would add something, don't you?" she asked.

Sarah smiled and nodded. "They certainly will. Thank you. I'll have Daniel back to the house by noon."

Ma waved as they rode away, pleased with herself for her contribution to what she saw as a growing romance.

When they arrived at the property, they unloaded the boards. Sarah didn't really have any plans for those right now, but knew they would come in handy when Mike got ready to build. She handed Daniel the shovel and took a rake herself, and they began clearing out the site of the old shack. They raked up the old pieces of wood, branches, and whatever else had accumulated on the site since the day old Miles had blown the place up.

When they had cleared it and leveled it out as best they could, she stopped and looked at the building site. The opening to the old tunnel was a bit of an eyesore. It lay right at the edge of the site, only partially covered. She had Daniel drag an old tree limb or two over to cover up what was still visible of the tunnel opening. Mike could do what he wanted with that tunnel later. At least the tree limbs would keep everything except maybe a few mice from making a home down there. She walked down to the creek bank and saw that the opening at that end was covered by a couple rocks. She told Daniel he needed to go on home. She had only a little left to do.

Sarah walked over and began digging two holes for the rose bushes. She smiled at the thought of Mike coming out here to see what she had done. Maybe the roses would have bloomed by then. That would make a pleasant welcome. She took her time, and when they were planted, she got a hatful or two of water from the creek to help get them started. She stood back to evaluate her work for a while, then got on her horse to head home. For the second time, she was unaware that Sharpe had watched her while she was out there. This time, he had kept her under observation from about the time she had sent Daniel home.

———

Sharpe kicked around briefly at the building site. It looked like the girl or maybe the cowboy Stone planned to build something here. Obviously, he couldn't let that happen. He didn't need any neighbors. He stared around the site. It had been completely cleared except for a tree limb or two laying at the edge. He supposed that had been too heavy for her to carry.

Sharpe walked down to the creek bank and began walking up the bank to the place where he had left some gold from the Nebraska train robbery. As he walked, he scanned the bank for footprints or any other sign that the girl or the cowboy had gotten anywhere near his gold. He came to a spot, maybe halfway from the old shack site to his gold, that made him stop. There were footprints every-where. He squatted on his heels to look it over. At least three sets of footprints. One smaller, the other two larger.

Probably the girl and two men, he decided. Loose soil covering a slight depression in the ground told him they had been digging here.

Sharpe continued down to the spot where he had left the Nebraska gold. The site was undisturbed. At least they hadn't found that. He returned to the first spot where somebody had been digging. He circled it one more time but found nothing he hadn't found the first time. He came to his decision. He would have to get rid of the girl and the cowboy too, if he showed up. He couldn't have anybody building a house down here, and he couldn't have them finding his stash.

Sharpe climbed back to the site of the old shack and looked up through the meadow to the hills on his right. He could see Pete riding back with the supplies. Angry that Pete hadn't taken a route that would have better kept him out of sight, Sharpe started back through the meadow to give Pete a piece of his mind.

———

Red looked at his latest telegram from Captain McNelly, telling him that they had identified Sharpe at a bank holdup in Round Rock. Red and his men were to come down from Ft. Worth immediately to join the search in the Round Rock and Austin area. Red glanced up at the clock on the wall. It was already four thirty in the afternoon, too late to catch a train to Austin today. He picked up his hat and started walking down toward the Hell's Half Acre area, where Stone and McKinnon were showing posters and hoping to pick up the trail. His other two men were over in the Dallas area, doing the same, and should return this evening.

Red's first several stops were unproductive as he searched the various cafés, saloons, and gambling dens in

Hell's Half Acre. Finally, he turned and began retracing the steps to his hotel when he saw Ash McKinnon emerging from the White Elephant Saloon, holding a piece of paper —Red was sure it was the poster for Louis Sharpe. Red hurried up to McKinnon, and a moment later, Mike Stone came out of the saloon as well.

Ash McKinnon turned his infectious grin in Red's direction. "No luck today, boss," he began.

Red cut him off with a wave of his hand. "Sharpe's been spotted down south of here," he began.

Stone turned immediately, focused on Red's next words.

"Somebody in Round Rock identified him after a bank robbery," he began. "Hang on, Mike." Red reached out to catch Stone's shirt sleeve as he started back for the hotel. "The fastest way you can get down there is on tomorrow morning's train. There's not another one running today. You and Ash can go down to Austin right away to check on Sarah. I'll take the other two and see if we can find a trail leading out of Round Rock. The sheriff down there said the trail was too cold, but we'll see."

Stone stood indecisively, shifting from one foot to the other and looking down the street toward the hotel. Red half-turned him to look into Stone's eyes. "First thing tomorrow, I promise. He hasn't been seen in Austin, just at the Round Rock bank. First thing tomorrow," he repeated.

Stone stopped shifting on his feet and nodded. He removed his hat, reached into his hatband, and took out a scrap of paper, passing it to Red. "Can you do one thing for me? Sarah's address is on that paper. Can you send a telegram to Captain McNelly and ask him to check on Sarah, and to tell her that Sharpe's been seen down there?"

Red opened the scrap of paper and looked at it, making sure he could read the writing. "I'll do it right now," he promised. They all turned and headed north. Red detoured to the telegraph office on the way. Within minutes, they sent the message to Leander McNelly. Mike Stone and Ash McKinnon walked back to the hotel. There was nothing more they could do, other than wait for that morning train.

CHAPTER SEVENTEEN

KIDNAPPED!

S arah was out in the kitchen with Ma Kirk, helping her prepare dinner for her guests, as she often did, now that school was no longer in session. A knocking at the front door interrupted both their conversation and the dinner preparation. Ma lifted her hands from a kneading bowl, she was up to her elbows in dough and flour.

"No," Sarah told her, "I'll get it."

"Okay," Ma agreed, "but if it's somebody interested in renting that empty room, come and get me."

"I'll do it," Sarah agreed over her shoulder. She opened the door to see a badge and a man she hadn't seen before.

The man on the porch, clearly identified as a Texas Ranger by his badge, removed his hat. "Ma'am," he said with just a slight drawl, "I'm looking for Sarah Statton."

Sarah's gaze traveled down, there seemed to be a poster rolled up in his left hand. "I'm Sarah Statton," she responded. She hesitated, then made a guess. "Are you Captain McNelly, by any chance?"

Captain McNelly looked at her in some surprise, then

nodded. "I am Captain McNelly," he confirmed. "Can I talk to you for a few minutes?"

Sarah nodded and led the way to the swing on the front porch. She had a sinking feeling this was going to be about Louis Sharpe. Her fears were confirmed when McNelly unrolled the poster in his hand.

McNelly saw the look on her face when he unrolled the poster—it made his first question almost unnecessary: "You know this man, I take it?"

Sarah shook her head slightly. "I don't really know him," she said, "but I've seen him. He was following me around in St. Louis, and I saw him briefly again in Ft Worth. I believe he broke into my hotel room in St. Louis."

McNelly sat back and listened as Sarah explained her history with Louis Sharpe. When she finished, he nodded and rolled up the poster.

Sarah searched his face. "Am I in danger?" she asked.

McNelly shook his head, considering his words before he answered. "I don't believe you are," he answered. "We're just being careful. Louis Sharpe was identified as one of three men who held up a bank in Round Rock a few days ago."

Sarah repeated the words "Round Rock" under her breath, looking puzzled.

"About fifteen miles north of here," McNelly explained. "We haven't been able to determine which direction they took after the robbery. They killed one of the three men. The other two, including Sharpe, got away." He paused briefly, watching as a buggy drove by on the street. "There's no reason to think he knows you're down here, is there?"

Sarah shook her head, then hesitated.

"What is it?" asked McNelly. Sarah crossed her arms and leaned back. "When I was in St. Louis, I went to see an attorney about my uncle's will. He left me some property just north of town. He mentioned burying something of some value and left a map showing where he buried it. The map was in my room when it was broken into. Nothing was taken, though, and I doubt anybody would have thought that my old mountain man uncle could have had much in the way of treasure to bury. We already dug it up, and it didn't turn out to be much."

"Okay," McNelly concluded. "I don't think you're in any danger here, but just to be safe, I would stay within a few miles of your house here, and maybe you can go to the busier sections of Austin during the day. If you see Sharpe, let me know right away." He started to write an address, but Sarah stopped him.

"Red already told me how to find you before he left for Ft. Worth. He told me to come to you if I saw Sharpe."

McNelly put away his pencil and paper, then put his hat back on. "Speaking of Red," he said, "he sent me the telegram to check on you. He is coming down from Ft. Worth sometime today, bringing four of his men with him. Red and two others will stay in Round Rock. Two others, Mike Stone and Ash McKinnon, are coming directly here to check on you. I take it you know these men and feel comfortable having them check in on your safety from time to time?"

For the first time since their conversation had started, Sarah smiled briefly. "Yes," she said. "I know them, and I trust them."

The smile wasn't lost on Captain McNelly, but he had no intention of following up with any more questions. Either Stone or McKinnon was a lucky young man, he concluded. He stood up and moved down the steps. "Remember," he said, "if you see this man Sharpe, I need to know. If Stone or McKinnon is here, you can just tell them and they will keep me informed. Ma'am." He tipped his hat, mounted his horse, and rode away.

Sarah re-entered the house, looking thoughtful. Ma Kirk noticed the change in mood right away. "Who was it?" she asked.

Sarah glanced over. "It was a Ranger captain named McNelly," she answered. For the first time, she told Ma the story of being followed in St. Louis, how she met Mike in Ft. Worth when she was worried about Sharpe's presence there, and she finished by explaining what McNelly had just told her. Ma listened to the entire story without interrupting. From time to time, she glanced at Sarah's face as she spoke.

"What do you plan to do?" Ma asked at length.

Sarah shrugged. "I'll do just as he said," she answered. "I'll be fine at the house and the area just around the house. I go down to the school once in a while to check on supplies or plan for next year. I ride into town once in a while to shop or pick up supplies for you. I can still do those things. Sharpe very likely doesn't even know I'm here, and I can't think of anything I have that he would want. Besides," she continued, "Mike will be here, and Ash too, by tomorrow or maybe even tonight. I'll be fine."

Ma chuckled slightly. "I'm thinking you'll be a little better than fine when Mike shows up."

Sarah had a feeling she had just blushed a little.

"Okay," said Ma, "but please take my horse if you go any distance at all, even just to the school. I'll feel better."

Sarah nodded her agreement and helped Ma wash the dishes they had used that afternoon. When the dishes were dried and put away, she glanced at some papers and a few books she had brought from her room that morning. She gestured at the pile of materials. "I think I'll run over to the school and store these for the rest of the summer," she told Ma. "There's really not enough space in my room for them."

"Okay." Ma nodded. "But take my horse, like we agreed."

"It's only a mile over there," Sarah protested. Her objections dried up when she saw Ma's look. "Right," she said, "I'll take your horse."

———

As she put the saddle and bridle on the horse, Sarah figured she didn't really save much time as compared to walking, but she reminded herself she was doing this to make Ma happy. She put the books and papers in the saddlebags and started to mount up before she decided on one more precaution she could take. She returned to her room and pulled her bags out from under the bed. After a short search, she was rewarded by finding her pistol and ammunition in one of the bags. She checked to be sure the gun was loaded, then slipped it into the pocket of her riding skirt. She went back outside, mounted, and rode down the street toward the school. She didn't notice when a buggy and wagon pulled out and began following her at a distance.

She hitched the horse outside the school building. She could feel the heat when she entered, so she propped the front door open and opened a side window for a little cross breeze as she put the books on a shelf and the papers in a drawer. She noticed one shelf of books she had been planning to re-arrange since school ended, she supposed this was as good a time as any.

Thirty minutes later, she stood back, satisfied with her work, and left the building, closing the window and pulling the door shut behind her. Dusk was settling in as she crossed the front porch. She walked down the steps and unhitched her horse from the rail. She had moved around to mount the horse when she thought she heard the whisper of footsteps in the grass behind her. She half-turned, but before she could see the source of the noise, she felt a sharp blow on the back of her head. She collapsed against the horse and slid down to the ground, unconscious.

———

The day had started badly for Sharpe. He had begun by explaining to Pete that they needed to get rid of the girl. Pete had voiced a few objections. Sharpe had concluded that Pete didn't like the idea of killing a woman. Sharpe had fixed him with a hard stare, hand hovering near his gun, until Pete shut up about it. Sharpe made a mental note that Pete would have to do the killing. He couldn't have anybody having an attack of conscience later on and maybe turning him in to the Rangers.

They had ridden into town, going to the livery stable. Sharpe figured he needed a horse and buggy to snatch the girl. And probably a tarp to throw over her in the wagon, at least until they got out of town. The guy at the livery stable had insisted that Sharpe had to rent a horse for the day to go along with the wagon. Sharpe had argued that he would use his own horse to pull the wagon, but the guy wouldn't relent. Horse and wagon or nothing at all. Angry to the core, Sharpe had finally agreed. Time was wasting. Making one more stop at the general store, he bought a tarp and threw it in the back of the wagon.

He'd made Pete leave his horse at the livery stable and drive the wagon. He had made it a point, the first time he'd come to Austin, to find out where the Statton woman lived. As they neared the boarding house, Sharpe caught the glint of sunlight reflected off a badge as a man rode by. Sharpe pulled his hat low, and they pulled to the side of the street. After waiting for several minutes, they saw no sign of the man returning.

Sharpe ordered Pete to drive on. They reached a spot just down the street from the boarding house and pulled to the side of the road again. Sharpe led his horse into the trees and hitched him to a tree limb, returning to take a seat next to Pete in the wagon. After a full hour or more of sitting in the wagon with nothing happening at the boarding house, Sharpe was growing angry again.

"What do you want to do if she don't come out?" Pete began. Sharpe silenced him with a glare from those scary gray eyes of his. Then, for the first time that day, his luck changed. The girl emerged from around the back of the house, leading a horse. He was sure it was Statton—her hair had a distinctive auburn tint to it. She mounted and rode down the street, heading away from them. That suited him just fine, there didn't appear to be any more houses in that direction.

They followed at a discrete distance for maybe a mile until the girl pulled off the road and rode up to a small, ramshackle-looking building. She dismounted and went in. Sharpe ordered Pete to move the buggy out of sight down the road. He got down and looked around, satisfied that there was no one around to watch what he was about to do. He cat-footed as quietly as he could to the side of the building. On the way by, he could see the girl moving about inside. She was alone. Sharpe pressed himself against the side of the building. The girl seemed to be in there for quite some time, but he could afford to be patient.

Finally, he could hear the girl emerging from the building. He heard the front door being closed. She came down the steps and unhitched her horse, her back to him as he had planned. He pulled his gun from the holster, and as she began to turn, he struck her on the back of the head with the gun. She slumped to the ground. He grabbed her under the arms and dragged her toward the street. Pete saw them coming, turned the wagon around, and pulled up in front of them. Together, they tossed the girl in the wagon and covered her with the tarp. Sharpe glanced at the sky. They had just enough time to take her back to her property. Soon to be his property, he corrected himself.

———

The train ride from Ft. Worth to Austin was agonizingly slow for me. Ash and I were on the train, along with Red, and Sims and Walters, the other men who had been a part of our squad looking for Sharpe in North Texas for the past three days. Red had been in a huddle with the other two up at the front of the car. They would have to ride with us to the station in Austin, then go back north to Round Rock to pick up Sharpe's trail. Red finished his instructions to the other two, then made his way back to me.

He perched on the arm of the seat across the aisle from me and tried to offer some assurance. "McNelly saw her just this morning and doesn't feel she is in any danger."

I nodded. "What about the fact that she saw Sharpe in Ft. Worth after she came down from St. Louis?" I asked.

Red stared at the floor for a moment. "We think that is a coincidence," he said, "but that's why we're sending you and Ash down to check on her. Stay with her as long as you feel you need to." He gave me a pat on the shoulder and moved forward again.

Ash came back and sat down across from me. "What do you want to do when we get there, pard?" he asked. "Your call. I'll do anything you want me to do."

I glanced across the aisle at him, comforted by his presence. I thought for a minute. "Maybe you could go to see Captain McNelly as soon as we get there," I decided. "I'll ride on down to the boarding house where she lives. You can meet me down there after you find out if the captain has any more news since yesterday. When we're sure Sarah is safe, we can start looking for Sharpe."

McKinnon stretched across the two seats on his side of the aisle, leaning his head back against the window. "I'll do that," he said, then closed his eyes.

————

We finally pulled into the Austin station and went back to claim our horses. Red told me he would be in touch with Captain McNelly by telegram or messenger, and we should stay in touch with McNelly. We would meet and join forces again when we were able. The other three headed north toward Round Rock while Ash and I turned south. Ash branched off to check in with McNelly while I rode on down to the boarding house where Sarah lived. Ma Kirk answered my knock and ushered me inside.

"Sarah's not here right now, but she'll be right back," she said in answer to my unasked question.

The uneasy feeling in my stomach must have translated itself to my face, because Ma immediately put a comforting hand on my arm. "She's just gone down to the school for a short while. She took my horse. Captain McNelly felt it was safe for her to travel a little right around here and in well-traveled areas in town. She'll be right back."

Ma urged me to take a seat in the kitchen while she served me a muffin and some coffee. I accepted and made a little small talk with her, though my ears were tuned for any sound of Sarah returning. After a few minutes, an uneasy silence settled in.

"Tell me," I said eventually, "what Sarah has been doing lately."

Ma brightened at the turn in my mood. "Well," she said with a smile, "I hope I'm not spoiling her surprise too much, but she's been out to your property a few times. I think her idea was to have a welcome home surprise for you when you came back. She'll be so pleased to see you."

I smiled despite myself, though my anxiety didn't go down by much. It occurred to me that if Sharpe had been following Sarah all along he would now know about our land. It might be a place to look for him. It was fairly remote and might make a hideout. Old Miles had said something about Sam Bass and rumors about Bass burying money out there on that night when Miles had died in the cabin. Suddenly the hair stood up on the back of my neck and my head came up. Sharpe had ridden with Sam Bass. There was a connection there.

"What?" she asked. The look on my face clearly alarmed Ma.

I was saved from having to answer when we heard a horse out front. Relieved, I leaped to my feet and ran to the front door, followed by Ma. I yanked the door open and looked out. Ma's horse was trotting into the front yard, riderless.

CHAPTER EIGHTEEN

TUNNEL

S arah's eyes came open slowly, and she struggled to make sense of things. She was lying on her side, and there was a sharp pain at the crown of her head. Trees swam around in her vision, then slowly came into focus. She thought to push herself to a sitting position, then heard the low hum of two male voices. She closed her eyes again and lay still, trying to pick up the words. She opened her right eye to just a narrow slit. One man was standing with his back to her, the other standing in a way that gave her a sideways profile view. She didn't recognize the man she could see from the side. She had a feeling that the man with his back to her was Sharpe, but she couldn't be sure unless he turned around.

She found that she could hear most of the words spoken by the man who was partially turned in her direction. He seemed to object to something—there was a pleading, argumentative tone to his voice. "Why do I have to do this?" The rest of his words trailed away.

The other man responded, but Sarah couldn't hear what he said. She watched through one eye while the man she could see shook his head, then stared away from her, into the trees. Sarah slid a hand carefully to the pocket of her riding skirt...the gun was still there. She breathed a silent sigh of relief.

"How long you going to be gone?" The man she could see had spoken again. The other man turned slowly to face her. She saw in an instant it was Sharpe, then she closed both eyes tightly.

"One hour," Sharpe said. Now she could hear him clearly, and his words sent a chill through her. "Because there's already a poster out there on me. I don't want you turning me in. You do this, they'll hang you too if they catch you. You've got one hour. If it's not done by then, I'll kill you both."

Sarah heard spurs moving away and tried opening the one eye to a slit again. Sharpe was mounting his horse, then he turned and rode away. Pete stood with his back to her now, watching Sharpe leave. She had no way of knowing, but Sharpe had put Pete in the position he had worried about from the time that he, Kendall, and Sharpe had talked in Ft. Worth. He really didn't think he could hurt a woman. Kendall would have done the dirty work if he were still alive, but Kendall wasn't here. Pete knew he would not kill a woman, but he didn't want to be killed by Sharpe, either. He stood there, his back to Sarah, his mind racing through all the possibilities he could think of.

Sarah's hand crept slowly back up toward the pocket of her skirt. She froze when she saw the man turn and start toward her. She saw that he was dawdling, his thumbs hooked in his gun belt. She was trying to decide if she could roll, grab the gun from her pocket, and have any chance of getting off a shot.

The man came to a stop a few feet away from her and cleared his throat. "Miss, you awake?"

Sarah decided that talking was better than whatever chance she had of getting off a shot. She opened her eyes and nodded her head. "Yes," she answered simply.

The man nodded his head. "I thought I seen you move a time or two..." He shuffled his feet a few times. "You can sit up if you want to," he offered.

Sarah pushed herself slowing to a sitting position, observing him. She anchored her weight on her left hand, leaving herself in the best position possible to pull the gun and fire. The man still hadn't moved. He turned and spat, wiping his mouth with his sleeve.

"Sharpe—the other man—he wants me to kill you, but I ain't gonna do it. Never hurt a woman before, and I'm not startin' now. So, here's what I'll do for you. I'm gonna give you a head start out of here. I'm gonna go over and start brushing my horse. You can take off. I'll let you get a head start, then I'm gonna fire my gun in the air. Sharpe will come back. My story's gonna be that I thought you were still passed out an' you got away when I wasn't lookin'."

Pete paused, looked at Sarah, then looked at the ground. "Sharpe's gonna come back. He'll be lookin' for you and he's gonna try to kill you. Maybe me too. That's the best I can do." He stopped, staring at her, looking for a reaction.

Sarah returned his stare and nodded slowly. "Okay," she said.

He stood there, waiting for something else, but when Sarah said nothing more, he turned around and started walking toward his horse. "Go now," he said over his shoulder.

Sarah gathered herself and jumped to her feet, nearly stumbling at first, holding her hand to her head as a stab-bing pain shot through her. She scrambled through the trees and down the hill in front of her, toward the meadow. There was no cover there, but if she could get down to the base of the hill and turn back toward the creek, there would be some tree cover. The best chance she had, she thought, would be if she could get to the old cabin site and hide in the tunnel Mike had shown her. She reached the base of the hill and raced across the open ground toward the trees in front of the creek. Her heart sank when she heard shouting from Sharpe and the man who had let her get away.

———

Sharpe arrived back on the scene faster than Pete thought possible. Pete realized instantly that Sharpe hadn't really gone anywhere. He had probably been just a few hundred yards away in the trees, waiting to hear the gunshot. When Sharpe arrived and saw Pete standing there, the Statton girl nowhere in sight, his face turned a near-purple color, his rage clear in his eyes even more than in his face. He screamed at Pete, "Where is she?"

Pete backed away, pointing toward the creek. "She was awake the whole time...I didn't know...she got away."

Sharpe turned his horse slowly toward Pete, his hand near his gun belt. Then he saw that Pete's gun was already drawn. It wasn't aimed at Sharpe, but he could lift it and shoot in a second. Sharpe moved his hand away from his belt and yanked the horse around. "I'll deal with you later," he shouted over his shoulder.

———

Sarah found stamina and speed she'd never known she had. She glanced behind her as she gained the safety of the trees and her heart sank once again. She could see Sharpe on his horse. He was galloping in her direction.

She was pretty sure he had seen her enter the trees. She darted behind a large, thick pine tree and peeked around it. Sharpe was galloping directly toward the spot where she had entered the trees. A quick glance behind told her she didn't have time to get to the creek, then get over to the old cabin site and crawl into the tunnel. She drew her gun from the pocket in her riding skirt, braced it against the tree trunk in front of her, and waited for Sharpe to get a little closer.

He slowed down as he approached the trees, searching for tracks in the grass, looking up frequently into the stand of oak trees in front of him. He stopped for a moment, then urged the horse forward, reaching down toward his gun as he did. Sarah knew she couldn't risk getting into a gunfight with him. The first shot had to count. She sighted carefully down the barrel and squeezed the trigger, seeing with dismay that he had turned the horse slightly as she fired. The bullet burned across Sharpe's left arm.

He yelled in surprise and pain, reaching toward the wound with his right arm. His horse, startled, reared up at the same moment, pitching Sharpe from the saddle. Sharpe hit the ground and rolled out of the way of his plunging horse, cursing and holding on to his left arm. He instinctively rolled behind a slight rise in the rolling meadow, out of her sight. Sarah dropped her gun back into her pocket, then turned and ran toward the creek.

There was nothing she could do about leaving tracks in the moist soil between here and the creek. She ran as quickly as she could, dodging around the trees and rocks in her path. Behind her, she could still hear Sharpe swearing loudly. She didn't dare waste any time looking back. She reached the creek and splashed through the water. At least she could cover her tracks for this stretch of her flight.

She kept an eye peeled for the rocks they had rolled up to the tunnel exit. She saw them at last and left the creek, doing her best to hop from rock to rock. When she reached the tunnel exit, she kneeled down and rolled one rock away. She crawled in and reached through to roll the rock back in front of the entrance. It took maximum effort to pull it back, but at last it moved, and she rolled it back in as far as she could.

She backed up in the almost total darkness inside. She was actually glad she hadn't been able to roll the rock back completely—it gave her a small amount of light. She felt something furry scuttle away from her ankles. She choked back a gasp of surprise and settled down, pulling the gun from her pocket again. She didn't think Sharpe would be foolish enough to pull a rock away from the exit now that he knew she had a gun. Still, she had to be ready for him if he did. She made herself as comfortable as possible in the small space she had and concentrated her senses on listening for any sound of Sharpe approaching the tunnel.

———

Sharpe gathered himself and made a crouching run to the trees. She could have fired again by now and she hadn't, but he wasn't sure what that meant. If she was waiting for a clear shot, he had to get to the trees. He reached the tree line and ducked down behind the thickest trunk he could find, hoping the tree was between himself and the girl. He looked out to see his horse trotting across the meadow, probably heading back to where they had made camp. He could see no sign of Pete, but he didn't expect any help from that quarter. Pete had let the girl go, and Sharpe would have shot him for it if Pete hadn't had the drop on him with his pistol already pulled. He could be halfway to the Austin train station by now, for all Sharpe knew.

He swore under his breath one more time, then used his knife to cut away the lower half of his left sleeve. The bullet wound was a graze, but a deep one. He tied the sleeve he'd just cut around it tightly to slow the bleeding. He used his right hand and his teeth to tie a knot as best he could. Then he looked cautiously around the tree trunk, keeping his head down at ground level. He saw no sign of her, so he moved cautiously from one tree to the next, gun up and ready. She had probably hidden somewhere by now. He shook his head. He had already planned to kill her, and it didn't bother him. This gunshot wound just meant he would never give it a second thought after she was dead.

He worked his way toward the area he believed the gunshot had come from. He needed to be cautious because she seemed to be pretty handy with the gun, but he had to push forward because the sun was setting and he would soon lose the light he needed in order to follow her tracks. He worked his way through the trees until he found the spot where she had fired the gun. Her tracks were clearly visible behind a large oak tree. There were multiple tracks, meaning she had been there for at least a while, and he could see tracks leading away from it toward the creek.

He followed the tracks to the creek where he lost them. Clearly, she had been smart enough to cover her tracks in the creek. He crouched down near the creek bank and considered his choices. She could have moved upstream, away from the old cabin. It would take her closer to the road to Austin, and maybe she had hopes of stopping a wagon or horseman on the way back to town. He followed the creek upstream, looking on both sides for tracks leading away from the stream. After ten minutes, he had seen nothing, so he retraced his steps.

Following the creek downstream, it was a matter of only a few minutes before he was nearing the site of the old cabin. He moved up the bank a bit and took some cover in the trees, wary of another shot. He studied the creek bank on both sides. On the far side, there was a heavy cover of underbrush, and he didn't think she would have been able to pass through there without leaving broken twigs and other signs of her passage.

He returned his gaze to the area on the near side of the creek. His gaze stopped at the sight of two large rocks, side-by-side, one standing slightly farther out than the other. There was an impression in the wet creek bank, maybe a foot in length and the exact width of the rock that stood out a bit. He studied it as best he could in the failing light. It looked like those rocks could cover a dugout area behind them. One rock may have been rolled out, then back.

Sharpe crouched behind a tree and studied what he could see. He could have really used his binoculars, but they were on his horse, and there was no telling where his horse was by now. He had only his gun and a knife with him. If the girl was crouched down in a hideout behind those rocks, he didn't dare walk up there and roll the rocks away. She had a gun and she could shoot.

The sun had set now, and dusk was settling in. The only thing in his favor tonight would be a full moon. Plus, he reminded himself, he was out here with room to move and go on the attack, and she was probably completely hemmed in behind those rocks. He decided he would start by staying quiet and trying to wait her out.

About an hour later, he wondered if she wasn't in the hideout over there at all. He had remained perfectly quiet, gun in hand, waiting for her to push those rocks back and crawl out. She had stayed perfectly quiet, if in fact she was in there. Sharpe wondered if there was an exit on the far end and if she had escaped again. He rose and circled around to the site of the old cabin, watching as he went for anything that looked like a tunnel exit. When he reached the area where the old cabin had stood, his eyes were drawn immediately to a large, heavy tree limb or two at the edge of the clearing.

He approached the tree limbs cautiously. He kneeled to the side, pushing a branch or two out of his way and peering through the dead leaves with the little help available from the rising full moon. Finally, out of frustration, he grabbed the heavy tree limb in front of him and pulled it back slightly. When it moved, he dropped to the ground and quickly crawled back to the side. When there was no gunshot, he crawled back on hands and knees for another look. A small smile crossed his face. He could see steps leading down into the ground. That limb had been heavy enough that he felt sure the girl couldn't push it aside from inside the tunnel. He had her trapped.

Sharpe walked back down to the creek and sat down with his back against a tree, about ten or fifteen feet to the side of the rocks, blocking what he now knew to be the exit to a tunnel. He had now gone back to waiting, which frustrated him. He had thought immediately of setting the tree branches and leaves on fire, back up at the entrance, hoping to smoke her out. Unfortunately, he had nothing on him to start a fire. He could have sent Pete back to camp for matches, but he knew better than to think that Pete would show up.

Finally, feeling like any kind of action was better than waiting, he walked into the woods until he found a thick tree limb, about six or seven feet. He carried it back and stood behind the two rocks, a little to the side of the underground tunnel. He extended the tree limb, setting the end against one rock, then leaned in and pushed it. The limb slipped several times, but after four or five tries, he could see he had moved it back a bit.

———

Sarah was growing cramped and anxious inside the tunnel. After she had been in there for ten or fifteen minutes, she was pretty sure she had heard someone splashing through the creek outside. The splashing had stopped, but she had heard a twig or two snap out there. She knew she had to assume that Sharpe was watching, waiting for her to emerge. The faint light spilling through from the full moon outside gave her a bit of comfort, and she focused all her energy on listening.

After more time passed, she heard a rustling noise behind her. She found that turning inside the tunnel, while not impossible, was both extremely difficult and time-consuming. She remained where she was, still focused on listening. If the rustling noise changed or sounded like it was coming closer, she would turn and fire a shot up the tunnel. Luckily, the rustling noise stopped after just a couple of minutes. She returned her focus to the rocks in front of her. She wondered where Mike was right now. He should have returned home a few hours ago from Ft. Worth and hopefully had gone to look for her at the boarding house. But would he know to look for her out here when he didn't find her at home?

A few minutes later, she saw a stick, or probably a fairly thick tree limb, appearing in front of her. She could see that Sharpe was bracing the limb against one rock and endeavoring to push it away from the mouth of the tunnel exit. She considered firing a shot into the tunnel wall at the place she estimated Sharpe was standing, then rejected the idea immediately. The bullet wouldn't get through that much dirt with any velocity, and it would only give away her position. She watched, with a certain helpless feeling settling in, as he pushed the rock away. She would hold her fire until she could see him. She reminded herself that he would have to be at least outlined in the moonlight in front of her to get a good shot off. She could remain here in the dark.

CHAPTER NINETEEN
SHOWDOWN AT WALNUT CREEK

B laze was at full gallop when I rode up to Captain McNelly's office at the boarding house. Ash was standing in the front yard talking to the captain when I rode up, and they both turned and started toward me when I reined in my horse. I jumped from Blaze's back and answered their unasked questions by shouting, "Sarah's been taken!"

Ash turned and sprinted toward his horse as soon as the words were out of my mouth.

McNelly grabbed me by the arm to calm me down. "When?" he asked. "Where?"

I slowed down, took a deep breath, and told him that Sarah had gone down to the schoolhouse and not returned. Ash led his horse up as I finished talking.

McNelly's brow was furrowed in concentration. "How long ago?" he asked.

I shrugged in frustration. "She went down to the school maybe an hour or hour and a half before dark. She didn't come back."

McNelly glanced around him at the lengthening shadows, knowing they had probably taken her at least an hour ago. "Do you have any idea where he might have taken her?" was his next question.

I explained the connection between our property and Sharpe.

McNelly decided quickly. "You and McKinnon go on out to look for her at your property," he told us. "I have one man in town coming over in the next hour. I'll send him out to the boarding house where Sarah lives. He can join me, looking around the area close to home and around the school. If we haven't found her by morning, I'll call Red and the other two boys down from Round Rock."

Ash had mounted and I was running for my horse by the time McNelly had finished talking. We turned and galloped down the road toward the land that Sarah and I shared.

We slowed to a walk as we left the road and followed the bank of Walnut Creek toward the old cabin site. We pulled up before long, probably half a mile short of the site. We listened for any sounds that could help guide us. Darkness had set in and we had only moonlight to light our way. When we couldn't detect any noises of any kind to help us, we conversed in low tones, making our plan of attack. We knew we had to be prepared for at least two of them. We agreed to split up and work our way toward the old cabin site, then swing north through the meadow, then finally toward the rolling hills and trees at the back of the property.

"You have the better woodsman skills," I told Ash, knowing that he had grown up in the forests and hills of Tennessee. "How about if you move up into the trees, and I work down along the creek bank? Take it up into the trees maybe a couple hundred yards, then work your way back and forth. Don't forget I'll be on the creek bank. We don't shoot unless we have an unobstructed view of what we're looking at."

Ash nodded and melted into the trees, Winchester in hand. I drew my Colt and worked down the creek bank. After just a few yards, I holstered the gun. I had better balance without the gun in my hand, and the going was getting difficult in the dark. I scanned the area in front of me constantly, still hoping for a few sounds to guide me. I could hear nothing.

———

Pete had taken his time working his way down to his present position. He had heard the gunshot and had seen Sharpe take a tumble off his horse. For a minute there, he thought maybe the girl had solved his problem for him. If she had killed Sharpe, he would get on his horse and ride out right now. Well, he thought, maybe in a couple days he would ride out. He had sneaked down through the woods the other day when Sharpe had made a trip to the creek down here without giving any explanation. He seemed to dig in the creek bank, though Pete couldn't get close enough to get a good look. He'd made a mental note of where the place was, then slipped back up to their camp before Sharpe could see him. He would check that place before leaving.

Unfortunately, he saw right away that the girl had only made Sharpe furious when she shot his arm. Pete had remained out of sight for quite some time while Sharpe had followed the girl into the trees. Finally, under the cover of darkness, he had crept down near the creek, slogging his way toward the old cabin site. He wasn't sure what he would do when he found Sharpe and the girl. If he saw a chance to take out Sharpe, though, he would do it.

Pete prided himself on his woodsman skills, and he inched his way, tree to tree, until he saw Sharpe standing near the creek, below the cabin site, staring at a slight rise in the ground. Pete came to a full stop and stretched out flat behind a log, watching Sharpe, whose attention seemed to be entirely concentrated on a couple of rocks, immediately to his left. His gun was out and in his hand. He seemed to be inching his way toward the rocks. A flicker of movement to his left caught Pete's attention, and he swung his head slowly, now seeing another man working his way along the creek. His head was down and he seemed to be unaware of Sharpe's presence.

Pete swung his head back downstream and saw that Sharpe seemed to be unaware of the other man. A gleam of light to his left caught Pete's attention, and he looked back at the second man, still working his way along the creek. Another flash of light winked in the dark, and Pete realized that the man was wearing a badge. Pete froze for a moment, deciding. Should he kill Sharpe or the lawman? A moment later, his decision was made. If he killed Sharpe, he would likely be arrested for bank robbery and train robbery by that Ranger or whoever he was. Pete would likely swing at the end of a rope. If he killed the lawman, maybe Sharpe would consider the score to be even. He swung his rifle toward the lawman and sighted down the barrel.

Pete considered himself a woodsman, but he didn't hear even a whisper of a sound. He suddenly felt the barrel of a rifle up against his right temple. A soft whispered drawl sounded from above him and to the right: "If I was you, I'd put that shootin' iron down. Or else you can swaller it if you want. I could prob'ly help you with that." Pete slowly released the rifle and put his hands behind his head.

———

Sharpe had pushed back one of the stones. He stood now to the side of the tunnel exit, wondering just exactly what he could do about it. He couldn't think of any way to drive her out of the tunnel, given that he didn't have any way to start a fire at the other end. The moonlight was bright enough that he couldn't risk standing across the creek or even getting into a lying position over there and firing into the tunnel. She would have the advantage of being able to see him and could open fire. He didn't have any way of knowing how far back she was in the tunnel, so he would be firing blindly. He had seen steps leading down from the entrance at the other end, so he didn't have any way of firing through the tunnel.

He stood in frustration at the side of the entrance, considering the only possibility he could think of. Other than waiting it out, of course, and he was far too impatient a man to do that. The only possibility that occurred to him now was to lean over, hold his gun upside down over the tunnel, and fire into it. That meant exposing his hand and wrist to fire at point-blank range, and he didn't relish that thought. It all depended on whether he could catch her by surprise.

As he stood there and debated what to do, Sharpe realized movement at the edge of his vision. He looked up and saw a man walking down the creek bank, coming toward him. His concentration on the tunnel exit had been so complete that the presence of anybody else took him completely by surprise. There was a flash of moonlight off something on the man's chest, and Sharpe realized with a start that this was a lawman. In the next instant, he realized that his own gun was drawn, and the other man was empty-handed. In that moment, the lawman looked up and saw Sharpe. Sharpe's lips parted in a sardonic grin. His gun swept up.

———

I made my way slowly along the creek bed, my eyes sweeping both banks as I went. If Sarah was Sharpe's prisoner, he could be keeping her anywhere. Or, I reflected grimly, if he had killed her, he could have disposed of her anywhere. That last thought was so scary and depressing I resolved not to think about it anymore. The full moon was an advantage and a problem at the same time. The light helped me move along faster, but I had to stay in the shadow of the trees in order to not expose myself to gunfire.

I came around a bend in the creek and knew I was getting close to the cabin site. I had to trust that Ash was keeping me clear of anybody lurking in the woods. As I rounded the bend and looked ahead, I got the shock of my life. Louis Sharpe was standing in full moonlight, locking eyes with me. I knew I was in the shadows a bit, but I also knew he could see me, and his gun was already in his hand. Those deadly gray eyes flashed a little as his head turned toward me, then an evil grin split his face and the gun was coming up.

I threw myself to the side and down to one knee as I drew. I felt a burning pain across the top of my left shoulder, then snapped off a shot. The movement had thrown my aim off a little, but the shot seemed to catch him in the shoulder and turn him slightly. Off balance, he stumbled into the shallow waters at the edge of the creek and brought the gun up again. His feet seemed to hit a rock in the water, and he came to an abrupt stop. His second shot whistled past me. I steadied down on one knee in the cool water of the creek and fired. My second and third shots sounded like one, they came in such rapid succession.

In the strange, eerie glow of the moonlight, I saw both shots strike him on the left side of the chest. He staggered backward, and his gun splashed into the water. Then he pitched over backward and a second splashing sound reached my ears as he fell backward into the creek. I rose to my feet, gun still ready, and walked slowly toward him. After a few steps in his direction, I could see him lying in the water on his side, stretched out, with his head tilted back. After another step or two, the current moved him gently downstream.

"Sarah!" I screamed.

"Mike!" The sound seemed a bit muffled and distant, but I knew in an instant it was Sarah.

I ran forward and pulled one rock away from the tunnel exit. I was still pulling on the second one when Sarah crawled out and we collapsed into each other's arms. My questions came spilling out, one after the other. "Are you okay? Did he hurt you? Was there somebody else with Sharpe?"

She assured me she was fine, and we clung to each other, standing in the shallow waters of the creek. Suddenly, the import of my last question struck her. "There was another man. I don't know where he is..." I pushed her away and pulled my gun again, spinning around.

"Easy, pard. I got the other one all trussed up over here." Ash materialized out of the trees, prodding a prisoner forward. The man had his hands tied behind his back.

I felt the relief wash over me, and I turned back to Sarah. I tried to say something, but the words wouldn't come. I cleared my throat a couple times and tried again. "I thought I had lost you..." The words trailed off.

Sarah put reassuring arms around me. "I'm right here. I'm fine."

I enveloped her in another hug. After a few seconds, I heard a harrumphing sound from Ash's direction.

"Never mind me. I'll just take this guy to see Captain McNelly. I need another horse though." He prodded his prisoner again. "You got a horse around here?"

Sarah turned and waved her arm up toward the old cabin site. "There's a horse and wagon just behind the site up there. You can toss him in the wagon and take him in. I'll ride back with Mike and bring your horse to you." She stood with her arms around me as Ash pushed the prisoner past us.

Ash gave me a mournful look on the way by. "Luckiest devil I know," he mumbled under his breath.

Ash's prisoner stopped at the top of the creek bank. He turned back and looked at Sarah. "Don't forget what I done for you," he told Sarah.

Sarah nodded. "I'll tell Captain McNelly tomorrow," she promised.

I looked at her in confusion, but she simply squeezed my hand.

The man turned back again. "Something else," he said. "Sharpe buried somethin' down there in the creek bank. I seen him diggin'. Mebbe fifty yards down, this side of the creek. Right behind a big log." He looked over at me. "Now I done you a favor, too. Don't forget. Tell your cap'n." Ash took him away, and Sarah and I turned to look at each other again.

"You're bleeding!" Sarah exclaimed. Now I remembered the burning pain across my shoulder and, looking down, saw the blood on my shirt. We climbed to the top of the creek bank and Sarah tore off both the sleeves of my shirt. She packed one into the wound, then twisted the second one under my armpit and across the top of the wound, tying it down to hold the first rag in place. We stayed for a few minutes, sitting at the top of the bank and holding on to each other. Then we collected the horses and started back to town.

CHAPTER TWENTY
AFTER THE STORM

W e decided, the next morning, on another picnic on our land. We left McKinnon behind this time, wanting this one to be just for the two of us. The last we saw Ash, he was stuffing his face at Ma Kirk's breakfast table and telling some tall stories about what an excellent shot he is with that Winchester.

When we reached our property, we found that Captain McNelly was already there with one of his men. They had pulled Sharpe's body from the water and loaded it onto a cart. He came over to tell me we had done a good job last night, and he checked to make sure that Sarah was fine. He glanced at my shoulder, which had been attended to by a doctor that morning. My left arm hung limply in a sling.

"I talked to the doctor this morning," he told me. "You'll work at a desk for the next three weeks."

I suspected he was pushing his paperwork on me and frowned slightly.

"Doctor's orders," he told me. "Besides, you'll be in town every day for the next three weeks." He glanced at me, then over at Sarah, then back at me.

I took his meaning and chuckled. "You're the boss," I told him.

He turned to go. "By the way," he said, turning back toward me. "We found all the money stolen from the Round Rock bank in a sack right over there in the woods." He pointed toward the back side of the property. "Great job," he said, clapping me on my good shoulder. He climbed into the wagon and left with the other Ranger, taking Sharpe's body back to town.

Sarah and I picnicked on the grass at the edge of the meadow, just a few yards from where old Miles had built his cabin. I finished eating with a contented sigh and rolled over onto my back. Sarah laid down next to me and put her head on my good shoulder. We lay there and talked about our plans for life in our brand-new home here in Texas. After a while, I gave her a kiss, pushed myself to my feet, and walked over to the wagon we had borrowed once again from Ma Kirk. I reached in and pulled a shovel from underneath a tarp in the wagon, holding it up with my good arm.

"I threw this in the wagon this morning," I announced.

"I know," she told me. "I saw you put it there."

"Humph," I said. So much for surprising her with my little plan. I walked down toward the creek bank, carrying the shovel. She hurried to catch up with me and took the shovel away from me.

"No, you don't," she said. "You'll hurt your shoulder. I'll dig. You watch."

I grinned and walked with her down the creek bank. We counted our steps and stayed on the lookout for a big log. We found a place that looked likely just a few minutes later. I sat down on a rock and watched as Sarah began digging. On the third thrust, her shovel made a noise as it struck something solid. She quickly shoveled more dirt away, revealing a small trunk.

I got up and moved over to help her lift it from the ground.

"Wait," she told me as I reached down and grabbed one edge of the trunk with my good arm. "Tell me what you're going to do if we find some money in here. I'm going to use it to build a nice little house on our land. What about you?"

I considered that one for a minute. "Well," I said finally, "I guess I could build a house too and maybe buy a few cows to run on the pasture."

She nodded and reached down to grab her end of the trunk.

"Or," I said slowly. She let go of the trunk and straightened up to look at me. "Or," I repeated, "maybe I could buy a ring and put your money together with mine and build just one house."

Her eyes twinkled, and then that beautiful face lit up in a smile. "Yes, you could," she told me. "Yes, you could."

VANISHING TRAIL

PROLOGUE

JANUARY, 1883—NEAR LAMPASAS, TEXAS

Holt Jacobs hunched down among the oak trees and studied the corral in front of him through his binoculars. He considered himself a fine judge of horses, and he had pretty much decided on the palomino mare and the tall gray gelding. He studied the gelding a moment longer. He guessed it must be a little over sixteen hands.

He swept his glasses over the other five horses in the corral, then returned to the original two. He grunted in satisfaction, put the binoculars away, and rolled over on his back to wait for darkness to settle in. If it were up to him, he would steal at least four of those horses, maybe all of them. It wasn't up to him, he reminded himself.

His orders came from someone he just referred to as The Boss. Holt had the impression The Boss was pretty respectable, maybe a pretty big man in one of these towns around here. He never got his hands dirty with the horse stealing. He had Holt to take care of that for him. Holt had actually never met or seen The Boss. He only got messages addressed to him at a hotel in Austin, where he checked in once in a while. When the horses were delivered, his share was given to him in cash at the drop-off place, and the rest was sent to The Boss in some way. That end of the operation was run through another man, but Holt intended to find out more about it.

A noise in the corral caught his attention, and he rolled over to check things out. A cowboy was returning from his day's work. He unsaddled his horse, rubbed it down, and turned it loose in the corral before heading for the bunkhouse. The door slammed shut behind the cowboy and things got quiet again.

Satisfied that his two theft targets were still in the corral, Holt Jacobs turned over onto his back again and waited quietly for full darkness to arrive and for everybody to settle down and go to bed in the house and bunkhouse. He had to admit, he reflected, that life was better since he'd been working for The Boss, whoever he was.

There were posters out on him throughout Arizona and parts of New Mexico. He'd not seen or heard of any posters in Texas, and that was fine with him. Especially, he thought, because the reward for him was of the *Dead or Alive* variety. He had, by his own count, killed seventeen men in fair, stand-up gunfights. He didn't mind the gunfights, in fact, he kind of liked them. Nobody had ever bested him, and he didn't mind the killing. It was the being hunted part that had worn him down.

The horse thieving had kept him pretty much out of sight, and the pay was pretty good. His time was his own between jobs, and he had several places he liked to frequent in Austin and San Antonio. It bothered him a little that he had to travel so far to each place where he was sent to steal the horses, and all of those places were pretty far away from the hideout. Still, he had to admit that The Boss had it organized pretty well, and life was pretty good. He didn't really want to do anything else for a while.

When the darkness had settled in, and the lanterns in the house and bunkhouse had been put out quite some time ago, he eased from his hiding spot and tiptoed toward the corral. He paused when the horses caught his scent and snorted, but they settled down pretty quickly and he worked his way over to the gate. The moonlight proved enough visibility to ease the gate open and slip inside.

He shook out a loop on the rope he'd brought with him. The palomino mare proved docile enough that he was able to walk up quietly and slip the noose over her head. He led her over and tied her to the rail near the gate. Taking down another rope that he'd observed earlier hanging over a fence post, he moved toward the tall gelding. This one proved to be a little more suspicious of him, snorting and tossing his head, then moving away.

Having neither the time nor the patience to slip up on the gelding, he shook out a loop and tossed it over the horse's head, speaking soothingly and casting a few anxious glances over his shoulder, first at the bunkhouse, then at the ranch house. His luck seemed to be holding, he saw no lights inside. He led the gelding quietly over to the gate, where he slipped the knot loose on the rope holding the mare and led them both out of the corral. He briefly considered scattering the other horses but decided the noise might cause too much trouble. He eased the gate shut and latched it behind him.

Leading the horses steadily out of the yard, he worked his way into the trees, headed for the place where he had tethered his own horse several hours earlier. The light cast by the full moon helped him again, and he found his horse quickly. He tied both stolen horses to his saddle horn and

led them away. He planned to ride for several hours, stopping to cover his trail now and then, before he stopped for
a little sleep. He wanted to be well away from any possible
pursuit.

———

Feeling something strike him on the cheek, Holt's eyes
fluttered open, and he rolled instinctively off the bedroll,
reaching under it for his gun. Bright sunlight caused him
to squint, and he stayed in the crouched position, blinking
furiously and trying to orient himself. He eventually registered a chattering noise overhead and looked upward to
see a squirrel scolding him and dashing back and forth on
a tree limb. He looked down to see several acorns lying
beside his bedroll.

He stood, rubbing his eyes, and put the gun away. He
moved to a small campfire he had made, about ten feet
away, and made preparations for coffee and some bacon.
He chewed a biscuit absently as he rolled up the bedroll
and tied it to the saddle. He glanced overhead, frowning.
He had clearly slept quite a bit later than he'd planned.

He finished a quick breakfast and moved out to the
west, anticipating a meeting at the hideout sometime
tonight. He'd hired a couple ne'er-do-wells to keep an
eye on the place and look after the horses until he could
move them for sale. He paid them as little as possible. If
they got greedy or too curious, he had ways of moving
them on. Holt was a small man, but they feared his
guns.

He glanced down before mounting his horse, a frown
breaking out on his face as he looked at his boot print. His
feet were exceptionally small, and it was a sore point with
him. He had even killed a man once for making jokes
about his *peg-leg* bootprint. He swore under his breath

and stepped up into the saddle. He had some ground to make up after his late start.

Leading the two stolen horses as he had done the previous night, Jacobs struck off again to the west, stopping to splash across a stream whenever he found one, feeling confident he could soon shake off any pursuit. He had to admit this is where it came in handy to steal only two horses. The owners were less likely to keep up the pursuit when the loss was comparatively small. Unless, he conceded, he had stolen someone's prize mount. Then they might pursue for a long time.

Moving up into some low hills, he took a break for a few minutes and watched his back trail. He tethered the horses and lay down at the top of a ridge, breaking out the binoculars and looking down over the ground he had just covered. He swept the glasses back and forth, then stopped to stare at a small dust trail in the distance. He focused on the spot where the dust had risen. He again swore softly to himself. A single man was riding along slowly, leaning over to read the tracks in the dust. Holt caught the glint of a badge in the sun.

Laying the binoculars aside, he ran over the possibilities in his head. He didn't want to run for it. The man was a pretty good tracker to have followed him this far. He prided himself on what he could do in a stand-up gunfight, but there was no point in letting it come to that. He needed to kill this man and move out. He stood and walked to his horse, pulling the Winchester from the scabbard and returning to lie down at the top of the ridge. Now he would wait.

He waited for an hour, watching the pursuer cast back and forth along a creek until he picked up the trail on the other side. He came on, looking up into the small hills in front of him from time to time. Holt made sure not to let anything metallic reflect a glare from the overhead sun. As the man drew closer, he pulled his Winchester in front of him and sighted carefully down the barrel. He exhaled slowly and gently squeezed the trigger.

The lawman, or whoever he was, pitched backward off the saddle and his horse bolted several yards. Holt Jacobs grabbed the binoculars and looked at the spot where the man had fallen. The man attempted to rise, not even reaching his knees before he fell and rolled over onto his back. He lay still.

Holt remained motionless for several minutes, sweeping the area with the binoculars. He felt sure the man below was dead, but he wanted to be sure there was no one else who had heard the shot and investigated. Finally, convinced that no one else was coming, he rose, mounted, and rode down to look at the man he had shot.

When he reached the spot and dismounted, he approached the body cautiously, pistol in his hand, looking around him. He prodded the body with his foot and got no response. Holstering his gun, he kneeled down and looked at the man. He was sure he had never seen this man before. He reached down and pulled the Texas Rangers badge from his shirt, then pocketed it. The longer he could keep anybody from knowing he had killed a Ranger, the better. He found a little money in the man's shirt and pocketed that as well. He covered the man's face with his hat.

Finally, he stood and re-mounted his horse, staring down at the corpse. A shock of bright red hair peeked out from under the man's hat. That, he knew, might be a dead giveaway in helping them identify the dead man. He shrugged and turned the horse to ride away. There was nothing he could do about the red hair.

CHAPTER ONE
ASH MCKINNON

JANUARY 1883—LANGTRY, TEXAS

I stood at the bar in an open tent saloon and surveyed the surrounding spectacle. A sign hung above the entrance of the tent with words proclaiming *Law West of the Pecos*. A smaller sign to the side identified the place as *The Jersey Lilly*. Several doubtful-looking characters were lined up at the bar beside me. The first was my partner in the Texas Rangers, Charlie Bass, and the rest were railroad workers or travelers passing through town. Most of us were drinking beer. A few had the misfortune of trying the house whiskey.

The activity caught my attention at the far end of the tent. This, I had learned, was a combination saloon and courtroom. Judge Roy Bean was holding court down there, and it appeared to be a wedding. I heard him asking the man and woman some pretty standard questions, and there were mumbled answers that I couldn't quite make out. Finally, the judge grabbed his gavel and raised it in the air. I leaned forward, knowing what he would say next.

Roy Bean slammed the gavel down and bellowed, "I pronounce you man and wife. May God have mercy on your souls!" With that, he shepherded the happy couple toward the bar and let them know they were expected to buy whiskey, besides the five dollars they owed him for the wedding.

I snorted into my beer and turned back around to the bar. Never having gotten married myself, I couldn't be certain, but I was pretty sure the *God have mercy on your souls* part wasn't something you would generally hear at a wedding. Seeing the judge headed in my direction, I slid my five cents across the counter and got myself a refill. The judge didn't like to see empty glasses, and this was the only place to get a beer for miles.

My name is Ash McKinnon, and I have been a Texas Ranger for about a year and a half now. They recruited me after a cattle drive from Central Texas to Kansas. It turned out that a Ranger named Red Corbin was one of the men on the drive. He had arranged for me to be hired by the Rangers, along with a friend named Mike Stone, because he liked the way we had handled ourselves on the drive.

I come from the hills in Tennessee, mighty close to North Carolina. Most folks have never heard of Ford Creek, the town I'm from, so I just say I'm from the hills in Tennessee. My ma claims I was big enough to sit at the dinner table when I was born. I don't know about that, but I stand about six feet three and weigh in at 235 pounds. People and things generally get out of my way when I want them to. I might also mention that my granny says I'm good-lookin', on account of my brown eyes and dark curly hair, but you know her eyesight ain't what it used to be.

I've spent three of my twenty-six years in Texas now, and I reckon I'll stay here. I had been sent out here to West Texas just a few months before, mainly to deal with bandidos from the south stealing cattle and horses from the ranchers in this remote area. Also, the railroad appreciated having a Ranger's presence if it was needed. It had been pretty quiet, all things considered. Quiet wasn't bad, but I felt a little cut off out here. My major source of entertainment had been watching Roy Bean conduct his *court*.

A disturbance down the line at the bar got my attention. I saw a man standing at the bar, arguing with Roy Bean. I knew that wasn't generally a good idea. I hadn't seen the man around here before, and he was dressed too nice to be a railroad worker, cowboy, or drifting miner. I had a feeling they had overcharged him for his beer. Bean fleeced the strangers around town sometimes. I exchanged a glance with my partner, Charlie Bass. So far, we had stayed out of these things, not really knowing what our authority was around town.

The stranger raised his voice. "I gave you a twenty-dollar gold piece for a beer. Where's my change?"

Roy Bean polished a glass absently and stared at the newcomer. "You kin have a refill. Just holler."

The stranger was turning slightly red around the gills. "I don't want another beer! Look at that sign!" He pointed at a sign behind the bar proclaiming beer for sale at 5 cents per glass. He waved his finger back and forth for emphasis.

Bean didn't bother to turn around and look at the sign. "This is my bar," he announced loudly. "Also, it's my court." He pointed at the Law West of the Pecos sign. "I like to keep the peace around here. It don't seem to me you're bein' peaceful." He slammed the glass down on the bar and leaned over the counter. "You need to pipe down."

The stranger, completely red in the face and almost at a loss for words, leaned in to get face-to-face with Roy Bean. "Where's my change?" he shouted. "You owe me $19.95."

Bean leaned down, fished around under the bar, and came up with a gavel. I glanced over at Charlie. We had no idea he kept a gavel under there. Bean lifted it up and rapped it down sharply on the counter. "I'm finin' you $19.95 for disturbin' the peace," he thundered. "I'd advise you to go back outside an' get on your train. If'n you disturb the peace anymore, I'll be chaining you to that tree out there." He pointed toward a large ash tree outside the bar. "That there is my jail," he finished.

The stranger whirled around, looked at the ash tree, then looked around the tent, hoping for some help from somebody. No takers. Nobody looked in his direction. Finally, he drained his beer, slammed the glass down on the bar, and headed off toward the train station.

"Probably a good idea," I observed. "No fun gettin' chained to that tree, I expect."

Charlie finished his beer, then glanced over in my direction. "Don't never let him chain me to that tree, McKinnon," he said.

"It's a deal," I agreed, finishing my glass and moving out of the tent with Charlie. "We don't pay more than a nickel for a beer around here, and we don't let each other get chained to that tree." Sometimes, I thought, it's good to wear a star on your shirt. Even Roy Bean hadn't tried to mess with us yet.

We left The Jersey Lilly/courthouse and ambled down to what passed for a main street in Langtry. We hitched our horses outside the only café in town. The menu ran heavily to beef and beans, but it beat anything Charlie and I might be cooking. Before stopping in to eat, we were interested in getting any mail that might have come in on today's train. There was no post office out here, nor was there a telegraph office. News came once a week in the mail on the train.

We lined up outside what passed for a railroad office. There was a tent stretched out next to the tracks. There was a table under an awning outside the tent, and once a week, they passed out mail. The wind kicked up heavy swirls of dust in the street as we waited. December and January were the driest months of the year around here, and we had just come through an exceptionally dry six weeks. I had to admit there were times when I longed for those green hills of Tennessee.

At long last I heard my name called and stepped up to the table to take the letter they held out for me. A quick glance told me the letter was from the captain of our division, Samuel McMurry. Most of the rest of our division, Company B Frontier Battalion, was stationed in El Paso. I glanced quickly at Charlie as I tore the letter open and slowly began to read.

I was to report to Captain Bill McDonald in Austin for reassignment. Charlie Bass, my partner, was to rejoin the rest of our unit in El Paso. I looked up from the letter and caught his questioning glance.

"You're to report back to the unit in El Paso," I told him. "I'm going to Austin."

I looked back down at the orders, and the next sentence jumped out at me.

Red Corbin has been killed, it said. *Catch the first train to Austin and report to Captain McDonald immediately*.

I reread the sentence, my lips moving wordlessly, then stared off down the street. Red had recruited me into the Texas Rangers and had pretty much taught me everything I knew about bein' a Ranger. A few memories of working with Red on the cattle drive, then on assignments with the Rangers swirled through my head.

I took a couple steps back toward the railroad office and read the handwritten sign posted at the tent entrance. The next train east left in two hours. I looked around to see Charlie watching me, saying nothing. I moved across the street.

"I'm having another drink," I said to him over my shoulder.

We both moved back into The Jersey Lilly. Looked like Judge Bean was done with court for the day.

The Southern Pacific line from Langtry back to San Antonio was close to empty on this trip. I sat alone in my row, huddled next to the window and staring out at some pretty dry, empty landscape as we rattled our way through West Texas. Being originally from Tennessee, I welcomed the idea of getting back to the hilly country around Austin, but I wondered why it was me they were bringing back to look into Red's death.

Following a cattle drive to Kansas, I had worked with Red, among others, on a case involving an old confederate of Sam Bass by the name of Louis Sharpe. Following a series of train robberies and bank robberies, we had tracked Sharpe to an area just north of Austin. On a piece of land belonging to my friend and fellow Ranger Mike Stone, we had caught up to Sharpe. Stone had killed him in a gunfight in the middle of a small creek on that property. I had been reassigned to the frontier division shortly after and hadn't seen Red since that time.

I was still wrestling with memories and questions as the shadows lengthened outside the train and darkness closed in. It would be late tomorrow before we arrived in San Antonio. I would probably need to stay there overnight and then catch another train to Austin. I reached up and pulled down my bedroll from the rack above me to serve as a pillow. I laid it between me and the window, then composed myself to get the best night's sleep I could under the circumstances.

———

Sleep hadn't come easily on the train to San Antonio. I kept remembering Red Corbin and some good times on the drive to Kansas. I wondered how he had been killed and whether they wanted me to track his killer. If so, why me? I wondered if my old friend Mike Stone would be assigned to the case. I had arrived at San Antonio completely exhausted. A night's stay at a hotel near the train station had helped. I was on my way to Austin now and figured I should arrive in a couple hours.

When the train pulled in, I was no more settled in my mind than I had been two days before, when the message first arrived. I hopped down from the train, carrying my bag, and went to claim my horse. The new captain in the area, Captain McDonald, was unknown to me, and I had to ask a couple people for directions to the address they had given me. Austin, I could see, had been growing a lot since I'd been gone.

Before long, I found myself outside a boarding house, by the look of it. I knocked on the door and was directed to a room at the end of a long hall. A deep voice told me to enter when I knocked on that door, and a short, blonde man with an impressive mustache rose to greet me when I entered.

"McKinnon?"

I nodded, and he pointed to a chair opposite a small, very cluttered desk.

"You knew Red."

It wasn't a question. I said nothing and waited while he stared out a small window. He turned and looked at me again.

"Red was bushwhacked. Shot from ambush while he was trailing a horse thief a little north of there. I'm assuming you want his murderer caught just about as bad as I do."

I leaned forward in my chair. "They shot him from ambush?"

McDonald looked down at his desk. His face was flushed, and the veins stood out in his forehead. He started to say something, then stopped. He nodded. "Bushwhacked. They found the spot where the horse thief laid down and waited for him."

The words spilled out of me. "I want him brought in just as bad as you, Cap'n, just like you said. Only I hope you're not too particular whether or not he comes in dead. I'd just as soon have him strapped over my pack horse as ridin' on his own horse." I sat back and waited for his answer. He'd have to send me back to West Texas if I couldn't have a free hand on this one.

McDonald looked out his window for a moment, then nodded slowly. He turned back to look at me. "You can defend yourself, McKinnon," he said. He shuffled a few papers on his desk. "You can defend yourself any way you need to. Does that answer your question?"

I nodded. "Is there anybody else workin' on this?" I asked. I thought for a moment. "Mike Stone? Can you assign Mike Stone?"

McDonald shook his head slowly. "I've got Stone working a case in North Texas right now." He shrugged. "Governor's request. Nothing I can do about it. If he frees up and you need the help, I'll assign him. Meanwhile, this is about tracking, and you're our best tracker."

He shoved the papers on his desk aside, then stood and spread out a map. I could see there were a few circles drawn in red on the map. I stood for a closer look. McDonald began pointing at the circles. "Lampasas—

that's where the horses were stolen that Red was tracking." He pointed, one after the other, at three more circles. "Georgetown, Bartlett, Leander. They stole horses in all three places. Don't really know if they're connected, but we think so. Two of 'em had a new hand start working a week or so before the robberies. Then he disappeared a few days after. Not the same guy, though." He paused. "We haven't been able to follow the tracks after any of the robberies. Tracks seem to vanish into thin air. That's why I brought you in, McKinnon."

McDonald stopped and dropped into his chair. I leaned over the map and studied the four circles. They weren't really all that close to each other. "Can you tell if they were headed in the same direction? I mean, as far as you could track? Could they have been headed to the same place to meet up with somebody or sell the horses?"

McDonald shook his head in frustration. "Don't know. Couldn't track 'em far enough to say." Another thought struck him, and he got up and began to pace. "Here's something else. None of the horses have shown up since they were stolen. I mean, a lot of times, a horse will show up later, and you can tell the brand was altered with a running iron or something, but you know it's the same horse. Not with these guys, though. Not one horse has shown up since being stolen, and we've had some guys keeping an eye out for a while, all over the state."

I was feeling some of the frustration the cap'n was showing. I leaned back over the map and shook my head. "No tellin' where they're going to hit next, not with that map." I sat back down. "Anything else you can tell me? Do they steal the same kind of horses every time?"

McDonald started to shake his head no, then stopped. "They steal all different breeds, if that's what you mean. Only top-dollar rides, though. These guys steal the best, most expensive horses wherever they go, and leave all the rest. That's if it's even the same guys doing all the robberies."

"I'm gonna assume it's the same gang doing all of it," I said, almost to myself. "If they prove me wrong, I'll just have to start over." I twirled my hat in my hand, trying to think of questions. "Did you find anything on Red, any notes?" I stopped, feeling embarrassed and not wanting to remember my friend as a dead man on a lonely trail.

McDonald quickly shook his head no.

I started to leave, then turned around with one last thought. "Is there a ranch, anywhere around any of these four spots," I said, pointing at the map, "that breeds really excellent horses? I mean, someplace maybe known as a ranch where you could go and get a top-notch horse?"

McDonald looked up, picking up on my idea. "You mean, someplace they might strike next?"

I nodded.

He looked at me blankly for a second, then shook his head. "I don't know, but I'll do some asking," he said. "Check back in with me sometime tomorrow before you go."

I stood on the porch outside the boarding house and collected my thoughts for a minute. I didn't really know anybody in Austin, not with Mike Stone somewhere in North Texas. I decided to grab a bite and check into a hotel. It didn't sound like I was going to be in town for all that long.

CHAPTER TWO
LONGHORN CAVE

S tanding outside the hotel the next morning, I realized there were actually two people in Austin I knew and remembered. One was a lady everybody called Ma, who ran a boarding house down the road. I knew she served a mighty fine breakfast down there, and I liked to think I was one of her favorites. The other person was Mike Stone's wife, Sarah, who I'd met at the same time Mike did. I decided to make a call on both of them this morning, then swing by to see Captain McDonald again in the afternoon.

Ma swung the boarding house door open and clapped her hands together with delight. "Ash McKinnon! Get in here!"

She ushered me through the door and herded me down the hallway, then introduced me to about a half dozen people having what appeared to be the best breakfast I had ever seen. Of course, I had to allow for the fact that I'd been eating at what passed for a café in Langtry for the last several months.

I'd never been a boarder at Ma's place, but I had parked my feet under her table for several meals. She ladled up a heaping spoonful of scrambled eggs, then another, then about a half dozen sausages, and finally some toast and coffee. When I came up for air, she pushed a giant wedge of apple pie onto my plate. When she asked if I wanted more, I could only moan softly, loosen my belt, and lean back. She surveyed her handiwork in satisfaction.

"Tell us what you've been doing," she said.

I entertained them for about a half hour with stories about West Texas and Judge Roy Bean's court. Nobody there had heard of him, but they all vowed to stay clear of the judge if they ever found themselves in Langtry. Finally, I pushed my chair back.

"I've got to be going," I told Ma. "I need to stop in and see Sarah."

Ma beamed. Sarah had been a boarder at her place at one time. "Just a second," she told me. She disappeared into the kitchen, then returned with a napkin stuffed full of cookies. I reached into my pocket for some change, but she wouldn't hear of it.

"Just make sure you come and see me the next time you're in town," she said.

I promised to do that, then mounted up and rode toward the land owned by Mike and Sarah Stone. They had jointly inherited the land in an odd twist of fate, and I knew they had made plans to build on it.

———

Sarah had her back to me, painting a new house that stood in the middle of a clearing on the creek that flowed past their land. Walnut Creek, if I remembered the name correctly. I started to call her name as I rode up, but she had already heard the creak of the saddle leather. She turned, then dropped the paintbrush into a can and sprinted toward me. I swung down, and she enveloped me in a hug.

"Ash!" she exclaimed. "What a pleasant surprise! How long have you been here? What brought you to town? Are you hungry?"

I answered the last question first. I patted my stomach. "I've just been to Ma's place," I explained.

Sarah laughed, knowing what that meant. "Maybe you could use some coffee," she said, leading me into the house.

I sat at the table, admiring the nice home they had built here, while she bustled around the small kitchen, making me a cup of coffee.

When she brought it to the table and sat down across from me, I took one more look around the house, then took a sip of the coffee.

"I always said," I reminded her, "that Mike Stone is the luckiest devil I know."

Her laugh rang through the small house. "What about you, Ash? Haven't you found a girl yet?"

That Sarah. She always got right to the point. "I've been in Langtry, Texas, for months," I complained. "They don't have anything but a railroad, some miners, a couple salty old cowboys, and a crazy judge. When was I supposed to find a girl?"

Sarah's laugh filled the house again. "Okay, I guess I can see where that would be a problem," she admitted. "You're back in Austin now, though. Maybe your luck will change."

"Not for long," I said rather sadly. "I'll be off on a case soon. In fact, I wanted to see if you can tell me anything that might help. It's about Red Corbin's death."

The smile faded from her face instantly, and I kicked myself mentally for not easing into the subject a little more slowly.

Sarah saw my expression and shook her head. "It's all right, Ash. You go ahead and tell me what I can do. Red stayed with us a few days before...well, before he went off on that last assignment."

I had been staring at the ground, but I lifted my eyes when she said he had stayed at their house. "Did he leave anything here?" I asked quickly. "Any papers or personal items or anything that might help me?"

She started to shake her head, then sat up suddenly. "There's an old cedar chest in the corner of the room where he slept. Let me look in there." She was on her feet in an instant and disappeared around the corner. I could hear a squeak or two from the other room as the lid of the chest opened and closed.

In a moment, she reappeared, carrying an old vest. She held it out to me. "I've never seen this before. I'm sure it's not Mike's vest," she said. "It must have been Red's."

I nodded and held the vest up, thinking it might be about the size Red would have worn. I didn't recognize it, but then I hadn't seen Red in a year or more. I put it down in my lap and reached into the small pockets in front. The first was empty, but my hand emerged from the second pocket with two slips of paper. The first appeared to be a receipt for a pair of boots. I set that aside and opened the second piece of paper.

At first, it puzzled me, holding the paper out in the light from a window. It appeared to be the tracing of a man's boot print. I looked up at Sarah, who also looked puzzled.

"It's a tracing of a boot print, I think," I told her. "I wonder if he saw this print more than once and thought it might have to do with the robberies."

On impulse, I set the tracing down on the floor and stepped on the paper, comparing my boot print to the one on the paper. My boot print engulfed the print on the tracing.

"Well," I said, "I do wear a size twelve boot." I gestured at Sarah. "You try."

She did as I asked. When she had placed her boot over the tracing on the paper, I could see that the one Red had traced was only slightly larger than Sarah's boot would leave. I sat back, puzzled.

"Either that is a woman's print, or a guy with a really small foot," I concluded. I folded the paper back up and put it in my pocket. "I'll keep this," I said. "Maybe it could help." I gestured at the vest. "I don't know what to do with that," I said slowly. "He didn't have any family that I ever heard him talk about."

Sarah folded the vest and placed it on the table, a few tears forming in the corners of her eyes. "I think the Rangers were his family," she said. "We'll keep it here for now."

I stood to go. "I need to get back to see Captain McDonald," I told her. "Make sure you give your best to Mike for me. I'm hoping the cap'n will assign Mike to this case when he finishes what he's doing."

Sarah smiled and gave me a hug. "I'll tell him," she said. "I guess I don't really need to tell you to be careful, but you remember what happened to Red. Keep your eyes open."

I mounted and walked my horse alongside the creek that ran past their new house, remembering an adventure that had ended right on the banks of this creek recently. I glanced back to see Sarah waving at me. I returned the wave, thinking that Mike Stone was probably still the luckiest devil I knew. Then I gave my buckskin a little kick in the ribs and took the road back to Austin.

———

Holt Jacobs rose early, made a quick breakfast, and started moving the horses down the trail toward the hideout. Longhorn Cave was tucked away to the east of the Colorado River and a little southwest of the town of Burnet. Burnet was growing quite a bit because of the arrival of the railroad just last year, but it was still small enough for the little horse-stealing operation to remain a secret. Holt hadn't known about the cave previously. He'd been told about it when he was recruited into the gang. He had been fairly impressed to find out that Sam Bass had used it as a hideout at one time.

Leaving his camp just as light filtered through the trees, Holt worked his way south for several miles, then struck a path due west to the Colorado River. Losing the trail of the stolen horses in the Colorado River had been his contribution to the operation. Holt moved steadily, pulling over frequently to check his back trail. Whenever he topped a rise, he stopped to scan the area in front of him as well. He didn't want to meet anybody or be seen by anybody. When it was mid-morning, he pulled off the trail and waited for evening before he began to move again. When he reached the Colorado, he made camp for the night.

Holt risked a small fire, heating his food and giving him a bit of warmth. He checked the horses and walked a small circle around his camp before settling down in his bedroll. When he didn't drift off to sleep immediately, he began reviewing in his head how he came to join up with this horse-stealing crew and what his own plans would be for the future.

He had been approached by a man who identified himself only as Lance several months earlier at the Sholz Garten saloon in Austin. Lance said he worked for a man who had money, connections, and a great plan to steal horses and sell them in another state. He said he'd been given Holt's name by somebody, but wouldn't say who.

He said Holt could make maybe $250 a month. His job would be to first recruit two other men to help steal the horses and bring them to a hideout. Holt would get instructions by mail or a telegram at a hotel in Austin, telling him which ranches to rob and the type of horses to steal. He would never know the identity of the man who sent those messages.

Holt, along with his recruits, would steal the horses and bring them to a hideout for a few days. After those few days, Holt, and only Holt, would meet Lance at a pre-arranged location and hand off the horses. His pay would come a week or two later at a pre-arranged pickup spot.

Holt was both interested and irritated with the proposal. Who was the guy in charge? That was his first question. Lance only shrugged. That, he said, would remain a mystery. Why the mystery? Lance shrugged again. They were all safer, he said, if all of them knew only as much as they needed to know. Those men he would recruit, for instance, would only have contact with Holt. They would get their instructions from him and would know nothing about Lance or the man in charge of it all.

Lance met his insistence on learning more with a stone wall. Holt could take the offer as presented, or he could move on and Lance would find somebody else. They agreed to meet the next night at the Sholz Garten and Holt would give his answer. The money had been too good for him to pass on it, so he had agreed.

Now, several months later, he had recruited a couple of guys to help him. They weren't along on this particular job because he didn't need them—not when he was only stealing two horses. He preferred to work alone, anyway. They would wait at the Longhorn Cave when he got there.

They were half brothers named Ike and Slade, and they were the right combination of greedy and lazy. Greedy enough to get the job done and lazy enough not to want more.

Holt, on the other hand, wanted more. He believed that if he could get rid of Lance and take his job, there would be a lot more money in it for him. His mind began working on the ways he could do that, and somewhere along the way, he drifted off to sleep.

———

Moving at daybreak again, he led the horses to the edge of the river, then looked back at the hoofprints left behind them. This, he thought, is the one time he would have liked having his helpers along. Searching along the bank, he led the horses into the water, then down to a sizable rock at the water's edge. He lifted the rock and placed the reins for his horse under it. Going back into the trees, he found a large branch and used it to cover the tracks, working his way from the tree line down to the water. He tossed the branch into the river when he was done, then mounted and splashed the horses through shallow water for a hundred yards.

After glancing around him in all directions, he swam the horses across the river, then splashed through the shallow water on the other side for another hundred yards. He then led the horses into cover on the far side, tethered them, and again covered the tracks. He would repeat this procedure twice more along the way as he worked south along the Colorado River.

Three days later, Holt approached Longhorn Cave from the west and south. As he traveled, he looked around him, realizing that this wouldn't work as a hideout for too much longer. More and more settlers had come into the area, and he, Ike, and Slade depended on being able to graze the horses on empty land around the caves for several hours each day. It was vital for them to be able to do that unseen. Holt decided that was a problem for another day. Who knew what he would be doing in a few years?

Topping a rise, he could see Ike and Slade waiting at the usual spot near the cave. He handed off the horses, telling them to graze and water them. He proceeded into the cave, spread out his bedroll and proceeded to take a nap. He would have some work to do later today or tomorrow with a running iron, altering those brands. In another three days, he would take the horses to Lance for sale. This time, he intended to find out more about where those horses were going. There had to be more money for him in this operation.

————

I found Captain McDonald muttering to himself as he weeded through some paper on his desk. He left me shifting back and forth on a tiny and uncomfortable chair while he finished up what he was doing. Finally, he glanced up at me, mumbled to himself, and reached for a paper or two at the edge of his desk. He glanced over at them, then handed them to me.

"Jessie Maitlin," he said. He leaned back and watched while I read the papers.

I'd never heard that name, but I settled down to read the papers he'd given me. The first page said that a woman named Jessie Maitlin owned a ranch near Belton, Texas, where she raised horses and grazed a few cows. I raised my eyebrows and looked at McDonald.

"Belton?" I asked.

"North of Austin, south of Waco," came the answer. "I hear she raises some pretty excellent stock, horse-wise."

It made sense. Maybe this ranch was a target. I turned to the second page, where I saw a handwritten note from this woman, saying she was worried about the number of horses being stolen and asking for any help the Rangers could give her.

I started to hand the papers back to McDonald, but he waved them off.

"Keep 'em," he said shortly. "You're headed up there to look things over. Maybe you'll get lucky enough to be in the area when they strike next. You got any other ideas? Toss 'em out if you do."

I knitted my eyebrows together and leaned back in my uncomfortable chair. Nobody had ever said that thinkin' was my strongest point, but I was starting to enjoy this detective kind of work.

"Does she have any hired hands on the ranch?" I asked.

The captain thought about it for a second. "Maybe one," he answered finally. "I think they said she had one hand."

"So maybe she can pretend to hire me," I suggested. "I can be there for a week or two, check things out, maybe be on the spot if they try to steal her horses."

The captain reached for a blank piece of paper, picked up his pen, and scratched a note on the paper. "Give this to her," he said.

He bent his head back down over some more papers on his desk and started scratching again with that pen. I realized our interview was over. I picked up my hat and left. I could ask somebody else how to get to the ranch.

CHAPTER THREE
JESSIE

I cantered north on the road toward Belton, my collar turned up against the cold wind beginning to blow in from the north. I began to regret my decision to start my trip immediately after my meeting with McDonald. I could, I thought, be holed up in a warm hotel room in Austin right now. I hunched down, leaned into the wind, and resolved to put in a couple more hours before making camp. At least, I told myself, I could make it to Belton and start working on the case sometime late tomorrow afternoon or early evening. I knew from my previous time in Central Texas that the weather could change at any time, with warm winds pushing up from the south.

I gave some thought to what I knew about these horse thieves. That was the disturbing part. I knew little—just that my friend Red had died trying to bring them in. I didn't really know how much help I needed. I had gone back to McDonald's office before leaving to ask if he could spare anybody to help me. He had told me to go up to Jessica Maitland's ranch and find out what I could. He promised to assign Mike Stone if he freed up. If not, he would bring Charlie Bass out from Langtry to help me. I was rooting for it to be Stone, but either one would be a welcome sight riding in.

I made a cold camp and started out early the next day. I decided to stop in at the saloon in Belton when I arrived there in the early evening. I needed some directions to the ranch, plus I didn't mind finding out what I could learn around town before showing up at the ranch with my letter from McDonald.

The bartender eyed me—slightly unfriendly, but not hostile—as I walked in. He came over when I took a seat at the bar. "You ain't been here before," he said.

"Nope." I didn't feel like telling him anything else. "Gimme a beer."

He shrugged, filled a glass, and shoved it down the counter to me.

About twenty minutes later, looking a little friendlier, he stopped in front of me. "Want 'nother?" he asked.

I nodded, and he brought the glass over to me this time. Some people, I'd noticed, just naturally didn't trust strangers, but he seemed to be warming up.

He stayed put where he was for a minute, looking down the bar at the other customers. I decided to ask for directions. "Can you tell me how to get to the Lazy M Ranch?" He stared at me blankly. "Maitlin Ranch," I explained.

"Oh." He pointed out the doors. "Take a right out those doors and go down the road mebbe three miles. Look for the sign on the left." He hesitated. "She ain't hirin', if'n that's what yore lookin' for."

I lowered my glass back to the bar. "How d'you know that?"

He shrugged. "Guy come in two, three days ago, asked me same thing you just asked. I was out on the front porch mebbe two hours later when he went by, headed in th' other direction. Didn't look none too happy."

"Oh," I said thoughtfully. "Well, maybe I'll try anyway. Maybe she'll like me better."

"Yeah," he said, a little doubtfully. "Well, that other guy did look a little shifty-eyed."

I chuckled, got up, and shoved some change across the bar. "I'll try not to let my eyes get too shifty."

He laughed and waved as I left. I made a note to ask about the man who'd been looking for work. He could have been part of a plan to rob the ranch.

––––––––––

Jessie Maitlin sat on the porch of the ranch house, rocking gently in the evening chill, enjoying having the moment to rest. She kept an eye out for her younger brother, Kyle, who had been out checking on the livestock. It was just about time to move some of them to a fresh pasture, and they needed to start feeding hay. When Kyle came in, she would go inside and help her mother start dinner.

She reflected on how tired she was at the end of every day, at the tender age of twenty-four. It was no mystery how that had come about. She had wound up running the family ranch at the age of eighteen.

A sudden barking from the dog got her attention, and she stood quickly, shading her eyes against the setting sun. After a moment, she sighed and sat back down, not sure if she was amused or annoyed. The dog, a retriever/collie mix, had succeeded in running another squirrel up a tree. She was more than a little jumpy these days, worrying that her horse ranch was the target for another of the robberies she had been hearing about. They simply couldn't afford the loss.

Her eyes traveled from the corral in the yard out to the

pastures beyond. She loved this place and knew she would never leave it, she just wished she didn't feel like everything was on her shoulders.

Her parents had come to Texas in 1855, moving from Northern Georgia, lured by the inexpensive land and the promise it held. Her parents, she reflected, had given their lives to their family and this ranch. Those two things seemed inseparable.

Her father had marched off to war when she was not much more than a baby. Coming from another southern state, her parents' loyalty had been to the Confederacy, like most families around them, even though nobody owned slaves around here or were that caught up in arguments about states' rights. And so, her father had gone off to war in 1861. Ironically, he had survived the battles and had come home with both arms and both legs intact. The war had killed him more slowly.

She shifted in the rocking chair and watched idly as some chickens clucked and scratched around in her mother's flower bed. She should have chased them away, but she didn't feel that energetic. Her thoughts returned to her father.

Harold Maitlin had marched away to war in May 1861 and, after fighting in some small skirmishes and waiting out the winter of '61-'62, had been involved in the first day of fighting at Shiloh. It was malaria, not injuries, that kept him out of the second and third days. Ironically, malaria might have prevented him from being killed at Shiloh. The southern troops had been pushed back after the North received reinforcements, and her father's unit had been decimated on the second day. The malaria had taken his life, it just worked a lot more slowly.

Harold had, like a lot of troops, been exposed to miserable, damp weather and swarms of mosquitoes as they waited in their camps for the inevitable battle. He'd been suffering from fever and chills the first day at Shiloh, but he wasn't yet incapacitated. On the second day, he'd not been able to answer the call.

Removed to a sick tent, fellow victims of malaria had surrounded him, along with victims of typhoid and dysentery. Jessie knew that disease had killed more soldiers in the Civil War than had actual battles. Her father was among those who died an untimely death from disease.

Luckily for Harold and the family, the army had found enough quinine to give her father to stop the malaria at Shiloh. He had somewhat recovered over the next several weeks and had eventually returned to his unit. He had finished the war in General Joe Johnston's army, surrendering a few weeks after Appomattox. Jessie had been seven years old when he returned.

Her father had lived for another eleven years, though he suffered greatly from recurring bouts of malaria. He fought through the fevers and weakness, usually managing to do a day's work before returning to his sickbed. She had seen, though, how the illness was wearing him down. She had done her best to go out to work beside him, learning everything she could about stock breeding, animal care, and ranching. The harsh winter of '75-'76 had left him with a lingering case of pneumonia, and he was too weak to fight it off. They lost him in the spring of 1876.

Jessie's mother had seemed lost for a year or more after her husband's death, leaving Jessie feeling isolated and alone. Her brother Kyle, born shortly after her father returned from war, had leaned on her for strength and comfort. Finally, her mother Iris had pulled herself together and resolved to make things work for her young family. Iris did most of the cooking and cleaning, and planting and harvesting a large vegetable garden. She looked after the chickens and milked the family cow every day. Kyle, now age seventeen, was becoming quite a help as well.

She heard hoofbeats and looked up to see Kyle riding up to the corral. He dismounted and led his horse into the corral, and Jessie went out to help him unsaddle and wipe down his gelding.

Kyle's horse was mainly of mustang blood, as were more than half the herd. Cowboys driving herds up the Chisholm Trail to Kansas were their best customers, and the cowboys prized the toughness and endurance of the mustangs. Jessie knew the railroad was likely to change that before much longer, and she would have to figure out how to replace the loss of that business. That, she decided, was a worry for another day.

Putting an arm around Kyle's shoulders, she began walking with him to the house. The sound of hoofbeats stopped them, and Jessie turned around to see a large, rugged-looking man riding into the yard.

Jessie glanced, almost automatically, at the shotgun she had left resting against the corner of the porch. The string of robberies, compounded by the stranger who had appeared two days ago looking for work, had left her on edge. Kyle sensed her tension and shuffled nervously.

The stranger followed her glance and lifted both hands disarmingly into the air. "Ash McKinnon, ma'am. Texas Rangers. Captain McDonald sent me."

He reached slowly into his jacket and withdrew a folded-up piece of paper. Dismounting, he handed her the paper and removed his hat, shifting it between his hands while he waited for her to read it.

Jessie took the paper and read, glancing up at him when she had finished. "Well, Mr. McKinnon," she began.

He waved his hands. "Please, ma'am, Ash. My daddy ain't here."

She relaxed, refolding the letter and looking at his disarming smile. There was a little more of a Southern accent in what he'd just said—maybe Kentucky or Tennessee, she thought. She wondered if he was able to turn that Southern accent on or off to relax people, or maybe throw them off balance. In any case, she tended to trust her instincts, and her instincts told her this one was a lot more trustworthy than the visitor from two days ago. Plus, he had the letter from the captain she had written to earlier.

The back door banged shut behind her, and Jessie turned to see her mother standing on the porch. Then she walked down the steps. She glanced at the stranger, then at Jessie.

Jessie, recovering her manners, turned and held out her hand toward the new arrival. "Mother," she said, "this is Mr. Ash McKinnon, from the Rangers. My mother, Iris," she finished, waving back at her mother.

Iris stepped forward and took his proffered hand. Jessie noticed that it basically disappeared in the stranger's grip. "Mr. McKinnon," she began.

"Just Ash," he corrected.

"Well," said her mother, with a slow smile. "Just Ash, please join us for dinner. We have plenty," she assured him when she saw his doubtful expression.

"I'd be obliged, ma'am," he said. "Although plenty takes a powerful amount of food for a guy my size. I promise I'll go easy on you."

Iris chuckled and turned toward the house. Ash fell in behind her.

Jessie hesitated only a moment, then followed them in, a smile beginning to spread across her face. That good-old Southern-boy accent was becoming more pronounced by the minute.

———

I held myself back at dinner as best I could, although the food was delicious. I was pretty sure it would be bad manners to let my belt out a notch at the table. I stole a glance at Jessie every once in a while. She was downright beautiful—dark hair and dark eyes. She caught me looking one time and I'm pretty sure I blushed.

Ash, I said to myself, *don't go getting hooked on this girl. You've got a job to do. Next thing you know, she'll be reeling you in and you'll just be floppin' around in the bottom of the boat.*

Actually, the next thing I knew, Jessie had said something to me, and I needed to answer. I searched my brain for the last thing she had said. Something about a man looking for work. My brain snapped back to the conversation with the bartender.

I nodded my head. "The bartender in town said someone had come through here looking for work."

The surprise showed in her eyes. "The bartender knew about that?"

"I asked him for directions out to your ranch," I explained. "He figured I was comin' out here to look for work, because he said somebody else had come through and asked for directions just a couple days before. I guess that guy was headed out here next, looking for a job."

"Okay, that makes sense." She seemed to relax a little, but I could see some strain and fatigue in her eyes. "Wait here," she said. "I want to show you something."

She returned with a piece of paper, which she pushed across the table to me. I picked it up and saw that it was a drawing—a man's face. The detail was astonishing. I was looking at a man about my age, with hair thinning out a bit, a full beard, and eyes set slightly too close together.

"Wow," I said. "You can really draw." My eyes

returned to the drawing, and I studied it a little longer. "I haven't seen this guy," I said, "but I'll send it to the captain. He might want to find somebody that can draw copies, then send them around to the other Rangers." I looked at it again, trying to memorize that face.

"Have there been other ranches where maybe a stranger came to work and then the ranch got robbed?" she asked.

I glanced up to see those pretty dark eyes locked in on me. I nodded slowly.

"There have been a couple," I said reluctantly.

She seemed on edge and upset about this stuff already, and that answer wasn't going to make her feel any better about things.

I looked down at the table, trying to gather my thoughts. "You did exactly the right thing, not hiring him and making this drawing. He could be one of the gang." I cleared my throat and set the drawing down on the table. "I'm going to be here to help you. Tell me more about the ranch and the horses. Start with where they are located."

Kyle cleared his throat and joined the conversation for the first time. He pointed toward the back wall of the house. "They're in the south pasture. It's the closest one we have to the house that has enough grass for them."

"Show me," I said.

We stepped out the back door, and I could see the horses, maybe one hundred yards away. "How many?" I asked.

They told me they had about seventy, including three foals.

"This gang seems to go after the very best horses and then leave the rest. How many do you have that are what you would call your very best?"

They looked to Jessie for that answer, and she took her time, thinking it over. "I would say ten," she answered.

"We have one stallion with Arabian bloodlines. He has a lot of speed. So, we have that stallion, maybe six of the best mares, and three colts that they might go after. What do you want us to do?"

I looked at a small, enclosed pasture off to one side. It was more like a big corral, but it looked to be large enough for ten horses from what I could see in the fading light. "What's that pasture for? If we threw out some hay, could you graze the ten horses in there, closer to the house?"

Kyle started moving, trotting off the back porch. "We call it the birthing pasture," he said over his shoulder. "I'll throw some hay out there and bring the horses in before it gets too dark."

I looked at some trees bordering the birthing pasture on the west side. "I'll get my bedroll," I said. "I'll be sleeping over in those trees."

———

Jessie came in the back door of the house, carrying a lantern. It had taken both of them, working together, to cut out the horses they needed and bring them to the birthing pasture while Kyle had finished throwing out the hay before darkness had completely settled in. She had gone back out to bring water and a little food to Ash.

She saw a glow of lantern light coming from the kitchen as she walked back to the house. She found her mother washing the dishes from dinner. Jessie put her lantern down and picked up a towel to help.

Iris turned her head as Jessie came in. "Is he settled down out there?" She looked out the window. "I hope it won't be too cold. What if it starts raining on him?"

Jessie took the questions one at a time. "He knows the way to the back porch if it rains. And I told him to come in and throw his bedroll down in the living room, next to the fireplace, if it gets too cold." She paused. "I have a feeling it would have to get really cold before he would come in, though."

Iris finished washing the dishes and picked up a towel to dry her hands. "I think he's a good man," she said. "He's kind of...ruggedly handsome, don't you think?"

Jessie felt herself blushing slightly and looked up to see her mother's amused smile. She smiled despite herself. "Yes," she said after a moment. "I guess that's a pretty good description of him. I'm glad he's here."

CHAPTER FOUR

HORSE HANDOFF

Holt Jacobs tore open the envelope in the Austin hotel lobby, surveying his latest instructions. The usual furrow of frustration on his forehead was even more pronounced than usual. He had two reasons for being irritated with this latest set of instructions.

First, the directions were very vague. Jacobs had long suspected that The Boss had somebody that traveled to the target ranches and hired on for a week or two prior to the robbery. When the man wasn't able to hire on, the instructions got a lot more vague on which horses to take. This note said to visit the Lazy M Ranch near Belton. So far, so good. Then it just directed him to take the stallion and three or four of the best-looking mares. Holt blew out a snort of exasperation. Noticing that he had drawn a few curious stares, he moved out to the street.

Having to look things over and choose the horses would require him to hang out in the area for an extra day or two, increasing his chances of getting caught. And if they weren't happy with the horses he took, they would blame it on him.

The second thing that bothered him was that the note said he had to make this happen within the next week or so. He had noticed that he was being given less and less time to pull off these robberies. Plus, he had planned to shadow Lance this time when he went to transport the horses for sale. Following the trail of the stolen horses was important to him. It was the first step in his plan—it would help him get a bigger share of the profits. Holt suspected they were being shipped by rail, which suggested that there was another guy on the robbery payroll working for the railroad. He at least needed to find out who that was.

Holt folded up the note, put it in his pocket, and unhitched his horse from the rail. He paused before stepping into the saddle, one hand on the pommel of his saddle. He had to decide what to do about the timing problem he had now. He couldn't follow Lance and get back in time to take one of his helpers to Belton and pull off the robbery. He stepped into the saddle and turned his horse out into the street. Holt knew what he would do. He would follow Lance first, then come back for the Lazy M robbery. He could make some excuse for the delay. They needed him too much to get rid of him for one late job.

Holt tied the rope from one of the stolen horses to his saddle horn. It was time to move the two horses he had stolen several days ago. It was barely light, but he always preferred to move the horses early. Looking behind him, he could see one of his men, Slade, doing the same with the other horse. Ike lounged against a tree, hands in his pockets, watching them. Holt had given up trying to figure out which one of them irritated him more. It was a tie, he decided.

"You," he said, pointing at Ike, "be ready to head out with me when I get back. Maybe in a couple days. I expect to have another job by then."

Ike removed a twig from his mouth, leaned over and spat, then nodded. He resumed leaning against the tree.

Holt shook his head and mounted up. He'd wanted people who were too lazy to get ideas about more money, so he'd gotten what he asked for. He kicked his horse in the ribs and moved out. The meeting point with Lance was north of Austin. He could be there tomorrow. Then he planned to send Slade back to the cave to wait. Meanwhile, Holt would go to see what he could find out about where these horses wound up after he handed them off to Lance.

———

Two days later, Holt met up with Lance for the handoff of the horses. The meeting spot was well hidden from any roads or trails, but Holt could always find it by moving north from the cave until he reached the Lampasas River. It was just a short distance east from there. Holt watched silently while Lance looked the horses over, grunted with what might have been approval, and tied a rope from each horse to his own. Occasionally, Holt had seen him come with a helper to transfer the horses, but today he was alone.

"Want some help?" Holt offered, sensing an opportunity.

Lance half-turned, sent a withering stare in Holt's direction, and shook his head. "Nope." He stepped into the saddle and began leading both horses away. "You'll get paid in the usual way," was his only other comment. He led the horses off in an easterly direction, glancing back once in a while to be sure there was no pursuit.

Holt shrugged and watched him ride away. He hadn't really expected to be invited along. Lance had been secretive, just like the man running the show, who never tipped his hand. Holt turned and waved a hand at Slade. "You can go back to the cave," he said. "I'm gonna go and see if we have any instructions on the next job. I'll meet you and Ike in a couple days."

Holt watched for a few minutes while Slade rode back toward the south, then wasted no further time in striking Lance's trail. Lance had followed a narrow game trail, winding through small stands of oak trees. Holt stayed out of sight, but had no trouble following tracks left by three horses. After two hours had elapsed, he found himself climbing a small rise. Holt dismounted and led his horse up to the top of the rise, where he glanced cautiously over the top. He could see Lance riding down to the bottom of a sloping meadow, where he turned onto a road and headed for a town not too far in the distance.

Holt took a seat at the top of the rise. He was pretty sure the town in the distance was Temple. He looked speculatively at the railroad tracks running through the town and leading off to the north. His job now was to find out who the contact at the railroad was and, if possible, to find out where the horses were being shipped.

After about ten minutes, Holt rose and trotted his horse down the slope and took the road to the edge of the town. He hitched his horse to a rail on the main street, pulled his hat down low over his forehead, and began to saunter toward the railroad station. He moved methodically, checking both sides of the street as he worked in toward the center of town.

As he neared the station, he saw the two stolen horses hitched across the street from the railroad and a few yards to the south of it. Holt retreated a block and sat down on a bench with his hat pulled low, awaiting developments.

It turned out he didn't have to wait long. After a few minutes, Lance emerged from the station house, accompanied by a burly man with an impressive black mustache. They walked over to the horses and exchanged a few words. Lance passed some money to the other man and walked away. The second man stood for just a moment, then unhitched the horses and led them to a corral inside the railroad yard, where he handed the reins to a stock handler and then returned to the station.

Holt remained on the bench as Lance walked away in the other direction on the street. Holt watched him until he ducked into a saloon. He returned his attention to the railroad yard, where the two horses had been turned out into a corral, apparently awaiting a train to take them away. He watched the handler speculatively as the man turned away from the corral and shuffled back to his post at the edge of the yard.

Taking a chance, Holt rose and sauntered over to the handler, who appeared to be no older than about twenty. He looked extremely bored, casting a curious glance in Holt's direction as he approached. Holt came to a stop beside him, took off his hat, and ran his hand through his hair. He pointed at the two stolen horses in the corral.

"Nice horses," he offered.

The youngster cast a bored glance toward the horses. "I reckon," was all he had to say.

"I was thinkin' about working for the railroad," Holt said. "Do you like doing this?"

The young man snorted and shook his head vigorously from side to side. "Hate it. Couldn't get no proper job cowboyin' for a ranch, so I took this. Still lookin' for something else, though."

Holt nodded and took a step or two away. Then he turned and threw a casual question over his shoulder. "Where are these horses going, anyway?"

The handler paused and glanced up at the horses. "The train stops at various places in the Nation and Kansas and Missouri," he said. "Those two are goin' to Parsons, Kansas." Seeing the ticket agent with the mustache emerge from the station, he made a show of picking up a broom and sweeping off the steps leading up to the station doors. Holt tipped his hat and retreated quickly out to the street.

Holt reached the street and placed his hat down low over his forehead again. He had found out everything he had come here to learn, but he felt like pushing his luck. Anything he could learn about Lance could work to his advantage somewhere down the road. He decided to return to his seat on the bench and watch to see what Lance would do after he emerged from the saloon.

His patience was rewarded after about a half hour. Lance emerged from the saloon, staggering slightly, wove his way down the street to his horse, and climbed aboard. Holt pulled his hat down a little farther as Lance trotted past on his way out of town. Feeling bolder after seeing the condition of his quarry, Holt hustled down the street to his horse and began trailing.

Lance struck a trail to the south, along the main road toward Austin. Not surprised, Holt followed at a comfortable distance. When the other man picked up the pace, Holt followed suit. He glanced overhead. It was a little before noon. He believed that Lance lived in Austin. Maybe he was trying to get there before dark.

After about four hours of pushing the horses hard, Lance entered a town and cantered down the main street, then hitched his horse to the rail. Holt pulled up at the edge of town, assuming that Lance had found another saloon on his way home. He leaned over to read the town name on the sign to his right. He was in Granger, Texas. Holt watched as Lance strolled casually up and down the street, looking over one business in particular. Holt couldn't quite make out what he was looking at. Finally, Lance mounted the steps and went inside one store.

Moving a short way down the street, Holt squinted against the sun and slowly read the sign on the storefront Lance had been eyeballing. His eyes widened when he saw the name: *First Bank of Granger*. Being an old, experienced bank robber himself, he was immediately suspicious. He wondered if Lance was holding up the bank right now. Holt relaxed slightly as Lance came back out of the building he'd entered just a few minutes before. Lance walked casually up and down the street, then seemed to walk down the path between two of the buildings, no doubt checking for any entrance or exit to the bank from the rear.

Now sure of what he was seeing developing, Holt watched until he saw Lance enter a boarding house. After about twenty minutes, he emerged from the boarding house and walked down to a diner. Holt turned his horse and rode out of town, looking for a spot to make a cold camp. He felt sure Lance planned to rob that bank tomorrow, and he knew how to take advantage of it. A small smile broke out on his face as he considered the possibilities.

———

I sat on the back porch of Jessie's house, sipping the coffee she had brought me while I looked at the drawing she had made of the man who had tried to find work at her ranch. The face was distinct. The nose was broad and flat, while the eyes seemed set unusually close together. I folded it back up and put it in my pocket, then walked out to the corral that now contained the best horses on this ranch. I called it a corral at this point. The Maitlins called it the birthing pasture, but they knew what I was talking about. I leaned against the rails, sipping slowly from my coffee cup.

A common pattern of these robberies was that they stole only a few of the horses, and those few were the best on the ranch. They left horses prized by most cowboys alone, those being mustangs or other horses that had a lot of endurance and wouldn't cost too much. I knew how that worked. My mustang wasn't gonna win any races.

Jessie showed up beside me, and it caught me by surprise. I felt pretty self-conscious as I began to ask a question, stuttered a bit, then dug in my heels and tried again. If she noticed how tongue-tied I was, she was nice enough to ignore it. I steadied myself down and motioned toward the horses with my coffee cup.

"Who buys these horses?" I asked. "I don't think most cowboys could come up with money for those."

Jessie nodded in agreement. "You're right," she said. "My stallion has Arabian blood, and I charge more for these than I do for the ones most cowboys buy." She stopped to think for a minute. "I sell some of these to other horse breeders. I've had a few people buy them to ship back east for racing. Quarter horse racing," she clarified. "Most of my money comes from other horses I'm selling to people for cattle drives. Mainly I breed these because my dad and I loved good horses."

I nodded absently, staring out at that Arabian stallion in the corral and the foals that came from him. I started to take another sip of coffee, then looked at the bottom of the cup in surprise when I came up empty.

Jessie chuckled and took the cup. "I'll get you another," she said.

"Much obliged," I told her. "The coffee I've been making for myself on the trail is just shocking bad." I shook my head at the memory. "My coffee pot is about twenty-five years old. My granddaddy gave it to me. Maybe that's the problem."

Jessie laughed and followed my gaze around the corral. Then she asked the question I had been thinking about. "Do you think the thieves have moved on because I didn't hire the man they sent around here?"

I looked over in surprise at how we'd thought the same thing. A plan was shaping up in my mind, though. "Could be," I answered. I couldn't read the expression in her eyes. I hoped I was seeing relief at not getting robbed and disappointment that I might move on. I was getting lost in those eyes, so I looked back out at the horses right quick.

I drummed my fingertips on the top of the rail. "Is there anybody else around here who raises some pretty pricey horses, maybe a little like what you've got out there? Somebody who might have horses these guys would want to steal?"

She thought for a bit, then nodded slowly. "There's somebody about a half-days ride south of here. He bought a colt from me about three years ago, and he's using that horse as a sire now. He got some pretty good mares from a brother in Kentucky." She looked over at me. "Are you wanting to move on down the road and look there?"

This time I was pretty sure I heard a little disappointment in her voice. That's what I wanted to think, anyway. I shook my head back and forth. "Not leavin' for good," I assured her. "I might ride down there with this picture you drew and see if the same guy tried to hire on down at that place. First, though, I'll check around here. Really thorough, to see if anybody's been skulkin' around out there."

A smile crossed her face briefly. "Okay, Ash. You look for those skulkers and I'll make you some breakfast. Mom would shoot me if I let you ride away from here hungry."

I circled the corral/birthing pasture on foot first, looking for bootprints all the way around the structure. I could only find the tracks I had made this morning, along with a few from Jessie, also this morning, and a couple others I knew must have been made by Jessie's brother Kyle last night.

I mounted up and began moving around in widening circles, looking especially for signs in the trees on the left of people passing through on horseback—broken twigs, tracks, and things such as that. In the pasture in the back of the corral, there were too many horse tracks to help me. I sat my horse for a moment, studying the land around Jessie's house. I felt sure that anybody intent on theft would have to pass through the trees on the west side where I had slept last night. There just wasn't enough cover if they came from any other direction.

Satisfied that nobody had tried to sneak up on the ranch and the horses last night, I headed on in for breakfast.

———

Jessie's mom wouldn't need to worry about me riding away hungry. They piled my plate to the rafters and I could barely finish it. Finally, I sat back and thanked them for the breakfast.

Iris lifted a plate of biscuits and started to pass them in my direction. I held up my hand and waved the biscuits off. "They're delicious," I told her, "but I'm worried about my horse. He could get hurt trying to give me a ride if I eat anymore."

Jessie came outside with me as I tossed my bag on the horse and led him around to the front of the house. She stopped me with a hand on my sleeve as I mounted up. "Come with me," she said.

I followed her around the corner of the corral, where I saw a big chestnut gelding hitched to the rail. I walked over to the horse, admiring the lines and the size of him. He was at least sixteen hands. I looked at her questioningly. "Is he from your Arabian stallion?" I asked.

Jessie nodded. "My Arabian stallion and one of my mustang mares," she answered. "He has good speed and a lot of endurance. Why don't you give him a try? You may need him to catch the guy you're after."

I took one more look at the chestnut, then I unhitched him and led him over, switched saddles, and prepared to mount up.

Jessie stopped me and gave me a brief hug. "Be careful," she said.

I grinned ear-to-ear and mounted the chestnut. I could feel that hug all the way down to my toes.

CHAPTER FIVE
NO HONOR AMONG THIEVES

Holt rose early the next morning, having a cup of coffee for breakfast along with a little beef jerky. Not that he was in a hurry, he reflected, he just couldn't afford to have Lance see him in town this morning. After he had paced impatiently for at least a couple of hours, he pulled the watch from his pocket and checked it for about the tenth time. He saw that he had only about fifteen minutes before the bank opened, so he quickly saddled his horse and began moving toward town.

Pausing frequently to check his pocket watch, Holt arrived in town exactly at opening time for the bank—nine o'clock. He rode across to the north side of town, hat pulled low over his forehead. He noted only one horse hitched to the rail outside the bank, and he was pretty sure he had seen it there yesterday. It probably belonged to the owner or manager of the bank.

Arriving at his chosen spot on the north side of town, he tethered his horse as far away from the bank as he could while he could still see what was happening down there. He made a show of tightening the girth on the saddle, checking his horse's hooves, and trying to look preoccupied with anything other than watching the bank.

Just as he was feeling like he needed to move his horse and get out of town, he saw Lance leave the boarding house. Holt mounted but stayed where he was, watching.

Lance unhitched his horse and led it across the street, where he hitched it to the rail outside the bank. He reached into his saddlebag and removed what appeared to be a burlap sack. Looking both ways, he climbed the steps to the bank.

Holt had seen what he needed to see. He turned his horse and left town, heading to the north. Holt was taking a bit of a chance, but he intended to ride north until he reached the turnoff that would lead to the place where he always met with Lance to hand off the stolen horses. He felt sure that's where Lance would go to shake pursuit. Besides, he couldn't take the chance of following Lance and being overtaken by a posse on his trail. He kicked his mare in the ribs and picked up the pace.

———

Pulling off the trail in a stand of burr oak trees just short of the Lampasas River, Holt dismounted, tethered his horse, and sat down to wait. Leaning against a tree and taking a swig of water from his canteen, he figured he had little to lose if Lance didn't come this way. He could still make the robbery at the Lazy M. He could come back once in a while to keep an eye on Lance, but Lance might not know much more than how to arrange the shipment of the horses. The one with the mustache at the railroad. That was the man with the next piece of information. If Lance proved to be a dead end, he would watch the railroadman for a while. At the end of this trail, Holt needed to know who was sending his orders—who was he stealing the horses for? That man was making a lot of money. And depending on who he was, Holt had a feeling that man could be blackmailed.

Patience was rewarded about forty-five minutes later when Holt heard hooves pounding toward him. He rose and peered through the trees as Lance galloped past him, slowing the horse as he splashed into the river. He reined the horse over to the left, working his way to the west, leaving no tracks for the posse that was sure to be following. Holt watched as Lance stayed in the water for about two hundred yards, then abruptly guided the horse out of the river and into the trees. Lance returned briefly with a tree branch, brushed dirt over his tracks, then disappeared again.

Holt was in no hurry to follow, still feeling confident he knew where Lance was headed. Holt untethered his horse and led it on foot, deeper into the trees and away from the trail. When he reached a deep thicket well back from both the trail and the river, he tethered the horse securely and made his way back, on foot, to his original vantage point. Unsatisfied with the view he had of the trail and the river, he selected a large oak with a low-hanging limb and climbed up the tree. Finding a wide, level limb, he settled in, leaning back against the trunk, and resumed watching the trail.

It was another two hours, by the time on Holt's pocket watch, before a posse showed up on the trail. Led by a man with a badge Holt assumed to be the sheriff of Granger, it was a ragtag bunch of five men, including one man who was barely hanging on to his horse. Holt chuckled under his breath, knowing the sheriff had probably had to make a sweep of the saloon to get himself a posse.

The group reached the bank of the Lampasas River and milled about uncertainly on the edge. The sheriff moved his horse uncertainly up and down the bank, then finally swam his horse across the river. The posse followed and spread out on the opposite bank, moving up and down, trying to find a trail. After a few minutes, the group moved off down the trail, away from the river, scouting for signs. Holt stayed where he was, certain they would return.

They were back just a few minutes later, re-crossing the river and splitting up to scour the bank for signs in both directions. Holt watched with interest as the sheriff and another man reached the place where Lance had left the river and moved into the trees. They passed the spot and moved on. After another thirty minutes of trying to pick up Lance's trail, they regrouped where the road met the river. After a few minutes of heated discussion, the sheriff led the group back toward Granger.

Holt waited for only a few minutes after the posse moved out of sight before shimmying back down the tree and starting for his horse. It was only about noon, and Lance might or might not hole up for the rest of the day at their meeting place. Things would get a little more difficult if he moved on from there today.

Holt mounted up and moved north to a point near the river bank, then moved west, casting back and forth until he struck the narrow game trail he was looking for. He held the horse to a walk, noting a familiar landmark here and there along the trail. After about an hour, he dismounted and led his horse forward.

After another ten minutes on foot, he hitched the horse one more time and crept forward, moving from tree to tree, watching the small clearing in front of him. He could see Lance seated on the ground, feeding small branches into a fire he had built. Holt smiled when he saw the whiskey bottle in Lance's right hand. Judging by the number of swigs the man was taking, this was going to be easy. He stayed behind a tree and watched as Lance finished the bottle and dropped it on the ground. After a few more minutes, he flopped onto the ground, rolled over, and began snoring.

Not bothering to step quietly, Holt drew his gun, reversed his grip, and moved into the clearing. When Lance stirred and rose, Holt struck him soundly across the forehead with his gun barrel. Lance slumped soundlessly back to the ground. Holt moved across the clearing and lifted the saddlebag from the ground at the far edge of the clearing. Flipping it open, he reached inside and lifted the bundle of bank notes and the small bag of coins.

Holt sat down and quickly counted the take from the bank robbery, then snorted in disappointment. The total came to only $634. Holt shook his head and stuffed the money into the pocket of his jacket. No wonder the posse had quit so easily. He reached back into the bag, then changed his mind and dumped the contents out onto the ground. Sorting through a random collection of ammunition, canteen, and bits of food, he stopped and picked up a small notebook. He glanced over his shoulder at Lance, who hadn't stirred.

He returned his attention to the notebook and hastily shuffled through the pages, ripping several of them as he went. He found his own name in there, along with the hotel address Lance used to communicate with him. He stopped at the next name he found: E. Pendleton. There was an address listed in Temple. He stuffed the notebook into his pocket and turned to go.

Holt stopped at the edge of the clearing, gun in hand, and briefly considered killing Lance. After a moment, he rejected the idea. He still needed Lance to hand off the horses and keep the operation going. His best bet now was to pay Pendleton a visit. Or maybe he could break into Pendleton's house first. Maybe he could find something that would tell him who was buying those horses up north. If he was really lucky, maybe he could find out who was giving the orders.

―――――

Mike Stone rode slowly toward the Denton County jail, his prisoner tied to the saddle and trailing on the horse behind him. It was the end of a very long pursuit, and he was looking forward to handing over the prisoner. Horace Beane, or *Three Finger Beane* as he was more commonly known, had left a trail of theft and shootings across half the state.

Stone had never heard the term *pecos* as anything but a reference to the West Texas river until he had started working on this case. Now, unfortunately, he knew what it meant. Beane had murdered two men, thrown them in the Pecos River, and fled. Apparently, when a man was murdered and thrown in the Pecos River, it was called a *pecos*. Most recently, Stone had caught up with Three Finger trying to rustle cattle from a herd headed north on the Chisholm Trail.

Reaching the county jail, Stone handed the prisoner over without ceremony. He was looking for a room at a boarding house and then a café, in that order. He found a room, stopped just long enough at the telegraph office to send a telegram to his captain in Austin, and crossed the street to a café. After living on beef and beans for the last three weeks, he was hoping for anything else for dinner. Seeing nothing but beef on the menu, he gave up and ordered a steak.

After breakfast at the same café in the morning, he crossed the street to check for a reply to his telegram from the night before. To his surprise, he found a long telegram waiting for him. He left the telegraph office, parked himself on a bench he saw outside, and settled down to read what his captain had to say.

Captain McDonald began by congratulating him on the capture of Three Finger Beane. The governor, he assured Stone, would be pleased. McDonald went on to tell him that he needed to partner with Ash McKinnon on a case involving a ring of horse thieves. A smile crossed Stone's face, he and McKinnon had worked a cattle drive, then joined the Rangers at the same time. The smile faded when he was reminded that his friend Red Corbin was killed while trailing one of the thieves.

Stone stood up, paced up and down for a few minutes, then settled back down to read the rest of the telegram. The horses being stolen were only the most expensive ones to be found on whatever ranch was being robbed. Several had Arabian blood, and they had found none so far in Central Texas, where the robberies had all taken place. They had attached a description of several of the horses. McDonald advised him to return on the train to Austin, where he could talk with the captain further. McKinnon, he was told, was looking for the thieves in the area of Belton, Texas.

Stone stood and moved down to the boarding house to pay his bill. As he stepped out of the boarding house, he stopped and looked at the telegram again. Several of the horses, it said, had Arabian blood. He drifted to unhitch his horse, then changed his mind and crossed to the tele-graph office again. He sent off a note to McDonald, telling him he wanted to check something there in North Texas concerning the ring of horse thieves before coming to Austin.

Stone mounted and rode north and slightly east, angling over toward the Chisholm Trail. He had seen a lot of impromptu horse race tracks set up along the trail during his drive a few years ago. And, from time to time, he had seen a few of them more recently, since he'd begun working as a Texas Ranger. Mostly, they seemed pretty harmless. He had ridden over to watch one of them during the cattle drive when the herd had stopped for a day in the Indian Territory.

A lot of the cowhands on the drives liked to race their horses. Usually there was a little betting going on—sometimes more than a little. The thought that had crossed his mind was that maybe the horse thieves were selling the stolen horses to men who were winning money at the race sites that had sprung up along the trail. Maybe that's where a few of them went, anyway. Maybe, he thought, if the horses were good enough, they could be sold for racing back east.

Cantering north and east on the road out of Denton, Stone struck the Chisholm Trail and followed it north for a few miles, remembering a crudely constructed racetrack he had visited a few years ago, hopeful it was still there. He held to the western edge of the trail. He was rewarded just a few miles later when he saw a carved wooden sign: *Shady Grove Races*, it announced. Written below in letters he could barely make out, it said, *Must bet at least 25 cents. No more than $2 allowed*.

Stone followed a faint, worn trail off to the west, nodding briefly at a couple of cowboys who passed in the opposite direction. He guessed they were returning to a herd somewhere up the trail. Trail bosses usually had a pretty tight schedule, but they knew they had to let the boys blow off a little steam once in a while.

After a few more minutes, he could follow his ears to the racetrack. The sound of pounding hooves and shouts grew louder until he rounded a bend and saw one hundred or so people standing around a dusty oval, with a tent pitched here and there. Stone knew they would be taking bets and selling beer in those tents.

He rode up to the track and hitched his horse at a rail, ignoring men shouting at him from the tents. He spotted a makeshift corral to one side, where he assumed they kept the horses before and after the races. He stopped briefly and scanned the telegram—there were a few of the stolen horses described there. He stuffed the telegram back into his pocket after a brief read and headed to the corral. Stone figured his best bet was to look for an altered brand rather than hoping to be lucky enough to find one of the few horses mentioned in the telegram.

Moving into the corral, he moved among the horses, hoping he looked like a serious bettor trying to choose the next horse to risk his money on. He patted a few before moving back to check a few of the brands. A black gelding caught his eye. It was a nicely built horse. Stone was guessing he was fast. The brand had really caught his attention. It was a circle R brand, but it looked like the brand had been something else before. Somebody had worked this one with a running iron.

Stone noticed motion at the corner of his eye. He turned to see a man advancing toward him out of the crowd. His face looked like an angry thundercloud. Stone turned slightly to face him. As he did, the man caught sight of the badge on his chest, turned, and disappeared into the crowd.

Stone moved after him immediately. He plunged into the crowd, glimpsing briefly the man heading toward a tent at the far end of the oval. He tried to follow, but men stood or moved into his way, moving only slowly as he pushed his way through. Emerging from a knot of people, he couldn't see the man anywhere.

Stone ran toward the tent where he had last seen the man headed, then ran to the entrance, shoved the flaps aside, and plunged into the tent. Bettors were lined up in front of two tables, shouting and waving money. Stone surveyed the crowd quickly, then checked under the tables. There was no sign of the man he'd pursued into the tent. His shoulders slumped in frustration. Then he noticed a flap at the back of the tent. He ran to the back and pushed through the flap. He saw nothing initially, then movement off to his left caught his eye. His quarry was sprinting into the corral.

Frustrated that he hadn't stayed with the horse, Stone ran toward the corral, where he saw the man leap onto the black gelding and bolt out of the corral bareback as another man swung the gate open.

Shouting for the man to stop, Stone knew the words were futile as soon as they left his mouth. He sprinted for his horse and jumped aboard.

Spurring his horse onto the trail, he gave chase. Within a few minutes, he knew there was no point in keeping up the pursuit. The black gelding had undoubtedly been stolen for his speed and racing ability. The dust trail Stone was following became less and less visible. It mingled with whatever tracks had been left with dozens of other tracks. There was nothing to follow. He slowed his horse to a stop, shaking his head in anger and frustration.

Finally, Stone reined his horse around to return to the racetrack. He would question the guy who had held the gate, if he could find him. He could look for any other horses with altered brands. He didn't hold out a lot of hope.

CHAPTER SIX

SCOUT'S TRAIL

My new chestnut gelding, which wasn't my horse, I had to remind myself, moved with a long, even stride. I urged him into a gallop for a few minutes, then brought him back down to a canter and began wondering how much it would cost to buy this horse. He covered the ground effortlessly, and he could really run. He hadn't even been one of the ten horses Jessie had brought into the corral in the back of the house. I realized how big a target her ranch could be for the thieves.

I rode into Belton and kept going. I estimated it was a little past noon when I saw the place I was looking for. A sign on the trail said *Atherton*. There was a ramshackle fence out front, and a small ranch house sat at the edge of a pasture. I could see a pasture behind, with maybe thirty horses and seventy head of cattle. There was a small bunkhouse at the edge of the pasture. A small, wiry man with a weather-beaten face and permanent crow's feet etched around his eyes approached me, neither welcoming nor unwelcoming as he stopped and looked me over.

I pushed my jacket to the side and let him see the badge hanging from my shirt pocket. He glanced at it and nodded, his expression never changing. He hooked his thumbs into his pants pockets and waited for me to say something.

I swung down from the horse, stretched for a minute, then fished in my pocket for the drawing that Jessie had given me. "McKinnon," I said, pointing a thumb at my chest.

His lips barely moved when he said, "Call me Zeb." He held his hand out for the drawing, and I could see the recognition in his eyes when he looked at it. He studied it for a few more seconds, then handed it back to me. "Yep, he was here, if'n that's what yore wantin' to ask me," he said.

I felt my heartbeat pick up the pace a little. "When?" I asked.

"Yestiddy," came the reply. "He were lookin' for work, but I told him I didn't have nothin' for him. It was gettin' on toward dark when he come, so I let 'em stay over yonder in the bunkhouse for the night. He rode outta here at daybreak."

My hopes rose and fell as I listened. I'd missed him by only a few hours. I folded up the drawing, pushed it back in my pocket, and rocked back on my heels, trying to figure out what to do now.

Zeb watched me through shrewd eyes. He cleared his throat and spat, then looked at my horse and nodded in appreciation. He looked back at me. "Is he a bad 'un?" he asked.

I nodded my head slowly. "Could be," I said. "Might be part of a crew that's been stealing top-notch horseflesh around these parts for the last several months. Any idea where he went when he left here?"

Zeb shook his head. "Said he was lookin' to buy some

good harrses." Zeb snorted and shook his head again. "I guess my horses wasn't good 'nough for him." He thought it over, then added grudgingly: "Maybe I was lucky. I guess he were plannin' to steal the harrses." He thought a minute longer. "I tole him about the Maitlin Ranch." He pointed up north, where I'd come from. "He didn't go thataway when he hauled outta here, though." He pointed to the south. "He went thataway."

I looked down the trail to the south. "Any idea where he would go down that way?"

Zeb shook his head again. "Don't know any harrses better'n mine that he'd want to buy. Or steal. I tole him he could bunk up here again if'n he passes back through in the next couple days, though."

I saw a little hope. "Can I stick around here today, maybe stay over in the bunkhouse, see if he comes back through here in the next day or so?" Zeb looked a tad bit doubtful, so I sweetened the pot. "I could do some work for ya."

Zeb's eyes brightened up, and he hatched a small smile for the first time. He looked me up and down. "I reckon a boy yore size could split a powerful amount of wood, if'n he put his mind to it." He pointed toward an enormous pile of logs off to the side of the house.

I looked at the woodpile, blew out a miserable breath, then nodded my head up and down in agreement. My big mouth got me in trouble when I was eatin' and when I was talkin'. Other than that, I didn't have any trouble with it, far as I could tell. I led the chestnut over to the corral and hitched him to the rail. Then I went over to the wood-pile, picked up the axe, and started chopping.

Morning found me sore and no closer to finding the guy in Jessie's drawing. He hadn't returned, and I couldn't hang around here anymore, waiting for him. Besides, I wasn't just itching to tackle that woodpile again.

I hauled myself out of the small, uncomfortable bunk, not sorry I wasn't spending another night in that thing. I stretched, dressed, and walked toward the ranch house. Zeb, who had warmed up to me some after he saw how much wood I'd chopped, stepped out the back door and handed me some coffee. He waved me inside, sat me down at the table, and put a mess of bacon in front of me. I had no problem finishing it off. I'd earned it at that woodpile.

When I finished, I pushed back and told Zeb I'd be heading out. I asked him one more time if he had any idea where the guy I'd been looking for might have gone. He started to shake his head no, then stopped. I watched him and waited.

"Well," he said finally. "You could mebbe check down there at Salado. Guy down there has some pretty good harrses," he said grudgingly. "Not as good as mine," he mumbled. "Name's Peterson, has a ranch down there at Salado. You can ask fer him at the Stagecoach Inn."

I rose, tossed the last handful of bacon in my mouth, and trotted out the back door. I knew that Salado was a stop on the Chisholm Trail, and I had heard of the Stage-coach Inn. It was something I could check on. I thanked him over my shoulder, saddled up the gelding, and headed down the trail.

————

When I reached Salado, I crossed a new bridge over Salado Creek, and I found myself looking at an impressive restaurant and hotel with white columns and white railings on the second floor. I dismounted in front and stopped to look at it. I'd been told that Sam Houston, Robert E. Lee, and Jesse James had all eaten in the restaurant. I looked down at my dirty clothes and muddy boots and decided I wasn't ready for it this time. Maybe next time I could clean up a little.

A clatter of wheels behind me got my attention, then a small cloud of dust rolled over me. I dusted myself off as best I could, then turned around to see a stage rolling to a stop in front of the inn. A hefty, sour-looking driver climbed down off the stage and opened the door for the passengers. I figured the stage driver might be a good source of information about the Peterson ranch and horses. I waited until all the passengers had emptied out of the stage and moved to the inn before I went to question the driver.

I walked over to the stage. The driver's irritated expression faded only slightly when he saw the badge on my chest. He waited impatiently for me to reach him, then folded his arms across his chest.

"Yeah?"

I was just a mite put off by that greeting, I must say. I folded my arms and stared him down until he shifted his feet and broke the stare. "I'm looking for a little information," I said. "In particular, I'd like to know about the Peterson ranch. Where is it, and what kind of horses do they have out there?"

He refused to look at me, staring across the road and shuffling his feet some more. He pointed toward the south. "Down the road, mebbe two miles, you kin see it from the road on the left. They got some harrses, but nuthin' I could use to pull this stage. Harrses that fancy folks might like to prance around on in a parade or somethin'. That's all I know." He turned abruptly and began to unhitch the horses from the wagon.

I started to ask if the stagecoach line had a prize for rude drivers, 'cause he must win every time, but I changed my mind. He'd told me what I needed to know, even if I didn't like the way he said it. I just got on the gelding and headed south.

The Peterson ranch showed up right where he said it would be. A sign hung from the gate after I'd ridden about two miles. A man was working right at the front of the property near the gate when I rode in. He was fixing the fence, and he stopped, put his hands on his hips, and waited as I rode over.

"Mr. Peterson," I asked.

He nodded, took in the badge on my chest, put down his tools, and walked over. "Gus," he said, extending a hand. "What kin I do fer ya?"

I shook his hand, then pulled Jessie's drawing out of my pocket. I opened it and started to hand it over to him. "Have you seen—" I started to ask.

He drew in his breath sharply and turned to his left, staring toward the barn I could see in the background.

"Wes," he said. "Leastaways, that's what he told me his name was. What's he done?"

I folded the paper back up and put it away, staring over toward the barn. "Well," I said, "I don't know if he's done anything yet, but he seems to keep showing up, looking for work, just a week or two before a ranch gets their horses stolen. Do you raise some high-dollar horses around here, show horses or race horses or some such?"

He was still staring back toward the barn, growing redder in the face by the minute. He tore his gaze away and looked back at me. "Yep," he growled, still glaring in the direction of the barn every couple of seconds. "Moved out here from Virginny, uh, Virginia, a couple o' years ago. Mostly I run cattle now, but I brought some top-notch breeding stock, an' I have some customers back east for my horses. I ship a couple back there every year."

I turned and mounted up. "He's in the barn, right? You keep looking over in that direction."

Peterson bobbed his head up and down a couple times.

"Mind if I go talk to him?" I asked.

Peterson waved at the barn. "Go ahead. I'm right behind ya."

As I approached the barn, I could see somebody saddling a horse over there, glancing over his shoulder from time to time. He looked to be in a hurry. As I got closer, he seemed to be trying to decide whether to jump on that horse and light out of there or stay and talk. He stayed, probably because I was only about ten yards away from him when he finished saddling.

I dismounted and strolled in his direction. "Your name Wes?" I asked.

He hesitated, like he was trying to remember what it was he was calling himself today.

Finally, his head kinda bounced up and down once or twice. "Yeah," he said. He took a long look at the badge, then turned and seemed to fiddle with his saddle.

I took a few steps closer. "How long you been workin' here, Wes?" He mumbled something I couldn't quite understand, so I took a couple more steps in his direction. "What did you say?"

He wheeled around suddenly with a riding crop in his hand and took a vicious swing at me. I barely ducked out of the way. He turned and jumped on his horse and spurred it away, heading for the gate and the road beyond.

I turned, ran back to the gelding and jumped aboard. We took off, down to the gate, then turned south to follow him down the road. After only several hundred yards, I could see it was no contest. That gelding could really move. We were catching up in a hurry. I could see Wes look behind, that riding crop still in his hand, and it didn't take no genius to see he wanted to use it on me.

I looked down and lifted my lariat off the saddle. I had carried one ever since my days on the cattle drive. I'd done a lot of practicing back then, and I kind of prided myself on it. As the gelding pounded closer, I shook out a loop and dropped it neatly over his shoulders, then pulled it tight. He had no choice but to slow his horse, but there at the end, he didn't slow it enough. He got pulled backward. He finally yanked his feet out of the stirrups, bounced off the horse's rump, then bounced on his own rump in the middle of the road.

He got up, but that gelding had gotten some fine training, I could see that right away. He backed right up, dumped the man back on the road, and kept that line taught. Every time that guy started to get some slack in the line, that gelding backed up again. I decided to let Wes roost there in the road for a while. I also decided I had to ask about buying that gelding. He was gettin' more work done today than I was.

After a while, I got down, took a short length of rope, and tied his hands behind his back. Then I tied his feet together, took off the lariat I'd lassoed him with, and put it back on the gelding. I walked over and squatted down beside him in the dirt. "Let's talk about horse stealing," I said.

He swore and spat into the dirt. "I ain't talkin' to you about nuthin'," he informed me.

"Okay," I said, "I'll just tie you into that saddle of yours and take you to the nearest sheriff around here. Maybe somebody's heard of you or knows something about you."

He swore some more for a while, then said: "I ain't

getting' back in that saddle. Ain't nuthin' you can do about it."

I picked him up, walked over to his horse, and chunked him face down across the saddle. I heard the air whoosh out of him when his belly hit the leather. I picked up the reins and started to walk him back to the gelding.

I heard a muffled voice from the other side of the horse. "Okay," he said. "I'll sit up and you can tie me in."

"Now ain't that nice," I said. "I love it when folks can agree on things."

I got my rope back out and tied his horse to my saddle. We walked back to the Peterson ranch, where I was told that the nearest sheriff was back in Belton. I was headed back that way, anyway. Peterson looked like he wanted to use my rope for a noose, but I just took my prisoner out of there and headed north to Belton.

———

Holt wasted no time getting away from the meeting spot where he had left Lance. He didn't want to take any chances on that posse coming back. He walked his horse back out to the river and stayed in the shallow water for several hundred yards before weaving through the trees and finally taking the trail back to Granger. If Lance found any tracks, he wouldn't make a connection. And chances were, heading back to Granger was the last thing Lance would think about doing, anyway.

A day and a half of hard riding brought Holt back to the Longhorn Canyon. He found Ike and Slade napping under a tree when he rode up in the early afternoon. One of them woke when he rode up to them, then nudged the other awake. They both stared at him wordlessly.

Holt jerked a thumb at Ike. "We're riding in ten minutes.

We'll be gone maybe three, four days. Pack up and saddle up." He rode away, not seeing the hateful glares that followed him. He wouldn't have cared if he had seen them, anyway.

Another two days' ride saw them pass through Belton and on down the road to the Maitlin Ranch. They rode past, Holt noticing as he did that there was a dog who barked at them as they rode by. He would have to remember the dog and do something about that.

They circled the ranch and came in from the west side as the sun was setting. Holt took out his binoculars and found a vantage point to look things over. The horses he saw were mustangs—cowboy horses, not what he was looking for.

Still keeping a respectful distance, he worked closer to the house. He spotted a small corral at the back of the house and refocused the binoculars. A small smile appeared on his face. These were worth stealing. He swept the lens back and forth, then stopped on the stallion. He looked up, then back down through the glass. A small whistle escaped his lips. This one, he thought, was worth keeping for himself. He lowered the binoculars, looked around in all directions, then moved in a little closer.

CHAPTER SEVEN
FOOTPRINTS

J essie sat on the back porch of the house, keeping one eye on the horses in the corral. She and Kyle had both worked closer to the house and corral these last two days, reluctant to leave her prize horses unguarded. Keeping them safe at night was a different matter entirely, she'd had very little sleep last night. The drowsiness from the late afternoon sun today was almost overpowering.

She found it very unsettling that the man who'd asked for work the other day may have been trying to size up the herd. Her instincts had been right. At least she had sent him away before he could have gotten a good look at her stallion and prize mares. That thought comforted her a little, but only a little. He could have simply asked around town in Belton to find out more about her herd.

She wondered if Ash had been able to find the man. She was also wondering when he might be back. It had been a great comfort to have him here. And, she had to admit to herself, it wasn't entirely about guarding the horses. A small smile spread across her face, and the drowsiness took over. She leaned back in her rocking chair and dozed off.

She came awake when her dog, who had been sleeping in the sunshine on the porch, growled. Jessie came awake and looked at the dog, who was looking off to the west, past the corral, alternating growls with an occasional bark. Jessie came to her feet, still watching her dog. "What is it, Rex?"

The dog came to his feet and trotted down the steps, still growling, his attention fixed on the trees west of the pasture. He disappeared into the trees. Jessie grabbed the Henry rifle she had propped up in the corner of the porch and followed the path taken by her dog. A moment later, the dog burst into frenzied barking. Jessie held the rifle out in front of her and broke into a crouching run, trying to follow the sound of the barking.

The trees slowed her progress as she entered the woods. She stopped from time to time and listened, but the barking was growing fainter. She reached the edge of the tree line on the far side of the woods but saw nothing in the pasture that opened up before her. She cast back and forth along the tree line and saw a few faint horse tracks leading out into the pasture. She could follow them for only about twenty yards before she lost the trail. She didn't want to leave the horses unguarded, so she didn't pursue it any further.

She returned to the trees and followed the horse tracks back into the woods. The earth was a little more moist here than in the meadow. She made some progress following the tracks until she found the place where the horse had been tethered. There were many tracks here, circling back and forth around an oak tree with a large, low-hanging limb. She began to look for human footprints leading away from the tree but found she couldn't make much progress. The man was obviously lighter than the horse, so the impressions left were much more shallow.

Jessie could identify only three faint prints leading away from the oak tree. She was pretty sure she could see partial prints from a boot heel for a few yards, but then she found nothing more. She blew out a breath of frustration, then a sound behind her caused her to wheel around, rifle at the ready. She felt relief wash over her when she saw it was her dog, Rex, returning. She called the dog and let him sniff around the oak tree, wondering if he could give her some direction.

Rex sniffed the ground around the oak tree, then trotted away toward the ranch house, pausing once in a while to sniff the ground and the bushes. Jessie followed slowly, stopping often to check the woods behind her, afraid there was a second man out there. Or, she thought, this first man could have turned around and come back.

She heard the dog snuffling eagerly near another large oak tree in front of her. She pushed through the branches blocking her way and scanned the ground where the dog had stopped. She caught her breath when she spotted a clear boot print on the ground near the tree. The point of the boot mark was aimed toward the ranch. She lifted her eyes and saw that the man, whoever he was, had seen the horse corral pretty clearly from here.

Jessie stood indecisively for a moment, then untied the ribbon she'd used to tie back her hair this morning. She wrapped it around a tree limb to help her mark the spot, then started toward the house. Something stopped her, and she turned around and went back to look at the boot print. She stepped a few feet to the side and pressed her own boot into the ground, then stood back to compare the prints. They were pretty much the same size. Puzzled, she took another look. Her brother Kyle would leave a much bigger print. Her mother, Iris, had a boot size a bit smaller than her own. She was sure the first print was not hers.

She turned and trotted through the trees toward the house. When she came out of the woods, she could see Kyle pitching hay just beyond the other side of the corral. She cupped her hands and shouted his name, then waved toward the house when he looked up. She ran up the back steps, left the Henry in the corner of the kitchen, then pulled a piece of paper and pencil out of the cupboard.

She was finishing the note as the back door slammed and Kyle moved over to look at the note. She reread what she had just written:

Ash,

> *Someone has been watching the house. I found a boot print in the woods, not too far from the corral. It's a small print, so I'm not sure if it was a man or a woman. Please come as soon as you can.*

Jessie

She let Kyle finish reading the note, then folded it up and gave it to him. "You've got to find Ash," she said. "Ride back to Belton first and ask for him there—maybe the sheriff's office and the saloon, anyplace else you can think of."

Kyle nodded, grabbed the note, and ran out through the back door. In just a few minutes, he had saddled a horse, and Jessie heard the hoofbeats dying off in the distance as he galloped away.

———

The sheriff stepped outside of his office in Belton as I rode up, leading Wes, or whatever his name was, behind me. The sheriff hooked his thumbs inside his belt as I untied Wes from the saddle, then untied his feet and pulled him off the saddle. Then I stood him up and pushed him toward the jail. The sheriff held the door and followed me into the office/county jail. He watched as I pulled out a chair and told my prisoner to sit down.

"Elmer Hutchins," he said to me, extending his hand. He waggled a toothpick between his lips. "Whatcha got here?"

I shook the sheriff's hand, then pointed at Wes, scowling from where he sat in the chair. I turned to look at Elmer, pulling Jessie's drawing from my pocket. I explained how Wes seemed to show up at ranches and ask for work just a few days before they stole valuable horses. His eyebrows lifted as he compared the drawing to Wes sitting in front of him.

"Where'd the drawing come from?" he asked.

I told him that Jessie Maitlin had drawn it when Wes had applied for work at the Maitlin Ranch. The name worked like I'd hoped it would, his expression changed to a frown when he looked back at Wes. He pulled a chair out, turned it around, and straddled it backward, his arms folded over the top of the chair back.

"I don't take kindly to folks coming to my county to rob people," he began. "What do you have to say for yourself?"

Wes's gaze went to the floor and stayed there. He shrugged and said nothing as Hutchins continued to fire questions at him.

"Who're you workin' for? What were you doing out at the Maitlin place? Where are you from?"

After several minutes of silence, Hutchins looked up at me, shrugged, and looked back at Wes. "Well," he said, "we can just lock you up in the jail an' see if you're less bashful in a few days." When he still got no answer, he stood up and pushed the chair away. "We'll give you a couple meals a day in here. Of course, the new cook down to the café just got hisself promoted from washin' dishes a couple days ago. We gen'rally let the new cooks practice on the prisoners for a few days before reg'lar folks eat the food."

Still getting no answers, he hauled Wes to his feet and pulled him back to the cells at the back. He pushed Wes through the door, locked it, then told him to turn around. He cut the rope around Wes's hands through the bars.

I stood in the hallway, then noticed the glare Wes sent in my direction. Pure hatred. I guess he didn't cotton much to getting yanked off that horse onto his caboose, back there in the road. I stared back at him, then took a couple steps forward. "If you show up at the Maitlin place again," I told him, "your tail end ain't the only thing that's gonna be ailing you."

Hutchins moved back out to the door, motioning at me to come out on the porch with him. "I can keep him here for a few days and send a description to some other sheriffs and marshals around here—see if anybody matches that description or if he matches any posters they have. If nobody claims him, I'll have to let him go after a few days."

I nodded. The prisoner hadn't actually done anything wrong that we could prove. I could just hope he was already wanted by somebody. If not, I hoped he would decide this wasn't worth it and move on.

I moved down the steps and mounted my horse. "Can you let me know if you have to let him go?" I asked. "I'll be out at the Maitlin place for a few days." Hutchins nodded and waved, and I moved across the street and down a few doors to the telegraph office. I dashed off a note, telling Captain McDonald about Wes and that the sheriff in Belton had him in jail right now. I told him I had a drawing I would send in if he wanted it. Then I mounted up and headed for Jessie's ranch.

As I reached the edge of town, I could see somebody coming from the other way, riding at a full-out gallop. I pulled over a bit and eased up on my reins, not wanting to sideswipe whoever this was coming at me. As the rider drew closer, I recognized him. It was Jessie's brother, Kyle.

Just as he was about to go past me, he saw me and began slowing the horse. He actually overran me by several yards before he could get his horse stopped and turned. I sat and waited, half-turned in his direction. He began to talk as he came alongside, the words just spilling out of him. I couldn't tell who was more out of breath, Kyle or his horse.

"Mr. McKinnon," he sputtered, "Jessie sent me. Somebody's been there, at the ranch, spyin' on things, lookin' it over."

That got my attention. "How do you know? Did you see somebody?"

"Footprints," he said. "Jessie saw footprints. He..." Kyle seemed to remember something and began fishing around in his pockets. He held a note out to me. "Here," he said. "Jessie said to give you this."

I grabbed the note and began to read. My eyes got big when I saw the part about the small boot print and I shoved the note into my pocket. "Let's go!" I shouted. We galloped out of town, heading north for the ranch.

———

Mike Stone waved goodbye to his wife Sarah and turned his horse to the trail toward Austin. His visit at home had been all too short. It was the one thing he didn't like about working for the Rangers. He was away from home too much. He supposed that he might be able to stay closer to home if he worked his way up to captain. He pulled his watch from his pocket and checked it. He had a nine o'clock meeting with Captain McDonald, and he needed to pick up the pace if he didn't want to be late. About twenty minutes later, he knocked on the captain's door.

McDonald waved him in immediately, pointing at a chair across the desk from him. "Good to see you, Stone," he said. "Everything good at home?" Stone nodded, surprised at any personal greeting from the boss. "I sent you a telegram about Red Corbin, right?" McDonald asked, changing the tone and subject immediately.

Stone nodded again and stared silently at the floor. Red's death wasn't something he wanted to talk about just yet. McDonald sensed the mood change and waited a few moments before continuing.

"I've got Ash McKinnon out near Belton right now, following up on a letter from a rancher out there, somebody who thinks they might be scouting her place out with a robbery in mind. I want you to go out there and join McKinnon for a few days, see what he's got." McDonald paused, suddenly remembering his last telegram from Stone.

"What did you find up there, up north? You said you wanted to look into something that maybe had to do with the horse stealing."

Stone nodded and explained about the small horse racing track built just off the Chisholm Trail in North Texas. The horse he'd seen might not have been one they were looking for, he said, but it looked like somebody had worked the brand over with a running iron. The guy riding that horse, he added, had left in a hurry when he saw a badge.

McDonald digested that information, leaning back in his chair and clasping his hands behind his head. "So," he said, "you think maybe they steal the horses and run them in races."

Stone nodded.

"Up north of here, along the Chisholm Trail?" he continued.

Stone shrugged, then nodded. "Some of them could be up there, being raced in the Nation, Kansas, along the Chisholm Trail. Maybe some of them are good enough that they ship 'em back east for breeding and racing. Maybe out to California too, for some racing or breeding." He lapsed into thoughtful silence for a moment. "Somebody would have to be pretty well organized. Stealing just the ones they want and shipping them out with nobody figuring out where they've gone. Somebody selling them, wherever that is they go."

McDonald turned his chair around and studied a map on the wall behind him. Stone could see several small circles drawn in red in a semicircle north and east of Austin. "That's where they've been stolen," he said over his shoulder. Stone got up and moved around the desk to get a closer look at the map. He could see circles in Lampasas, Belton, Salado, and another down to the south near San Antonio.

"I wonder where they're going?" McDonald said, half to himself. "We've been on the lookout for them all around Central Texas, some in East Texas, North Texas. That one you saw at the race up there, if it was one of them, is the first one we've run across." He turned back around and pulled two written sheets of paper from the desk.

"That's the descriptions of the horses taken," he said. "See if maybe the one you saw matched up with anything on that list."

Stone ran his finger down the first page, then turned the page over and started on the second one. Halfway down the page, his finger stopped. "This one could be it," he said. "Black gelding, rocking R brand, about fifteen and a half hands. That one had a circle R brand, but that could be done with a running iron, easy enough."

"That's probably one of 'em then," McDonald said thoughtfully, still staring at the map. "Where do they go? Railroad?"

Stone walked around the desk again. "The Missouri-Kansas-Texas Railroad runs right down through here," he said, tracing a line from Kansas, down through the Indian Territory, and through the Dallas-Ft. Worth area to Austin. "I guess they could put the horses on the railroad somewhere down here and ship them out." He stopped and gazed at the map. "I don't know how they would get them to the railroad with nobody seeing them, or how they would get the stolen horses on the train."

"Mmmph," McDonald said, turning back around. "Don't know how they get them sold, either, when they get where they're going. Who could get all that set up and keep it running?"

Stone shook his head and walked back around to stand beside his chair. He sensed this was just about over. McDonald never went in for any chit-chat.

McDonald stared absently at his desk for a minute, then raised his head, picked up a pen, and pulled over a stack of papers. "Okay, keep thinking about it," he said. "Go see what McKinnon's got going out there. Maitlin Ranch, a little north of Belton." He picked up the paper on the top of the stack, muttering to himself.

Stone half smiled and nodded, knowing he'd been dismissed. "Cap'n," he said, half under his breath. He put on his hat and let himself out.

CHAPTER EIGHT
ROBBED

When we were about a mile away from the ranch, I slowed my horse to a stop. Kyle pulled up alongside me. "If there's anybody watching the ranch now, which I'm guessing there are some folks doing just that," I began, "I don't want them to know that I'm here." I pointed down the road. "I'm going to ride past the house and come back in through the trees on the west side. That's where you said the boot prints are, right?"

Kyle nodded. "Yes, sir. In the trees, on a line with that corral where we put the horses. Maybe seventy-five or a hundred yards away."

"Good," I said. "That's where I'm headed. I'll take the last part of it on foot once I'm into the trees. You can tell Jessie to meet me over there and show me the tracks."

Kyle wasted no time, clucking to his horse and trotting on down the road. I waited several minutes, then followed, but moved on past the entrance to the house and pulled over into the woods to the west. I dismounted and wove in through the trees. When I reached a place even with the corral on my right, I tethered my horse and waited.

I heard footsteps coming after about ten minutes and watched carefully through the trees to be sure it was Jessie coming before I revealed myself. After I saw both Jessie and Kyle coming toward me, I stepped out from behind a tree and called to them. They altered course slightly and walked over. Jessie stopped beside a large oak about twenty yards away and motioned for me to come over.

I walked to her, and she pointed to the ground. There was a clear boot print, tiny for a man's print. I pulled Red's drawing from my pocket, squatted down, and compared the two. The print on the ground was exactly the size of the one in the drawing.

Jessie kneeled beside me and stared at the drawing. "Where's that from?" she asked. I handed her the drawing and let her compare it to the print on the ground.

"That was drawn by my friend Red just before he died," I said sadly. "He was the Ranger working the case before me. He was bushwhacked, shot from ambush, over west of here after a robbery near Lampasas."

She folded the drawing back up and handed it to me. "And this was in his pocket?"

I shook my head. "No, whoever shot him must have taken everything in his pockets. He left this with some clothes at the last place he stayed. Friends of mine, Mike and Sarah Stone. I'm hoping they will send Mike to join me on this case," I added as an afterthought.

I stood and continued to look at the boot print. Jessie stood and waited for me to say what I was thinking. "I want to stay out here until nighttime, then I'll be watching for them to come back. Tonight seems likely. Not much moon out these next few days. That'll help them." I looked around. "I'll move back from here a little, where there's good cover. Good chance he'll come back to get another look from this spot before he moves in."

Jessie moved a little closer. "Do you have a bedroll with you?"

I nodded.

"Anything else you might need? A couple blankets? It's been cold at night," she reminded me.

I said yes to the blankets. She turned around to Kyle. "Can you run in and get a couple blankets for Ash?"

Kyle trotted off to get the blankets, and Jessie turned back around. "Are you hungry? I can bring you some food in a bit."

I said yes to the food as well. There was a little smile on her face. "I didn't think you would turn down the food," she said.

Was it my imagination, or was she standing a little closer to me than she needed to? I hoped she was, but I doubted myself a bit on that one. I mean, what with bringing in the prisoner and hustling to get over here, I hadn't even had a shave in about three days. I figured my face must be getting a mite bristly.

I glanced at her and passed a hand over my face without thinking about it. Her laugh was a very pleasant sound. She patted my shoulder.

"Don't worry, you're a very welcome sight to me. I'm glad you're here." She turned to go. "And not just because I'm worried about the horses." She turned and walked back to the house. The door closed softly behind her.

Well, I thought to myself, if that don't beat all. I moved back farther into the trees, searching for a spot to pitch my bedroll and keep an eye out for whoever made that small boot print.

———

Holt squatted in front of a small fire, warming his hands against the January chill in the night air. They had retreated more than a mile away from the Maitlin Ranch, he estimated. Tonight was the night he wanted to make his move. He glanced over at Ike, who was whistling tunelessly while he whittled away on a stick. Holt rolled his eyes in irritation, then stood up and walked away from the flames. He never looked directly into the fire—he didn't want to be blinded if anyone walked up on the camp. Still, he needed a minute to let his vision adjust.

A small plan was forming in his mind. It was a little risky, but he wasn't a patient man, and the risk seemed worth it just to get things moving. He wanted more money, and he wanted it quickly. To do that, he needed to get some information. Maybe he could use the horses they would steal tonight to help him do that.

Maybe he could shortcut the handoff to Lance and the connection in Temple. Lance was probably still licking his wounds after getting his bank robbery money stolen. Maybe he would even be a little slow to get in touch with The Boss, whoever that was, after Holt didn't show up with the horses.

Meanwhile, he would have to break into the railroad agent's house in Temple to find out, if he could, who these horses were going to. What was the name of that town? Oh yes, it was Parsons, Kansas. If he could get a name to work with up there, maybe he could take these horses, hide them out while he broke into the agent's house in Temple, then get on the train with the horses. He would have to do that farther north, maybe Waco. And maybe he could make a deal for himself with whoever it was in Kansas to buy the horses from him. It was risky, but it could be a pretty sweet setup.

Satisfied with his idea, Holt turned and saw Ike asleep on the ground. The knife and whittled stick were lying beside him, and he was snoring. Holt walked over and kicked him, none too gently, on the leg. "Let's move," he snapped.

They saddled quickly and began riding toward the ranch. Holt went over his plan for the second time, wanting no misunderstandings or mistakes. "I'm coming in from the west. I'm going to look things over first from the woods over there. You will circle around to the north and get close to the corral, but not close enough to disturb the horses. You wait for me. When I come over and give the signal, you ride over and open the corral. I'm going to rope the stallion. You pick one or two mares, rope them, and we get out of there fast." Holt looked over but couldn't see Ike's face in the dark.

"Got it?" Holt snarled. He hadn't heard an answer and felt his temper rising.

"Sure, sure," came the answer. "I wait until I hear from you, I open the gate, we steal the horses." They rode the rest of the way in silence.

They parted near the ranch. Holt rode to the woods, going in on horseback only a few yards before dismounting and moving forward on foot. He found it much harder to find his way in the dark. He cursed softly to himself as he cast back and forth, trying to find his way back to his vantage point. He couldn't count on Ike to do as told if it took too much longer, he knew. After about ten minutes of searching, he finally spotted the tree he'd stood beside when he had been here earlier. He moved over to it.

He unslung his binoculars and checked the house. Everything seemed quiet. Satisfied, he turned to check Ike's position before moving out to give Ike the okay. Then he would move to the corral. His mouth dropped open, and he stifled another curse. Ike was at the corral gate, reaching down to open it. Holt stood stock still for a moment, trying to decide what to do. Then he heard a stick snap behind him. His hand dropped to his gun, and he drew as he turned.

———

It was a cloudy night with just a sliver of a moon showing. It couldn't have been a better night for horse rustling, unfortunately. I had grown up in the woods, and I was counting on those skills to help me tonight. They had the advantage—they knew what the plan was. All we could do was wait for them and hope to stop 'em. I glanced over toward the porch, knowing that Jessie was sitting up there with her Henry rifle. She would fire only toward the corral, if she fired at all. I would fire only away from the house. She wouldn't come into my field of fire and I wouldn't go into hers.

As the hours wore on, the coffee Jessie had brought me for dinner had long since worn off. I couldn't walk around keeping myself awake, for fear of making noise. I swung my arms back and forth, both to stay awake and to keep warm. From time to time I stopped and picked up the blankets and wrapped them around me.

Mostly I kept focused on that spot where somebody had left prints. I moved my eyes back and forth, not locking in, hoping to pick up movement from the corner of my eyes. Finally, I heard rustling noises. They were very faint at first, then I was sure they were coming in my direction. Finally, someone in black clothes passed by, moving slowly and only briefly illuminated by the faint glimmer of moonlight breaking through the cover of the trees overhead. I held still and watched as he took up a position under the oak tree.

He appeared to be half-turned toward me, but he seemed to be focused completely on the house. Then he turned a little more toward the corral. I eased out of the thicket where I'd been standing and started cat-footin' it in his direction. I had to crawl, but I knew if I didn't keep coming, he was bound to start toward the corral soon. I picked up the pace a little, testing each step before putting my weight down on my foot. It was so dark out here, I knew I needed a little luck.

When I was still a few steps away, he shifted and seemed to mutter something under his breath. I figured one more cat-step and then I'd rush... My foot came down on a stick and there was a loud snap. I came the rest of the way with a rush, my hand dropping to my pistol, but as he turned, I could see that his gun was already out. I swung a haymaker left hook and connected with a solid crunching noise to the right side of his jaw. He spun and fell backward, but I heard the roar of his gun just as I felt a crashing blow to my head. Then I blacked out.

———

Jessie was sitting on the back porch with her Henry rifle cradled across her lap. She was bundled up against the January cold, and it seemed like several hours had passed. She regretted that she hadn't taken Kyle up on his offer to take her place and watch for the second half of the night.

She shifted, then sat up straight, staring out past the corral. Someone was approaching slowly on horseback. She leaned forward and balanced the Henry on the railing, sighting down the barrel. The man seemed indecisive, sitting on his horse just beyond the gate at the far side of the corral. Then he reached down to open the gate. She aimed the rifle at his shoulder and slowly squeezed as the gate swung open.

Suddenly, there was a gunshot from the trees. Startled, she pulled the rifle just slightly and missed her target when she fired. The horses, startled by the shots, bolted from the corral. She swung the Henry back to the man on the horse and fired again. He was moving now, but she saw him arch his back suddenly. She was pretty sure she had grazed him. Then he grabbed his rope, shook out a loop, and dropped it over the neck of one of her mares as the horse galloped past. The man disappeared in the darkness before she could get off another shot.

Leaping down from the porch, she whirled as Kyle bolted out through the back door. "Get the horses!" she shouted, then turned toward the woods where Ash had taken up watch for the night. She ran toward the trees, then stopped, then began trotting quietly toward Ash's position again. She didn't dare call out his name. There was no telling who had fired that shot.

She reached the tree line south of where she had been that afternoon, working her way silently forward. After a few minutes, there was a thrashing noise off to her right. She lifted the Henry, then held her fire. More thrashing noises followed, then she faintly heard a horse galloping away. Feeling more confident that only Ash was out here now, she began calling his name softly. She heard no answer.

Jessie felt a little disoriented in trying to find the spot where Ash had set up camp in the near-total darkness. She decided to come back out of the trees and enter the way she had before—farther north. Coming from that entry point, she felt sure she could find it.

Bending down and holding low, just in case Ash heard noises and fired toward the corral. That was assuming he was in any shape to fire. She found her entry point and came back into the woods, moving west and looking for the large oak tree where she had seen the boot print. As she worked in closer, a low moan guided her for the last twenty yards. Now she could see someone lying on the ground and moving one arm back and forth in the leaves. She risked striking a match and saw that it was Ash, lying on his back with a nasty, bloody furrow across the side of his head.

Jessie kneeled down beside him, touching his arm and saying his name softly, but he didn't respond, and his eyes remained closed. She looked around, then struck another match and found her way to his camp. Jessie looked through his saddlebag and found his canteen, then picked up the lantern she had brought out earlier this evening. She bent down and picked up one of the old blankets she had brought him, then returned to where Ash was, tearing a small piece off the blanket as she walked.

She again kneeled and looked around. Feeling sure the attackers had left when the horses stampeded, she struck another match and lit the lantern. She turned his head gently to examine the head wound, then poured some water from the canteen onto the torn-out piece of the blanket. She washed his face and forehead gently. After about a minute or two, he stirred and his eyes opened.

He started to rise, then moaned and fell back on the blanket. "Easy, Ash," she whispered. "It's me. I think they have gone. Just lay there for a minute." He nodded his head slowly, even that small motion causing more pain, judging by the look on his face. After another minute or two, she resumed washing his face and hands with the moistened piece of blanket.

He stopped moaning after a bit, and Jesse stopped. His eyes were still open, and he seemed to track her movements when she changed positions. She took his wrist and felt the pulse. It was strong and steady.

She whirled when she heard a rustling noise behind her. She felt for the Henry with one hand, rising and turning. She sighed in relief when she saw the light of another lantern.

Iris came through the trees and kneeled beside them. "Is he okay?" she asked.

"I think so." Jesse turned and looked at Ash. "I think I need to pour a little water on that wound to clean it out," she said. "Do you think you can let me do that?"

Ash looked a bit puzzled, then raised a hand toward his head. He felt gently on his scalp, wincing when his fingers touched the furrow where the bullet had passed. He winced and put his hand back down. Reaching with his other hand, he grasped Jessie's free hand. "Go ahead," he breathed.

Jessie opened the canteen again and poured a little water on the wound, letting the bits of leaves and dirt wash away. Ash made no sound as she poured. When she had cleaned it as best she could, she stopped and put the canteen away. She looked at Iris.

"I'm afraid to move him right now," she said. "Can you stay with him and keep him as comfortable as you can? I'm going for the doctor."

"Yes," Iris whispered.

Jessie turned back to Ash and squeezed his hand, a little surprised to realize she was still holding it. "I'm going for the doctor, Ash," she said. She reached out to pick up his pistol, lying on the ground just a foot or two away. She placed it beside him.

"Here's your gun," she said. "Mom will be here, and she'll have my Henry. I'm riding into town for the doctor." She leaned down and gave him a kiss on the cheek. "I'll be right back."

CHAPTER NINE
RECOVERY AND REVENGE

I was only partly aware of the people crowding around me. I knew Iris had been talking to me, and I knew that Jessie had come back with an older guy I hadn't seen before. He set a black bag down next to me, and I figured out he was the town doctor. I stared up at him. But it was hard to see, as some sunlight was filtering through the trees. I squinted at him, feeling a little dizzy and clenching my teeth against the headache.

"How you feeling?" he asked. "I'm Doc Linden." He grabbed my jaw and turned my head to the side.

"I been better," I said, letting out a grunt when he turned my head. "Except I feel a little addle-headed."

"Mmmph," he said, fixing me with a stare. "More addle-headed than usual, I guess." He stared into my eyes for a while. "I expect you've got a rock-hard head and you're gonna be fine." He turned my head again. "How many do you see?"

I rolled my eyes at Jessie and stared at him. "I only see one of you, doc, and I'm thinkin' maybe it's one more than I wanna see."

He snorted again and waved his hand in the air. "Fingers, man. How many fingers do you see?"

"Oh." I looked at his hand. "Two. I see two."

He put his head down to my chest and listened for a while. "Sounds okay," he said. He sat back and looked me over. "Anything else you got complaints about?"

I lifted my left hand in the air. "I don't think it's broke," I said, "but maybe you can look it over." He took my hand and looked at it. It was bruised up and swollen some. "What did you run into with this?" he asked.

I grinned for the first time in a while. "I ran that into a horse rustler's jaw," I said with satisfaction. "Punched him good, right in the jaw. Right before he shot me in the head, I mean."

Doc Linden chuckled a little and looked at my hand. He told me to wiggle my fingers and wave my hand up and down. Everything seemed to work.

"Yeah, he's okay," he announced. "Help me get him up." He stooped down to give me a hand, but I wasn't a whole lot of help. He waved at Jessie and Iris to give him a hand. Between the three of them, they got me up, and we took a slow walk to the house.

We reached the front room, and the doc looked at Jessie. "Where do you want this big lug? He weighs a ton," he added.

Jessie steered us toward her bedroom. "On my bed," she said.

The doc's eyebrows went up, and I guess mine did too.

"You don't wanna put me in there," I said. "I might break that bed or something." I started to point at the couch in the front room.

Jessie laid two fingers across my lips. "Ash," she said, "this is my house, and you got hurt stopping horse rustlers from stealing my stock. You just go where I say. You'll get the best sleep in the bed. I'll sleep on the couch."

The doctor chortled at that one. "I guess she told you," he said.

They laid me on the bed, and I gotta admit, it felt pretty good. Until the doc started washing off the wound, that is. I clenched my teeth again and tried not to whimper out loud. After that, he wrapped a big bandage around my head, kinda made me look like one of those mummies in Egypt.

Finally, he finished. He waggled a finger at me. "Three days of rest," he said. "No running around punching people on the jaw. Unless, of course, they're trying to shoot your fool head off again."

Jessie saw him out the front door and came back to stand by the bed.

"I think I'm his favorite," I told her.

She laughed pretty hard. Then she sat down beside me on the bed. "He's a little grumpy, I know, but he's been a good doctor for us. I actually think he likes you. Besides, who knows, maybe you can be somebody else's favorite."

I wasn't sure what she meant, but I knew what I hoped she meant. I let it go, though, on account of my addle-headed condition. I had to allow for that. I started to talk, but it seemed like my eyelids just kept rolling down on me. I dropped off to sleep before I knew it.

Holt rode west, clinging to the saddle horn with one hand, reins in the same hand. His other hand was holding his jaw. It jarred him and ached savagely each time his horse's hooves hit the ground. He had the vague impression he had shot a man with a badge on his chest as he went down. He remembered the roar of his gun, but he had blacked out immediately afterward.

When he had come to, he had heard a woman's voice

calling someone's name. He assumed it was the name of the man he had shot. He gathered himself together, stumbled to his horse, and got out of there. He had a pre-arranged meeting place with Ike, and he just hoped to get there before he passed out again.

When he came close to passing out, Holt reined in the horse, dismounted, and put his head between his knees. He wondered if he had killed the man he'd shot. If not, he wanted to find him someday and finish the job. He touched his jaw gingerly and wondered if it was broken. Finally, he remounted and pushed on.

As the sun came up behind him, Holt recognized both their meeting place and the figure of Ike, who was dismounted in a small circle of trees. He was squatting in front of a small fire, warming his hands. When he turned slightly, Holt could see a bloody streak across his back. Ike's jacket and shirt were torn. Holt found a twisted satisfaction in knowing that Ike had been injured too. Until that moment, Holt had been torn between killing Ike for opening the gate too soon back there, or letting him live because he still needed him.

Holt dismounted and walked up to Ike with his hand balled up into a fist. He'd intended to hit Ike, but two things stopped him. One, Ike was bigger, and two, if Ike hit him back on the jaw, the pain would be excruciating. Holt settled for raking him over the coals for about fifteen minutes. Ike accepted the tongue-lashing quietly, but Holt thought he looked absolutely bored.

Finally, Holt's jaw couldn't take any more screaming and he lapsed into silence. He walked over to look at what Ike had brought away from the corral. There was a mare that looked pretty valuable and a colt that had apparently followed his mother after Ike lassoed her. Somewhat mollified, Holt went back and stood with his back to the fire. The wound across Ike's back was clearly the result of being grazed by a bullet. Holt didn't ask. He splashed water from his canteen onto a rag and bathed his jaw gently.

As the morning wore on, he could see that he was having trouble making himself understood when he talked to Ike. He knew the jaw must still be swelling and probably turning colors by now. He decided he would have to change plans and take a few days here to recover.

Holt turned to Ike, speaking slowly in order to make himself understood. "Go back to Longhorn," he said, irritated that Ike kept looking at his jaw while he talked. "Wait a few days, then go back to that ranch with Slade and steal the stallion. Take it back to Longhorn and wait for me there." He waved a hand in anger when Ike objected. "Do it," he hissed. "Leave these horses with me. Go now."

He watched as Ike shrugged, gathered up his horse's reins, and swung aboard. He couldn't choke back a moan of pain as the movement pulled on the bullet wound running across his back. Holt stood, arms folded, and watched him ride away. Then he touched his jaw again, gently. He would stay right here for a couple days, then find a place to hide the horses near Temple while he broke into the station agent's house. Maybe then he could figure a way to take these horses north himself and sell them.

Holt opened his saddlebag and began looking for something he could eat. He cursed softly to himself, wondering how long it would be before he could chew again. Whoever that was, wearing the badge back there, Holt promised himself, would pay for this.

———

Three days later—his jaw feeling a little better, but his mood not improved at all—Holt left his hiding place. The stolen horses were roped and trailing along behind him. He had used a running iron to alter the brands somewhat. He had to admit that he wasn't all that skilled with the iron, but he hoped he had changed the brands enough to cover up the theft. He suspected that his buyers at the other end of this, wherever that was, didn't really care that much about brands.

Holt struck a course to the north and east, angling back toward Temple. He needed to break into the railroad agent's house and find some information and how to sell these horses. What was the name again? He puzzled over that one in his head for a few miles, then remembered: Pendleton. He would take his time getting there. That would give a few more days for his handiwork with the running iron to heal over on the horse's hindquarters, and it would give a little time for any pursuit from the horse rustling to settle down.

He decided his jaw had healed enough to do a little more chewing than he'd been doing, so he pulled the horses off into a stand of post oak trees and picketed them, then settled down with his rifle to wait for the whitetail deer to start moving at sundown. He had seen them everywhere the last couple of nights. He didn't have long to wait, dropping a small buck with the first shot. He field-dressed the animal, taking just a few choice cuts, which he grilled over a small fire.

By morning, he was ready to move the horses back east. He didn't want to board the train at Temple, but he needed to move in that direction, north and east, then hide the animals while he went to see what he could find at Pendleton's house. He spent the entire day drifting east. When he came to the railroad tracks for the Missouri-Kansas-Texas railroad, he pulled back into the trees and followed alongside the tracks. By mid-morning the next day, he had built a makeshift corral in a small clearing in a thick stand of post oak and cedar trees. He stood back from the corral to evaluate his work. It wouldn't win any prizes, but he decided it would hold the horses for a couple days and they should be able to graze sufficiently in the area within the corral.

Holt waited until it was nearly sundown before proceeding into Temple. His plan was to wait near the railroad station and, if possible, follow Pendleton home from a distance. If it looked like Pendleton lived alone, he would break into the house or boardinghouse room the next day after Pendleton went to work. If there was a wife at home during the day, he would have to think of something else.

Before leaving for the trip into town, Holt knew he needed to disguise himself as best he could. He had been at the train station, hanging around and asking questions, just a week before. He ran a hand over his beard, then reluctantly poured some water into a pan he used for boiling water and cooking, then pulled the knife from his belt. Twenty minutes later, after several nicks and much cursing, he ran his hand back over his face. It felt strange to his touch, but he knew he would be hard to recognize without his usual heavy beard.

Riding into town, he stopped first at the telegraph office and sent a message to his normal contact, Lance, to tell him that the robbery at the Maitlin Ranch had failed. He gave no details, but promised he could rustle the horses within the next week. He sent off the message, confident he had bought himself a little time. He hoped that within a week or two, he would have no further need for Lance.

Holt crossed the street and moved down to a saloon. He took a seat near a window, giving him a view of the street. The railroad office was just a few blocks away, and he hoped that Pendleton would come in this direction when he left work. Most of the houses and boarding houses seemed to be on this side of town. Holt remembered Lance talking to a burly man with a thick mustache when he'd brought the horses from the last robbery. He felt pretty safe in assuming that man was Pendleton, and he would be able to recognize him if he came in this direction.

Half an hour later, his hunch proved correct. The man with the luxurious black mustache came down the street toward him. Holt had a moment of panic when he saw that Pendleton was coming into the saloon, but he reminded himself that the man probably hadn't really seen him when he was in town before, and if he had, Holt had shaved his beard since then. He pulled his hat down a little lower and nursed another beer as Pendleton sidled up to the bar. He threw down three whiskeys in rapid succession, then walked out, seemingly none the worse for the house whiskey.

Holt threw a couple coins on the table and left just a couple minutes later. The bulky form of Pendleton was still easy to follow from a distance. Holt's luck held when Pendleton entered a shack at the edge of town a few minutes later, slamming the door shut behind him. Holt slowed, then walked past the shack, glancing casually sideways as he did so. He was willing to bet no woman lived there. The place appeared to be just barely standing up. There were no flowers planted around the house anywhere, and Holt had the feeling he could pull one board loose just about any place he chose, and the whole shack would collapse. Whatever Pendleton was making from this horse rustling business, Holt concluded, it wasn't going into this place.

Holt turned and walked back past the house, headed for a boardinghouse he had passed on the way. He would be back in the morning to see what he could find in that shack.

————

Holt took his time over breakfast at the café the next morning. He finished his coffee leisurely and took a trip to the railroad office, sticking his head in the door just long enough to see that Pendleton was at work. He turned and meandered down the road to the shack where Pendleton had gone last night. He approached the door, looking slowly in both directions. There was no one in sight. He knocked loudly on the door and wasn't surprised when nobody answered. He tried the handle and found it open, so he went inside after glancing around one more time.

A small desk in the corner got his attention, but after shuffling through the papers for about five minutes, he found nothing of interest. He wondered if there might be a loose board in the floor with a hiding place under the house. He began tapping the boards in various places, without result. He stopped and glanced at the bed. It was simply a mattress resting on the floor, but on a hunch, he went over and lifted the edge of the mattress. He saw an envelope underneath and pulled it out.

There were no windows inside, and he didn't want to light the lantern. He moved instead to the back door of the shack and let himself out. Standing on what passed for a back porch, he reached inside and pulled out a single piece of paper. It read: *Sam Starr. General delivery, Fort Smith, Arkansas.* Beneath that, he saw several lines of notes. They appeared to refer to horses sent through on the railroad at various dates in the past. Holt smiled to himself and pushed the paper back into the envelope. He went back inside, tossed the envelope back under the mattress, and left by the back door, circling the house and proceeding back to the saloon for a premature celebration.

The next piece of the puzzle had fallen into place nicely, he reflected. Sam and Belle Starr were known to run an organization in the Nation that included fencing stolen horses, among other things. He felt certain he knew now where the horses were going.

———

Pendleton was a careful man by nature. He was saving his money from this rustling operation being run by a couple of old buddies from his childhood. After he had enough money, he planned to move to San Francisco and live in style. Meanwhile, he mumbled to himself for the hundredth time about the place he was living in as he opened the front door. He stopped immediately and looked around. Somebody had gone through the papers on the desk, he was sure. He looked quickly at the mattress on the floor in the corner. They had moved it. He stepped over and lifted it, reassuring himself that the envelope and paper inside were still there.

Pendleton sat in a chair in the corner for a few minutes, thinking things over. Something just didn't feel right here. And, he reminded himself, he was a careful man. He picked up his hat, put it back on, and walked down to the telegraph office.

———

Sheriff Hutchins escorted the man who called himself Wes out the front door of the jail in Belton. Three days had passed since Ranger McKinnon had brought the man in, and he couldn't hold Wes any longer. He had contacted other sheriffs in the area, and no one knew anything about the man. There were no posters out on him. Hutchins strongly suspected Wes was up to no good, but he couldn't prove a thing.

He walked the prisoner out to the boardwalk in front of the jail, shook the bullets out of his gun, then handed it to him. Hutchins put the bullets in his pocket, then handed Wes his gun belt.

"Ride out of town," he said shortly. "I don't want to see you around here no more." He turned, then turned back. "Oh, and Wes," he said, "don't even think about going back around the Maitlin Ranch." He turned on his heel and went back in the jail.

————

Wes stood on the porch and watched Hutchins disappear inside the jail. He then walked over, mounted his horse, and rode slowly north toward the Maitlin Ranch. He checked over his shoulder once in a while, but Hutchins wasn't following. Wes vowed he would settle that score he had with the big Ranger.

CHAPTER TEN
GANG FROM SCYENE

I was lounging at the table after breakfast, and I had to admit, I was enjoying it. Actually, I couldn't remember ever having lounged much, and I wasn't even sure I was doing it right. My family back in Tennessee was dirt-poor, and I had pretty much had to earn my keep, even when I was growing up. I ran the trap lines, hunted for food, and had to take care of the garden. I was lucky I'd gotten as much schooling as I had.

I looked up to find Jessie's eyes on me, a little smile on her face. She walked over and refilled my coffee cup. "What are you thinking about?" she asked.

I hemmed and hawed for a while, then finally got around to answering what she asked. "Well," I said, "I've never been taken care of like this. I've got my big feet stowed away under your table all the time, and I...well, I feel like I should be doing something around here."

She sat down in the chair next to me and patted my arm. "Don't worry," she said. "The doctor said just one more day to do nothing but rest. He'll be back out tomorrow to look at you, and if he says it's okay, I'll have some light work you can do for a while."

I nodded. "Whatever the doc says," I said a little doubtfully. "As long as he doesn't talk about somebody shootin' my fool head off again..."

Jessie laughed and reached over to help me to my feet. "Would you like to go out to the back porch?" she asked. "You can sit out there in the sun. It's a pretty nice day. I can come and join you after I've done a few chores."

I agreed, and she walked me outside. As I was sitting down, I had a little dizzy spell and sat down a little faster than I'd planned on. Jessie reached out to steady me, concern on her face.

"Ash? You okay?"

I nodded. "I'm okay. I was just dizzy for a bit when I leaned over. Okay now."

Jessie lingered over me for a moment. "You're sure?" I held onto her hand for just a second.

"I'm sure," I said. She looked at me for a moment, then leaned in and kissed me on the lips. I reached out and pulled her back in for another one, then she leaned back and we both smiled.

"I took advantage of you, didn't I?" she asked.

"Yep," I said. "I think you did. Took advantage of a poor, sick country boy, and I hope you make a reg'lar thing of it."

She laughed and leaned back. "That country boy accent of yours just comes and goes, doesn't it?"

Well, she had me there. She was on to me. I smiled a little sheepishly and waited while she went and got my gun belt. She brought it out and left it lying across my lap. Then she went back into the house. I leaned back in the chair and couldn't stop smiling.

The morning sun made me drowsy, and I found that I could tilt back in my chair and pull my hat down over my forehead to make myself comfortable. After a while, my eyelids became heavy, and I drifted off in the chair.

Sometime later, a noise to my right brought me half-awake. I pushed my hat back and sat up. At the same time, I heard Jessie's brother Kyle shout my name as he came out of the barn. I registered the sound of his voice at the same time I saw someone stepping around the corner of the house, gun out.

I saw the man on my right stop and half-turn toward the barn when he heard my name shouted. The drowsiness fell away from me completely as I sat up and yanked my Colt.45 from the holster. He turned back toward me, and our two shots sounded like one as we both fired at the same time. I heard his bullet whine past me and bury itself into the side of the house. My shot spun him around and he fell to his knees.

I didn't trust myself to stand, so I leaned forward, put both hands on the handle of the Colt, and squeezed off two more shots as he tried to turn and bring his gun to bear. Both shots found their mark, and he pitched over backward and lay still in the grass.

I heard Jessie's shout from inside the house and heard her footsteps running toward the back door.

"Hold it!" I shouted, keeping the gun trained on the form in the grass. When he didn't move after several seconds, I lowered the Colt. "Okay," I said, "you can come out now."

Jessie and Iris both came from the house, and I could see Kyle moving in cautiously from the barn.

"Help me up," I told Jessie, and she helped me get to my feet. I trained the gun on the man lying in the grass as she helped me slowly step down off the porch and walk over to him. I kneeled and felt his wrist. When I was certain he was dead, I rolled him over onto his back. It was Wes, the man I had arrested a few days ago.

I heard a sharp intake of breath from Jessie, and I turned and looked up at her.

"Is this the man who came here looking for work?" I asked.

She nodded her head, then looked away from the dead body.

"Do you think he came here to get even with me for not hiring him?" she asked.

I rose slowly to my feet, and she stepped over and slid an arm around me to steady me.

"No," I said. "I think it's more likely he came here to get even with me for arresting him and putting him in jail over in Belton."

Just then, I heard a voice shout, "Hello! Ash?"

A man moved out slowly from the other corner of the house. I raised my gun instinctively, then relaxed when I realized I knew that voice very well.

"Come on around, Mike," I called out.

Mike Stone came around the corner and took in the scene of the dead man in the grass, me wobbling on my feet with my gun pointed at him, and the woman standing at my side, holding me up. His face broke into a grin.

"Well, Ash, I've always known you to be a little irritable, but you seem worse than usual today. And that's with a beautiful lady putting her arm around you, too." He made a reproachful noise that sounded like "ttsskkk" and shook his head.

Jessie broke into a laugh and kept her arm right where it was.

I grinned and lowered my gun. "Mike Stone," I said. "I woulda said you're just jealous, but I know better. You showed up just in time. We could use a little help around here right now."

———

Milo Wills leaned back in his chair and stared out his office window on Houston Street in San Antonio, wondering how many of these people had voted for him in the last election. Whether any of these people had voted for him, there were enough people in the state who had voted for him to make him the newest Texas State Senator. He wasn't actually sure if he would have won fair and square without the votes he'd paid his *fixer* to get for him, but that really didn't matter. He'd won.

The sign out front said *Milo Wills, Attorney*, and in fact, it was his law office. He'd hired a kid named Barrett to do most of the legal work for him. He divided his time between trips to Austin and some work he did as a senator with another enterprise he was running that was far more profitable than the law office or the pay for being a senator. As a matter of fact, that third enterprise made almost all of his money for him. The other two just gave him a good public image and fed his ego.

Wills got up and crossed the floor to close his office door. He returned to his desk and pulled out a telegram he'd received from one of only two people in this world he'd chosen to trust. Well, he had to admit, there were three if he counted his *fixer*, a man named Shaw. It wasn't that Shaw was honest or loyal, but Wills could always count on him to do what he was told to do if the money was right. He got things done, and he kept his mouth shut —that's what really mattered.

Wills returned to the telegram from his boyhood friend, Pendleton. Pendleton was an important part of that third business that made him a lot of money, but the news on that front wasn't good today. Wills scanned the telegram again:

House here was broken into. Stop.
Believe intruder might have found info on Belle S. Stop.

Lance or the guy he hired might have gone into business for themselves. No new merchandise coming. Stop.

Wills tore the telegram into shreds and dropped it into a trash basket. He folded his hands behind his head and stared out the window again. He had set this up so that only three people knew he was running this operation. One was the guy he called his fixer, Shaw. The two of them had run a little cattle rustling operation for a while, stealing cows in South Texas and running them up the trail to Kansas. When he'd made enough money, he got respectable. Shaw would never be respectable, but he was useful, so Wills had brought him along.

The other two people were a man and a woman he had known since his childhood days in Scyene, Texas. Scyene, near Dallas, had been a pretty busy little town back in those days. The railroad had caused the town to boom for a while, but then folks in Scyene had refused to build a depot for the train, so now the railroad stopped in a place called Mesquite, and the town of Scyene was drying up. Wills suspected it would be gobbled up by another city one of these days.

While he was living there, though, Wills had made two friends who were very useful to him now. One was Pendleton, who had lived next door. When Wills had found out that Pendleton had gotten a job shipping things on the railroad, it hadn't been hard to persuade him to send a few stolen horses up the line to Kansas. Pendleton was greedy, but not too ambitious. Greed made a man do some crazy things sometimes, so Wills kept an eye on him. So far, he still trusted Pendleton.

The other friend from Scyene was a girl named Myra Maybelle Shirley. Folks called her May Shirley. May was friends with the Younger family, having grown up with them in Missouri, but Wills had steered clear of the

Youngers, and now he was glad he had. Too many head-
lines in the newspaper. Wills like things to be quiet and
profitable.

May Shirley had married a man named Reed, and they
had moved around, mostly staying ahead of the law, from
what he'd heard. Reed had gotten himself killed in a
stagecoach robbery a few years later. There was a story
that May had then married one of the Youngers for a few
weeks, but he didn't really believe that story. Then, a few
years ago, May married a man named Sam Starr and
moved to the Territory. Nowadays, she was known as
Belle Starr, and they had themselves an operation in the
northeast corner of the Territory, moving stolen horses
and doing some bootlegging, mainly. It was perfect for
Wills.

It had been a pretty sweet operation, so far. Only
Pendleton and the Starrs knew who they were dealing
with. Wills sent messages out to Wes, the scout, then to
Holt and his boys, the horse thieves. The horses got
passed along through somebody named Lance to Pendleton, who shipped them to Parsons, Kansas. The Starrs sent
the money for the horses directly to him, and he
distributed it. He was running the whole show while
staying removed from it.

Until now. A scowl returned to his face and his
stomach rumbled as he rummaged around in a desk
drawer for some whiskey. All of this had a bad feel to it.
First, the scout, Wes, hadn't reported in for more than a
week. Then Wills had gotten word that the next expected
robbery hadn't happened. He had thought there would be
a few more horses headed north right now. And, to top it
off, somebody had connected Pendleton with the Starrs
and might be looking to move in on the operation.

He spilled the whiskey slightly as he poured a second
glass and cursed softly to himself as he wiped off the desk

with his hand and downed the drink. He had to decide what to do about this, and he probably needed to do it soon. He wasn't yet prepared to roll up the entire operation and move on to something else, but it sounded like he needed to make some changes. The first thing would be to make sure that nobody was taking the horses directly to Parsons, Kansas, and selling them to the Starrs. He grabbed a piece of paper and began composing a telegram to Belle:

> Belle:
> I may have an employee going into business for himself. Stop.
> Name is Holt. Stop.
> If he contacts you about buying horses, I want him to get a
> very unfriendly reception. Stop.
> M

He set the telegram message aside and leaned back in the chair again. He would get Shaw to send that in a few minutes. There was something else still bothering him, but he couldn't quite put his finger on it. He reviewed in his mind how he had set up this operation. He sent messages directly to Wes, the scout, Holt, the horse thief, Pendleton, and Belle Starr. Only Pendleton and Starr knew who he was and could send him messages. He scowled into his whiskey glass and reached for a refill. Then he stopped with the whiskey bottle in midair.

He had no communication whatsoever with Lance, the go-between for Pendleton and Holt. Pendleton had no connection with Holt directly. So, he wondered, how did Holt know to break into Pendleton's house? Or were Lance and Holt working together, and it was Lance who had broken into Pendleton's house? He slammed the whiskey bottle down on the desk and rose to his feet.

"Shaw!!!" His voice echoed in the office, which he had never bothered to furnish other than with the desk, desk chair, and one well-used side chair.

Shaw, who usually lounged on a bench outside the office, came through the door. He had his usual disheveled look, and he wiped his mouth with a greasy sleeve from his buckskin jacket as he entered. His appearance slightly repulsed Wills, as usual, but he knew how, uh...effective Shaw was at what he did. The man had no scruples. He got things done, and he kept his mouth shut. A man like that was hard to find.

Wills picked up the telegram message and waved it impatiently in the air. "Take this down to the telegraph office and send it to Fort Smith—the usual place."

Shaw grabbed the message and turned toward the door, but Wills stopped him.

"Wait a minute, there's more. Go to Temple and find Pendleton. Tell him you want to know where to find Lance. Tell him you're going to watch Lance and make sure he isn't going into business for himself. Tell him if that's happening, you're going to straighten out Lance, and I'm not going to be happy."

Shaw nodded and moved to the door, then waited to see if Wills had anything else to say, triggering a fresh bout of temper.

"Get going!" Wills shouted. He threw two gold pieces in Shaw's direction. "Make sure the telegraph operator keeps his mouth shut."

Shaw nodded and left, glad to escape Will's foul temper. It was a good thing, he thought, that the pay was so good.

———

Ike rode into the Longhorn Cave hideout, still grimacing from time to time from the pain caused by the furrow across his back. He would carry that scar for the rest of his life to remind him of the rustling job at that ranch near Belton. He dismounted and tethered his horse, then walked into the cave. Slade could hear him coming but didn't bother to get up. He kept one hand on his pistol and watched until he could see it was only Ike coming in. He leaned back against the cave wall, noting the rip across the back of Ike's jacket and the dried blood beneath it.

Slade watched as Ike rummaged around in his blankets until he found the flask he was looking for. "Didya get any horses?" Slade asked finally.

Ike cursed at length and took a very long pull from the flask. "Two," he said sullenly. "A mare and her colt. Didn't get the stallion we was after. Holt said we have to go back for him."

Slade digested that news for a while and watched as Ike finished the flask. "Well," he said finally, "we're going back for the stallion?"

Ike laid down carefully on his stomach and stretched out on the blankets. He didn't bother to give Ike an answer. There was time to think about that tomorrow. Slade stared at him and shrugged when he realized he wasn't going to get an answer to his question. He stretched out on his bedroll and soon was snoring even more loudly than Ike.

CHAPTER ELEVEN
BELLE STARR

W e sat around the kitchen table, enjoying the heat from the stove in the kitchen. Iris was baking, even though we'd all just had as much food as anybody could possibly put down for dinner. That included me, and that was saying something. Kyle moved out to the porch to keep watch. The stallion and remaining best mares and colts were still in the corral behind the house, and none of us felt sure there wouldn't be another try at rustling the stock we still had out there.

Stone told us about his meeting with McDonald, and we filled him in on the robbery here just a couple days ago, what I had learned about the scout Wes, and how he had tried to hire on at ranches before the robberies happened. We agreed that he probably hadn't been involved in the actual thefts. He seemed to have been sending information to somebody. Then he moved on before the rustlers moved in. We had been hoping there would be something in his pockets or in a saddlebag telling us who he was working with, but we'd been disappointed there. We found nothing at all to help us.

When we were done, he told us about the racetrack

just off the Chisholm Trail up north and how he had seen a horse that might have been one of the rustled animals. He told us he thought the horses were being moved out of state on the railroad, where they were maybe being sold as racehorses or breeding stock.

Stone got up and walked over to the burlap bag he always carried with him when he was out traveling. He rummaged around in it for a bit, then came back with a map which he spread out on the table. I leaned in to take a look. It was a map of the central part of Texas. I could see Austin in the middle and Dallas and Ft. Worth on the north side. It ran down a little below San Antonio at the bottom. Stone asked Jessie for a pencil and she went to get him one.

When she came back with the pencil, Stone began drawing circles on the map and explained that McDonald had a map like this back in his office. The circles, he said, were where he knew there had been horses stolen— horses like the ones taken from Jessie's ranch, not just random rustling of cowboy ponies. I leaned in and saw that he had drawn circles around Lampasas, Belton, Salado, and a place just a little north of San Antonio.

Jessie moved a lantern to the table as darkness fell outside. "Were the robberies one after the other, moving up or down this half-circle?" she asked hopefully.

Stone shook his head slowly. "Nope," he said. "They're too smart for that, I guess. They've hopped from north to south and back again. This probably can't tell us where they're going to strike next. Here's what I'm hoping." He took the pencil and drew a big circle, using the robberies on the map as a guideline. When he had finished, there was a circle around the middle of Texas, with Austin roughly in the middle.

"What I'm hoping," he continued, "is that this gang is operating somewhere near the middle of the circle. Not exactly the middle, I'm sure, maybe a little north or a little south, but maybe they're coming from a hideout somewhere in the middle, like spokes on a wagon wheel. They steal the horses, hide them somewhere for a while, alter the brands maybe, then load them on a rail car and sell 'em somewhere up north. Out of Texas, probably."

I stared at the map, nodding my head slowly. "That could be," I agreed, "but that circle covers a whole lot of ground. How would you suggest we start lookin' for 'em? I wasn't in any shape to trail them after they took the mare and her colt from here. Does anybody have an idea which direction they head after they rustle the horses?"

Stone shrugged in frustration. "Nobody's got a good idea," he admitted. "Somewhere toward the middle of that circle is probably fair to say." He drummed his fingers on the table for a minute, then looked up at me.

"You're an excellent tracker, Ash. How would you hide tracks and keep from leaving a trail? Just in general, I mean."

I sat back in the chair, distracted for a minute by the apple pie I saw Iris lifting out of the oven. Jessie followed my gaze, laughed, and got up to get me a piece of it. Stone just rolled his eyes and waited for me to answer his question.

"Water," I mumbled, half to myself. "Water is good for covering tracks. You wait and move them after it rains, or you splash through water in streams and rivers." I looked back at the map. "There's a lot of rivers and streams there. I don't know where I would start."

Stone nodded, then drew a line north and south on the map. "This is the rail line for the Missouri, Kansas, and Texas Railroad," he said. "Most folks call it the KATY. Don't get too far away from the KATY rails. They still have to move the horses out of here and sell them."

Stone got up and moved back to the window, staring

at the horses in the corral in the fading light. "I think I want to start checking at the railroad stations around here," he said over his shoulder. "I'm going to start here with the closest stop in Temple and work my way north. I'm going to see if I can get any clues about how the horses are loaded and moved and where they might be going."

He turned around and came back to the table. "How long before you're up and around, Ash? Any idea?"

I glanced over at Jessie and Iris. "I'll know more tomorrow," I said. "The doc is supposed to come back and take another look at me tomorrow." I paused. "You want me to try to figure where the horses are held until they go to the railroad? Maybe I can get working on that in a few days. Maybe there are a couple tracks still out there after they hit this place."

"That's what I'm hoping," Stone said. He stared at my empty plate. "I could have sworn there was a piece of pie on that plate," he mumbled. He looked at Iris. "You're never going to get those enormous feet out from under your table, you know."

Iris dished up a piece of pie for Mike and pulled my plate over to give me another piece. I protested just enough to sound polite. Iris ignored me and loaded me up with seconds, just like I'd planned it.

"That's just fine, Mr. Stone," she said. "We enjoy having your friend at this table."

———

Holt halted near the edge of the town of Waco. It was dusk. There were few horses entering town and, for that matter, few on the streets of Waco. He was getting very tired of building makeshift corrals to hide the mare and colt while he tried to make arrangements for getting them out of Texas. He hesitated, then thought how much he would like to put the horses into a stable and head on down to a pub. He dismounted and checked the altered brands. They seemed to be pretty well healed over. He abruptly re-mounted and proceeded into town. He paused when he saw a livery stable.

There was an old man sweeping up near the stalls, paying no attention to Holt. Making his decision, Holt led the mare and colt into the stables. The old man looked up, chewing on a piece of straw, waiting for Holt to say something. He glanced at the horses with no expression on his face.

Holt swept a hand, including all three horses in his gesture. "How much for all three for one night?" he demanded.

The old man removed the straw from his mouth, barely glanced at the horses, and said, "One dollar."

Holt started to protest the price, which seemed a little high, then decided he didn't want to say or do anything that might cause the old man to remember him. He simply shrugged, dug a coin out of his pocket, and handed over the reins.

Moving out of the livery stable, he began walking the several blocks toward the train station. He paid for his ticket first and sized up the situation while he did so. He hoped to slip the stolen horses onto the train without paying the agent. He stepped up to the booth and bought a ticket for himself to Parsons, Kansas, on the morning train.

Moving into the train yard, Holt searched the area, his eyes resting on a short, seedy-looking man leading a horse away from one of the train cars. Holt approached the man, then stepped in front of him, tossing two silver dollars in the air and catching them as the man stopped and stared at him.

"I've got three horses I want to put on the train tomorrow morning," Holt said casually. The man watched the silver coins for a moment, then nodded toward the ticket window.

"You kin buy passage for yer horses over there," he announced, watching Holt carefully, then looking back at the silver dollars.

"I don't really want to pay over there," Holt said smoothly. "I was hoping maybe you could help me. These silver dollars are getting a little heavy in my pocket."

The man's face broke into a gap-toothed smile very briefly, then he looked around. "If'n you was to have those horses here at about eight o'clock in the morning, I could prob'ly hep you with that," he muttered in an undertone.

Holt passed him the two dollars. "We understand each other," he said. "I'll have them here in the morning."

———

Holt was up early and brought the mare and her colt to the train yard. He handed off the two stolen horses, along with his own horse, and watched as the handler loaded them onto a railroad car. Satisfied, he went to the telegraph office. He had a message to send before he was ready to board the train himself.

Holt took his time over the message he wanted to send to Sam Starr, or Belle Starr. He wasn't sure exactly who he was dealing with, but it didn't matter. He just needed to establish a way to sell horses in the Territory. He had decided he didn't want to try to take over any business that The Boss, whoever that was, had going on here. He knew that might be pretty dangerous. He would just try to set up a connection for himself, selling directly.

After several messages that he tore up, Holt finally decided on a direct approach:

Arriving in Parsons, Kansas, on Tuesday the 3rd. Stop.
Will have two fine horses. Good for racing. Stop.
Arabian bloodlines. Stop.
Meet me at the train if interested. Stop.
Ask for Holt. Stop.

He read the message over several times, then had it sent out. Satisfied, he boarded the train and looked out the window as they passed through the central part of Texas. In a couple of days, he hoped he would have found someone to fence all the horses he could steal. He tipped his hat down over his eyes, leaned back, and drifted off to sleep.

————

Sam Starr looked down at the two telegrams in his hand. They had come together, delivered from Ft. Smith to the saloon operated by the Starrs. They had opened the saloon near the ranch they called Younger's Bend in the Territory. A fight broke out in the saloon and he paused, watching to make sure nothing else was going to get broken. They were still cleaning up from the last fight in here. When he saw one fighter go down and pass out on the floor, he returned his attention to the telegrams.

He frowned when he saw that the first had come from Belle's old friend from Texas. She always insisted on dealing with him personally. The frown deepened when he saw the second message. Things seemed to be getting complicated, and Sam liked things to be simple. He saw Belle watching him from across the saloon. She walked over, eyebrows raised, and looked at the messages in his hand. He handed them over and waited.

Belle read them, then read them again. She folded up both messages and tucked them into a pocket. "Send

Victorio to Parsons," she said simply. "Have him take care of this." She stopped and turned before walking away. "Have him bring the horses here."

When she had turned and left the saloon, Sam Starr allowed the scowl to deepen across his face. He passed a hand across his forehead. Parsons, Kansas, was a long way to go in the first place. The railroad was building a station in Eufaula now, so maybe that would make things easier if they had to keep dealing with this guy Wills. He sighed and looked around the bar for Victorio.

When he found Victorio leaning on the bar, an empty glass in front of him, Starr motioned to him, then turned and went outside. He waited for Victorio to catch up to him. Starr handed him a few coins, then leaned forward to whisper. "Go to Parsons," he said. "There will be a man on Tuesday's train named Holt who will want to sell us two horses. Kill Holt and take the horses. Bring them here."

Starr didn't wait for a response. He walked away and went back into the saloon. Maybe, he thought, the two horses would be worth all this trouble after all. He was tiring of keeping Belle happy when she insisted on dealing with Wills.

———

Stone observed the ticket agent, then repeated his question. "Has there been somebody come through here in the last couple days wanting to ship a sorrel mare and a colt, and maybe go north along with the horses?"

The agent, who had given his name as Pendleton, was making a production of cleaning out a drawer behind the window where he sat. He hadn't made eye contact since Stone had walked up to ask him questions.

Pendleton's hands stopped moving when Stone asked about the horses, then went back to re-arranging the drawer. He glanced up briefly, seeming to take a moment to think about the question.

"No," he said clearly. "Nobody came through shipping a mare and colt. Why?" He stopped and waited for the answer.

"Horse rustlers," Stone stated flatly. "Shipping stolen horses, taken from a ranch near here. You're sure?"

Irritation showed in Pendleton's face. And maybe, Stone thought, a bit of fear. "Of course, I'm sure," he said brusquely. "Anything else?"

Stone shook his head slowly, still watching Pendleton's face. Something told him it might be worthwhile to come back here and keep an eye on this one. He reached into his pocket for a coin. "Ticket to Waco," he said.

———

Riding the train north, Stone began to re-evaluate his strategy. He wasn't likely to get a corrupt ticket agent to confess to shipping stolen horses. He might do better by trying to find somebody who had seen the horses or loaded the horses. Plus, he still didn't know what the destination might be. Where were they actually going? He had found one of the horses near the northern border of Texas. They might go farther north than that.

By the time the train had chugged into Waco, Stone had decided to stay in town for a day or two, asking questions and deciding just how far north he was willing to go in pursuit of the stolen horses. He waited for his horse to be unloaded from the train car, then walked him down to a livery stable he'd seen as they pulled into town.

The old man at the stables took his horse and his money without comment, and Stone turned and started for the street. He stopped and turned back. It didn't seem likely, but he might as well ask. "Did anybody come in here in the last few days with a sorrel mare and a colt?" he asked.

The old man forked some hay down for Stone's horse, taking his time, then leaned over and spat. He straightened up slowly. "Aye," he said. "Sorrel mare an' her colt, mebbe two days ago. Somebody'd been workin' over them brands if you ask me." He whistled tunelessly and moved past Stone, heading for the chair he'd been in when Stone arrived.

"Hang on," Stone said. "What do you mean working over the brands? They'd been altered?"

The old man took a seat, letting out a little grunting noise as he did so. "Aye, they'd been worked over, pretty recent, I'd say. It were a Circle M brand, but I'd say it were a Rocking M not too long before. Pretty sloppy job with the runnin' iron, I'd say," he added scornfully.

He picked up a stick and a knife and began whittling. He stopped and looked up at Stone, taking in the badge on his chest. "Was he a rustler?"

"Probably." Stone kneeled down beside the old man. "What did this guy look like? Tall, short, what color hair?"

"Yeller hair, it was." The old man squinted at the afternoon sun. "Kinda short. Pretty dang grumpy, if'n you ask me. Tiny little boots. Tiny. Big ol' bruise on his jaw. I'd say somebody punched him good." He resumed the whittling and the tuneless whistling. Stone left the livery stable at a trot, headed for the train station again.

A few quick questions to the station ticket agent told Stone everything he needed to know. A short, blonde man with a nasty yellowing bruise on his jaw had bought a ticket for Parsons, Kansas, two days ago. The agent didn't recall that the man was shipping horses, and he had given his name as Smith, which probably didn't mean anything.

Stone was set back for a few minutes when the agent said that *Smith* hadn't paid to ship any horses north. Then he remembered what the old man at the livery stable had said about the altered brands on the horses. He looked around the train yard and saw a man unloading cargo from one car. He approached the man, who took one look at Stone's badge and ducked around the train car, trotting in the other direction. Stone didn't bother to chase him. He had a pretty good idea of how the stolen horses could have gotten on the train.

CHAPTER TWELVE
DEATH IN KANSAS

Sheriff Hutchins showed up at the house not much past daybreak. He said he wanted to take the corpse back to town. He said he would get it buried properly. I'm guessing he also wanted folks to know, come election time, that he didn't allow horse rustling around here. That was okay with me. He tossed the body into a wagon he'd brought along, then came up to join Jessie and me on the porch.

Jessie handed him a cup of coffee, and he warmed his hands around the cup for a minute. "You folks doing okay now?" he asked. "Do you think they're done rustling horses here?"

Jessie and I look at each other, neither one of us feeling confident about the answer. "They didn't get the stallion," I said, "and I'm guessing they wanted him most of all. He was the biggest prize around here."

Hutchins nodded that he understood and took a long, loud slurp of his coffee. "I've got a deputy I can spare in a couple days," he offered. "He's lookin' into something for me out east of town right now, but I could send him out when he gets back."

We agreed, and Hutchins finished up his coffee, then drove the wagon out of the yard. As he left, Doc Linden rode in, stopping to exchange a few words with the sheriff. He rode on up to the porch and dismounted.

I touched my hand to the bandage on my head, hoping he would tell me I could go back to work.

Doc climbed up onto the porch, glancing back at the wagon being driven away by the sheriff. "Well," he said, turning back around to look at me. "I guess there's no shortage of folks wanting to shoot your fool head off." He softened the words with a chuckle when he finished.

"I'm popular," I agreed.

He unwound the bandage on my head, turning me to get a better look in the morning light and making a few noises—I had no idea what they meant. He moved his hand back and forth in front of me, watching my eyes. "Any headaches?" he asked abruptly.

"I've had several," I admitted, "but yesterday, and so far, today, my head doesn't hurt anymore." I looked at him hopefully.

He took his watch out of his pocket and glanced at it, then tossed it up and down while he took one more look at me. "Okay," he said finally. "You can get up and around, do some light work for a few days. If you still feel good after that, consider yourself healed up. The wound looks good," he added.

He stopped after stepping down from the porch and looked back at me, then at Jessie. "Nice to see somebody helping to look after this little family," he said. He glanced at both of us again. "Might make a good full-time job for somebody. I'm just sayin'..." He chuckled at the quick blush that appeared on Jessie's face, mounted up, and rode out.

"Well," said Jessie, the blush on her face fading away. "I told you the doc actually likes you." She took both my hands to help lift me up from the chair. "Come on," she said. "I promised I would put you to work when the doc said it's okay."

I trailed after her into the house. I didn't seem to have anything to say, but that silly grin was back on my face.

———

Holt folded his coat and pressed it up against the side of the train car. He was used to being out in the open. Being confined in this train car for two days was getting the best of him. He hadn't gotten a lot of sleep, and he'd had too much time to think about things. He reviewed in his mind what was bothering him the most.

He didn't want to cross the Starrs, and he didn't know what the connection was between whoever had been sending him the telegrams and the Starrs. Whoever The Boss was, he seemed like somebody who didn't get his hands dirty. Holt knew he could handle that. The Starrs, though, ran a pretty big operation in the Territory, from what he'd heard, and he didn't want to cross them. Besides, if they didn't buy the horses, where was he going to get good money for them?

The train swayed suddenly around a bend, and Holt swore under his breath. He didn't feel like taking this ride very often. He would have to set up a way to send the horses and get paid without traipsing off to Kansas every time. He reassured himself that his plan was a good one and leaned back up against the train window. Sheer fatigue was taking over, and he felt his eyelids rolling shut. This was going to work out, he told himself...

The train's whistle brought him wide awake, and he saw that the sun was dropping in the west—he must have been asleep for several hours. He turned and saw the conductor coming down the aisle. He waved his hand to flag the man down. "Where are we?" he blurted out.

The conductor paused only to glance at him before moving on. "Parsons, Kansas," came the reply. "We'll be stopping here for about an hour. Going to load some wood for the engine and let those off who are stopping here." He turned and moved on.

Holt jumped up and grabbed his bag from the rack above him. He hopped off the car as soon as it stopped moving, then trotted down to claim the mare and colt after he had them unloaded. A quick glance told him they had survived the trip without a problem. He claimed his own horse next and began leading all three animals away from the tracks. He looked around and saw a man in leather breeches and a vest watching him closely. He paused and took in the long scar across the man's face and the hair tied off and falling halfway down his back. This, he thought, could be somebody sent by the Starrs. He turned slightly and headed toward the man, who was clearly sizing him up.

———

Victorio watched silently as the stranger approached him. A quick glance at the mare and colt convinced him that this was the man wanting to sell horses. He turned his unblinking stare on the man himself. Victorio noted that he was a small man with two tied-down guns at his hips. He knew instantly that this man prided himself on these guns. He would never challenge Victorio to a fistfight and wouldn't rely on a knife. Victorio glanced down at his own gun, hanging from a rawhide strip around his neck. He was surprisingly good with the pistol, but he would always prefer to use the knife inserted through a leather band around his waist.

Victorio was the son of an Apache father and a white woman who had been carried away captive by the Apaches when she was just a girl. Victorio had grown up with his tribe in Arizona, but he was smart enough to know that their way of life was ending there. He had known enough of the white man and his ways to leave the Apaches and travel to the Territory. He had become useful to the Starrs for just this kind of work. He knew what to do.

The small man with the two guns stopped in front of him. "I have two nice horses here," he said, studying Victorio's face. "Maybe you could use a couple horses like these."

Victorio watched him, his face remaining impassive. He nodded almost imperceptibly. "Maybe I could," he said.

He walked around the mare, running his hands over her shoulder and looking at her teeth. "I need to ride her before I can know if we will buy her." He glanced over his shoulder and pointed toward some open pasture land, away from the railroad and town. He had to get away from the town to do his job.

The stranger hesitated, looking doubtfully in the direction indicated by Victorio, who felt himself growing impatient. He lifted the hackamore rope in his hand. "You can hold my horse while I ride." He watched as the stranger's expression gradually changed from suspicious to one of agreement. Holt motioned for Victorio to lead the way.

Victorio moved ahead, glancing back only occasionally to be sure the stranger was following. He walked for several minutes, then veered around a stand of cottonwood trees. He felt sure the trees would block the view from the town. He took a few more steps, involuntarily

touching the handle of the knife at his side. Now, he
decided, was the time...

———

Holt had a bad feeling as soon as he started talking to the
man with the scar on his face. That it was somebody who
worked for the Starrs, he had no doubt. The man was
part-Indian, he was sure, and he looked like a man who
could handle himself in a fight. Holt had no intention of
getting into a fight. At the moment, he just wanted to sell
the horses and get away with his hide intact. He forced
himself to look as relaxed as possible and followed the
man out of town.

The farther they went, away from the view of anyone
in town, the more he glanced back and felt his tension
rising. They skirted around a stand of cottonwood trees,
and he knew no one could see them now. Then he saw the
man's hand touch the knife. He released the reins he held
in his right hand and rested the hand on one of his pistols.
When the stranger stopped and whirled, Holt drew the
gun and fired point-blank.

Starr's man wore a completely startled expression
when the first shot struck him in the chest. He dropped
the knife and staggered backward. Holt's second shot
went straight through the heart. By the time the stranger
hit the ground, Holt was looking around, deciding what to
do with the body. He led the mare and colt back to the
cottonwood trees and tethered them, then did the same
with his own horse, which had run off only a short
distance. He shooed the dead man's horse away and ran
him off a short distance. Then he dragged the body under
the trees. It would have to do. He didn't want to stay out
here any longer.

———

Back at the train station, there was only one employee for the railroad. He sold tickets, loaded and unloaded baggage, helped load firewood, and did whatever else he had to do. He had made some nice extra money for the last year or so by unloading some horses that didn't seem to belong to anybody and holding them for people he was pretty sure were fencing stolen horses.

He had watched the exchange in the train yard and was pretty sure they had stolen the mare and colt. Plus, he recognized the guy who had waited for the train. He'd delivered several horses to this man before. When he heard a couple gunshots and saw the train passenger coming back with the mare and colt, with no sign of the man who had waited for the train, he had a decision to make. Did he keep his mouth shut or not?

Greed won out. He dashed off a telegram to the man in Temple named Pendleton. Maybe it would be worth a few extra dollars. He already knew what he would do with the extra money.

———

Two days later, Holt was getting more than just a little worried. Because the Chisum Trail ran to the west of here and Parsons was such a small town, he had had no luck in selling the horses on his own. Horses of the kind he was selling were mostly good for outlaws who needed the speed or cowboys who liked to race them, and there was a shortage of both around here. Mostly, he had just looked for a place to hide out for a couple of days, hoping that any danger to him after the shooting would die down.

He'd spent the time camping in a small grove of trees

west of town, close to a stream. January nights got a little too cold for him here, but he kept a fire going. It wasn't really the cold that got him moving. He knew that before too long, word was likely to get back to the Starr outfit that their man was dead. He didn't need to be hanging around Parsons, Kansas, when that happened.

On the third morning, he decided. He would go back to Texas, stopping at Dennison on the northern border. He would get the best price he could for the horses, whatever that was, then go back down to Longhorn Cave and lie low for a while. This would blow over eventually, then he would figure out what to do next. He gathered the horses and rode back into Parsons, leading the mare and the colt. He bought passage for himself and the horses back to Texas. There was only one man working the depot, and Holt ignored his curious stares. He needed to get home. When the train arrived, he boarded and heaved a sigh of relief.

The agent at the train station watched as the south-bound train pulled away. He checked the watch in his pocket. Two hours until the next train. He had time to send another telegram.

————

Stone chafed at the delay in getting to Parsons. The locomotive had broken down yesterday, and they had spent almost a full day sidelined just south of Ft. Worth. Stone worried that whatever was going to happen with those horses in Parsons had already happened. He knew there was very little chance of recovering them if they had been moved already.

On the other hand, sitting on the train for nearly a day had given him a chance to think, and Stone had a gift for analyzing things. His mind kept returning to the question of why the destination picked by the horse thief was Parsons. It was a tiny little stop on the route. If the thief was looking to fence the horses, it seemed a very unlikely destination. And yet, he reasoned, there had to be a reason.

When the engine had finally been repaired and the train had started to move yesterday evening, it had hit him like a thunderbolt. One of the biggest operations for fencing stolen horses, among other things, was in north-eastern Oklahoma. The woman now known as Belle Starr, along with her husband Sam, were known to buy and dispose of stolen horses. What if the horses stolen in Texas had found their way to the Territory, or for that matter, places north and east of there? The Starrs probably had that kind of reach. It fit together in Stone's mind.

By the time the train stopped in Dennison to load up firewood, Stone had reviewed in his mind what he knew about the Starrs. Sam Starr was native to Oklahoma, as far as Stone knew, but Belle had Texas ties. The Rangers had kept up with Belle, although she was now living and working entirely in the Territory. Stone knew that Belle, or May Shirley, as she was mostly known then, had grown up in a town near Dallas called Scyene. Maybe the Texas connection was there?

Stone stared out at the train yard in Dennison and decided to go out and stretch his legs. They had another forty-five minutes before moving out. He thrust his hands in his pockets and began walking vigorously, though aimlessly, around the train yard. The Younger brothers had come from Scyene, but they had gone to prison a few years ago after that bank robbery in Minnesota.

After about fifteen minutes of walking and turning things over in his mind, Stone decided it might be worth going over to Scyene when he came back from Parsons. He could do a little checking around over there and see if he came up with anything from Belle Starr's background that might tie her to the horse rustling in Texas.

Stone turned to re-board his train, vaguely aware of activity from a train that had arrived from the north. Passengers were getting off the train and baggage and horses were being offloaded. Stone glanced over and stopped in his tracks. There was a man across the way with sandy-blonde hair, standing a little on the short side, leading three horses away from one of the baggage cars. There was a sorrel horse and a colt. It all fit the descriptions he had been given. As Stone started to move toward them, the man glanced over, then spun and began moving in the other direction.

———

Milo Wills stared at the telegram he held in his hand, his stomach turning over as he read it. He set the telegram on his desk, then forced himself to sit down and think calmly. The telegram from Pendleton told him that the horse rustler, Holt, had killed Belle Starr's man in Parsons. A few days later, he had gotten back on the KATY railroad train, along with the rustled horses, to return to Texas. It was, it forced Wills to admit, the worst news he could have received today.

He had no doubt that the Starrs would have revenge in mind when they found out their man was dead. They might even blame him. He had to do something about this before the Starrs found out. More than that, he had to wrap up this operation now and walk away. It had become too dangerous. He needed to get Holt out of the picture immediately. Pendleton, he still felt he could trust.

The man that worked for Pendleton, though, Lance some-body—he had to be taken out of the way too.

Wills opened the door to his office and motioned to Shaw, his fixer, who was lounging in a chair outside. As soon as Shaw stepped in, Wills handed him three gold pieces. He didn't bother to sit down or even step away from the door.

"Pendleton had a man working for him, first name Lance. He isn't useful to me anymore. Find out what you need to know about him from Pendleton, then make him go away. After that, go to Longhorn Cave. Find out who is there and if they have any horses there."

Shaw took the gold pieces, a smile touching the corners of his mouth. This was what he did best. He put on his hat and went outside to mount up.

That took care of one problem. Wills sat down behind his desk again and stared out the window. What to do about Holt? It occurred to him that with Lance out of the way, there was no possible way for anyone to tie Holt back to him. He drummed his fingers on the desk and turned a couple of possibilities over in his mind, then rejected each one as being too dangerous.

Suddenly, his fingers stopped drumming, and a smile spread slowly over his face as he looked out the window. Maybe the Texas Rangers would like to know a little about a horse rustler named Holt. They could do his work for him. With any luck, there would be a shootout and they would kill Holt. Even if they just arrested him, the Starrs would avoid trying to come after him for revenge. Too dangerous for them, he mused. The more he thought about it, the better he liked his plan.

He swung around to his desk and picked up his pen to compose a telegram. What was the name of that Rangers captain he had met in Austin earlier this year? He frowned and stared at the opposite wall. McDonald! That was it. He grabbed a piece of paper and composed an anonymous telegram for Captain McDonald. When he had finished, he swung around and looked out the window. Shaw was already gone, so he rose and picked up his hat. He could send this telegram himself.

CHAPTER THIRTEEN
WHAT GOES AROUND...

Holt collected his horses at the Dennison station as quickly as he could, feeling like he was being watched. He knew it was probably too soon for the Starrs to have caught up with him, but he was getting more and more jumpy. The thought had struck him on the way down on the train that maybe somebody there in Parsons was in touch with Sam or Belle Starr. He told himself that wasn't likely, but he wasn't entirely convinced. Despite the cool temperatures on this winter day, he felt a trickle of sweat run down the back of his neck.

He led the horses away, trying to get his bearings. He wasn't sure which direction he wanted to go, but decided it would be enough for right now just to get away from the train station and the town of Dennison. It was a little unusual to see a man leading two horses and a colt, and he felt conspicuous any time he drew a second glance from anybody. It wasn't helping, he admitted to himself, that he was returning those curious glances with hostile stares.

He resolved to look down and not draw eye contact,

but the sound of another train arriving and unloading across the yard caused him to look up. The sight of metal flashing in the sun drew his eyes, and he stopped his sweeping glance to look back at what he'd seen. His stomach began to churn when he realized he was looking at a badge. He froze momentarily, then quickened his pace to reach a couple of outbuildings at the edge of the train yard. He turned the corner, looking back over his shoulder as he did so. The man with the badge was following.

Holt fought down the panic as he broke into a trot, urging the horses to keep up. His gaze swept left and right. He was having trouble deciding what to do. A small voice inside him kept telling him the lawman wasn't really following him, he needed to calm down. The rest of him didn't seem to listen to the small voice. He saw a short hitching rail outside the final of the outbuildings he was passing. On impulse, he trotted over and tied up the horses.

He turned and retraced his steps, forcing himself to calm down. If the lawman was still behind him, the man would probably just walk past him and keep going. He probably wouldn't even realize it was the same guy he'd just seen with the three horses. Holt continued to talk to himself while his heart pounded faster. His mouth felt increasingly dry.

The man turned the corner, and Holt could see the badge again. He took a couple more steps in that direction, but the guy with the badge had stopped walking, and he was staring directly at Holt. Reflex and pure panic set in. Holt's right hand swept down for his gun. He cleared the holster and a mixture of relief and excitement swept over him. He would shoot the lawman and get out of town. Problem solved.

A blow hammered him in the stomach, and he staggered back, staring down in confusion. He could feel pain in his shoulder, too, and he wasn't holding his gun anymore. He stared at the blood pooling on the ground and wondered who had been shot. He looked up to see the man with the badge holding a gun in his right hand and stepping toward him. Holt reached down for his other gun with his left hand and tried to claw it free. He never registered the third shot that struck him. He was dead when he landed on his back in the alley.

———

Mike Stone stood in the alleyway, gun still in hand, watching for any sign of movement from the man he had followed around the corner. When several seconds passed and he saw no movement, he approached the man slowly, gun still drawn. As he came closer, he put the gun back in the holster. There was no chance the man was still alive. When Stone heard footsteps coming from behind him, he removed his badge and held it in the air.

"Texas Ranger," he announced. "Do you have a sheriff in town?"

When he heard a voice telling him they would find the sheriff, he nodded and kneeled beside the body. He didn't recognize the man, but he hadn't really expected to. His eyes traveled down and stopped when he saw the boots. They were exceptionally small. He looked around at the prints left in the dust of the alley. He felt sure he had found the man who had ambushed Red.

Remembering that he had started to follow this man when he saw the three horses, including a colt, Stone stood and walked farther down the alley. He saw three horses tethered at a rail at the side of the last building. He walked over and inspected the brands on the mare and the colt. Someone had altered them, he could see that clearly. He untied the stolen horses and walked back toward the corpse, where he saw the sheriff standing and waving people away from the body.

Stone approached, introduced himself, and asked the sheriff if he would take charge of the body, explaining that the man was a horse thief and had very likely been the killer of a fellow Ranger. The sheriff agreed and gave orders for somebody to bring him a wagon. Stone then led the horses away, quickening his pace when he heard the train whistle. He needed to get his bag and his own horse off the train before it left. There was no need to continue on to Kansas.

Stone arranged for the stolen horses to be sent to Temple, then he moved on from the train station to the telegraph office. There, he composed a lengthy telegram to Captain McDonald. He explained about the shootout and the death of the man who had the stolen horses. He also explained why he believed the dead man had been Red's killer. Finally, he told the captain why he wanted to go to Scyene. He sent the telegram, then went to a café nearby. He would wait for a reply from McDonald.

———

McDonald sat in the boarding room he used when he had to sit at a desk in Austin. These days, he reflected with some frustration, that happened more often than he wanted. He longed for the days when he had spent his time in the saddle. Unable to get himself started on a report to the governor, he went over to the telegraph office and checked for messages. He found two waiting for him when he arrived. The first was a message from Mike Stone. He dashed off a response, telling Stone to proceed to Scyene. He made a mental note to let the governor know that Red's killer had been killed in a gunfight with Stone.

The second note caused his eyes to widen in surprise. He returned to the desk with the message and handed it across to the clerk. "Can you tell me where this was sent from?" he asked.

The clerk glanced at it briefly. "I can tell you where this one came from," came the quick answer. "The operator puts his initials on them. This came from San Antonio."

Surprised at how easy that had been, McDonald started to leave, then turned back. "Can you tell me where in San Antonio I can find this office?"

The clerk glanced at McDonald's badge, then typed out a message. He waited a few minutes for the reply, then picked it up and read it. "Commerce Street, near the river," he said.

McDonald, who had never been to San Antonio despite his years of service as a Ranger, stayed by the desk, debating his next question. Finally, he asked, "Which river would that be?"

The clerk didn't pause or look up as he typed out a new message. "San Antonio River, sir."

McDonald thanked him and let himself out quietly.

———

Back at his boarding room office, McDonald sipped from a fresh cup of coffee and stared thoughtfully out the window. Clearly, whoever had sent this message was unaware of what had just happened up in Dennison. He spread the message out on his desk and read it again.

To McDonald. Stop.
A horse rustler named Holt is traveling on the KATY
Railroad with two stolen horses—mare and colt. Stop.
Headed south from Parsons Ks. two days ago. Stop.

Believed to have killed a man in Parsons. Stop.

The message didn't say who the sender was, of course. The part about coming south with stolen horses had turned out to be true. There were a few questions that came to mind. Who sent the message was an obvious one. Beyond that, why did this person want the horse rustler caught? If it was an honest citizen who wanted to see the rustler caught, why not identify themselves? And who was the man killed in Kansas, if that part was true?

Too many questions to deal with right now, he told himself. The first thing to do was to send somebody to that telegraph office in San Antonio and see what they could find out about the sender. McDonald frowned as he considered who he could send. He didn't really have anybody to spare right now. Then a smile crossed his face as he thought of an answer that would solve two problems. He could send himself. He could get out from behind this desk and get back to doing what he liked about this job.

———

A return to light work suited me just fine. I spent a day or two repairing some fences alongside Kyle, then spent another day checking on the horses and the small herd of cows with Jessie. It was too cold to move them to the higher pastures at the north end of the property, but Jessie and I decided it wasn't too cold for a picnic alongside the stream cutting through those pastures. Iris had packed the lunch for us with a knowing smile on her face. We spread out a blanket beside the stream and Jessie began unpacking the lunch.

"My mom likes you, you know," she told me. There was a teasing smile on her face.

"Of course she does," I said, leaning back with a smug smile on my face. "Mothers always love me." I settled back on the blanket and dropped the smug part of my smile. "I just have to do a better job of getting the daughters to love me."

"Daughters?" Jessie said, pausing mid-way through the unpacking. "Daughters? Just how many of those daughters do you plan on getting to love you?"

Well, that hadn't come out quite right. "Daughter," I said. "I just need one daughter." I leaned past Jessie, reaching for the cookies in the basket, and got a playful slap on my hand.

"That's for dessert," she said, leaning into me as she reached to put a plate of chicken on the blanket.

It seemed to me that she stayed that way, leaning into me longer than necessary while she re-arranged the chicken on the plate. Me, I wasn't complaining.

"Did you have any mother and daughter in particular in mind?" she asked. "I'm just curious. Is this a long list or a short list?" Jessie turned and looked at me, one eyebrow arched.

I started to say something, got a little tongue-tied, and started over. "That Iris, for instance," I said haltingly. "She's a fine lady. She, uh, would be the mother, of course."

Jessie chuckled and let me flop around, watching as my face turned red. I dug in and tried again. "That makes you the daughter, of course, and I'm, well, what I'm trying to say is..."

She finally put me out of my misery and leaned in to give me a long kiss. "Are you trying to say that I'm the only one you've got your eye on? Is that what you're trying to say? Because I like the sound of that, Ash McKinnon."

I heaved a sigh of relief. "That's what I'm trying to say. There's nothing in my life I've liked better than this time

I've spent at your ranch. And it's not just because I'm an old country boy at heart. It's because of you." I searched for something else to say, then decided to quit while I was ahead. The look in Jessie's eyes told me I'd managed to say what I needed to.

I'd have to say I don't remember a whole lot about the lunch, but I won't forget the couple of hours we spent eating the lunch and cuddling on that blanket. It was cold, after all. We had to stay warm, didn't we?

———

We rode back to the ranch a couple hours later and found Kyle waving a piece of paper at us as we came into the yard. "Telegram from Mr. Stone!" he shouted. "He got the horse thief and found our horses. The horses will come into Temple on tomorrow's train!"

We swung down, and Kyle handed me the telegram. It was from Captain McDonald, telling me that Stone had caught up with the horse rustler, or one of them, at the train yard in Dennison, and had killed him in a shootout. The man's boot prints matched the ones Red had traced, so the dead man was likely Red's killer. The recovered horses were coming to Temple on tomorrow's train.

I handed the telegram to Jessie, knowing there was grim satisfaction in my eyes at realizing that the man who murdered my old friend Red and who had taken a shot at my head had met his end by drawing on my old friend and partner Mike Stone.

We gathered around the table in the kitchen, trying to decide who would go into Temple to get the horses. Jessie, Kyle, and I were all volunteering to go, but I had some concerns about going in myself and leaving the family to watch over the ranch. Jessie finally convinced me that they would all be fine, considering that they had caught the horse rustler. I argued that somebody else might be out there waiting to try again, but I had to admit that it had been quiet around here for quite a while. If there were other rustlers still out there, they had probably moved on. Besides, I would be back by tomorrow night.

———

Jessie saw Ash off in the early morning light. He was mounted on the horse he'd been riding when he first came to the ranch. She smiled as he waved goodbye and headed out the gate. She planned to make the chestnut gelding a present to him when the time came for him to move on to a different assignment. She hoped she would still see that gelding in her corral often. She was pretty sure he would come back to see her when he could.

Jessie walked into the kitchen. Iris saw the smile on her daughter's face and chuckled knowingly as she handed off a cup of coffee. Jessie had given up protesting when Iris teased her about Ash. She knew the mutual interest was perfectly obvious to her family, and there didn't seem to be any point in denying it. The fact that she couldn't stop smiling was a dead giveaway.

The family settled down to breakfast, and Jessie and Kyle discussed what had to be done today. The family garden needed to be hoed and planted with potatoes and onions. That was the least favorite job for both Jessie and Kyle. The fences also needed to be checked today after last night's heavy wind. When both Jessie and Kyle had volunteered for the fence line job, Iris sighed and went over to break a piece of straw off the broom leaning in the corner. She knew from experience there was only one way to settle this.

Iris turned her back and broke the straw into two pieces—one shorter and one longer. She palmed both pieces in her hand and turned around. "Okay, you two," she announced. "Choose one."

When Kyle went first and drew the short straw, Jessie threw one hand in the air in celebration, then patted her brother on the back. "Make sure you get all those weeds out first," she reminded him. Seeing the defeated look on his face, she relented slightly. "I'll do the first weeding after you're done with planting," she promised. Then she went outside to saddle up.

As she traveled farther from the house and climbed a little in elevation, moving toward the back of the property, Jessie realized that the wind must have been stronger than she had realized. She had taken the first watch on the back porch, and the wind hadn't really kicked up that much by the time she was sound asleep. Now, she began to see large tree limbs down. She pulled up short when she saw what she had been hoping she wouldn't.

An old, fairly-large oak tree had blown down and landed squarely across the fence on the east side of the pasture. The small herd of about fifty head of cattle had drifted across the fence line and scattered out. Jessie sighed and sized up the situation. She would need Kyle's help to herd the cattle back into the pasture and repair the fence. She reined her horse around and started back for the house.

———

Ike and Slade had been at the ranch for a day, arguing back and forth over how they were going to steal that stallion. After Ike had explained the difficulties during the first try, Slade was arguing against trying to steal the horse at all. Ike then asked his partner if he, Slade, wanted to explain to Holt why they hadn't stolen the stallion.

Slade thought about the two tied-down guns that Holt liked to wear and agreed that they should try to steal it.

The main problem, as they saw it, was the stallion himself. He was a fast, powerful horse, and they were likely to each have to drop a lasso over him to lead him out of there. Watching the house last night, they had learned that there was a guard posted on the back porch all night. Now it was an arithmetic problem. They needed two people to steal the horse and one person to deal with the guard on the porch. Neither one of them liked the odds.

The situation had gotten a little brighter this morning when the Ranger had ridden off at first light. Then, the girl had ridden out shortly later, leaving only the boy digging in the garden and the woman somewhere in the house. Still, it was now broad daylight, and nobody in their right mind, they agreed, tried to rustle horses in broad daylight. Especially, they agreed, when horse thieves generally got hung in Texas.

They were hunkered down in the trees to the west of the corral when the thunder of hooves told them the girl was coming back to the ranch at a gallop. They saw her ride up, waving at the boy, and heard the words "fence down". The boy dropped the hoe, dashed into the house for a couple minutes, then came out, saddled up a horse, and rode away with his sister. The mother came out of the house a minute later, propped a shotgun up against the corner of the porch, and began peeling potatoes.

Ike and Slade glanced at each other, then began easing back through the trees toward their horses. They wouldn't get a better chance than this.

CHAPTER FOURTEEN
INTO THIN AIR

Iris settled down in a chair on the back porch. She glanced at the shotgun in the corner from time to time—she could use it if she needed to. She picked up a paring knife, glanced out at the corral, and started peeling. After about fifteen minutes, she went into the kitchen and started some water boiling on the stove. She went back to the chair on the porch and started in on the potatoes again. About twenty minutes, she estimated, and she could move on to something else. Frequent glances at the corral told her that the horses were undisturbed.

As she leaned over to pick up another potato, Iris heard the unmistakable sound of steps creaking on her left. She froze and glanced over her shoulder. A man was standing there, covering her with a rifle. A bandanna covered his face and his hat was pulled down low. Another man appeared on her right. He reached out and picked up the shotgun. He emptied the shells and tossed the empty shotgun over the railing.

"Stay where you are an' take it easy, mum," were the first words either of them spoke. The man on the right advanced toward her. "Put your hands behind your back. Behind the chair. Keep 'em there."

She did as she was told. One of them produced a leather strip from his pocket and tied her hands behind the chair. The second one walked over to a sheet drying on the line at the side of the house. He produced a knife and cut two strips from the sheet. He returned to the porch and used one strip as a gag. With the second, he covered her eyes.

Satisfied that the woman would cause them no trouble, Ike and Slade moved to their horses, which they had tethered in the trees. They mounted and moved to the corral. They watched the stallion moving around inside, then both men, remaining mounted, moved into the corral. They both shook out a loop and tossed it at the stallion. Slade missed by a wide margin, but Ike was luckier. His noose settled over the stallion's neck. Two tries later, Slade landed his noose also, and they moved out of the corral. The stallion bucked and plunged behind them, but they kept moving away from the gate. The combined strength of their horses eventually won out, and they began moving steadily as the stallion's bucking slowed. Eventually, they settled down to a steady gallop with the stallion trailing behind them.

They slowed a bit after a while but kept moving at a brisk pace, trying to put as much distance between themselves and the ranch as they possibly could. Undoubtedly there would be some tracks left behind, but they were counting on the dry ground to make pursuit a little more difficult. It would be a few hours before they came to a stream where they could begin to cover their tracks. Until then, they just wanted to put some miles behind them.

By mid-afternoon, they had again slowed the pace, this time to a trot. When they spotted a small stream in front of them, they relaxed. They eased the horses into the stream and splashed through the water for half a mile before emerging on the other side. They felt like things were looking good now, but they wouldn't really feel they were in the clear until they reached the Colorado River.

————

I returned to the ranch from Temple in the early afternoon and found the place in an uproar. Jessie had saddled two horses—hers and the chestnut gelding. I knew the chestnut gelding was for me, but I wasn't sure where we were going. Kyle was hovering over Iris in the kitchen, asking her if she was okay. Then a glance in the corral told me that the stallion was no longer there, so I now knew why Jessie had saddled our horses. The part I hadn't figured out yet was the concern for Iris. I went in and sat down next to her in the kitchen.

Iris smiled and reached out to take my hand. "Before you ask me, Ash, yes, I'm fine. Two guys showed up on the porch while I was watching the corral and tied me up, then stole the stallion. Mostly I'm upset they got the horse while I was watching." She glanced up at Jessie, who had appeared behind me in the doorway.

"I'm assuming you want to go after these guys," Jessie said, crossing the kitchen to put a hand on my shoulder. "I was mad enough to go after them myself, but common sense told me to wait and even up the odds a little. I have saddled your horse, too." Her face was showing strain, but she bent down to kiss me on the cheek. "And I do mean YOUR horse, by the way."

I looked back at Iris. "You're sure you're fine? I guess the sheriff's assistant will be here before long," I said, remembering the sheriff's offer to send a man out. That conversation seemed like a long time ago now.

Iris waved me away. "I'm fine. They got what they really wanted, so they won't be back. Go get those guys."

I jumped up from the chair so quickly that I almost tipped it over. I righted the chair and waved at Iris as we left the kitchen. Something Jessie had said hit me in a delayed reaction, and I glanced over at her as we trotted toward the horses. "MY horse?" I asked.

Jessie gave me a wan smile and handed me the reins of the chestnut gelding.

"This is a fantastic horse," I said, not quite believing he was mine now. We moved toward the corral. "Let's go get your stallion back," I said.

We struck the trail they had left as soon as we pulled away from the corral. It was clear from the tracks left that the stallion was fighting as they led him away him. There were chunks of turf torn up where he had kicked and plunged. The trail moved away toward the west, and things seemed to have settled down before too much time had gone by. The three sets of tracks were clear—the stallion was being led by two horses. He was trailing behind them in the center. No doubt both rustlers had a rope around the stallion's neck and had tied the ropes off to their saddle horns.

A little farther along the trail, they seemed to move in a straight line, and judging by the horse's strides, they were proceeding at a full gallop. I knew they couldn't keep that up for too long, but they were making good time, and they knew where they were going. We didn't—we had to follow their trail. I knew we were losing a bit of time for as long as they could proceed at a gallop.

After about an hour, we rested our horses for a while and gave them some water. Jessie looked at me as we remounted, then pointed toward the trail in front of us. "Any idea where they are going?" she asked.

I urged the gelding into a canter, not wanting to take

my eyes from the tracks. "If I were them," I said, "I'd be heading toward water soon to cover the tracks. Stream, river, something... They have to know this trail is pretty easy to follow."

———

An hour later, my guess turned out to be true. I would have rather been wrong about this one, but the tracks came to a small stream and disappeared. I knew they had waded the horses along, then left the stream and covered those exit tracks as best they could. There was nothing to do but walk our horses into the stream, watching the banks on both sides for signs of our quarry coming back out of the water.

We eventually found it about a mile downstream. They had dragged some branches over the tracks on the bank and had woven back and forth in the trees near the shore. We sorted that out and struck a small but faint trail left in the woods. I was frustrated because I knew we had probably lost an hour, and we wouldn't have that much more daylight.

Another hour down the trail and they entered another stream, a bigger one this time. We did as we had done before, splashing through the stream, but after following this stream for some time, two things had dawned on me. One, I could hear more water, and I was afraid it was the Colorado River this time. And two, our light was fading rapidly, and we would soon need to make camp.

Once again, I was right and wishing I was wrong. This stream merged with the Colorado River. I knew it would be very difficult to find their exit point from the river, but we would have to try tomorrow. For now, we had to make camp.

We built a small fire, not too far back from the river. I

tried to sound more confident than I felt when Jessie asked me about our chances of finding the stallion tomorrow. There was still a decent chance that we could find their tracks leaving the Colorado. A small voice inside me, though, said that things had just gotten a lot tougher.

The night was clear and cold. We laid the bedrolls side by side for warmth, and I told Jessie as we drifted off that we would do better tomorrow. I hoped I was right.

———

As the sun climbed up higher and higher the next morning, a lot of my confidence was gone. The farther we proceeded down the river, the more both of us were wondering if we'd missed the tracks when they exited. The thought of going back and re-covering the same ground again was unbearable. We called a halt, and I stared out over the expanse of river in front of us, and a sudden thought struck me. I started to talk, then stopped and thought it over a little more. Jessie just watched me and waited.

"Maybe," I said haltingly, "we're going about this the wrong way. Maybe we just need to work on figuring out where the hideout is. We can't be that far away. Maybe the thing to do is start asking the locals around here where rustlers might be hiding out."

Jessie gave a tight smile. Her frustration was really showing, and I didn't blame her. "That's great," she said, the doubt sounding heavy in her voice. "But how are we going to do that? Rustlers don't go around telling people where they hide out. And if somebody else who's not a rustler knows, will they really tell us? They won't want these guys coming after them."

A little smile grew on my face. "Maybe we just have to ask the right questions," I said. "We don't ask where rustlers might be hiding out now. Probably only the rustlers know that. What we can do is ask where rustlers and outlaws might have hidden around here in the past. There might be an old-timer or two who knows about that and would be happy to tell us about it. Maybe this place they're using has a history."

A bit of hopefulness appeared in Jesse's eyes. "Okay," she said thoughtfully. "Maybe that could work. But where are we going to find old-timers that want to talk to us about horse rustlers and hideouts?"

The smile kept growing until it was a full-blown grin on my face. "That," I told her, "is what saloons are for."

————

Pendleton found he was deeply disturbed by the presence of Wills's *fixer*, Shaw. The man had shown up unannounced at the train station that afternoon and stated that the two of them would have a talk about Lance. There was no shred of a request in what he said—he had simply informed Pendleton it would be happening. Then he had clearly expected Pendleton to walk out on his job for the talk. When Pendleton had insisted it would wait until he was off work, there had been a long and uncomfortable stare-down. Shaw had finally mumbled something about meeting him at the saloon and walked out.

Now Shaw slugged down a shot of whiskey and stared across the table. He reminded Pendleton of a rattlesnake staring at its prey. Shaw waved the shot glass at a waiter, then went back to staring at Pendleton. "I need to know where this guy Lance lives."

"Why?" Pendleton didn't really expect to get an answer to his question, but he was stalling for a little time. He had to decide what would happen if he refused to give the information. He had the uncomfortable feeling he wouldn't live very long if that happened. He also had the feeling he would never see it coming. He would just be dead.

"Boss said to come and get it from you." Shaw got his refill and threw it down instantly. He wiped his sleeve across his mouth and went back to the rattlesnake stare.

Pendleton took a pull from his beer and decided. He wanted to live. Lance could fend for himself. He took another glance at Shaw. Lance would probably never have the chance to fend for himself.

"Round Rock, north of Austin." He fished in his pocket for the address he had written down and brought with him. He slid it across the table and watched as Shaw glanced at it, then shoved it in his pocket. Pendleton tried another question: "What is happening?" He had little hope of getting an answer to that question, and he didn't.

Shaw shrugged and stood up. He didn't bother leaving any money to pay for the whiskey. "Ask The Boss yourself," he said, and then he disappeared through the batwing doors.

Pendleton stayed at the saloon for quite a while after Shaw left. He switched to whiskey, but it didn't help all that much. Something must have gone wrong with this operation, and Wills had clearly got rid of anybody he couldn't trust. The big question, of course, was whether he, Pendleton, was among those people that Wills would decide couldn't be trusted. Pendleton stayed at the saloon and drank until he could barely find his way home. He crashed through the doorway and fell onto his mattress. His brain was working just enough to tell him he would have a big decision to make by morning.

In fact, by the time the morning sunlight coming through his one window finally did its job and woke him up, he wasn't feeling any better than last night. His brain was barely working, that was for sure. He rose, moaning with each step, and fumbled around until he had a cup of coffee strong enough to take the paint off the walls. Well, if he'd had any paint on the walls, the coffee would take it off.

He lurched over to the table and slumped over it with his coffee in front of him. He took a few scalding hot sips and waited for some cobwebs to clear from his brain. He assembled the facts in his head. He had saved a pretty fair amount of money from working this racket with Wills. He certainly hadn't spent it on any luxuries. He had known, in the back of his mind, that Wills was ruthless. Pendleton was pretty ruthless himself, but he didn't have the people to do his dirty work like Wills. Maybe that was a mistake on his part.

He had the same gut feeling that he'd had last night— that Wills was getting rid of people he didn't trust. Pendleton wasn't one of those people yet, but he had a feeling it was only a matter of time. He really didn't think there would be any more stolen horses passing through to help fatten his wallet, and he really didn't care about the railroad job. That left only one conclusion: it was time for him to pull up stakes and get out of here. Out of Wills's reach.

He was a careful man, and he knew how to walk away. He would ride north to Dallas and catch a train ride on the Texas and Pacific Railroad to El Paso. That might be far enough to get away from Wills, or it might not be. He would go on to California if he needed to. The money he'd saved was buried out back. Part of him acknowledged that the bank was a safer place, but the rest of him said that he might need the money in a hurry with nobody at the bank taking notice. You just couldn't trust people not to run their mouths.

Mind made up, he walked outside to the old wreck of a barn he had out back and saddled his horse. It wasn't much of a horse, but he just needed to get to Dallas. He would stay out of sight as much as possible on the way up there. That done, he picked up the shovel in the corner and walked out to the spot where he had buried his money. Being careful was about to pay off. Next time, maybe he needed to get himself a cutthroat like Shaw. It was something to think about.

CHAPTER FIFTEEN
UNEARTHING THE PAST

Shaw had been following Lance for two days now. Finding him had been pretty easy after getting an address from Pendleton. Round Rock wasn't a big place. Wills had been clear that Lance had to go away. Shaw had no illusions about what that meant, and he never questioned Wills. The money was too good. He had to put up with an occasional tantrum, but that was easy enough. He'd never really had it so good for getting so little work done.

There was really just one big reason why he hadn't done this job yet, he had to kill Lance and get away without getting shot or having a posse on his trail. The first morning, for instance, Lance had been in town the entire morning. Like most small towns, the businesses were pretty much on one main street. The jail and sheriff's office were pretty close to everything else in town. He could afford to wait for a better chance to do this and still ride away with no bullet holes in him.

That problem had been solved yesterday afternoon. Lance had mounted up and ridden out of town, heading north. Shaw had followed at a distance, just waiting for a good shot. Lance had ridden for quite some time, stopping by the railroad tracks just south of the town of Georgetown. Shaw could see that Lance had stopped at a water stop for the railroad. He seemed to wait for a train. Shaw, sensing his opportunity, had veered off into the woods and found a spot where he could rest his rifle over a low-hanging limb. He was preparing for a shot when he heard the whistle of a train. He watched as Lance ducked behind a rail fence, then he noticed that Lance was keeping an eye on the train as it approached.

The train stopped and began taking on water. Shaw watched in curiosity as the door of the express car opened. He saw Lance getting to his feet, then ducking back down behind the rail fence. Shaw nearly laughed out loud. There was an armed guard on the express car. Lance must have planned to rob the train at the water siding. The armed guard had convinced him that it wasn't such a good idea. Forty-five minutes later, the train rolled away, and Lance came out from his hiding spot. He mounted up and rode back toward Round Rock. Shaw let him go.

He still planned to do his job, but holding up the train while it was stopped didn't seem like such a bad idea. For all he knew, Lance was out here every day, trying to pick the right train. Shaw would give it one more day. Maybe an armed guard would do his job for him, or maybe he would just rob Lance after Lance robbed the train, then get rid of him. One more day wouldn't matter that much. If he could make a little money on the side, Wills didn't need to know about it.

As he suspected, the next day played out much like the day before. Lance rode out in the early afternoon and hid out at the water siding. Shaw settled down with his rifle resting across the same branch, hidden back in the trees, and awaited developments. The whistle sounded shortly, and the train rolled around the bend and into view.

This time, things played out differently. The train stopped and took on water. The engineer climbed down and walked alongside the train, apparently just stretching and taking a walk. When he did, Lance came out from his hiding spot and pulled a gun on the engineer. They went to the express car, where Lance rapped loudly on the door and demanded that the door be opened.

There was some shouting back and forth for a while. Shaw couldn't really understand the words, but it was obvious that the man inside didn't want to open up. After a while, the engineer shouted, and the door rolled open. Lance reversed his gun and struck the engineer on the head with the gun butt. The engineer slumped to the ground and Lance stepped inside the car. After several minutes went by, he came out carrying a burlap bag. He sprinted over to his horse and mounted up.

Mass confusion prevailed. As Lance rode away, a young guy showed up in the express car doorway and took a couple shots at Lance as he rode past. Lance stopped and fired back, but nobody seemed to hit anything. A couple more shots sounded, and Shaw decided this was getting too messy. He couldn't wait and take the money from Lance. He needed to do his job and get out of there.

He sighted down the barrel of his rifle. Lance was half-turned away from him, firing again at the doorway of the car where the kid seemed to duck in and out, taking an occasional shot. Shaw let his breath out slowly, then squeezed off his shot. Lance jerked backward, then tumbled out of the saddle and lay still on the ground.

Shaw turned, trotted to his horse, and mounted. He hesitated for just a moment, looking back at what was going on at the train siding. The kid had come out of the express car, waving his pistol in the air. A few people spilled out of the train, and they seemed to congratulate the express car kid on shooting the robber. Shaw smiled grimly, then retreated into the trees. If they thought the kid had shot Lance, it was better for him. Nobody would look for him.

The first thing he wanted to do was to get away cleanly. He stayed under the cover of the trees for a while, then finally crossed the tracks and struck the road north. He would stay with the road for a while, then turn west toward the cave. He wasn't exactly sure what Wills wanted him to do there, but he would check things out. If Wills didn't show up or send someone with a message for him, he would go on back to San Antonio after a couple days at Longhorn Cave.

———

Mike Stone reined in his horse at the edge of the town of Scyene. The sheriff had taken care of things in Dennison after the shooting of Holt and the recovery of the Maitlin horses. A short train ride to Dallas, an overnight stay, and then an hour's ride to the east had brought Stone to Scyene. He surveyed the main street, which was named Scyene Road. He rode along the street until he spotted a café, where he decided to stop off for breakfast.

Taking a table near the window, he pulled out a couple pieces of paper and a pencil, making a few notes about what he knew so far. Scyene had a population now of around 250 people, which was down a little from what it had been at its peak. The town had refused to build a depot for the railroad and seemed to be declining now as a result. They had built the depot in nearby Mesquite.

Stone knew that Myra Maybelle Shirley, or May Shirley, had come to Scyene maybe twenty years earlier and had lived near the Younger family. She had also known the James family in Missouri, though she didn't seem to have had any part in the James-Younger robberies. Neither family seemed to be around here now, though he thought it would be worth checking around near the farms where they had lived.

A café server interrupted him briefly to bring coffee and to take his order. When she left, he began scratching a few more notes on the paper. May Shirley, now known as Belle Starr, had come here at around age 18, then married a man named Jim Reed two years later. Reed, who had known the Starr family, had been killed in a holdup about six years after marrying May Shirley. Her connection with Sam Starr came a couple years after that. She had married him and moved to the Territory.

Stone decided that the best thing would be to look for friends and acquaintances of May Shirley during those two years after she came to Scyene, before she married Jim Reed. Maybe there was a connection from those early years. If he turned up nothing there, maybe there was someone she and Jim Reed had both known during that timeframe of fifteen to twenty years ago.

Where to start? That was the question. He could try the saloon, but he needed to find someone who had been a friend or acquaintance of May Shirley. The saloon didn't sound like a good place to find somebody like that. He eyed the server as she came back to get his money for the breakfast. Maybe he could start by asking her.

He put a couple of coins on the table, then held out a hand to stop her as she walked away with the money. "Could I ask you a question?"

She stopped and waited, saying nothing. Her expression also told him nothing.

"I'm wondering where I could find someone who knew May Shirley, maybe fifteen or twenty years ago." When he got a blank look, he tried again: "Folks call her

Belle Starr now, but she was May Shirley or Myra Shirley back then."

The expression turned from blank to slightly suspicious. She glanced at the badge on his chest, then seemed to stop and think about the question. She shrugged. "I didn't know her at all. She's a little older than me. I have an uncle and a neighbor who talk about her from time to time. You could find them both at the lodge tonight." She pointed across the street.

Stone looked across the street and saw a Masonic Lodge. It didn't seem much better than the saloon as a place for asking questions, but he could give it a try. He looked back at the server hopefully. "Can you tell me where she lived when she was here?"

"Sorry." She walked away to take an order from a couple who had just arrived.

———

After stopping several people on their way down Scyene Road, Stone was finally directed to two small neighboring farms on the east side of Scyene. Here, he was told, was where the Shirley and Younger families had lived during their days in Scyene.

He knocked at the door of the first house for a long time, hearing no answer from inside. Walking around the corner, he found an older woman weeding in the garden. She stopped and watched as he crossed the yard toward her.

She said nothing as he introduced himself and ignored the handshake he offered. She waited impatiently as he explained that he was looking for someone who had known Belle Starr as a young woman. Her expression hardened at the mention of the name.

"You some newspaper fella, tryin' to get a story again? How many times are you people gonna bother me?"

She was building to a full-fledged tirade when Stone stopped her by waving his arms and pointing at his badge. She subsided only slightly, then ignored all further questions as she went back to hoeing her garden.

"Don't know nothin'," she informed him over her shoulder.

———

Stone got only slightly better reception at the next door, and nothing more in the way of answers. By early evening, he was getting thoroughly discouraged. He decided to try the Masonic Lodge. He had no intention of interrupting their meeting, but maybe he could meet somebody on their way in if he waited out in front of the lodge.

Finally, his luck changed. A man coming in for the meeting stopped to answer his questions and directed him to another man who turned out to be the uncle of the woman who had served him in the café. He stroked his beard thoughtfully when Stone asked for anybody who had known Belle Starr.

"Old lady Greer," he said, pointing down the street. "White house with the pink shutters. She was kind to May Shirley, and May didn't have many friends. Ask old lady Greer. Watch out for the fruitcake, though." He chuckled as he walked into the lodge building.

Not sure what that last remark meant, Stone walked down the street to the house they had directed him to. A wizened old lady answered the door and squinted at him as he explained why he had come. Her eyes lighted up at the mention of Belle Starr/May Shirley and she threw the door open, then waved him to a table in the kitchen.

"May Shirley, huh?" The voice was hoarse and

sounded a little like a croak. She hovered over him, offering a drink, which Stone declined. "No whiskey?" She sounded very disappointed and poured one for herself.

"Okay," she conceded. "No whiskey. You got to have some of my fruit cake, though." She dropped a loaf of something onto the table. Stone pulled back slightly when he heard the solid *thunk* of the loaf hitting the wooden table. She produced a knife and began to saw away at it.

When she had hacked off a piece of the cake, she dropped it onto a plate and pushed the plate in front of Stone. He had to admit that it smelled good and didn't look too bad, but the sound of the single piece thumping down onto the plate had him a little scared. He picked up a fork and prodded at it. Seeing a slightly hurt look on her face, he took a bite, mainly just to keep her talking.

Old lady Greer settled down into a chair opposite Stone and finished off her whiskey. "Belle Starr," she reminisced in a gravelly voice. "She were somethin'. Rode up and down the street in that black velvet ridin' outfit, shootin' off them pistols. She were really somethin'." She reached around for the whiskey bottle again.

Stone couldn't help but notice that she wasn't eating the cake. It was feeling a little heavy in his stomach, but he had to keep her talking. He swallowed another piece.

"Didn't have many friends, she sure didn't. She liked to come over here from time to time, an' I'd always talk to her. Didn't have no boy takin' a shine to her, not till that no-good Jim Reed. Can't blame the boys, though. All that shootin' and cussin' and spittin' she always done. And that black velvet..." Old lady Greer shook her head and lapsed into silence.

Stone took a deep breath and swallowed two more bites. "Good cake," he lied. His stomach was complaining.

Old lady Greer brightened up noticeably. "I soak it in rum. That there's the secret," she confided. "Let's see now,

May Shirley. She taken up with the no-account Jim Reed, an' then Sam Starr. I don't guess no other boys was interested, though. Them other two used to hang around with her, but I don't think they was up to no good, neither."

Stone's attention homed in on her immediately. "What other two?" he asked. She looked at him blankly, then looked at the cake on his plate. Stone shoveled down another bite.

"Them other two...what was their names?" she mumbled to herself. "One of 'em was Pendleton...Ed Pendleton, I think. The other was Mort Wilson. He wasn't no good, neither. I think maybe the three of them was rustlin' cows or horses, or they was up to some kind of no good back then. Pendleton was the smart one. Wilson fancied hisself to be the leader. May should've stayed away from them, too."

Stone put the fork down and leaned forward. She was starting to fade out, probably from that third shot of whiskey. "What became of those two? Do you ever hear anything about Pendleton or Wilson?"

She roused herself briefly and shook her head. "Haven't heard nothin' about Pendleton," she said. She gazed blankly at the opposite wall. "Wilson, I heard he don't exackly go by that name no more. Heard he got hisself elected to somethin'. Mayor, or sheriff, or senator, or somethin'. I still say he ain't no good." Her eyes closed and her head slid down onto the table. Moments later, there was a loud snoring noise.

Stone let himself out and walked over to his horse. He swung aboard and moaned slightly as he did so. Tomorrow, he would send a telegram to McDonald. Meanwhile, he steered his horse toward the saloon. Maybe some whiskey would soak up some of that fruitcake. McDonald would never appreciate what he had gone through to get this information. How much did that cake weigh, anyway? Ten pounds?

———

Back in Austin, McDonald stopped off at the telegraph office and sorted through three messages. He set aside two of them. The third message, he saw, was from Mike Stone. He opened it and glanced at it briefly. The names Pendleton and Wilson meant nothing to him, but he felt strongly that he needed to follow up on it. He would do that himself, he decided. He dashed off a message to Stone, telling him that he would follow up personally. He paused for a minute, tapping his pencil thoughtfully on the counter. He finished by telling Stone to return to Austin.

Grabbing up his bag, he made a dash for the train station just down the street. He was catching a train to San Antonio this morning to see if he could get any clues about who had sent that anonymous telegram to tip him off about Holt. Something really didn't smell right about that one. He had to get to the bottom of it.

A train whistle sounded, and he picked up the pace to a full-out sprint. He swung aboard just in time and plopped down onto one bench. With any luck, he would be home tonight, but he wasn't counting on it. He had a strong hunch about this. He would stay in San Antonio as long as he needed to.

CHAPTER SIXTEEN
GENTRY

We struck a trail south along the banks of the Colorado. I could tell that losing her prize stallion was weighing heavily on Jessie, and I questioned whether my plan was going to work. The trail of the rustlers was only growing colder by the hour, and they had succeeded with as many robberies as they had pulled off because they were good at covering their tracks and moving the horses. We traveled south for a day, pausing only occasionally when we spotted tracks near the river bank. By evening, nothing had panned out, but we came to railroad tracks running east–west. We stopped to talk things over for a while and agreed that in the morning we would follow the railroad tracks east to the nearest town. Maybe there we could pick up a clue about where rustlers might hide out in this area.

We made dinner over a small fire, then we leaned back against a log, covered by a blanket against the evening chill. I wondered what Jessie would do if we couldn't find the stallion, but didn't want to ask. I got up to put a little more wood on the fire, and she seemed to guess at my thoughts.

"I'll always have that ranch," she said thoughtfully. "At least, as long as I'm able to keep things running and hold on to it. It was my dad's dream, and it's what my family does now. The horse breeding I was doing with that stallion was what I loved doing, but I can still breed and sell mustangs for cowboys and probably graze a few more head of cattle than I have been. I can keep it going."

I returned and sat next to her in front of the fire again. I thought about my time in Texas, spent on a cattle drive and working with the Rangers. "Well," I said eventually, "you'll always have a place that's home. That's what I miss the most since leaving Tennessee. Home and family."

She reached under the blankets and took my hand. "That's right," she said. "You don't have any family in Texas, do you?"

"No," I said regretfully. "What family I have left is all back in Tennessee."

She gave my hand a squeeze under the blankets. "You never know," she said. "Maybe we can do something about that."

The fire burned down after a while, and the evening grew colder. We laid out bedrolls near the coals and fell asleep, hoping tomorrow would bring us closer to finding that Arabian stallion.

———

The railroad tracks led us east to a town called Burnet the next morning. I can't say I'd heard of it, but I hadn't been in Texas all that long. It was a pretty small little town, but the local news was that the Austin and Northwestern Railroad had come to town, and things were busy because of the railroad. They had built the tracks from Austin to Burnet, and they were building more tracks to the north, up to the town of Llano. So far as I could tell, there weren't many trains going through yet, but there were jobs for track layers and such. They even had themselves a new telegraph office, and they were building a hotel.

We stopped for breakfast at the only café I could see in town, and I figured that was as good a place as any to ask questions, seeing as how the saloon wouldn't get busy until later. We got disappointed in a hurry though, as the girl that brought our breakfast just shook her head and left when I asked a couple questions. The other two tables had railroad workers who had only come here a couple months before. It was getting hard to shake off the discouragement and the feeling that the rustlers had simply vanished. Again. They were good at it.

We killed some time until the early afternoon, then went down to the saloon. There were only three or four people in there, but the owner had a tip for us.

"You need to talk to Gentry," he told us. "Old rascally coot has a little spread west of here that don't keep him nearly busy enough. That's why he's in here every night. I think he might have rode the outlaw trail hisself back in the day. He might tell you somethin' or he might not, but you could ask him yourself in a couple hours."

Gentry came in as promised a couple hours later, thumbs hooked behind his suspenders, slumped over slightly as he made his way to a table in the corner. His face was leathery from many hours spent in the sun. The crow's feet at the corners of his eyes were deep and pronounced. He looked up, only mildly curious, as Jessie and I approached.

"Can we ask what you know about outlaws who've been around these parts?" I began. "Maybe horse rustlers who've been around here?"

Gentry glanced away from me as a beer was brought to the table. He glanced at Jessie, then back at me. He drained half the beer in one gulp. "Don't know nothin' about rustlers." He waved for another beer. "Horse thieves get hung."

"Outlaws, then. Have there ever been any outlaws working these parts?"

He hesitated, and I tossed a coin onto the table.

"I'll buy you a couple," I said.

He shrugged and waved at the table. I held a chair for Jessie and dragged another one over for myself.

"Don't know nothin' about outlaws around here lately," he said. "Maybe there was a few several years back, but that probably don't do you no good now." He shoved my money at the boy who brought his beer and drained the new one.

I dropped another piece of silver on the table. "That's okay," I said. "It doesn't have to be recent. What can you tell me? Has anybody used these parts as a hideout?"

It was a shot in the dark, but he stopped with his beer halfway to his lips. He shot a blurry-eyed look at me over the beer, then at my badge.

"I might have heard tell of something," he mumbled. "Didn't do no outlawin' myself, you know."

Now we were getting somewhere. "I don't care what you have done or haven't done." I leaned forward. "Tell me what you know."

Gentry seemed to think things over for a minute. I was wondering if I needed to up his order to some whiskey to loosen his lips, but it turned out that one more beer did the job. He looked back and forth between Jessie and me, then put the empty glass down.

"There's a place right near here that was used by outlaws a time or two. I mean, I..." He seemed to think better of what he started to say. "I mean, I heard tell, is all," he said evasively.

I waved my hand in frustration.

"There's a cave," he said finally. "Rebs used it to make

gunpowder durin' the war. Sam Bass used it as a hideout, they say. Rode their horses right in there to hide out. That's what I heard, anyway. Folks say he hid two million dollars in there one time, but that ain't true. I don't believe it no ways," he amended.

The part about riding horses into the cave had our attention. I glanced at Jessie, trying to keep the excitement out of my voice. "Where is the cave?"

Gentry waved his arm vaguely. "West of here. Ride west. It's out past my spread. Easy to miss, though."

"Will you take us there?" I asked. I was aware of Jessie's hand tightening on my arm.

Gentry immediately shook his head. "Nope."

I asked again, and he shook his head again. He moved to get up, and I wondered what else he might know about that cave. I dropped the subject, bought him one more beer, then moved to another table with Jessie.

"He's scared, I think," I told Jessie. "He's afraid of somebody that's been in that cave. Maybe afraid of somebody that's using it now." I drummed the tabletop in frustration. "That place could take a while to find."

Gentry stood up to leave, and Jessie rose and walked across to stop him before he could get to the door. "I run a small ranch with my mother and my brother," she told him. "The most valuable thing by far that I had on that ranch was an Arabian stallion. He was stolen, and it will be hard for us without him. Can't you help us?"

Gentry looked at Jessie for a long moment, then stared at the floor. "Okay," he agreed. "You come out to my place in the morning, and I'll help. Bud, over there, can tell you how to get to my place." He pointed at the barkeeper, then left.

———

McDonald leaned back against the seat and waited for his breathing to come back to normal. It was another sign he was sitting down behind the desk too much—running for the train had left him completely winded. He stared out the window. It wasn't too long ago he would have been riding his horse down here to San Antonio. He preferred to ride his horse, but he had to admit the trains were faster. It made it a little easier for the Rangers to get around, too. The train tracks were being laid everywhere. Unfortunately, it also made it easier for the outlaws to get around.

He pulled a stack of papers out of his bag and started to read. He made a mental note to tell the governor he wanted to go back out and do his work from the back of his horse. There had to be somebody who could stay in Austin and do his job. He'd only worked this job as long as he had at the governor's insistence. A new job, the governor had called it. Somebody else could have it as far as he was concerned.

After a while, he put the papers away, except for Stone's telegram from Scyene. He studied it again. The names Pendleton and Wilson still meant nothing, but Stone had passed along a comment from the woman in Scyene that Wilson had gotten himself elected to something. McDonald tapped the message thoughtfully on his knee. He shuffled through his papers again and pulled out a list of statewide elected officials for Texas. He had requested it a few days ago, back in Austin. He looked at the list again. Neither name was on there.

He stuffed the papers back in the bag when the whistle sounded in San Antonio. He hopped down, pulled out the slip of paper with the telegraph office address, and immediately asked for directions. It turned out to be a walk of about a mile, but that didn't bother him. He liked to walk.

A bell sounded quietly when he entered the office, and

a clerk looked up from behind the desk. McDonald walked across the room, holding the anonymous telegram he had received, tipping him off about Holt. The clerk held out his hand to take the message from him. He prepared to send it, then looked up in confusion. "Uh, what do you want me to do with this, sir?"

McDonald leaned against the counter. "Somebody in your Austin office where I received this message said that it was sent from here. Was it you that sent this message?"

The clerk glanced back down at the telegram and nodded his head. "Yes, sir, I sent this message. It has my initials on it." He looked back up, still wearing a look of confusion.

McDonald reached out and took the telegram back. "What I need to know is, can you remember anything about the man who sent this? Anything at all that you can tell me would be helpful."

The clerk reached for the message again, and McDonald gave it to him. "Sent two days ago," the clerk said, mainly to himself. He tapped the paper on the countertop and thought. "I remember only a little. I hadn't ever seen him in here before, I'm certain. He was tall—maybe your height. Slim."

"Age?" McDonald asked.

He stared at the countertop, shaking his head slowly. "Hard to remember, sir. Maybe forty or so." He handed the message back, spreading his hands in an apologetic gesture. "Sorry, there's just nothing else I can remember."

McDonald folded up the telegram, thanked the clerk, and let himself out the door of the office. He dawdled along the street, trying to focus his thoughts. That had been little to move forward with. He walked past the county courthouse and stared at it blankly for a moment. Stone's message said that the man Wilson had gotten himself elected to something. He moved along a little farther, passing the mayor's office, then a small office for city records. He stopped and retraced his steps.

The clerk in the records office looked at him in confusion when he made his request. The man centered his glasses on his nose and repeated McDonald's request. "Elected officials in San Antonio, sir? Elected to what, exactly?"

"Elected to any city offices. You'd have that, wouldn't you?" The clerk nodded slowly. "Yes, most of them, anyway." He eyed McDonald's badge, then nodded again. "I'll make a list of all the elected city officials for San Antonio. Can you check back with me in the morning?"

McDonald thanked the man, then made the same request at the county courthouse for anyone elected to a county office. The clerk there also promised to have a list in the morning.

Feeling somewhat better, McDonald found a place to stay for the night. He would go back to Austin tomorrow.

———

Milo Wills looked up as Shaw came into his office and slumped down in a chair in the corner. There were a couple things about Shaw, Wills reflected, that really irritated him, and he had just seen two of them. First, Shaw always came in without knocking, and second, he didn't bother to speak to Wills or even look at him. Wills stared at him for several seconds without result, then curiosity got the better of him.

"How's our friend Lance doing?" he rasped, not bothering to look at Shaw. Two could play this game.

"You won't see Lance no more," Shaw said in an indifferent tone. "He got shot during a train robbery." He glanced up, gratified to see the astonished look on Will's face. Shaw nodded. "Yep, he was robbing a train durin' a water stop. The kid in the express car thinks he shot Lance, so I got away clean. It was me who got him with my rifle."

Wills leaned forward, elbows on his desk, thinking that one over. He felt considerable relief, he realized. Lance was out of the way and nobody could tie it back to him. Holt hadn't been heard from, and he felt good on that score, too. Maybe he could just rebuild this operation with Pendleton. He'd have to make nice to Belle Starr, though. Lost in thought, he mumbled something to Shaw about taking a walk and left the office.

There were a few loose ends he would still have to tie up. Holt had hired a couple of no-accounts to steal the horses and then look after them at Longhorn Cave. He didn't know exactly what had happened to his scout, who'd been out there looking for horses to steal. He felt sure nobody could tie the scout back to him, but he would have to find somebody else. Maybe, he thought, he should just let things settle down for a few months, then restart the whole rustling operation.

Walking down the street, Wills glanced across the road at the telegraph office where he had gone to send the telegram to the Ranger captain, McDonald. He stared at the man coming out of the office, then forced himself to stop staring and keep walking. The man was wearing a badge, and Wills was pretty sure it was Captain McDonald himself. He had been dressed up for an event when they had met, but it looked like McDonald. Wills walked another hundred yards, then looked back to see McDonald going into another building.

Wills took the long route back to his office, then burst through the door. "Pack up what you need and meet me here in fifteen minutes," he growled. "We're leaving town for a while." He grabbed a gun and some papers from his desk, then went home to pack up.

Next morning, Captain McDonald visited both offices from the day before—the county records office and the city records office. Both had given him a list, and he scanned the names eagerly. Disappointment set in when he failed to see a Mort Wilson on either list. He pulled the state list he had brought from Austin, glanced at it briefly, then folded the three together and put them all in his pocket. He crossed the street, headed for a café he had seen down the block.

As he walked, head down, he nearly collided with a shopkeeper who was sweeping the dirt and leaves away from his shop entrance. McDonald looked up, apologized, and started to move on when a sign on the office next door caught his eye. McDonald stepped back and read slowly:

Milo Wills, Esq.
Attorney, Texas State Senator

A surge of excitement swept through him as he pulled the lists from his pocket and shuffled through them to find the names he'd brought on the state list from Austin. He kicked himself mentally for not thinking of this before. Wills and Wilson were pretty close, and a lot of men changed their names to hide their past. He whirled back to look at the shopkeeper, pointing at the sign on the window. "Where—"

The shopkeeper looked at the sign, then back at McDonald. "He's gone. Him and that thug that works for him. Done gone yesterday. Had a couple horses packed up. I'd say they'll be gone for a while." He finished sweeping and went back inside.

McDonald stared at the shopkeeper's back, then

turned and began trotting back to his room at the boarding house. He would get back to Austin on today's train. Mike Stone should come in today. He would get Stone on the trail. Wills, or Wilson, or whatever his name was, could be the key to everything.

CHAPTER SEVENTEEN

CLOSING IN

Wills slumped in his seat on the train, resisting the urge to kick Shaw, who was sleeping in his seat with apparently no worries in the world. This was the first time Wills had made the trip to Longhorn Cave since beginning the horse-stealing operation nearly two years ago. The train tracks to Burnet had been laid since that time. Maybe, he reflected, that was a reason all by itself to get out of the horse-stealing business for a while. The train would bring a lot more people to the area. More people meant more chances someone would find the cave.

Wills didn't know the guys that Holt had used to steal horses and hide them. He knew they operated in and around the cave, and he didn't figure they would be hard to find. He would run them off and keep any horses they might have there. If they objected, well, he didn't plan to make it a fair fight. He would make sure he had the drop on them, and besides, that's why he had Shaw. He really didn't plan to let anybody get away from the cave that might identify him later.

After what seemed like an eternity spent chugging

north on the rails, someone came by to inform them that the train would shortly arrive in Burnet. They rolled in, and Wills and Shaw disembarked, then retrieved their horses and mounted up. As they rode through Burnet, Wills glanced over and noticed a beautiful young woman standing outside the telegraph office. He tipped his hat to her, and she nodded. Burnet, Wills thought, was a more interesting town than it had been on his last trip up here. But business came first, he reminded himself. They trotted their horses out of town and turned toward Long-horn Cave.

———

McDonald arrived at his office to find Stone waiting for him. He trotted into the room, waving at Stone to take a seat. McDonald dropped the list of elected officials for the state of Texas in front of Stone, then hauled his chair around the desk to sit beside him. He ran his finger down the list, then stopped at the name of Milo Wills.

"I think this is your boy Mort Wilson," he informed Stone. "People change their names sometimes to hide what they've done. That woman up in Scyene said he'd gotten himself elected to something, right?"

Stone nodded thoughtfully. "She did. Initials are the same, MW either way. Could be him. Where is this guy Milo Wills located?"

McDonald explained how the state senator was located in San Antonio but had left town in a hurry yester-day. He thumped the desk in frustration at the fact he didn't know where to look now.

Pulling his watch from a pocket, McDonald jumped up and headed for the door.

"I've got to talk to the governor," he said. "You can go on home for a couple hours, if you want to. I'll check for messages after my meeting. If we haven't heard from McKinnon by the time my meeting is over, you can go back to the Maitlin Ranch and see what has been happening there."

Stone followed him out the door, wondering if he had enough time to go home and come back. He decided it was worth it to make the trip.

————

I took my time in the telegraph office, trying to figure out exactly what I wanted to tell McDonald about where we had gone and why. I settled for saying that the stallion had been stolen from the Maitlin Ranch, and I had followed the trail to the Colorado River, where the trail had gone cold. I tapped the pencil on the countertop for a while, then settled for saying that I believed they could hide the stallion at a place called Longhorn Cave. I could explain the rest of it another time. I started to hand it over to be transmitted, then pulled it back. I added a sentence to say that Longhorn Cave is near the town of Burnet, and there was a guy named Gentry who would guide us. I scanned what I had written one more time, then handed it over to the clerk.

Jessie was waiting on a bench outside the telegraph office when I came out. She linked her arm through mine as we stepped off the boardwalk. We unhitched the horses, but she paused before mounting.

"Do you think we should get some food and supplies before we go out there?" she asked. "You said it could take a while to find it. Maybe we should make sure we can stay for a while and keep looking if we need to."

I agreed, and we made a stop at the general store before leaving town. Jessie picked up some food while I laid in some extra ammunition for both my Colt and

Winchester. I figured if these guys had gone to this much trouble to steal the stallion, they probably wouldn't want to give him up peaceably. More time had passed than I had figured on, so we hurried to get back to the horses and on the trail.

We followed the directions they had given me to Gentry's place. We found him about forty-five minutes later, standing on a falling-down porch with his thumbs hooked into his suspenders. He watched us ride up, but there was no smile on his face.

Jessie leaned in to me as we reined in the horses. "Do you think he's had second thoughts about helping us?"

"Looks like it," I mumbled. I kept my eyes locked on his as he came down slowly from the porch.

Like he was reading our thoughts, Gentry looked first at me, then at Jessie. He dropped his eyes to the ground after looking at her, then stared off down the trail behind us. Finally, he cleared his throat, looking back at Jessie.

"I said I'd hep ya, and I will, a little," he said in a soft voice. "I mean, I'll get you close to that cave and point the way for the last bit. That's the best I'll do," he said defiantly. "Take it or leave it."

I exchanged glances with Jessie—we really didn't need to talk about it. I looked off toward the west, assuming that the cave lay in that direction.

"Take us to it," I said.

Gentry mounted up, and we followed him, moving to the west as I had thought we would. None of us said anything. The creak of saddle leather was the only sound to be heard. The ground stayed level for a while, then rose slightly. Stands of oak trees became more frequent and a little thicker. In another fifteen minutes, we were weaving in and out among some large boulders, and the terrain became more rugged.

Finally, Gentry stopped and half-turned his horse to

face us. He pointed off toward the northwest, then waved his hand in that direction.

"I ain't goin' no further," he announced. "T'ain't gonna be that hard to find it from here. Just keep yore eyes open." He turned and rode off.

I watched his retreating back for a moment, then turned back to look in the direction he had pointed. I started to tell Jessie we could just spread out a few yards apart and work to the north and west. I stopped halfway through what I was saying and we both ducked down over our saddles when we heard nearby gunshots.

———

Mike Stone was back in McDonald's office when the door popped open and McDonald walked in, pushing a telegram into Stone's hand.

"Telegram from McKinnon," he said. "Just got it this morning. I think maybe you need to go to this cave."

Puzzled about the cave remark, Stone took the telegram and read it. He hadn't heard of Longhorn Cave, but that's what would make it a good hideout—if very few people knew about it.

"I can take the train to Burnet," Stone said, rising from the chair and grabbing his hat. "What about this Milo Wills guy? Or Mort Wilson, or whatever his name is. Want me to do anything about that?"

McDonald shook his head and dropped into this chair.

"You just go find this cave and see if McKinnon needs any help. If we have a lot of luck, that's where Wills went yesterday. I'll see what I can find out about Senator Wills and where he came from. And Stone...the shopkeeper yesterday said Wills has a thug that works for him. Keep your eyes open and tell McKinnon that goes for him too."

———

The trip to the train station was a quick ride, then Stone could catch a late morning train to Burnet. McKinnon's telegram had said they were being guided to the cave by a man named Gentry. He would take time to ask around town about Gentry and where he lived. He slid down in the seat and pulled his hat down over his eyes. Today was shaping up to be a long day.

———

Wills and Shaw were approaching the entrance to Longhorn Cave—Wills felt sure of it. He had last been there a year or two earlier, so he was a little fuzzy on the landmarks, but he knew they were getting close. He pulled Shaw aside and explained his plan for dealing with the two men Holt had used to steal and watch the horses.

"I plan to ride up to the entrance of the cave by myself," he told Shaw. "Your job is to move along beside me, using the boulders for cover. When I run into these two guys, I need you to cover me from someplace where they can't see you." He added an afterthought as Shaw pulled his rifle out of the scabbard. "They don't really need to be around to point us out to the sheriff or Texas Rangers later on."

Shaw dismounted without answering and tethered his horse in a stand of oak trees. He knew what to do. He returned, carrying his rifle, and began moving from boulder to boulder, staying about thirty yards to the left of Wills.

Wills moved forward, holding his horse to a walk to allow Shaw to keep up. He followed a slightly weaving path, staying alert for the cave entrance. He really didn't want to stumble into it. As it was, he nearly stumbled into Holt's men before he found the cave.

Emerging from a stand of trees, eyes scanning from left to right, Wills jerked his horse to a halt suddenly when he saw two men standing in front of him, side-by-side. Wills's horse crow-hopped a time or two at the sudden yank on the reins and Wills soothed the horse as he eyed the two men. Both held rifles in front of them. They pointed the muzzles at the ground, but Wills knew he couldn't make any sudden moves. It wouldn't take that long to bring those rifles to bear.

"Howdy," he said conversationally, resisting the urge to look over his shoulder to see if Shaw was in place. "I'm looking for a lost horse. Wandered out this direction this morning. Either of you boys see a horse wandering around here?"

"Nope." The speaker was the one on the left. He leaned over to spit on the ground. "Long ways for a horse to wander off, mister. You sure he was lost?" He sneered a bit as he asked, and Wills had no doubt these were Holt's horse thieves.

Wills sized up the situation. The one on the left was itching for a fight. He had raised the muzzle of the gun slightly and was trying to stare Wills down. The one on the right still looked to be fairly relaxed. His gun muzzle remained pointed at the ground, but he was scanning the trees and boulders on both sides. That was the smart one, Wills decided. He was more dangerous.

Wills gave the one on the left a disarming smile. "Yep, he just wandered off," he said. "You trying to say I'm a horse thief, mister? Because you sure look like a horse thief to me." He finished with a hard edge to his tone.

It took a second for the words to register. The one on the left had a smirk on his face that changed to anger as the words sunk in. The muzzle of the gun came up, then the man was driven backward by Shaw's shot. The rifle clattered to the ground, and he slumped sideways, dead instantly from a shot through his chest.

Wills palmed his pistol, prepared for a shot at the second man. Shaw's gun sounded again, but the second man had leaped to the side and dropped behind a boulder. He snapped off a quick shot at Wills, who dove from his horse and crawled behind another boulder. After several seconds passed with no further shots, he eased his head around the base of the boulder for a look. He could hear a faint rustling of leaves and twigs somewhere ahead of him, but the second man seemed to be gone. Wills rose to his feet, remaining crouched behind the boulder, and waved for Shaw to come forward.

Shaw came forward, but Wills chafed at how long it was taking. Eventually, Shaw came into view, using the trees and boulders for cover. Wills waved his pistol impatiently, but Shaw ignored him completely, focusing on the ground in front of him until he had worked to a position parallel to the one held by Wills. He continued forward, and Wills moved forward after a moment, lagging a little behind Shaw. He intended to let Shaw take the risks.

Shaw reached the place where the two men had been standing, and Wills covered him from behind a tree while Shaw checked the dead man, then the tracks left by the second man. The two of them followed the tracks for just fifty yards or so, but the prospect of somebody returning the favor and shooting them from cover proved to be too much. They returned to the mouth of the cave. Wills walked inside briefly, then came back out. There were fresh horse droppings inside, but he wasn't going to chase after a horse at this point. The second man, the one who had gotten away—that was more important.

Wills came back to stand beside Shaw, relieved at not getting shot, but not all that happy about that horse thief that got away. He had pretty well decided to order Shaw to go after the man while he himself waited in the cave. He started to say so, irritated that Shaw didn't seem to listen to him.

"Somebody else comin'," Shaw said as he ducked and scrambled to the top of a small rise, taking cover behind a boulder. Wills could see his rifle resting in a niche at the top of the boulder. Wills broke in the other direction, taking cover behind a large oak tree. In a few minutes, he could see the man Shaw had seen just a few minutes earlier. He was on foot, leading his horse and coming along slowly. The sunlight reflected off the badge on his chest.

Shaw stayed motionless where he was. The man he'd spotted earlier was still coming forward, although slowly. He turned slightly, giving Shaw a better look at him, and Shaw caught the glint of sunlight reflecting off the badge. He smiled slowly and crouched a bit, shifting just a little to sight down the barrel. Shooting a Ranger would be a first. He was going to enjoy this.

———

We had drifted in the direction of the gunfire. The more ground we covered, the more worried I became. Not for me. I'd been shot at before, and no doubt I would be again, but I was worried for Jesse. Her mother and brother needed her back at the ranch. There was nobody at home waiting for me. I stopped and started to explain why I wanted her to stay back.

"It's dangerous," I began. "We don't know how many of them are out there or who they're shooting at." I could see by the set of her jaw I wasn't getting anywhere.

"I'm coming with you," she said firmly. "Anyway,

who's saying they're not coming in this direction and they'll find me here after you're gone?"

Well, she kinda had me there. We really didn't know where these guys were or what their problem was. Finally, I worked out a compromise with her.

"Okay," I said finally. "Come with me, but will you let me go first? Stay off to my side and maybe thirty or forty yards behind me. If anybody draws a shot, I want it to be me. Will you agree to that?"

She thought it over and agreed. We proceeded on horseback for maybe a mile, then we dismounted. I used the trees for cover a little more and urged Jessie to do the same. She stayed back as agreed, and I slowly worked my way forward, thinking maybe we were getting close to that cave.

———

Jessie stayed back as asked, but kept her rifle ready as she moved from tree to tree. There were boulders now as well, and she wove back and forth among them. Things had been quiet for more than a half hour now since they had heard the gunshots, and she wondered if the horse thieves had cleared out and taken the stallion with them.

Moving toward a large boulder, she scanned from left to right, seeing Ash on her left. She swept the ground on her right visually, then froze. She drew a deep breath and moved forward to the boulder in front of her. There was a man ahead of her, maybe sixty yards away, using a boulder for cover as he took aim at Ash. She didn't have much time. She dropped to the ground, laid her rifle across the boulder, and squeezed off a shot.

CHAPTER EIGHTEEN
HUNTERS AND HUNTED

Ike couldn't believe he was still alive. He had spent several months with Slade, stealing horses and hiding them at this cave. He knew he wasn't any smarter than Slade, and he was sure he wasn't any faster with a gun. He liked to think he had a better sense of self-preservation. When the man on the horse had showed up outside the cave, he really wasn't too worried because he and Slade had the numbers in their favor.

Slade had a quicker temper, and Ike could tell he was getting ready to shoot the guy. That was okay with him, it saved him from doing the dirty work. When somebody they couldn't see had opened up with a rifle on Slade, Ike had lit out of there like a scared jackrabbit. But, he reminded himself, he was still alive and Slade wasn't.

He hadn't tried to cover his tracks at all. He'd just run in a zig-zag pattern, using trees or rocks for cover if he could. He was surprised they hadn't come after him—he knew he'd made a lot of noise, and it couldn't have been that hard to follow his tracks. Now, he was just lying in some underbrush, peering out through the leaves, not quite believing his own luck.

He was jolted into action when he heard more gunfire coming from the direction of the cave. He wormed out from the underbrush and began running toward his horse. Once in a while, he leaped from boulder to boulder in an effort to cover his tracks, but it was a halfhearted effort at best. Mainly he needed to get out of there. Maybe they could occupy themselves with shooting at each other.

In another few minutes, he could see his horse. He slowed down, looking in both directions, afraid that somebody lay in ambush, waiting for him to reach his horse. After a brief pause, he knew he had to keep moving. He ran for his horse at full speed, once again hugely relieved when there were no further gunshots. His saddle was back in the cave, no time to mess with that. He untied the rope he had used to tether the horse and leaped up bareback. He trotted away, passing Slade's horse and the Arabian stallion.

He stopped and looked at the stallion. That was one fine horse. Did he dare take it with him? Greed won out, and he untied the Arabian's rope from the tree. The other end was still looped around the stallion's neck, and the horse followed along quietly enough. Ike swung a wide circle around the cave, then settled into a steady trot, headed for Burnet and the railroad.

———

Thirty minutes later, he was relaxing and congratulating himself. He had pulled off the trail from time to time, checking his back trail. Nobody seemed to follow him. Maybe those guys were busy, what with another gun battle breaking out before he'd left. He could get a good price for this stallion somewhere and start again.

After another few minutes, as he was drawing close to

Burnet, he saw another rider coming down the trail. He pulled his hat low, feeling fairly confident that the other rider couldn't be anybody who would recognize him. He and Slade had kept to themselves around here. He kept his gaze down on the trail, but he sensed that the other rider was slowing down. He risked a glance upward.

Ike's heart sank when he saw that the other man wore a badge. To make matters worse, he really seemed to be looking pretty hard at the stallion. His gaze traveled from the stallion to Ike. Several thoughts raced through Ike's mind at once, but one thought trumped all the others: horse thieves got hung in Texas, and he didn't want to get hung.

———

Mike Stone had directions to Gentry's house scratched onto a piece of paper, and he pushed his horse along at a brisk pace, following the directions they had given him. He didn't know exactly what Ash had found in Longhorn Cave, and he didn't know if the girl Jessie was with him, but something told him he needed to get there as soon as he could.

He saw the other rider coming down the trail and thought nothing of it at first. This didn't look to be a well-used trail, but occasional travelers were to be expected, and nothing seemed unusual at first glance. As they drew closer, he noticed that the other man had no saddle and was leading another horse with a rope he was holding with his left hand. Another look at the horse the man was leading told him this was an exceptional horse. In another instant, Stone knew this could well be the Arabian stallion missing from the Maitlin Ranch.

The other man seemed to mostly stare down at the trail. He pulled his horse slightly to the left, intent on passing Stone without looking at him. Stone moved his horse over to block the path.

"Hold on," said Stone, dismounting slowly, keeping his right hand near his gun belt. He noticed that the other man seemed to be keenly aware of Stone's gun hand.

"I need to have a look at that horse you're leading," Stone said shortly. "Go ahead and dismount."

The other man sat still for a moment, and Stone had the feeling there were several ideas going through his head at once. For an instant, Stone thought he was going to kick his horse in the ribs and make a run for it. Then he seemed to settle down. He shrugged and dismounted. An alarm went off in Stone's head when he saw the man was dismounting on the far side of his horse.

A small voice sounded in Stone's brain: *He's going to shoot under the horse!*

When the other man's feet hit the ground on the far side of his horse, Stone kneeled and drew in one motion. When the man's knees bent, Stone knew he'd been right. A gun appeared underneath the horse, and Stone fired. His shot hit the man in the thigh and he pitched backward, his gun going off in the air. The man's horse reared and raced away. Stone could see him now, raising up on one elbow and trying to bring the gun to bear. Stone fired again, and he slumped to the ground.

Stone rose slowly and moved over to the other man, keeping his gun out in front of him. A quick check told him the man was dead. Stone holstered his Colt and looked around. The horses hadn't gone far. His priority, as far as Stone was concerned, was to find McKinnon. He rounded up both horses and tossed the dead man over his horse. Then he led both horses over to a stand of trees and tethered them. He would come back to get them after he knew McKinnon was safe.

I was slipping through the trees and going from boulder to boulder, intent on the path in front of me. I felt pretty sure I could see the cave opening now—just a dark space from where I stood, but there seemed to be some footprints in front of that space. I moved from behind an oak tree, intent on getting a better look, when two rifle shots sounded.

The first shot was fired very close to me. I knew immediately it was Jessie. I registered movement in front. A man tumbled from behind a rock formation, his rifle sliding down through the boulders. The second shot came at the same time, and I felt the impact on my left shoulder. It spun me around and down. A third shot whistled through the air above me. I had the presence of mind to grab my rifle and roll behind a boulder, but it cost me. The pain in my shoulder was so intense I nearly passed out. I curled up behind the rock and fought to stay conscious.

There were a few searching shots as I lay there. A couple of them struck the boulder in front of me, then there was a shot on either side. I knew that he knew where I was, but I also knew the rock protected me in front. Otherwise I would have been dead by now.

I looked around me to size up my situation. There were two boulders protecting me in front, lying side by side, one slightly higher than the other one. I took a breath and crawled slightly to my left, feeling waves of nausea wash over me. There was a slight crevice between the rocks. I swallowed hard and risked a peek between the boulders, fearing the shot from above that might send rock fragments into my eyes.

After a couple quick glances, I realized that he probably couldn't see me watching from between the boulders. He was too far away and above me. I settled down to look for the shooter through that crevice. I felt thirsty, besides the weakness and shock passing over me after the gunshot. I looked longingly at my horse, cropping grass about fifty feet away. I could see my canteen hanging from the saddle horn, but I didn't dare try to call the horse over. My attacker would kill the horse in an instant. I was probably lucky he hadn't thought of it yet.

I settled down and concentrated on looking through that crevice between the rocks, trying to figure out exactly where the shooter was located. For a few minutes, nothing seemed to move. I felt sweat trickling down on my forehead and cheeks, and I knew it wasn't from hot weather. It was a pretty cold winter day, actually. I might not have that much time before I would pass out. That could be the end of both Jessie and me.

In the end, it was the reflection of sunlight off the gun barrel that gave him away. He was in a nest of boulders up there, closed in on three sides, shielding him from both Jessie's position and mine. He was back in the rock's shadow on my right, too far above me to offer a decent shot from where I was lying. I could see only the top of his head, but an idea came to me. I waited for my chance, hoping I would be strong enough when the moment came.

Finally, he seemed to lean away and down. The top of his head disappeared for a moment, and I got to my knees and laid my Winchester across the boulder. When the top of that head came back into view, I laid down several shots in a row into that nest of boulders. I knew how much damage flying rock chips could do. A moment later, I heard cursing, and he burst out of the nest of boulders, then he ducked around behind them. I got off one shot that might have grazed him, because I heard a fresh round of cursing, then silence. Now came the hard part.

I had to move and get to a new position. He knew

exactly where I was, and he had me completely pinned down here. I needed the ability to raise up and get a clean shot at him without, as Doc Linden would say, getting my fool head shot off. I had spotted a place in front of me with protection from a couple large trees and a long, flat rock, maybe two feet high. The shooter disappeared behind the boulder nest and I got up and broke into a stumbling trot toward my goal. I half tripped, half dove behind the rock. A moan broke from my lips and I passed out for a few seconds.

I came to and rolled closer to the rock. I found myself looking in a different direction, to the right of the nest of boulders I'd been watching before. My eyes widened when I saw Jessie, crouched in a small trough, sheltered by a few rocks and some underbrush. She stayed low, waving her arms to get my attention. When I locked in on her, she pointed toward the shooter's new position.

I scanned the area where she was pointing, and I could see him behind yet another rock. It sheltered him from Jessie and from where I had been lying before, but I could see his shoulder from my new spot. He was facing away from me, and it looked like he was going to try to circle around and come in from the side or from behind us. My eyes traveled along the path he needed to take. There was enough cover that he might just make it. I motioned to Jessie to stay where she was. I would have a clear shot when he moved. I just hoped I would be conscious and able to take it.

———

Wills crouched in his new spot, knowing he probably couldn't stay there for too long. There were two of them out there, and they both knew how to shoot. He could see Shaw from where he was crouching now, and it wasn't pretty. He had probably raised up just enough for somebody down there to get off a shot at his head, and that's where he'd been hit. Wills shuddered and looked away.

He knew he had hit the one on his right down below. He'd seen the man go down and there was blood on the ground next to where he had taken cover. The man could still shoot, though—blood was dripping from Wills's right cheek where he'd been stung by rock fragments, and there was a long nasty bullet furrow across his back.

The one on the left had been quiet for a while, and Wills was wondering if one of his shots down there had hit the mark. He couldn't stay here for much longer. This had to be finished, one way or the other. The one he'd shot earlier had a badge on his chest, and Wills was assuming he was a Texas Ranger. If there were any more of them around here, he had to get out.

He would make a dash to circle around the one on his left. If he could get down there, off to the side or behind them, he would have the advantage. A sudden rush might just catch them by surprise. He gathered a deep breath and lunged out from behind the rocks.

———

I worked my way up to my knees and to the left, mainly using one tree for cover. I was partially exposed, but I could see him from this spot, and he was looking the other way. I held the rifle barrel up against the tree to steady it down. My shoulder was throbbing with pain and I knew I had lost a lot of blood. The trickle of sweat had turned into something more like a river, running down my forehead and into my eyes. I ran my sleeve across my face and struggled through waves of dizziness. I had to wait for him to make his move.

There! He came to his feet and broke out from behind

the rocks, running in a zig-zag pattern toward the trees on his left. I moved the Winchester slightly and drew a bead on him, following his motion. I drew a breath and exhaled slowly, squeezing the trigger. The shot knocked him down, but he came up on his hands and knees and continued crawling toward the trees. I'd been too weak to hold my shooting position and landed on my back after the shot. The rifle clattered to the ground.

I scrambled to my knees and picked up the Winchester. There was no time to steady it against the tree again. He'd gotten to his feet now and was staggering toward the trees. I brought the Winchester up, sighted in, and squeezed the trigger one more time. He grabbed his chest, fell on his side, then slowly rolled over on his back, staring at the sky.

I slumped to my knees and fell back against the rock I had been using for cover. The surrounding trees seemed to swim in and out of focus. I heard footsteps running toward me, and then I heard Jessie calling my name...

I think I had only been out for a few minutes. Jessie was patting my hand and splashing water on my face. I shook my head to clear my vision and tried to move, but my shoulder was telling me not to try that again. I looked up to see Jessie's beautiful face. My head seemed to be cradled in her lap.

"Stay with me, Ash." She splashed a little more water on my face and smiled when she saw me open my eyes and focus on her. "Stay with me," she repeated.

A smile spread slowly across my face. "When you said to stay with you, did you mean just for now, or did you mean it permanent?"

I closed my eyes and heard a soft chuckle, then felt the cool pressure of her lips against mine.

"We can make that happen," she said.

CHAPTER NINETEEN

HOME AT THE RANCH

We were sitting on the back porch in a little swing I had put together with my one good arm. Of course, I had made it to be a swing for two. We could fit in it with a little room to spare, but it seemed like the extra room was never between us when we sat there. Doc Linden had visited this morning and said that my shoulder would heal up just fine. The bullet hadn't hit the bone. He told me to wait a few weeks before I tried to use that arm very much. I pointed out that I'd been hit in the shoulder this time, not the head, and he allowed that I was making some progress in that respect.

We had managed to get me in the saddle that day back at the cave, and we had run into Mike Stone on the trail back to Burnet. We stopped to get the Arabian stallion on the way into town, along with the other member of the horse rustling gang. He'd been in no condition to go anywhere. Five of them were dead, and we knew that Pendleton had left his railroad job in Temple and had disappeared. So far, we had found no sign of him anywhere.

We watched as the stallion and a few mares galloped across the pasture in the back of the house. They were no longer confined to the corral, of course, but it seemed that Iris had been giving them some carrots most days they had been there, so they were hanging out closer to the house than they had been before all the horse stealing had started. Watching them run was becoming one of my favorite pastimes while I was healing up. One of my favorites, but not my top favorite, of course. That swing for two was awfully nice.

Jessie and I had continued to talk about a future together, and I knew the next step was up to me. The doc had told me I should be able to saddle up and ride after another week, and my first trip was going to be to go into town and find a ring. I had taken Iris into my confidence, and she had told me what size I should get and what kind of rings Jessie liked. Jessie knew something was up and asked me some leading questions once in a while. But a guy has to have a few secrets, doesn't he?

We heard horses coming, and after a few more seconds, Mike Stone and Captain McDonald rode in and tethered their horses at the corral. We had known they were coming. Captain McDonald had sent me a telegraph saying they wanted to talk to me, but he hadn't told me what it was about.

We had set up chairs for them on the porch, and Iris bustled about, getting them coffee and cookies. We made small talk for a few minutes. McDonald told me that Milo Wills and Mort Wilson had in fact turned out to be the same person. It seems that he, Pendleton, and Belle Starr had done a little rustling in their days back in Scyene. Belle Starr was, of course, out of our reach up in the Territory. Pendleton had been seen buying a ticket for El Paso, but we didn't know if he was still in the state or not. At any rate, the gang had pretty much been put out of business.

McDonald paused and eyed Jessie and me sitting in the swing, then allowed himself a small smile. "I would ask how you're doing, McKinnon, but you seem to be doing fine."

I glanced over at Jessie, who gave me a smile. "Sometimes, cap'n," I said, "a man just has to make do the best he can."

Stone snorted loudly.

McDonald shook his head and chuckled. "Well, anyway," he continued. "We came to talk to you about a couple of changes that we're going to make." He glanced over at Stone, who was watching the horses in the pasture. McDonald looked back at me. "I've been in charge of special projects, reporting to the governor directly, for the last year or so."

I nodded—this wasn't news. I began to wonder what this had to do with me.

"So," McDonald continued, "I guess you know I haven't really wanted to spend so much time behind a desk. I've really been wanting to get back out and command some men in the field, like I used to." He cleared his throat and glanced over at Stone again. "I asked the governor if I could return to doing what I had done before. He agreed on the condition that I find somebody to replace me." He looked over at Stone again, and it dawned on me.

"You going to have Mike take your place," I said.

McDonald nodded. "Captain Stone is now the special assistant to the governor."

My mouth formed the words *Captain Stone*, but no sounds came out. I looked back and forth between them.

"Congratulations, Mike," I said. "Does this have anything to do with me? It seems like a long way to ride..."

Mike spoke for the first time. "The captain here," he said, pointing at McDonald, "has been pretty much buried trying to keep up with things. He can request help from the other units, but there's been no one else working on this...this special force. I've been told I can have one man to help me. I came to ask you if you'll work with me."

I looked at Jessie, then at Stone, chasing the thoughts around in my head. "It sounds great," I said, "but I've been planning to spend a lot of my time around here. And, well... this is a long way from Austin."

The two of them exchanged glances. They seemed to have thought about it already.

"That's not going to be a problem," Stone said. "We're using the trains more and more to do the job, and you're pretty handy to the railroad lines right where you are. When you need to come into Austin, you can, but it might not be all that often."

I took a minute, thinking things over. I looked at Jessie, who nodded and squeezed my hand.

"Come on, Tennessee boy," Stone said, needling me. "What do you say?"

"Well, cap'n, it sounds purty good," I drawled. "Cain't see no problems with it 'tall."

Stone rolled his eyes. "He's mending just fine," he told Jessie. "He only does that thick Southern country boy accent when he wants to irritate me."

————

After we'd all had lunch and McDonald and Stone were on their way back to Austin, I walked out to the back porch again, watching that stallion run. Jessie came out and took my hand, standing beside me.

"I really liked that part about wanting to spend your

time around here," she whispered. "Are you really going to do that?"

"Let me say it this time," I told her. "We can make that happen."

A LOOK AT: MCCABES'S LUCK
JAKE MCCABE BOOK ONE

Some men wait on luck—Jake McCabe makes his own.

Jake McCabe has always been no stranger to hardship. From the blood-soaked battlefields of the Civil War to a bitter family feud that haunts his Kentucky past, trouble seems to shadow his every step. Some say the McCabes are cursed with bad luck—but Jake refuses to believe in fate.

Seeking a fresh start, he sets his sights on the promise of Texas, forging ahead with a strong-willed woman and her family by his side. Together, they dream of peace, prosperity, and a ranch to call their own. But the frontier is no place for dreams alone— danger rides the same trails as opportunity, and Jake soon finds that trouble isn't so easily left behind.

When old enemies resurface and new threats emerge, Jake must fight for his land, his future, and the woman who holds his heart. In the vast, untamed West, survival means standing your ground. And McCabe has never been one to back down.

AVAILABLE MAY 2025